PRAISE FOR *THE BI(*

"A nonstop actioner with cosmic overtones painted in consistently broad strokes."

—*Kirkus Reviews*

"Another A-plus thriller from a writer on a serious winning streak."

—*Booklist* (starred review)

"A twisty, mystifying, suspenseful, expansive and, ultimately, entertaining read."

—CultureFly

PRAISE FOR DEAN KOONTZ

"Positively twitching with suspense. Another sure-fire hit from a thriller master."

—*Booklist* (starred review)

"Dean Koontz is not just a master of our darkest dreams but also a literary juggler."

—*The Times* (London)

"Dean Koontz writes page-turners, middle-of-the-night-sneak-up-behind-you suspense thrillers. He touches our hearts and tingles our spines."

—*Washington Post Book World*

"Koontz has a knack for making the bizarre and uncanny seem as commonplace as a sunrise. Bottom line: the Dean of Suspense."

—*People* magazine

"If Stephen King is the Rolling Stones of novels, Koontz is the Beatles."

—*Playboy*

"A superb plotter and wordsmith. He chronicles the hopes and fears of our time in broad strokes and fine detail, using popular fiction to explore the human condition [and] demonstrating that the real horror of life is found not in monsters but within the human psyche."

—*USA Today*

"Far more than a genre writer. Characters and the search for meaning, exquisitely crafted, are the soul of his work. This is why his novels will be read long after the ghosts and monsters of most genre writers have been consigned to the attic. One of the master storytellers of this or any age."

—*Tampa Tribune*

"Dean Koontz almost occupies a genre of his own. He is a master at building suspense and holding the reader spellbound."

—*Richmond Times-Dispatch*

"Demanding much of itself, Koontz's style bleaches out clichés while showing a genius for details. He leaves his competitors buried in the dust."

—*Kirkus Reviews*

"Koontz has always had near-Dickensian powers of description and an ability to yank us from one page to the next that few novelists can match."

—*Los Angeles Times*

"Tumbling, hallucinogenic prose."

—*New York Times Book Review*

THE BIG DARK SKY

ALSO BY DEAN KOONTZ

Quicksilver · The Other Emily · Elsewhere · Devoted · Ashley Bell · The City · Innocence · 77 Shadow Street · What the Night Knows · Breathless · Relentless · Your Heart Belongs to Me · The Darkest Evening of the Year · The Good Guy · The Husband · Velocity · Life Expectancy · The Taking · The Face · By the Light of the Moon · One Door Away from Heaven · From the Corner of His Eye · False Memory · Seize the Night · Fear Nothing · Mr. Murder · Dragon Tears · Hideaway · Cold Fire · The Bad Place · Midnight · Lightning · Watchers · Strangers · Twilight Eyes · Darkfall · Phantoms · Whispers · The Mask · The Vision · The Face of Fear · Night Chills · Shattered · The Voice of the Night · The Servants of Twilight · The House of Thunder · The Key to Midnight · The Eyes of Darkness · Shadowfires · Winter Moon · The Door to December · Dark Rivers of the Heart · Icebound · Strange Highways · Intensity · Sole Survivor · Ticktock · The Funhouse · Demon Seed

JANE HAWK SERIES

The Silent Corner · The Whispering Room · The Crooked Staircase · The Forbidden Door · The Night Window

ODD THOMAS SERIES

Odd Thomas · Forever Odd · Brother Odd · Odd Hours · Odd Interlude · Odd Apocalypse · Deeply Odd · Saint Odd

FRANKENSTEIN SERIES

Prodigal Son · City of Night · Dead and Alive · Lost Souls · The Dead Town

MEMOIR

A Big Little Life: A Memoir of a Joyful Dog Named Trixie

DEAN KOONTZ

THE BIG DARK SKY

This is a work of fiction. Names, characters, organizations, places, events, and incidents are either products of the author's imagination or are used fictitiously. Any resemblance to actual persons, living or dead, or actual events is purely coincidental.

Published by Thomas & Mercer, Seattle

www.apub.com

ISBN-13: 9781542019927 (hardcover)
ISBN-10: 1542019923 (hardcover)

ISBN-13: 9781542019910 (paperback)
ISBN-10: 1542019915 (paperback)

Cover design by Damon Freeman

Interior illustrations by Edward Bettison

Printed in the United States of America

First edition

Where love rules, there is no will to power;
and where power predominates, love is lacking.
The one is the shadow of the other.

—Carl Gustav Jung

PART 1
RUSTLING WILLOWS

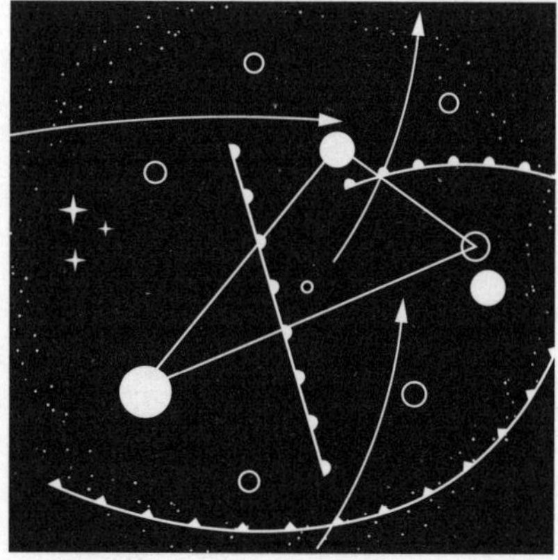

Incredible coincidences without apparent cause are called synchronicities.
They might better be called the stuff of life.
—*Ganesh Patel*

1

Twenty-Four Years Earlier

In every life, there are strange coincidences, occurrences that we find inexplicable, and even moments that seem supernatural. On this occasion, in the lonely vastness of Montana, the heavens were moonless, the blind face of the night pressed against the windows, the only light in the room issued from a television, and a young girl sat in communion with the dead.

Nine-year-old Joanna Chase, Jojo to everyone, was a happy child and a stranger to grief—until twelve days earlier, when her mother, Emelia, died. They were more than parent and child. Emelia taught Jojo to read and dream; they lived many lives in books, imaginations braiding like two vines, Jojo's ebullience an inspiration to Emelia, who by nature was more reserved with others than with her daughter.

Alone in the family room at two o'clock in the morning, Jojo was curled in an armchair, dressed in pajamas, wrapped in a colorful Pendleton blanket, watching home videos on the television, which had become her postmidnight routine for seven days. Jojo needed this immersion in the past because she regularly woke from ugly dreams, yearning for the beautiful face and mind and heart of her mother.

Tears flooded and receded and overflowed again. During the first five nights of these Chase-family movies, Jojo's tears had been bitter, her misery complete. On this occasion, however, as had happened the previous night, there were times when she smiled and the tears were sweet, when something her mother said or did reminded her of a precious moment that must never be forgotten.

In fact, that is why she subjected herself to the videos. She hoped the pain they inflicted would exhaust her grief, would be a kind of vaccine against endless torment. Maybe eventually she would be inoculated against tears and would thereafter always smile when she thought of her mom. She couldn't bear being weighed down by deep sorrow for the rest of her life.

Among the moments that brought a smile was a scene, shot months earlier. Wielding a video camera, Jojo interrogated her mom, who was sitting in a rocking chair on the porch, reading a book.

"Why do you read so much?" Jojo asks.

"For one thing, to keep my mind sharp."

"Is your mind very sharp?"

"As a razor."

"What's another reason?"

"I read to be entertained."

"What's another reason?"

At last her mother looks up from the book and smiles and says, "I read to keep from being sad."

"You're never sad. Are you sad? What're you sad about?"

"Sometimes I get sad when I think how you'll grow up and get married and move away from the ranch, and I'll be without my Jojo."

"Well, that'll never happen. I don't need any stupid boy when I've got horses."

"Maybe you'll find a boy who's a horseman."

"Like Daddy."

"Yes."

The camera circles three-quarters of the chair, and Mother's head turns with it, as Jojo says, "If I went away with some silly boy, what would you miss the most about me?"

"The way you pester me when I'm trying to read."

"Oh, very funny. If I was bad to the bone, I'd stick my tongue out at you."

"Only my Jojo would think that's bad-to-the-bone behavior."

Mother puts her book aside on a table and leans forward in the rocker. "Give me the camera. I have a question for you."

Jojo surrenders the camera, and now her face appears full frame as her mother asks, "Will you promise me something?"

"Promise what?"

"That you'll never change."

"Why would I change?"

"People do."

"Did you change when you grew up?"

"Big-time. When I was a young girl, all I wanted was a dog. When I grew up, I wanted a daughter."

Jojo says, "Dogs are nice, but daughters are better."

"Maybe. Though that's not what dogs say, and dogs don't lie."

"Zinger! I'm wounded. Could my own mother be bad to the bone?"

Mother winks.

Swaddled in the Pendleton blanket, smiling through tears, motherless Jojo rewound the video and watched the sequence again.

When she rewound to watch it a third time, everything proceeded as before until Mother, operating the camera, asked if her daughter would promise her something and Jojo asked, *"Promise what?"*

The video froze on a close-up of Jojo.

Although the image was locked, the audio continued, but the former dialogue between them was gone. Voice unmistakable, Mother instead said, "You will soon be going away, Jojo, going away to grow up elsewhere. I might reach out to you many years from now and ask you to come home."

Electrified, Jojo slid forward in the armchair, and the blanket slipped off her shoulders.

Mother said, "Before you, it was terribly lonely here, and I had little hope. For so very long, I had little hope."

Jojo rose, the blanket puddling around her feet. "Mommy?"

"One day I may be ready to do what I was born to do," Mother said. "And then I may need you at my side."

Jojo was shaking uncontrollably. Her mother was dead and gone, yet was somehow here now. Her mom would never hurt her. There was no threat in the words just spoken, but Jojo was shaking as much with fright as with wonder, gripped by a weirdly exhilarating anxiety.

The frozen video image thawed. On the TV, Jojo said, *"Promise what?"* Her mom said, *"That you'll never change,"* and the recording proceeded as it had the first two times that the girl watched it.

With the remote control, she rewound and then pressed PLAY, watched and waited. But if a haunting had occurred the third time that she'd viewed the piece, if a message had come through from the Other Side, it didn't repeat during the fourth viewing. Or during the fifth, the sixth.

Jojo knew that what happened was real. She hadn't imagined it because of lack of sleep or because grief had made her crazy. She would tell no one, as if the visitation was too sacred to share.

You will soon be going away, Jojo, going away to grow up elsewhere.

Four days later, she was taken to Santa Fe to live with her aunt Katherine, her mother's sister.

I might reach out to you many years from now and ask you to come home.

The years passed, and the vividness of that episode on a moonless night in Montana inevitably faded. She didn't forget it altogether, but eventually she came to believe that it wasn't what it seemed to be at the time, that it was most likely a fantasy spawned by desperate grief. She had always possessed a rich imagination.

One day I may be ready to do what I was born to do. And then I may need you at my side.

That made no sense. Her mother had been born twice, once into the world of the living and once into the world of the dead, from which she would never return and would never have reason to call her daughter to her side.

So the years passed, and the years passed . . .

2

Eventually, Joanna Chase would realize that the madness had begun on Monday evening, the thirteenth day of July.

As she'd been preparing dinner—hearts of palm salad, buttered pasta with pine nuts and peas—she thought she heard her car start with a roar of the engine.

Because she lived in a safe neighborhood of a peaceful city, because she was self-reliant and not given to paranoia, and because her security system was currently set in the at-home mode, she had no concern that someone could have gotten into the garage to steal the vehicle. Besides, both electronic keys were hanging from a pegboard in the laundry room, and the car would unlock itself only for someone in possession of a key.

More puzzled than worried, certainly not fearful, Joanna went through the laundry room and opened the door to the garage. Her black Lincoln Continental was idling, its running lights aglow, headlamps splashing across utility cabinets. The car was unoccupied.

Beyond the sedan stood her SUV, a white Lincoln Aviator, as quiet and dark as it ought to be.

She had previously owned a Lexus that had problems with its electrical wiring. Her Lincolns were superb machines that never gave her trouble—until perhaps now.

"What the hell?" she wondered.

She went behind the Continental, around to the port side, opened the front door, and settled into the driver's seat. The navigation-system map had loaded. On the screen, an orange square and the word START invited her touch, as if an address had been entered.

Although she didn't respond to that prompt, the car's mellow female voice advised her to obey all traffic laws and to follow vocal instructions to her destination.

"My destination is dinner, honey, and I can walk there," she said as she pushed the ignition button.

The engine fell silent, and the screen went dark after the car said goodbye with its programmed sign-off video and audio.

She got out and returned to the connecting door between the garage and the house. She stood there, watching, until the running lights and headlamps self-extinguished. She waited a minute or so, dreading that the Continental had caught the Lexus virus and would mock her by starting up again.

When the sedan remained quiet and dark, she returned to the kitchen, where she opened a bottle of good cabernet. She didn't indulge in wine every night, but the prospect of having bought another lemon on four wheels made a glass or two necessary. Maybe three.

As she ate, she listened to Rubinstein playing Mozart, and she read from *Kolyma Stories* by Varlam Shalamov. He had spent seventeen years slowly starving in a Soviet death camp deep in Siberia and, though released in 1951, had lived another thirty years under the jackboot of Communism. The music lifted her heart, and the stories made her grateful for the food before her.

Most nights, she slept well, and on this occasion, the wine drew her into a deeper slumber than usual. She hadn't dozed off with the TV on, but the gray light of a dead and silent channel filled the screen when she opened her eyes at 2:00 a.m. She fumbled with the remote and switched off the set. Sleep-sodden, hardly awake, she couldn't be sure if the distant sound of a racing engine was real or part of a lingering dream. She drifted off again before curiosity could motivate her to throw aside the covers and get out of bed.

3

Sunrise in Santa Fe, New Mexico, sometimes offered a peacock sky that opened the heart to wonder, even if the day included an appointment for a root canal procedure or, in Joanna's case, the prospect of a car mechanic issuing a diagnosis almost as unsettling as bad news from an oncologist. At dawn Tuesday, she stood in the small walled courtyard of her house, drinking coffee as she watched the new day spread its colorful plumage across the eastern sky.

At eight o'clock, she left the Continental at the Lincoln dealership and was provided with a loaner. Her morning was filled with errands, but she returned home at eleven thirty.

She took lunch—a turkey sandwich—at her desk in the study, while she worked on her current novel. The story centered on a heinous crime, and she was determined, as always, not to glamorize or to any extent romanticize criminals, which was in her estimation a problem with many contemporary novels and films. The stories by Varlam Shalamov, which she'd been reading, often featured gangsters who ran the Soviet gulags, portraying them with anger and bitterness that had the sting of truth, and his work helped to keep her honest.

Wednesday morning, the repair-shop manager at the dealership called to report that they were unable to find anything wrong with her Continental. She returned the loaner to them and collected her sedan. During the short drive home, the navigation system didn't offer any unsolicited directions.

That night, if the car started spontaneously in her garage, Joanna was unaware of it, for even without wine, she was lost in deep sleep. Sometime, as Wednesday melted into Thursday, the strange dreams began. Maybe she opened her eyes and saw the pale-gray light on the TV screen, or maybe that was part of the dream. Just part of the dream. *Yes, relax, Jojo, it's just part of the dream.*

4

Harley Spondollar would have died violently if he hadn't gone outside at 1:10 Thursday morning to climb over the picket fence and urinate on his neighbor's prize roses. He had been favoring the roses with his bladder water every night for five weeks. All that uric acid had at last begun to have a satisfying effect: the leaves grew spotted, the number of roses declined, and the flowers dropped their petals even as they struggled to open from buds to blooms.

Spondollar had nothing against roses. His hatred was reserved for Viola Redfern, who lived next door. She was seventy years old, maybe ninety—who the hell knew?—and Spondollar was convinced the old bitch would never die. She was indefatigable, giving her neighbors homemade cookies and cakes, roses from her garden, and sweaters she knitted. When Spondollar was sick, she provided him with pots of homemade soups. She never complained when he played music at high volume or sat on his front porch and loudly cursed everything from squirrels to passing children. She had legions of grandkids and great-grandkids who were always visiting her; they were so polite and quiet and well behaved that they made Spondollar want to puke.

Wednesday evening and early Thursday morning, Spondollar had made a special effort to consume such quantities of beer that he would be able to pay a deathblow to his neighbor's precious roses. Burdened by all her wrinkles and wattles, Viola reliably went to bed promptly at nine o'clock every night and fell asleep reading books, as boring a biddy as any ever born. On this occasion, however, she was staying overnight with a granddaughter to celebrate a great-granddaughter's tenth birthday.

One of Harley Spondollar's greatest joys in life was annoying the hell out of people and then playing psychological games with them until they regretted their impatience and indignation to such an extent that they found themselves apologizing for objecting to his boorishness. Viola refused to be annoyed, seemed impervious to insults, and had an inexhaustible supply of patience. Living next door to the likes of her was no fun.

So there he was in the second hour of Thursday, standing in her garden, facing his property, favoring her roses with a powerful stream of his finest in the mild summer night of the Oregon coast, when suddenly the air was filled with an electronic hum like the feedback from an enormous amplifier. At first the sound was the only phenomenon, with no detectable source. A crackling noise arose, as if a hundred yards of cellophane were being crumpled into a ball, which became louder than the hum. The lights went out. Then his house imploded. The front porch and walls and roof collapsed inward as if built of wet sand on a beach, imploded with such force that there might have been a black hole at the center of the structure, sucking it away into another universe. The crackling stopped first and then the humming. Perhaps fifteen seconds after the event began, it ended. Where his house had been there was now a mound of debris, its shape if not its size reminiscent of a giant anthill.

Harley Spondollar's response to every setback in life—as well as to any positive development—was to curse it exhaustively, but in this case, obscenities and blasphemies failed him. Dumbstruck, he stopped raining on the roses and tucked himself away and, without any awareness of having taken a single step, found himself wading into the ruins of his residence.

Initially, disbelief repressed fear. He dropped to his knees and scooped up a handful of what was left of the house. Beads. Beads of various sizes—some as small as air-rifle pellets, others as big as peas, a few the size of grapes, mostly smooth. In the light of the moon, he couldn't see them well. Some felt like wood, and others crumbled like plaster, and still others were as hard as metal. He realized there was no heat in the ruins, as might be expected, nor any dust. Mesmerized by the strangeness of the situation, he dug into the immense mound with both hands, searching for a nail or a screw or maybe a door hinge, anything that he would recognize as having been part of the house. He dug faster, more urgently, seeking an object, any object, that the house had once contained: a dish, a spoon, one of the DVDs from his porn collection.

Suddenly aware of a new alarming sound, he thrust to his feet and turned and swept the street with his gaze, but he realized that what he heard was his own desperate, ragged breathing. Disbelief gave way to fright and incomprehension. He was terrified, his grip on reality eroding. He faced the unknown, something mysterious, maybe occult. He had no interest in the unknown, no curiosity about it. To hell with the unknown. He wanted his house back.

He needed everything to be as it had been throughout the evening: watching slasher movies, drinking beer, and pissing on the roses.

When he had been killing Viola's rose garden, there had been lights on in a few houses along the street. Now about twice as many neighbors than before appeared to be awake, perhaps roused from bed by the loud hum and the crackling noise. He saw faces at windows. People were watching, wondering. Even in the dark, they could surely see that his house was gone, and they could most likely see him standing alone in the moonlight. Yet none ventured outside to learn what had happened. If he'd been anyone but Harley Spondollar, they might have hurried to the scene with first-aid kits and sympathy, might have set up tables on his lawn and provided casseroles and baked goods for an early we'll-get-through-this-together breakfast. But he was who he was, and they stayed in their houses. That was all right with Spondollar. He despised the lot of them; there wasn't one whom he would have invited into his home even when he had a home.

With the piercing wail of approaching sirens, a much-needed sense of reality returned to the night. A fire truck turned the corner, though no fire raged to be fought. Behind the truck came an ambulance with its emergency lights flashing, though no one had been injured. Close on the tail of the EMTs were police in three patrol cars. Spondollar despised cops, whom he considered to be nothing more than the enforcers of a tyrannical system.

None of these first responders had previously seen a house reduced to a mound of small beads. Although they were mystified, they began to wonder if Spondollar had destroyed his own home. He was obviously a victim, not the villain, at least not in this case, but the cops began to doubt him when he said that he'd stepped outside to enjoy the stars just before whatever happened to the house had happened. He couldn't very well tell them that he'd been pissing on Viola's roses. Apparently he didn't strike anyone as a stargazer, for it was this claim that made them suspicious. In the face of the unknown, they strove to deny that anything inexplicable had happened, tried to hammer the fantastic into the mundane. The fact that he was a chemist intrigued them, though he hadn't worked in that field—or any other—for years. No illegal methamphetamine lab ever exploded without a roar and fire, but they weren't willing to let go of that ludicrous theory.

He didn't tell them that he was a chemist. They had learned that on their own, which meant they must have run a background check on him and therefore knew about the embezzlement charge brought against him nine years earlier. He had been guilty, but he'd known worse about his employer than his employer had known about him, so the bastard called a truce.

As if they'd never heard of constitutional rights, the cops moved him from one patrol car to another, trying to keep him off balance, questioning him politely at first, then more aggressively. When he accused them of being fascist vermin, they threatened to take him downtown to grill him further, which they would have done earlier if they hadn't worried he would demand to have an attorney.

They needn't have worried about that, because the last thing Spondollar wanted was to put his fate in the hands of a lawyer. He despised lawyers, who in his estimation were unscrupulous ambulance chasers or servants of the ruling class.

They called this patrol-car-to-patrol-car ordeal "crime-scene interrogation in situ," although there had been no crime, although there had been instead a spectacular eruption of the unknown into an ordinary Oregon night. After more than four hours, just when Harley Spondollar thought they were at last going to take him in and book him on some bogus charge, the mystery man arrived, whereupon the needle on the scale of weirdness pegged out at the top.

Four black Suburbans swept into the street, the kind that the FBI employed in movies, except none was marked with an official insignia or bore license plates. Sixteen agents of some clandestine service, men and women, got out of the vehicles. All were dressed in black suits, white shirts, and black ties. Whoever these people were, they outranked the guys in uniforms. Spondollar was escorted to a Suburban by an attractive blond newcomer with eyes as gray as brushed steel. "The worst is over, Mr. Spondollar. Everything will be made right." She sounded as insincere as any politician. She left him alone in the front passenger seat. The patrol cars departed.

Maybe two minutes later, a moving van arrived and parked in front of the lot on which Spondollar's house once stood. Men in black boots and black uniforms, again lacking insignia, spilled out of the big truck, while the agents in suits departed in pairs to all the houses on that block, with what intention Spondollar could only surmise. Soon the men in uniforms were erecting an eight-foot-tall chain-link construction fence around the property, with fabric sheeting that prevented the curious from seeing anything beyond.

In the last minutes of darkness, as these busy worker bees finished installing an opaque gate across Spondollar's driveway, a white Suburban arrived. It cruised through the gate, around the great mound of finely rendered debris to which the house had been reduced, out of sight onto the backyard. One of the construction crew closed the gate and stood beside it as if on guard.

Harley Spondollar watched all this with amazement and interest that for a while displaced his fear. Gradually, however, a profound uneasiness gathered in him.

In the half-light that preceded sunrise, the icy blonde with gray eyes returned. She escorted Spondollar through the gate and around the ruins. He asked questions as she shepherded him, but she ignored him. He almost used the C-word and several lesser insults on her, but intuition warned that he might deeply regret doing so.

Although his house was gone, the concrete patio behind it remained intact, and the Suburban was parked on it. Beside the vehicle stood a four-foot-square white folding table and two white wooden folding chairs. The blonde instructed him to sit in one of them. He said, "What if I don't?" As if speaking to a stubborn dog, she said, *"Sit."* While in the custody of the police, he had been allowed to urinate behind a tree, but his bladder felt half-full again, and he considered her shoes as a target. Once again, with some disappointment, he yielded to intuition and sat in the chair.

As the woman departed, the sky filled with peach light in the east, and a man came around the front of the SUV. He was tall and slim, his face and hands the color of tea, his hair and eyes jet black. White shoes, white suit, white shirt, bright-red necktie. His smile was whiter than his clothes. He appeared to be from India.

He seemed to float down into the chair. He carried a sheaf of papers and a white ballpoint pen, which he placed on the table. His fingers were long, well manicured. His hands moved with the grace of a close-up magician's hands. He was the epitome of elegance. During Spondollar's chaotic life, he'd made attempts at elegance, sought to develop good taste and acquire refinement, but he had never pulled it off. He hated those who, like this guy, were naturally graceful, lithe and trim and confident in their skin.

"Mr. Spondollar, I am told that your cell phone was in the house when this event occurred. Is that correct?"

"Who the hell are you?"

"My name is not important. Was your cell phone in the house?"

"Shit, yeah. Destroyed with everything else—the house, the garage, my car. What does that matter? What happened to my house?"

"Mr. Spondollar, are you wearing an Apple watch, any health-monitoring device, or any device that has internet connectivity?"

"I'm in perfect health, a bull, no reason to monitor anything. My watch is an off-the-shelf piece of shit. What's it matter?"

"It matters that you're not putting out any GPS locator signal, so your attacker can't target you, might even think you're dead."

"My attacker? What attacker?"

Raising one eyebrow, casually gesturing toward the mound that had been a house, the stranger said, "You don't think what happened here was a spontaneous, natural disintegration?"

The eyebrow was so subtly ironic, the gesture so economic and elegant that Spondollar wanted to grab the red necktie, yank, and slam the guy's face down hard into the tabletop.

He restrained himself. *"What the hell happened to my house?"*

"I am not at liberty to say, Mr. Spondollar. This is a matter of national security and of the greatest secrecy."

"Let me see your ID. Who're you with? The FBI, the CIA?"

"I myself am not an agent of the government. I'm part of a rare cooperative effort between the federal government and the private sector. Both are required to meet a unique threat."

"What unique threat?"

"I'm not at liberty to say. Anyway, you wouldn't want to know, Mr. Spondollar, because if you knew, you'd never sleep well again."

"I don't *have* anywhere to sleep even if I could."

"I'm here to take care of that. We will spirit you away into a witness-protection program and provide you with a new identity that can't be traced. We will—"

Spondollar interrupted. "What've I been witness to? I haven't been witness to shit except what happened to the house, and I don't even know what that *was*."

"It's called a witness-protection program only because it functions like one. We will move you to Arizona—"

"Hey, you know, I've got a life right here."

"And quite a life it is," the stranger said without the least offensive inflection, smiling and nodding as if he truly believed that Spondollar had deep ties to this town and was a treasure to his neighbors. "Therefore, we will reimburse you for twice the value of this property——what it was when the house existed. We will provide you with a better house in Arizona, without a mortgage. We will pay you a monthly stipend of four thousand dollars for life and also make a cash settlement equal to twice the funds you currently have in the bank and in an investment account."

"Are you nuts? That's a fortune." He leaned forward in his chair and pointed an accusatory finger at the stranger. "So you must want something from me. What is it you want from me?"

"We want to limit collateral damage. If you were to try to go on living as Harley Spondollar, you would be attacked again, and there might be collateral damage. May I be frank, sir?"

"Be what you want."

The man in white leaned back in his chair. "We have no special affection for you, Mr. Spondollar. However, if you went to the bank to withdraw funds, the transaction would involve a verification via the internet. Before you received a cashier's check, you would be destroyed along with the bank and everyone in it. I don't know anyone in the bank branch you use, but as a fellow human being, I do have special affection for *them*."

Spondollar chewed on his lower lip for a long moment before he said, "That wasn't worthy of you."

"I know. A low blow. I regret it. But it's true. You are not a man who inspires affection. All I need from you is your signature on the documents I've brought. They include a nondisclosure agreement that, if violated, could lead to your immediate imprisonment."

"That's damn harsh."

"Yes, isn't it?"

"What if I said I'll take everything you've offered as long as I can also have my money in the bank?"

The stranger sighed. "I understand those funds have sentimental value for you, because you embezzled them from a man who made the mistake of treating you like his son. But the answer is no."

Spondollar winced. "That's even lower. I wouldn't expect that of someone like you."

"I apologize, but I don't regret having said it. I am growing impatient, Mr. Spondollar." He pushed the sheaf of papers and the pen across the table. "Sign where they're marked with the yellow tags."

Spondollar picked up the pen but hesitated. "It's just that I have this thing about authority."

"I am aware. I have taken no personal offense."

After signing one of five documents, Spondollar paused. "Okay, there've gotta be a few people who want me dead, not just one."

"No doubt," said the stranger.

"But what the hell was done to my house, and who in the name of God has the power to do what was done?"

"I am not at liberty to say."

"So . . . you don't know who it is, do you?"

"We know *how* it was done, with what technology. All you need to know is that this power is extraordinary—and who seized control of it is ruthless. Sign the papers, come with me, or be obliterated."

As Spondollar signed the remaining documents, the stranger opened a large white envelope and withdrew an eight-by-ten photo. "I'm sure I know the answer, but I must ask if you know this man."

If he had spent hours guessing the identity of the person in the photograph before it was revealed to him, Spondollar might never have gotten around to the right name. "*Him?* Asher Optime? He's a useless feeb. I could break his neck with one hand."

"He didn't wreck your house. But he must know who did. We need to find him. It's people like you, his enemies, being targeted."

"I haven't seen that sick sonofabitch in years. I wouldn't know where the hell he is."

"I thought as much."

Because it seemed he had no choice, Spondollar signed the documents without reading them. When he noticed Blue Sky Partners listed as the "grantor," however, he frowned and read the first two words aloud and said, "What's this?"

"The entity buying a house for you and paying a stipend."

"My mother's name was Skye. She was born in Arizona, where you're sending me. My ex-wife's maiden name was Blue."

"Synchronicity. A Jungian coincidence," the stranger said.

"A what coincidence?"

"Carl Jung, the famous Swiss psychiatrist and psychologist. He theorized that meaningful coincidences reveal that our collective consciousness creates reality at least to some degree. Together we make reality, and effect can come before cause—that kind of thing."

"Sounds like a load of horseshit," Spondollar said.

"Yes, doesn't it? Here's an example I like. Edgar Allan Poe wrote a story about a shipwreck, in which starving sailors killed and ate a cabin boy named Richard Parker. Fifty years later, there was a shipwreck uncannily like that in the story in every detail—and the starving sailors killed and ate a cabin boy named Richard Parker. Hundreds of thousands of people read that story over those fifty years and were horrified by it. Is it somehow possible that unconsciously they *dreamed* the story into the fabric of reality?"

Spondollar scowled. "How the hell could that happen?"

"Beats me. I've no idea of the mechanism. I'm just wondering."

"You're a weird sonofabitch."

"Yes. That's been said before."

As the stranger put away the photograph and gathered up the signed documents, songbirds began to celebrate the colorful peaches-and-cream clouds.

The birdsong saddened Spondollar, because it brought home to him that nothing in his life would ever again be as it had been. On certain other mornings, he had sat on this patio with his air rifle, picking off birds on their perches and even sometimes in flight. His guns had been destroyed along with the house and everything in it. He could buy another air rifle, and there would be birds in Arizona, but it would just never be quite the same.

5

Every night for three weeks, Joanna Chase dreamed of Rustling Willows, both the ranch itself and the groves of trees for which it had been named long ago. Although none of these fabrications of her slumbering mind descended into a nightmare, they were ominous and filled her with a foreboding that lingered after she woke. The dreams were set in the fullness of night or at twilight, or in the purple daytime shade of the forest that broke like an evergreen sea on the north and east shores of the grassy prairie that constituted much of the property.

She was always a child in these dreams, sometimes as young as six, at other times perhaps as old as nine, which was the last year that she'd lived on the ranch. For seven nights, there were only the trees and young Joanna as she wandered or else hurried among them, under their fragrant boughs and leafy branches. Rustling trees, soughing trees, whispering trees . . .

After a week, when the dreams failed to relent, animals began to populate them: great flocks of rock doves winging through the conifers in the last orange light of day, a herd of elk encircling her as she proceeded with them through a misty dusk. Frequently, a pack of lantern-eyed coyotes swarmed around her, under a polished-pearl moon; and though the mood was ominous, the threat she sensed did not come from those creatures, but from something unknown in the starlit currents of the deep, cool night.

She didn't wake in alarm from these eerie scenarios until the grizzly bear entered them. She sometimes encountered it in the dream woods at twilight, where it loomed eight feet tall, shambling along an aisle of trees parallel to a deer path that Joanna followed. Its wet black nostrils were flared, the better to gather her scent, and its eyes glimmered with golden light as it watched her.

In the early hours of Thursday, the sixth of August, in another sleep-crafted fantasy, as she plucked wildflowers from a hillside a hundred yards beyond the horse stables, with the sun an apocalyptic red ball balanced on the horizon behind her, a long and vibrant snort caused her to look up from the petaled riot of color and discover that the bear towered over her, no more than fifteen feet away. She was a small girl, maybe seven years old, and the grizzly was enormous, perhaps twenty times her weight, with four-inch claws that could kill her with one swipe. As with the raw-boned coyotes, she didn't fear this creature, not in the dream, but smiled at it and held forth the bouquet. The bear cocked its head, as if it found her unique in its experience, a puzzle to be solved. When it didn't come forward to meet her, she slowly approached it with the offering of flowers. The behemoth raised its head and let out a wild sound—part hoot, part rattling honk, part fierce blat—which made young Joanna giggle. Undeterred, in the crimson light of the setting sun, she followed her frail shadow to within a few feet of the monstrous figure, holding the bouquet high, and then the bear—

Joanna woke with a cry of alarm. She sat up in bed, threw aside the covers, thrust to her feet, and stood trembling.

Although usually she slept in darkness, recently she had been leaving the bathroom door ajar, projecting a simple geometric of pale light on the red-and-black Navajo rug. Shadows ruled the chamber, but none was deep enough to conceal an intruder.

She had been sleeping in a T-shirt and panties, under a thin coverlet and top sheet, because the room wasn't cold. The chill that stippled her with gooseflesh was a response to the dream rather than to the air temperature.

During more than nine years at Rustling Willows, she had never been threatened by an animal, by neither a coyote nor a bear, nor even by one of the rattlesnakes that were common to the territory. The vividness of these dreams and the intensity of her reaction to them had nothing to do with threats that she had survived. However, though she'd never seen a grizzly except in photos, she understood why that beast, if not the others, might haunt her dreams.

The bedside clock offered her a time that she didn't want to accept—2:40 a.m. When she fully woke from these dreams, she could never nod off again. This would be another night in which she got less than five hours of sleep.

The TV wasn't on. She didn't know why she thought it would be.

She slipped into a pair of yoga pants and, barefoot, went through the house to her study, switching on lamps along the way.

In these hours of lost sleep, Joanna wanted coffee prepared with cinnamon added before brewing, then poured black, not because she needed it to stay awake, but because the aroma and the flavor reminded her of mornings at Rustling Willows, in the kitchen with her mother, whom she'd lost when she was nine, the same year she'd also become fatherless. Her mother, Emelia, had drunk coffee this way, and Joanna had been allowed her own cup by the time she was six, though her coffee was diluted with condensed milk.

A coffeemaker stood on a corner table in her study. She brewed eight cups. She wouldn't drink that much, but she took comfort from the sight of it in the Pyrex pot and from the aroma that lingered as long as the Jamaican blend remained on the warming pad.

At her desk, she booted up the computer and opened a document titled *The Color of Never*, a manuscript in progress. At thirty-three, during the eleven years since graduating college, she had written six novels. The most recent two were modest bestsellers. Her sales increased novel by novel in an age of high-tech barbarism when it seemed that books might fade entirely from fashion and that vast fields of information, digitized but rarely accessed, would soon become graveyards of once essential knowledge.

She sipped the coffee, which warmed away her chill, but her creativity remained frozen. Her fingers could find no words in the keyboard. The current novel had gone well even when the strange dreams became a nightly occurrence, but she'd made no progress whatsoever after the animals became a part of them.

Never before had Joanna suffered from writer's block. Her frustrating inability to create suggested that the exceptionally vivid dreams might be either a symptom of some physical malady—perhaps related to the brain—or evidence of a psychological knot that needed to be untied. Slowly, day by day, she had ever more seriously considered seeking help.

She had no fear of doctors or therapists. Yet each time she'd picked up the telephone to make an appointment with John Wong, her physician, misgiving had quickly swelled into a peculiar, urgent dread. She was convinced that if she sought help with this matter, her life as she knew it would change drastically for the worse. She wasn't a superstitious woman nor one given to irrational fears. Her attitude at first surprised her, then annoyed her, and recently began to worry her as much as the dreams themselves.

Now, as she stared at the computer screen, at the last sentence she'd written almost two weeks earlier, her desk phone rang. Only a few friends knew her cell number; she shared her home number more widely. She had landlines as backup because . . . well, things fell apart. One day your mother was at your side, the next day dead. As reliable as it seemed, the entire cell-phone system was vulnerable to hackers, solar flares, and other disruptions. She had two lines, the second a rollover that ensured she wouldn't miss a call from an editor or agent while talking on the first. The line-one indicator blinked insistently, but the phone display reported Caller Unknown.

Robocalls were a problem, though not usually at three o'clock in the morning. She let it go to voice mail, but the caller hung up before leaving a message. Half a minute later, the second line rang. Again, no ID was provided. No message.

Lying to the right of the computer, her cell rang. Although the caller was *again* unknown, Joanna was intrigued enough to accept. "Hello?"

The woman's voice sounded vaguely familiar, but it wasn't that of a close friend. "Jimmy Two Eyes. You remember him?"

"No. Who is this?"

"You were six, and Jimmy Two Eyes was nine."

"I don't know him. What do you want?"

"Now that you've heard his name, you'll soon remember."

"Who is this?"

"I need your help." Those four words were spoken less as an emotional plea than as a simple statement. The caller sounded as calm as someone taking a survey regarding preferences in laundry detergents, even as she said, "I don't know who else to turn to. Just you, Jojo."

When she was a child, Jojo had been the nickname her mother gave her. Whoever the caller might be, this wasn't Emelia, her mother. The dead did not phone from the Other Side.

This was a century of frauds, fools, hucksters, and hackers. Joanna had dealt with her share of them. She had no patience for deceivers. Yet the weirdness of the call seemed somehow related to the dreams that had recently tormented her. So instead of hanging up, she asked again, "Who is this?"

Still employing a matter-of-fact tone, the caller said, "I am in a dark place, Jojo."

"And where is that?"

"It's a mental darkness."

"Yeah? All right. But *where* are you calling from?"

"You know."

"How could I know?"

"You know."

"I'm not playing this weird game. Tell me who you are or call nine one one."

"Only you can help me, Jojo."

Joanna terminated the call. Her hand trembled. The chill with which she'd awakened had returned.

She crossed the room to the corner table and poured more coffee. She stood there, the mug in both hands, sipping the hot brew.

She knew no one named—or nicknamed—Jimmy Two Eyes. But when she whispered the name into the steam rising from her coffee, the chill that disturbed her intensified and rilled down her spine from the base of her skull to her tailbone.

Where are you calling from?

You know.

How could I know?

You know.

With a sudden new insight, she found herself considering the contents of the room, with which she had lived for twelve years. The colorful Navajo rug seemed to float on the pale-gold maple floor, its pattern suggestive of mystical meaning. A decoratively painted colonial *trastero* stood against one wall, doors open, its shelves laden with folk-art objects: Pueblo pottery; fancy tinwork frames holding black-and-white photos of old Santa Fe; a *bulto* of the Christ Child carved from cottonwood, covered in fine gesso and painted by Luis Tapia. Fringed Pendleton blankets—with soft beige, red, and blue designs—draped two comfortable leather armchairs.

She hadn't merely furnished this house; she had *curated* its contents, as if this were a multiroom installation in a museum. She'd thought she was putting together a version of Santa Fe style reflective of this storied city that she loved. Now she realized that the result was a rustic yet sophisticated decor that could be found to some extent beyond the borders of New Mexico; that in fact it wasn't uncommon in humble, rural homes as far away as Wyoming and Montana, in those parts of the True West that had not yet succumbed to modernity as fully as the New West beyond the Rockies.

She realized as well, and with greater astonishment, she had surrounded herself with things reminiscent of the furnishings in the native-stone house at Rustling Willows, where she had resided during the first nine years and four months of her life.

Although she'd left the ranch twenty-four years earlier, and though her childhood memories were partly obscured by the dust of time, she found it incredible—inexplicable—that she hadn't until this moment recognized the influence of Rustling Willows in this home she'd made for herself. It seemed as if she'd subconsciously suppressed her recollections of that place, perhaps as a defense against the emotional pain of the tragedies that had occurred there.

Her mother's favorite form of exercise had been rowing a skiff on Lake Sapphire, which their house overlooked. She went onto the water at first light nearly every morning—and one day did not come back. The six-hundred-acre lake was as much as three hundred feet deep in places, but the authorities didn't need to drag it to find her body, because she washed up on a shingle beach, in the shade of cottonwoods. The county coroner determined that she must have rocked the boat and fallen overboard, and in falling had knocked her head against the gunwale, drowning while unconscious.

Following the loss of her mother and, two weeks later, the death of her father, Samuel, Joanna had gone to live for twelve years with her mother's unmarried sister, Katherine, in Santa Fe, in a sort of Victorian house crammed full of heavy furniture and bric-a-brac, a place that some might have thought was an affront to the graceful Pueblo-influenced structures that largely defined the fabled city. Soon after graduating from St. John's College, Joanna inherited the contents of a trust that included the proceeds from an insurance policy on her mother's life. She had bought her current home, furnished it, and lived frugally until her attempt to build a career as a writer bore fruit.

She couldn't understand how one mysterious phone call from a nameless woman had restored color to the faded memories of Rustling Willows, but maybe it was no coincidence that the recent dreams had been followed by the caller's quiet entreaty.

Which meant—what? That the dreams had been somehow induced? How? With drugs? Absurd. She was not a writer of paranoia-drenched fiction. She didn't traffic in the conspiracy theories that, like a series of tsunamis, washed through the internet. Surely the timing of the call was coincidental, not related in any way to the dreams.

Only you can help me, Jojo.

Where are you calling from?

You know.

How could I know?

You know.

And of course Joanna *did* know. The unknown woman had called from Rustling Willows—or had implied as much.

But that place was twenty-four years in Joanna's past, and she was not obligated in any sense to anyone in Montana. No one there could possibly be in a situation that only she could resolve.

She put the mug of coffee down. She toured the house, marveling—with increasing uneasiness—at how many objects echoed items in a ranch house twelve hundred miles and a quarter of a century away, at least as she now remembered them.

If she'd repressed other memories, some event or relationship that would explain the phone call, she must have done so for good reason. Although her imagination would now bedevil her with colorful theories, she would be wise to resist the temptation to seek an explanation. For all its natural beauty, the ranch had made an orphan of her. It wasn't likely to be a place of bright promise for her future.

In spite of all that, something about the years she spent at Rustling Willows must have inspired an inexplicable nostalgia; otherwise, she would not have made this house in Santa Fe a reflection of the one in Montana.

She'd often accompanied her mother in the skiff, and she had enjoyed those outings. However, even though she'd been spared the sight of Emelia's bloated corpse, the lake seemed polluted and unwholesome in the aftermath.

Neither had she seen her father's body, two weeks later, but the horror of his death had finally robbed the ranch of whatever charm it possessed. Samuel had gone for a ride on Spirit, his favorite horse. The theory was that they surprised a bear with its cub or encountered one half-starved; the panicked stallion threw its rider and bolted, and the bear chased Samuel down. Only the vicious claws of a grizzly could have made such grievous wounds; only a ravenous eight-hundred-pound bear would have devoured so much of its kill.

There were sound reasons never to return to Rustling Willows. Nevertheless, a strange yearning for Montana overcame her as she returned to her office and stood staring at the Navajo rug.

The desk phone rang. The first line.

"No," Joanna said.

When the call went to voice mail, the caller disconnected.

The second line shrilled. Again, the caller left no message—and resorted to the cell phone.

She picked up the mug that she'd earlier set aside. The coffee was cold. She refreshed it with hot brew from the Pyrex pot.

She went to a window and pulled open the curtains. Beyond was the stucco-walled courtyard. By the magic of moonlight, various specimen cactuses—some tall, some squat—seemed to have been imbued with animal life, standing or crouching in wait for her, eyeless sentinels, a few hydra-headed and others with numerous limbs, their moonlight-frosted faces implacable, their bodies barbed and needled.

After closing the curtains, she sat at her desk, staring at the computer screen, at the last sentence she had written: *Intelligence is dangerous without common sense, but common sense can never be learned by those who have been educated into arrogance, who lack the humility to believe in and trust their intuition.*

Every time she read those words, she knew them to be true, but she also sensed that something was missing from that statement.

Reluctantly—or perhaps not—she picked up the cell phone and found that the caller had left a message this time.

The voice was that of the woman with whom she'd spoken earlier, still oddly calm, considering the words. *"I am mentally in a dark place. I'm lost. I'm a danger to myself and others. Only you can help me, Jojo. Please come and help me."*

6

The Montana night is silent except for the occasional cries of coyotes or the inquiries of owls or the shriek of an unidentified night bird, as those creatures mourn the fate of the Earth.

The stars burn toward the heat death of the universe in however many billions of years, and the dead moon sheds cold light on the dark buildings that stand testament to the folly of the human race.

Asher Optime walks the weed-prickled main—and only—street, savoring the cool clean air. He relishes the peace here and regrets the screaming that must come later, though it will be brief.

Most nights he is not awake at this hour. He usually sleeps from midnight to dawn, as soundly as the unborn in the womb. His thrilling dreams take place in three-dimensional evolving versions of the artworks of Marcel Duchamp, Joan Miró, Robert Rauschenberg, and others. In the dreams, those artists of deconstruction wrench from him or cut from him or erase from him pieces of himself, until it seems that he will cease to exist before he wakes. This pleasant expectation is always disappointed, for every dream ends while a part of him remains: one hand crawling past a heavy door framed by brickwork, one sorrowing eye floating in a void where a dog barks in the dark, fragments of his face floating in a field of color. On this night, he will not sleep or dream, because it is *his* role to be the artist who erases the meaning of a life, the life of a twenty-eight-year-old woman named Ophelia Poole.

Five months earlier, a week before his forty-second birthday, Asher had found the road to nowhere, which had led to everything he wanted.

In Montana, the prairies appear endless, and valleys sprawl as wide as plains. The immense forests are so primeval, it's possible to believe that creatures said to be extinct for many thousands of millennia still live here in these densely grown and deeply shadowed reaches. The soaring, castellated mountains are forbidding ramparts that, silhouetted in a bloody sunset, might be the strongholds of an evil kingdom in a fantasy novel, and gorges plunge to depths where mist gathers as though to obscure passages to secret civilizations beneath the crust of the planet.

In human terms, Montana offers more lonely places than can be counted, some of which were once occupied by people with pluck and aspirations. They came for gold, found it, exhausted the veins; came for silver; came for copper in the mines that had been depleted of silver. They built small communities that they thought would grow to become hubs of commerce and transportation; some did, many didn't. In the state's 147,000 square miles, some of the loneliest places aren't the farthest from all traces of civilization, but are those where men and women had hoped to make a future before being forced to face reality and abandon what they had built.

Of the several remote settlements that Asher Optime has found and explored during months of preparation for his new life, this one is the most suitable for his purpose. A road of compacted earth and broken shale withers away in a meadow, where decades earlier a high crest of earth in the west, perhaps weakened by heavy rains and dislocated by seismic tremors, collapsed and buried the approach to the abandoned town under thousands of tons of dirt. Where the track continues through a forest, generations of undergrowth obscure it, so a trained eye is required to recognize it. Only a determined seeker in a Land Rover with fortified tires can follow the trail through three miles of thick, descending woods to a hundred or more clear acres by a rushing river, where unknown but hardy settlers once came with some purpose in mind that he cannot confirm.

Of the fifty-six buildings, only twenty-two have collapsed entirely or fallen into such ruin that it is dangerous to enter them. Those that remain are mostly simple, decaying houses. The largest structure might have been a modest lumber mill, though all of the equipment and internal features that could have positively identified it were stripped out and taken away at some point during the settlement's demise.

As best he can determine, the first residents staked their claim here around 1860. The settlement, which was never formally designated as a town, was abandoned by the last of its citizens in the late 1890s. He can't help but be impressed by the quality of their masonry and carpentry; for if they had possessed any less skill, nothing whatsoever would be standing. They employed native stone and heavy timbers and masterful joinery. Evident dedication marks everything they constructed, so that he wonders if they might have been members of a religious sect.

At the entrance to the town, he'd found a weathered plank mortared into the face of a stone plinth. Eight letters had been burned in the wood. He believes this is the name of the place: Zipporah. On one of his visits to buy supplies in the nearest center of commerce—over thirteen miles from here—he researched the word and learned it was the name of the wife of Moses. This discovery, combined with the fact that by far the most formidable building in town is a stone church, seems to confirm his speculation.

However, another building is a saloon, which on his first tour had sung in many voices when the wind was high and sieving through it, before he made repairs to the structure. Why would a town of religious types sanction such a den of iniquity? That question amuses Asher, although he spends no time pondering it. He isn't surprised that the settlers were hypocrites, for in his estimation, all human beings are hypocrites, himself excepted.

Ghost town.

Such a location is not just conducive to the work he has set out to accomplish, but it is also properly symbolic. His purpose is to ensure that Earth becomes, from pole to pole, a collection of ghost towns and cities, a planet where not a single human presence disturbs the peace of any continent or sails on any sea.

Here, in this place, the end will begin.

No. The end already *has begun*. Four are dead and another waits to die.

Having walked the length of the street, Asher returns to the saloon, which is at the heart of the settlement. The weathered walls of time-silvered wood glow softly with reflected moonlight, a gray ghost of a building. Most windows are broken out and boarded over from inside; others are etched by dust, like cataractous eyes.

After finding Zipporah on the second day of April, Asher had spent a month hauling in supplies and weatherproofing the saloon for the coming winter. With thirty-four large tubes of caulking, several rolls of insulation, and a lot of plastic sheeting, he has banished the wind that had enjoyed easy access for decades. He has installed a cast-iron pot-bellied stove to provide heat and used a chain saw to cut a firewood supply from dead trees in the forest.

From the exterior, the saloon looks as it did when he first came upon it. Inside, a spare yet cozy living space is furnished with an armchair and footstool. Two straight-backed chairs stand at a simple plank-top table he constructed himself, where he can sit to take his meals and spend hours every day writing the manifesto that will change the world and bring an end to human history.

Ophelia will be where he left her: sitting on the floor, her hands zip tied in front of her. A padlocked chain around her neck shackles her to a wall stud.

He climbs two steps onto the wide veranda. Approaching the front door, he expects to hear Ophelia weeping softly. Sooner or later, they all weep, the men as well as the women. If ever Asher abducts others who strive to meet their fate with tearless courage, he will employ whatever methods are required to break their resolve. They must not go to their deaths with the illusion that dying means something. He intends for them to understand that they are nothing, that they mean nothing. He needs them to die twice, first to suffer the death of the spirit and only then the death of the body. This is the path that all of humankind must follow in order to ensure that the future envisioned in his manifesto comes to pass.

This Ophelia bitch is not yet weeping.

He opens the door.

7

Most days at dawn, Joanna Chase took a long, brisk walk to clear her mind for a session of writing. Santa Fe was a city with a richness of museums and churches and missions, with much beautiful architecture to distract a fitness enthusiast from the tedium of morning exercise.

That Thursday in August, under a cloudless pale-blue sky, she took a shorter walk than usual, a mere ten minutes to Katherine Ainsley's house. Even though retired as the general manager of one of the city's best hotels, Aunt Katherine was always up before first light. Joanna passed under the spreading branches of the thirty-foot juniper that shaded the house, and went around back. Through panes in the kitchen door, she saw Katherine dressed in red silk pajamas and matching robe, sitting at the breakfast table with a bagel, a plate of lox, a pot of tea, and the newspaper.

She knocked and let herself inside, and Katherine said, "If I'd known you'd stop by, I'd have fired up the Keurig and made coffee."

Joanna loathed tea. She said, "It's an impromptu visit. I only decided to annoy you en route."

"Dear, you couldn't annoy me if you tried. Well, not since you were sixteen. In those early teen years, you could be a pisser."

Joanna crossed to the coffeemaker. "Gee, I don't recall that."

"How convenient. There's plenty of lox in the fridge. It's sugar cured, the kind you like."

Selecting a single-serving vanilla-bean coffee from a drawer full of choices, Joanna said, "I'll just have caffeine."

"The dreams again?"

"I went to bed at ten thirty, woke before three."

"Sleeping alone for a long period is unhealthy. It causes nightmares among other things."

"Is that the finding of a peer-reviewed Harvard study, Auntie Kat, or just your personal experience?"

"I worry about you, child. You're alone and lonely."

"I don't recall complaining of loneliness."

"Not directly. But in so many words. In so many, many words. One can be a feminist and still believe life is better with the right man."

At sixty-six, Katherine was vibrant, attractive—and planning her third wedding. Her first husband, Bernard, walked out on her thirty-five years earlier when her career became more successful than his. He was the wrong man. Harry married Katherine the year that Joanna graduated college; he was a lovely guy, and they enjoyed eleven years together before cancer took him. A year after Harry passed, Katherine met Saul, a second Mr. Right.

Watching the hot coffee drizzle into her mug, Joanna sighed. "Auntie Kat, men my age are different from those in your generation. A lot of them can't commit to anything but themselves. This coffee machine is more reliable."

"But no fun to snuggle with." In sheeny swishes of scarlet silk, Katherine went to the refrigerator, produced more lox, and put it on the table with a plate and utensils. "A bagel? Cream cheese? Salmon does for the female libido what oysters do for men."

"Not in my experience," Joanna said as she brought her coffee to the table and sat opposite her aunt.

Putting aside the newspaper, Katherine said, "Did you dream of the grizzly bear again?"

"Yeah. But it wasn't a nightmare. It didn't scare me. I picked a bouquet of wildflowers for it." She stirred coolness into her coffee. "It kills my father, so I give it flowers? What's with me? Seems sick, doesn't it?"

Katherine's blue stare, as clear as Santa Fe skies, fixed on Joanna's eyes, like a laser reading code. "You loved your father."

"Well, of course. He was my *dad*."

"How well do you remember him?"

"I was so young. And after all this time . . ."

"He was not an outgoing man. Your mother said shy, but I thought . . . well, something else. I believe he married your mother because he was unsure and somehow empty, while she was so centered and complete. Your life at Rustling Willows was idyllic, wasn't it?"

Joanna shrugged. "It was a beautiful place. Idyllic? I guess so. My memories of it are . . . misty."

"I was there for a week, when you were seven. I remember it well. The natural beauty. The relaxed pace of life. I'd say it was one step away from paradise."

"Until it wasn't."

Picking up a bagel and spreading cream cheese on it, Katherine said, "I'm not a psychiatrist, and I've never played one on TV, but I suspect that to some small extent, subconsciously, you blame your father for leaving you alone, for having to leave the ranch."

"What sense does that make? He didn't *want* to die."

"The subconscious isn't always rational, sweetie." Katherine reached across the table and put the bagel on Joanna's plate. "The book you're working on . . . does it draw on any childhood experiences that might have stirred up all this?"

"No. Nothing like that. Anyway, something's happened that puts the dreams in a different light."

When Joanna finished recounting the phone call she had received a few hours earlier, Katherine said, "How peculiar. You're right to be wary of this woman, whoever she might be. There's a world of scam artists these days. But surely you do remember Jimmy Two Eyes?"

Having picked up what remained of her bagel, Joanna put it down again without taking a bite. "He's real? You remember him?"

"Jimmy was three years older than you, the child of Hector and Annalisa . . . something. Alvarez! Hector and Annalisa Alvarez."

"Hector . . . he was the ranch manager," Joanna said, as in her mind's eye the figure of the stocky, broad-faced, ever-smiling Alvarez formed like an apparition coalescing out of mist.

"Yes. And Annalisa was cook and housekeeper. She and your mother were close, more like sisters than employee and employer."

Although she hadn't thought about them in a long time, in fact perhaps not in twenty-five years, Joanna's memory now conjured the faces of Hector and Annalisa with such clarity that she wondered why they *hadn't* come to mind—and often—since she'd moved from Montana to Santa Fe. Annalisa had been like an aunt to her, Hector an honorary uncle. Although she had been only nine when she'd last seen them, it seemed inexplicable—even perverse—that she had deleted them from her life as if they were old data of no further use.

Unsettled by all this, Joanna was further bewildered that, in spite of a concerted effort, she could not recall their son, Jimmy. "It's like . . . like I've had some kind of selective amnesia and haven't been aware of it. Jimmy, huh? Jimmy. Jimmy Alvarez, right? So why the 'Two Eyes'?"

"That's what the ranch hands called him," Katherine said.

There had been four of them, lean men with sun-weathered faces and calloused hands. Joanna remembered them, although not vividly.

When her father inherited the ranch from his old man, the year she was born, maybe sixteen or eighteen men had worked the place, because it had been a cattle operation in those days. Her dad sold off the livestock, a few hundred head, and cut down on the staff and turned Rustling Willows into a horse ranch. He bred superior quarter horses to be sold for racing, as well as certain breeds of show horses for those with the money to indulge in that expensive hobby.

"They never used the nickname in front of Jimmy's parents, but they didn't mean to mock the boy," Katherine continued. "There was something affectionate about it. They pitied Jimmy, as most people did. They feared him a little, too, though the poor child wasn't a danger to anyone. It was what he represented that they feared."

"What do you mean? What did he represent?"

Katherine regarded her with concern. "Dear, you really can't remember him?"

"I really can't."

Although some bagel and lox remained on her plate, Katherine pushed it aside. She stared at her empty teacup, reached for the pot that stood on a warming rack serviced by a candle, evidently decided she didn't want more tea after all, and slid the cup aside, as well. Although she didn't suffer with a tremor related to age, her hands trembled now.

"Jimmy represented the infinite varieties of chaos that we know might at any moment erupt into our lives, the chaos we mostly don't allow ourselves to think about. The sweet boy suffered severe birth defects. His head was malformed, as if he'd been born with a skull of wax that too late solidified into bone. His face, with all its problems and those eyes, it was . . . well, an unfortunate face."

"'Two Eyes.' Why call him that? Everyone has two eyes."

"Not like Jimmy's. The left was set an inch higher in his head than the right. It was blue and clear, but the right was black and perpetually bloodshot. Mack Northland, the most interesting of the ranch hands, said that when Jimmy stared at you, even though you knew he was harmless . . . it was nevertheless like being watched by both an angel and a demon." As though the kitchen had turned chilly, Katherine pulled the panels of her scarlet robe together at her throat. "I can't imagine how you've forgotten that."

"Neither can I. But I have."

"You see, Jimmy's IQ was very low. He was incapable of learning language. He grunted and whimpered and made other wordless sounds to indicate what he wanted. He had no sense of any social norms, of boundaries. So he'd often stare at you boldly for the longest time. Understand, Jimmy might not even have been aware of you. His mind, such as it was, might have been on something else entirely, but that stare could be disconcerting. He wasn't strong, but weak, wasn't quick, but slow, and yet the longer he stared at you, the more you felt that he was . . ."

"Was what?" Joanna asked.

"Planning something. That's very unfair to the child. He wasn't capable of planning anything, of any intentional wickedness. He was just one of nature's victims. But, sad to say, that's too often the human way, isn't it—to judge by appearances?"

8

In this former saloon where the end of the world has begun, Ophelia Poole sits now in a chair, her zip-tied hands resting on the plank-top table built by Asher Optime. He sits across from her, in his role as the scourge of that disease known as humankind.

Still she does not weep, as if by denying him the satisfaction of her tears she can deny him power over her.

Soon she will learn that he can't be denied.

The two windows that remain intact, glass frosted by decades of hard weather and dust, admit a feeble imitation of sunshine. Of what illumination there is, most comes from a Coleman gas lantern. With its bag-like wicks aglow, the pressure turned down, the lamp is less bright than it could be. In fact, Ophelia sports a summer tan, but here her face is moon pale, and her hair, which is actually golden, appears somewhat silvery, as if the subtly pulsing light is imposing a patina on her.

In the farther reaches of the large room, shadows gather like black-robed witnesses to an inquisition.

Twenty-eight-year-old Ophelia is a highly attractive woman whose twin sister, Octavia, was killed in a traffic accident when she was twenty-three. Having overcome blackest grief, Ophelia believes that she is virtuous and thinks she should "give back" to her community by serving as the counselor to a group of people who have recently lost loved ones. They meet the second Tuesday of every month at their church, for mutual support and light refreshments. Two nights previously, Ophelia made the mistake of being the last to leave the session, alone, just when Asher was trolling for a fifth person to serve as proof of his personal commitment to eradicate the horrid pestilence of humanity from this stressed planet.

She woke from a chloroform sleep the previous morning and found herself in this room, chained to the wall. In addition to drawing from her the story of her life, Asher has fed her three meals since then and escorted her to the outhouse, where he's waited while she toileted. He is not cruel in his righteousness. The only thing he requires of her is to read the part of his manifesto that he has thus far written: fifty-two pages in his meticulous cursive. She's read it all and wishes to discuss it.

She thinks he desires her feedback, but he does not. He only wants her to understand his purpose and her place in the magnificent task he has undertaken.

Now, as they face each other across the table, in the bleaching light of the gas lamp, Asher explains that during the conversation they are about to have, she must not chatter on. She must answer his questions as succinctly as possible. He will not tolerate an attempt to persuade him of anything, for he cannot be persuaded to believe anything but what he already knows to be true.

For her edification, Asher recounts his résumé: undergraduate degree from one Ivy League university, medical degree from another, the decision not to practice medicine. He speaks passionately about his lengthy internship with Xanthus Toller, guru of the Restoration Movement, and about the profound insights he gained from judicious experiments with mescaline and alkaloid psilocybin, which led him to the realization that not just animals and plants but indeed *all matter* is alive and *aware*.

She listens quietly, as she has been told to listen. However, Asher is the most observant and perceptive of men, and he can read her every thought in the smallest of facial expressions, in changes in her posture, and of course in her malachite-green eyes. She is afraid of him, thinks him insane, and so resists understanding the importance of her role in his great undertaking.

Her problem is that, even in her dire circumstances, Ophelia entertains hope. She doesn't understand that hope is a worthless currency, the fool's gold of the ignorant. Hope is like the blinders put on a dray horse to focus it on the way ahead. Hope prevents her from seeing the horrors of life to the left and right, horrors that may befall her at any moment; even worse, hope prevents her from seeing the meaninglessness of her own existence and the damage she does merely by being alive.

The purpose of this conversation is to take from her all hope, so that when he writes of her in his manifesto, she will serve as a convincing lesson to those who read his work and are moved to join the revolution.

"You're a pretty girl. Do you know how very desirable you are?"

She indulges in rebellion. "I'm not a girl. I'm a grown woman."

On the table lies a switchblade. He picks it up, presses the release button, and the blade springs forth. The softly pulsing light seems to transform the razor-edged length of steel into a blade of quicksilver.

"Do you understand how very desirable you are?" he asks again.

"Yes."

"Do you think I abducted you because of your good looks?"

"Yes."

"I have taken two men. And two rather plain-looking women. I took you only because you were careless and therefore made taking you convenient. Your looks mean nothing to me."

She is silent.

He smiles. "You didn't respond because it wasn't a question. Good girl. Smart girl. You expect me to rape you. Is that correct?"

Now mindful of his instruction to be succinct, she merely says, "Yes," but with her expression informs him of her contempt.

He closes the blade and sets the knife aside. "I have no sexual interest in you, Ophelia. Do you believe me?"

"No."

"You read the portion of the manifesto I've so far written. You know I'm in rebellion against all things human. Do you know this?"

"That's what you've written."

He nods. "The implication being that I don't really believe what I write. But I do, Ophelia. My motives are pure. Can you guess the extremes to which I've gone to make certain that my motives remain pure?"

"I'm sure you'll tell me."

The lantern hisses continuously, but at times the sound seems to come from elsewhere in the room, as if a serpent of substantial size slithers through the surrounding shadows.

"I took up medicine because it was expected of the men in my family, but my heart was never in it. A trust was established in my name the very month I was born and my father made contributions to it every year. I've no need to earn a living, which has given me the opportunity to do something of very great importance, which I came to understand during my time with Xanthus Toller. I'm in rebellion against destructive humanity, against all things human. And what is the quintessential fixation of humanity? What is the species' most manic compulsion, its most morbid drive, its ruling passion, the obsession that overwhelms all other obsessions?"

"Money," she says.

He shakes his head. "You know better. Money is second. Sex, Ophelia. Humankind is obsessed with getting off. Sex, sex, sex, and still more sex. Our sick culture is saturated with it. And sex leads to breeding. Other animals have sex only in that brief time of the year when the female is in heat, but human beings are always at it, until now we number in the many billions. However, I'm not of their ilk, not of *your* ilk, Ophelia. Because of your beauty, your ripe sexuality, you hold on to the hope that you can wound me or even kill me in the act, when I mount you and become vulnerable because of sexual obsession. But that is a false hope, Ophelia. Can you guess why I will never mount you or have any kind of sex with you?"

"No," she says, still clearly disbelieving him.

He leans across the table. "When one has a first-rate medical education, the money to obtain any drugs one requires, and a mission of greatness such as I have, a double orchiectomy can be performed with little pain and less blood than a bad nosebleed."

She stares at him uncomprehendingly, as if perhaps she does not know the word *orchiectomy*.

"More than a year ago," he continues, "I injected my scrotum and surrounding tissue with a strong local anesthetic. With the assistance of one of Xanthus Toller's wisest associates, I cut off my testicles. A double orchiectomy. Self-castration. I don't merely espouse the philosophy of the Restoration Movement, Ophelia. I *live* it to the fullest extent possible."

He believes that her expression is one of awe that she should be in the presence of such a courageous man. She's astonished speechless by the profound nature of his commitment.

Asher continues: "The prophet Xanthus has foreseen that one day a savior of the world will arise to eradicate the infection that is humanity, restoring our suffering planet to health. He thought this person might be a scientist who would design and unleash a plague capable of wiping out our species. But the savior is no scientist, Ophelia. The savior is me."

9

After the troubling conversation with Katherine, followed by a brisk half-hour walk, Joanna returned to her house. She took a quick shower, dressed, went to her study, and sat at her desk.

She didn't switch on the computer, because she knew she would stare for hours at the half-finished page eighty-eight of *The Color of Never*, without being able to advance the story by one word. She could not stop thinking about Jimmy Two Eyes.

Although it had been twenty-five years since Katherine had seen the boy at Rustling Willows, he had made such an impression on her that she had been able to provide considerable detail about him. The malformed skull. The misaligned eyes of different colors. Small ears set tight against his head, but a prominent nose. A mouth maybe half again as wide as a mouth ought to be. Those were not all indices of any particular birth defect with a formal name to be found in the medical literature. Burden upon burden had been piled on poor Jimmy Alvarez, as though he'd been conceived in a genetic storm. Mother Nature had been in a wicked mood, showering him with afflictions. He was severely hunchbacked, as well. His hands were abnormally small. His bones developed so slowly that he would never be taller than five feet, and his canted hips would always leave him with a hitching gait.

His parents, Hector and Annalisa, had blamed themselves for Jimmy's condition. They were people of deep but simple faith who perhaps could not blame Nature because that was, to their way of thinking, like blaming God.

In spite of all the information that Katherine had provided, Joanna could not quite picture Jimmy Two Eyes. Stranger still, with so many details to prod her memory, she nevertheless could summon no recollection of him whatsoever. To a young girl with an especially vivid imagination, Jimmy would have been not merely a subject of pity, but also a figure of great mystery, like a character in a fairy tale, perhaps a seer with knowledge of both dark and white magic.

She soon grew weary of staring at the dead gray screen of the computer and rerunning in her mind all that Auntie Kat had told her. She went out to the market and bought all the makings for both an enormous pot of vegetable beef soup and a casserole of vegetable lasagna. Cleaning and cutting all the veggies would take hours in which she might be distracted from the recent puzzling events, allowing her subconscious to mull them over and perhaps shape them into something meaningful.

When she returned home, before setting to work in the kitchen, she went to her study to check her emails. Among them was one from Katherine: Joanna, I saved all the letters I got from your mother back in the day, and this one was among them. I've marked the pertinent lines. You would have been eight when this was written. What do you make of it?

She printed the two-page PDF and read the lines that Katherine had highlighted in yellow.

Jojo is such a fine girl. She makes me proud, how she neither fears Jimmy Alvarez nor finds him off-putting. You know how she looked after him when you were here last summer, making a snack for him each time she had one herself, even wiping his mouth after he'd eaten. She spends more time than ever with him these days. They sit together on the bench in the apple orchard or down by the lake, and she reads stories to him. She's in third grade but reads four grades above that, smart as the dickens, although I doubt that poor Jimmy understands much of anything she says to him.

10

The ancient, clouded windowpanes render the Montana morning sunshine into a bleak Antarctic dusk, and the softly hissing gas lantern radiates séance light in which spirits might be called out of the shadows, if such things as spirits existed, which they do not.

This girl, Ophelia, wants to be stone, wants to be steel. Maybe she used all the tears when her twin sister died five years earlier; or she's seriously churched up, convinced there is an afterlife. Whatever the case, she won't reward Asher with her tears, not even when he describes what he will do to her with the switchblade.

Xanthus Toller explains that humankind is evil because of two qualities that are unique to the species: hope and ambition. The hope is for a better tomorrow and ultimately for a life beyond this one. No other living creature on Earth has a concept of time, let alone a belief that they can conquer it through resurrection or with longevity science. Hope breeds ambition, the desire to build and achieve and acquire, activities that lay waste to the planet. The most enlightened human beings must lead the way by abandoning hope and ambition in order to be able to persuade the selfish masses to participate in the extinction of their species. Asher has led four others into hopelessness and death, and one way or another, this woman will be the fifth.

"You think you're really something," he says.

"Is that a question? You said I can speak only to answer your questions."

"Assume it is."

"Then, yeah, I'm something. Something more than you."

Asher props one elbow on the table and rests his chin on the palm of his hand. "Why do you think so?"

"You're a eunuch. You've made a nothing of yourself."

"Exactly, I am nothing of value. You are nothing of value. I've faced the truth, and you haven't."

She glares at him with the contempt and anger of someone who still expects to be alive tomorrow. In her arrogance and self-assurance, she serves as the perfect example of why humanity is an existential threat to all other species.

He says, “You’ve read what exists of my manifesto, and yet you still don’t understand.”

“Freak,” Ophelia says defiantly.

“You’re nothing. I am nothing. We’re lice, tapeworms, parasites infesting the planet. We are disgusting. It tortures me to consider what our species has done and is still doing to this world.”

“Then kill yourself, why don’t you?”

“I will when my manifesto is completed and the testamentary necropolis is filled to capacity—and I’m the last on Earth.”

“What gibberish is that?”

“Testamentary necropolis? Perhaps your failure to understand my manifesto is a consequence of too little education. A necropolis is a graveyard, a community of the dead. The necropolis I’m creating is testamentary because it will serve as a testament to the truth of my philosophy and to my commitment to seeing the world restored to its unsullied prehuman condition.”

In spite of her dire circumstances, she sneers. “You mistake insanity for philosophy.”

Xanthus Toller teaches that of all the myriad species on Earth, only human beings indulge in hatred and anger. Therefore, it would diminish the message of Asher’s manifesto if he became enraged at this disrespectful bitch and killed her for the wrong reason. That would be murder. So very human. Justified killing is not murder, either in self-defense or in defense of the planet. But it must be done with regret, solemnly, without rancor and certainly without satisfaction of an erotic nature. He is a priest, not of any faith, but a priest in service to the whale and the wasp, the deer and the dormouse, an archbishop of seaweed and sycamores. He must at all times be measured in his response to provocations of the kind in which this woman traffics.

Asher raises his head from the pedestal of his palm and shakes it slowly, mournfully. "It pains me, saddens me, to say that by your ignorance and hostility, by your refusal to give up hope, you have earned special treatment. Not the quick and merciful knife."

Because her wrists are bound together, she has to prop both elbows on the table to mock him by resting her chin on a hand. "So tell me, you nutless freak, how does a pained and saddened eunuch kill someone if he doesn't use a knife? Will you set me on fire?" She fakes a look of surprise. "Oh, gee, I'm asking the questions instead of answering them. Still, I'd like to know."

Asher Optime has not understood this snarky bitch since she first woke from a chloroform sleep. She isn't behaving like the two men and two women whom he'd brought here before her. Those four had been properly terrified of him, respectful and eager to please. The longest he'd taken to bleed the hope from any of them had been four days, and one of them had fallen into black despair in less than six hours. This smart-mouthed slut isn't stupid, so she must be a little crazy—or she's faking this irrational confidence to put him off his game and keep herself alive in hope of escaping or somehow taking him out. He'd like to punch her in the face a few times, smash that smug smile into bloody pulp.

No. No, no, that would be wrong. That would be an act of anger and would reduce him to the miserable human condition that he has transcended under the instruction of Xanthus Toller and through the act of self-castration. He is above anger and resentment and all of that, high above it, flying on his mission of world restoration. He kills not for his own gratification, but for Mother Earth.

"Will you set me on fire?" she asks again. "Do you have some enormous vat of acid into which you'll slowly lower me? Is there maybe a pit of alligators, and you'll throw me among them after you wrap me in bacon?"

She's mocking him as if he styles himself after a comic-book villain, some nemesis of Spider-Man. Such impudence is infuriating. Rather, it might be infuriating if he wasn't incapable of violent and vindictive emotions. Having transcended such human weaknesses, Asher merely smiles and nods and says, "You hide your fear behind sarcasm and ridicule. But you'll be begging for your worthless life soon enough. Excuse me while I step outside to commune with Mother about how you should suffer for the sin of your existence."

She feigns astonishment. "Your syphilitic *mother* is here?"

"Mother Earth," he clarifies. "She's here. She's everywhere."

The necklace of heavy chain, which earlier anchored Ophelia to a wall stud, now padlocks her to the headrail of the chair. Thus shackled, with wrists zip tied, she isn't fully immobilized. But if she were to get up from the table, she would be able only to hobble clumsily around the room, the chair on her back, too slow and noisy to escape.

Asher carries his straight-backed chair outside, places it on the saloon veranda, and sits facing the ghost town's only avenue.

In a sky as pale blue as a robin's egg, the sun is at its apex, so neither the buildings nor the weeds in the unpaved street cast shadows. The warm summer air is so perfectly still that Zipporah might be a diorama under a glass dome. The scene looks flat and unreal.

From a pocket of his lightweight denim jacket, Asher extracts a silver cigarette case and a lighter. The case contains hand-rolled joints spiced with PCP, an animal tranquilizer that, in combination with weed, can often facilitate visions and profound communion with Nature. He already knows to what well-deserved torment Ophelia Poole must be subjected. He doesn't need Mother's counsel on the matter. But if the woman is given five or six hours to wonder about what horrors he is contemplating, her unfounded confidence might falter and her hope begin to fade by the time that he takes her down the street to the necropolis and forces her to spend time as the only living person among the decomposing dead.

11

Earlier that Thursday morning in August, Wyatt Rider, a licensed private investigator, had met with Liam O'Hara in the billionaire's signature building, in his personal apartment high above Seattle. The study was a large corner room with floor-to-ceiling windows and spectacular views of both Puget Sound to the west and, to the north, lesser skyscrapers than O'Hara's own, shouldering one another along the streets of the metropolis.

The vistas beyond the windows might have rendered the study furnishings unmemorable if they had been any less dramatic than the massive steel desk, which had a quartzite top the white of fractured ice with veins as blue as arctic seawater. The enormous

David Hockney paintings, from his California swimming-pool-art period, provided warmth in contrast to the steel and quartzite, a warmth that was a quality of O'Hara himself.

The forty-six-year-old billionaire had come from a family of modest means, the son of a lumber-mill worker and a diner waitress. Brilliant and driven, he had made his fortune fast in the high-tech revolution, but he never forgot where his roots were.

Wyatt Rider, too, remained always aware of his origins, but his father and mother hadn't been as humble and hardworking as O'Hara's parents. Although smart enough to know the risks, they had sought the easy money that could be snatched up by deceiving the naive and vulnerable.

Wyatt had done jobs for Liam six times, not the least of which had involved serious threats against the two O'Hara children, Laura and Tavis, and he was accustomed to being greeted with a broad smile and vigorous handshake. The lumberman's son was reliably energetic and in high spirits, as if his gratitude for such good luck would not allow him to indulge in a moment of anxiety or depression.

On this occasion, however, when the butler showed Wyatt to the study, Liam O'Hara's smile and handshake were perfunctory. He didn't offer his guest coffee, didn't engage in small talk, but escorted him directly to one of four leather armchairs encircling a steel-and-glass coffee table. The billionaire settled in the chair to the left of Wyatt's and sat forward on the edge, his hands clutching the padded arms much as he might have held fast to the security bar in a roller-coaster car.

He lacked even the shadow of a beard, as though he must have American Indian genes in his lineage, but his face was freckled, his hair rust red, and his eyes as green as shamrocks.

He spoke rapidly, as he often did, but not with his customary ebullience, instead with quiet anxiety. "For a couple years, I've been buying land in Montana—ranches, contiguous properties. Not in or around the town where I was raised, but in the adjacent county. My parents have passed away, as you know, and I don't really have friends back there. Anyway, I'm trying to put together maybe ten or twelve thousand acres, not just for sentimental reasons and not just as a place to get away to now and then, but also to preserve the land. It's so beautiful there. Have you ever been? No, that's right, I asked you that before, and you've never been. Well, I'd like you to go now, today, or as soon as you can, and look into a certain situation for me. Lyndsey and the kids and I went there last Friday, meant to stay a week at this ranch called Rustling Willows, roughing it, just the four of us, no entourage, but we got the hell out of there on Monday. The last few days, I've been trying to make sense of what happened, but I can't. Damn if I can. What happened—it was kind of magical at first, but it got weird pretty quickly, and then it scared the shit out of me."

When Liam took a breath, Wyatt said, "Tell me what happened."

The billionaire met Wyatt's eyes, but then looked quickly away and hesitated, though his habit had always been to make direct eye contact and speak forthrightly. His attention seemed to be caught by a helicopter moving parallel to the superbly insulated windows, as silent as if it were a hallucination. But Wyatt sensed that Liam was less distracted by the aircraft than he was *seeking* a distraction to delay making what revelation he intended to impart.

Finally, he said, "I don't believe in the supernatural—ghosts, spirits, possession, any of that. Do you?"

"Not actively," Wyatt said. "But I keep an open mind."

As he followed the receding helicopter, Liam said, "Anyway, whatever it was, it wasn't any of that."

After perhaps half a minute, Wyatt said, "I'm growing old here, Liam. Soon you'll need to hire a younger gumshoe."

Liam met his eyes and didn't look away this time. "None of what I tell you can ever be repeated in any public forum. They'd think I've lost it, slid into drugs or something, and the company's stock price would plummet."

"If I'd wanted to sell the story of that threat against Laura and Tavis, as sensational as it was, I could've gotten seven hundred thousand—maybe eight, hell, maybe a million—from one tabloid or another. I wasn't tempted for even a minute."

Liam grimaced. "I'm sorry. I didn't mean to imply . . . Damn, Wyatt, this experience has fucked with my head. You and I go back a long way. I know you're solid."

"We go back to before you were who you are." He reached out and put a hand on Liam's shoulder. "Do I have to get you drunk before you'll tell me what you need to tell me?"

Liam sighed and settled back in his chair and told it all.

Now, six hours later, Wyatt was in the Treasure State. Liam's Learjet had flown him from Seattle to Spokane. From there, a chartered propjet carried him, the only passenger, to Helena, Montana, where the runway was too short for the Lear. A new Range Rover, purchased from a local dealer by Liam while Wyatt was in transit, waited for him at the airport. When money was no object, getting from anywhere to anywhere else could be as easy as going nowhere at all.

He would be at Rustling Willows well before nightfall.

12

Six days a week, Wendy Sharp worked the lunch shift at an Italian family restaurant and the dinner shift at an upscale place with good Mediterranean food, but all she had on Thursdays was a lunch shift. By three o'clock, she was hurrying through traffic in her VW, eager to free Cricket from Jolly Bertha and go to the park and watch people, especially people with dogs, because it was her and Cricket's fondest dream to one day have a house with a yard and a dog, and they were still unsure what breed they most wanted.

Wendy Sharp had no one in the world except Cricket Moon; and she would die for her if ever it came to that. Cricket Moon Sharp was seven years old, with her father's auburn hair and her mother's blue eyes. She resembled her mother in every regard except for the hair, which was fortunate because Wendy might not have loved the child so intensely if every time she looked at her she was reminded of *him*. His name wasn't Snake, but that's what Wendy called him when she walked out of the hell that he built and ruled. Snake was the name he earned. Snake was not a part of their life anymore, and he never would be, not if Wendy had anything to say about it. In fact, she had *everything* to say about it, because Snake knew she would kill him hard if he ever came around, and he was scared of her.

She loved Cricket Moon with a passion that surprised her because for so many years before this child came along, Wendy had been dead inside. Well, her organs worked and her blood flowed and all that, but she didn't *feel* anything. Or she didn't feel much, not anything worth feeling: sadness, a quiet and persistent anxiety, self-loathing. She left home with all that bad psychological baggage and little else when she was fourteen. Anyway, it wasn't really a home that she left, just a place where her mother did dope and her father drank. Often the old man was in a mean mood, and the only thing that cheered him up was hitting someone too small to hit back. When Wendy got out of there, she lived on the street with a paper bag over her head, holes cut in it to see and breathe, and she had a special corner where she sat with a donation jar and a hand-printed sign that said: SEVERE FACIAL DEFORMITIES. SO UGLY NO ONE WILL HIRE ME. GOD BLESS YOU FOR CARING. Some people took her claim seriously, as if she were the girl version of the Elephant Man, while many others thought it was a scam but a funny one, and both types dropped coins and singles in the jar, sometimes larger bills. By concealing her face, which was actually pretty enough, she remained able to panhandle without much risk of being taken into custody by child-welfare authorities. She slept in churches and bathed after midnight in public fountains and reflecting pools, and she had money for food, movies, whatnot. Nothing really terrible happened to her, but nothing good enough happened to make her feel better about herself, which was why she was so susceptible to the Snake when he pitched her on the glories of his mission and his pure heart, and brought her to live in his compound at the eastern end of the San Fernando Valley.

She was fifteen when she became the Snake's "bride." In her mind, she always put quotation marks around the word because there was never a wedding and because she wasn't his only "bride." He had four or five at any one time, although this was not known by those beyond his inner circle of advisers, the so-called First 10. The other "brides" were often pregnant, and the Snake had a doctor in his mission, one who performed ultrasound scans to be sure that the mothers and their unborn babies were okay. The Snake wasn't a gentle husband, nor did he appear interested in a wife's needs or emotions. However, his concern for their health during pregnancy suggested that he cared about them more than he could easily express. If something was wrong with a baby—something often was—an abortion ensued. If the baby was healthy, its arrival was celebrated by all the "brides" as the birth of another right-thinking missionary who would grow up to help their father lead the world to its destiny. Wendy became pregnant when she was sixteen. Her unborn baby passed its ultrasound test. She was seventeen when she reached term. When her labor began, two other wives attended her. In the penultimate moment, as her child was about to enter the world, she woke to the terrible truth of what she had done.

Falling under the thrall of the Snake and becoming part of his mission had done nothing to alleviate her sadness, anxiety, and lack of self-worth. If anything, her anxiety increased, for the Snake's greatest talent was instilling fear of many things in others. Being pregnant had not been a source of joy, had not given her a sense of purpose. However, as her contractions grew more violent and as she felt the baby's head emerge from the birth canal, she realized something she had known but repressed: Of the children born to the "brides," all were girls, as was Wendy's baby. And this was no accident. The Snake claimed to know the future—what it should be, what it would be—and the future he meant to create for himself included a harem without regard for the crime of incest. Horror gripped her as she gave birth to Cricket Moon and saw that sweet innocent face, for she suddenly understood that she would be responsible for delivering her daughter into a life worse than the one she had fled at the age of fourteen. If she ever hoped to value herself, she must value her child; they were each other's salvation.

Three months after giving birth, Wendy began to worry that she had slimmed down enough to be attractive to the Snake. She wouldn't risk being mother to a second child of his, nor would she let him have partial custody of—or even visitation rights with—their firstborn. None of his "brides" ever spent the night with him; each was dismissed once used, and he slept alone. At two o'clock in the morning of the day when she began to become herself at last and find dignity, Wendy swaddled Cricket in a blanket, settled the infant in a large basket, carried her to the garage, and left her, basketed and sleeping, on the floor in front of the passenger seat of a Mercedes sedan, one of fourteen vehicles owned by the mission.

From the adjacent mechanic's shop, she fetched a three-gallon bucket and a length of flexible siphon with which she half filled the container with gasoline from a Lexus SUV. She went to the Snake's private quarters and cautiously opened the door. He snored softly in the low lamplight, for he was unable to fall asleep in darkness. She threw the gasoline on him—and then the bucket. He scrambled awake, gasping for breath in the fumes. She struck a flame with a butane lighter and told him that she'd spare him this time as long as he stayed on the reeking bed and listened to her. "But if you ever try to find me or my child, I'll know. For the rest of my life, I'll carry a knife, two knives. I'll know if you're trying to find us, and I'll find you first, find you when you least expect to be found, and disembowel you."

Then she threw the lighter on the bed. He screamed, but of course the flame went out the moment she was no longer depressing the gas lever, and he was not immolated. She left him sobbing with terror even as he continued gasping for clean air.

She drove into Los Angeles that night, abandoned the Mercedes, and boarded a bus to San Diego. For a while then, she and Cricket Moon lived in a home for unwed mothers, growing into a recognition of the wonder of the world together.

Her promise to the Snake that she would know if he tried to find her, that she would find him first, made sense only if she had a supernatural power like clairvoyance, which she didn't. But she'd meant it when she'd said it with such conviction. Evidently he had believed her, for neither he nor any of his acolytes had come after her in all these years. His real name was Xanthus Toller, and his resources were significant; if he'd wanted to find her, he could have done so long ago.

Now Cricket was seven and, during Wendy's working hours, the girl was being cared for and homeschooled by Bertha Jean Mockton, a retired schoolteacher, who lived just three blocks from the building in which Wendy had an apartment.

At 3:15 p.m. on that Thursday, after she finished waitressing the lunch shift at Geppeto's Little Italy, she picked up Cricket at Bertha's house and drove to their favorite park, one with a bay view. At a snack shop, they bought Cokes and two chocolate-chip cookies the size of saucers, and they sat on a bench together. There were little white clouds and lots of sunshine and a pleasant breeze and palm trees swaying and great swards of green grass. Beyond the grass, blue water sparkled. People walked, jogged, rode bikes, swept past on skateboards: women and men, all ages, all races.

Many dogs pranced by at the end of leashes, to be admired and coveted.

"Was there good business today?" Cricket asked.

"Pretty good business."

"Did you get a doorknob?"

"Two doorknobs and the hinges. Maybe even a whole door."

They were in the habit of translating Wendy's tips into pieces of the house they hoped to buy one day.

"That doesn't suck for a Thursday lunch," Cricket said.

"It sucketh not," Wendy agreed.

"We don't need a mansion like Mr. Toad has." Although just in second grade, Cricket read at a fifth-grade level and was currently breezing through *The Wind in the Willows* at Bertha's house and also in the evenings with her mother. "All we need is a nice little place with a big dog. We gotta name the dog something. Mr. Toad is called Toad 'cause that's what he is, you know?"

"Makes sense. But Mr. Dog isn't good enough for our dog."

"Bertha says her mom named her Bertha 'cause it's like this old German word that means someone who shines. She asked why my name is Cricket Moon Sharp, and I don't know. So why is it my name?"

Wendy had expected this question for some time. "Sharp is my maiden name. Your father chose the others. He liked unusual names."

"He was a really bad man, wasn't he?"

"Very."

"Like Dracula or something."

"Better you don't know his name. Trust me about that."

"I trust you about everything. So do you like my names?"

"Do you?"

"I kind of do. Anyway, it's who I've always been."

"I like them, too," Wendy said. "A cricket is sprightly and quick, and so are you. Crickets sing, and you're always singing."

"I sing better than crickets."

"You do indeed."

"Crickets know one song. I know like a hundred. Why Moon?"

"Why not? The moon is beautiful, and so are you."

"So did you ever think about changing my names?"

"At first. And then I thought, just because someone names you doesn't mean they own you. Nobody owns you, Cricket."

The girl thought about that, nibbling her cookie, and then said, "We have to name our dog. So then won't we own him?"

"No one owns a dog, sweetie. We adopt them. They're family."

"I think I'd like a sister. A dog sister, I mean."

They had been sitting on the bench for fifteen minutes when Wendy noticed that the number of people in the park had declined dramatically. By the time she and Cricket finished their Cokes and cookies, and discussed possible dog names at length, the joggers and cyclists and skaters all but disappeared. Wendy became aware of men and women in dark suits and sunglasses, who were sitting on distant benches and loitering along the pathways, like morticians who had left their funeral homes in search of business prospects among the melanoma-courting sun worshippers and head-injury-prone skaters who refused to wear helmets.

She said, "I think they've closed the park."

"Who did? They can't close a park. There's no doors on a park."

Although Wendy didn't believe the Snake would come looking for them after all this time, though operatives in black suits were not how those true believers in his cult chose to style themselves, she was nonetheless disconcerted. "We better go," she said.

"But we just got here, Mom."

As Wendy rose from the bench, a man behind her said, "We mean you no harm, Ms. Sharp."

She pivoted, suppressing a small cry of alarm. She never let anyone know that anything frightened her. Bad people thrived on your fear, saw it as a weakness, and moved in fast on you.

The guy was tall and slim and handsome, dressed in white from head to foot, with a fresh red carnation pinned in the buttonhole of his suit coat. Nature had given him a kind face and a sweet smile—but it was wise to remember that oleander bushes produced beautiful flowers so poisonous they were as lethal as a bullet in the head.

"Who are you?"

"Ordinarily, I withhold that information. But in your case, considering what you've endured, I know you'll need to be reassured that I'm trustworthy." He produced a business card. "Google me. But use my phone, not yours. Your phone is most likely hacked. It won't be good for either of us if your name is connected to mine."

Wendy surveyed the park. Now she saw no one but men and women in black suits. They remained at a distance but watchful. The man in white gave her his iPhone and his password.

Having gotten off the bench, Cricket studied the stranger while Wendy googled him. "You look like you sell ice cream."

"I guess I do," he said.

"Do you sell ice cream?" the girl asked.

"No, but I love to eat it."

"Why do you dress all in white?"

"So I don't have to waste time thinking about what to wear."

"Do you always wear a flower?"

"Not always. Only when I'm going to meet a princess."

"You know a princess?"

"I just met her," he said.

"Wow. Cool. I never knew a princess."

"I'll introduce you to yourself."

"You're a little silly. Do you have a dog?"

"I've got four dogs."

"Four!"

"Two golden retrievers, one Belgian sheepdog, and one humongous Newfoundland."

"If you really have four, what're their names. Tell me quick."

"Butterscotch, Lollipop, Peppermint, and Licorice."

"You named them candy names!"

"They're very sweet creatures."

"My name's Cricket. What's your name?"

"Ganesh."

"I know what a cricket is. What's a Ganesh?"

"A Ganesh is a man who doesn't sell ice cream."

Wendy discovered that, if she wanted to know everything there was to know about this man, she'd need to take a few weeks off from work. She lost track of his conversation with Cricket, and when she finally backed out of the internet, she heard her daughter say, "Which one is named Gumdrop? Must be one of the golden retrievers, huh?"

"No Gumdrop. The retrievers are Butterscotch and Lollipop."

"Oh. I thought you said there was a Gumdrop."

"No you didn't. You were testing me."

"Okay, yeah, but I needed to be sure I should like you."

"Do you like me?"

"Well, yeah, you got four dogs."

Wendy said, "Okay, I'm impressed. Google needs a dedicated server just for you. What's this about?"

From an inside coat pocket, he produced a folded sheet of paper, opened it, and showed her a photograph. "It's a matter of national security. You remember this man?"

She grimaced. "Asher Optime. He's the Snake's right hand. Sorry. I call Xanthus Toller 'the Snake.' You know who he is?"

"Toller? Yes."

"Optime was the craziest of Toller's true believers. A vicious enforcer in the cult."

"Bad things are happening to people who knew him and had some conflict with him, people whom he had some reason to hate. He seems to be a dedicated hater."

"What bad things?"

He looked at Cricket, and Wendy said, "She's no frail flower. I raised her to handle whatever."

Meeting Wendy's eyes again, he said, "Seven have been . . . murdered. And not in a way it's ever been done before. Like I said, this is a matter of national security. We've recently gotten ahead of the curve, trying to identify who might be on the list."

"What list?"

"The death list. We've got a nationwide manhunt for this guy. In the meantime, we're trying to save anyone we think is in danger."

"What—we'll have to live with bodyguards?"

"Bodyguards won't do any good. They'll just die with you. Your only hope is to go into a witness protection program."

Wendy didn't like that. "You'll make us disappear."

"Not the way you're afraid of. You'd get a new identity, a cash settlement, a generous monthly stipend, and a paid-off house."

She was dubious. She surveyed the park again, wondering if she should grab Cricket and run, but there were too many of the suits.

"A house? What house? Where?"

"A lovely town in Georgia."

The bole shadows of the palm trees were long in the afternoon light, and silhouettes of the fronds fluttered on the grass like broken-winged birds.

She said, "Money, a house? Who pays for all that?"

"The government."

"You're not the government."

"But I speak for the project, a rare government collaboration with the private sector. You know who I am. You know my reputation."

Cricket said, "Does the house have a yard?"

"Yes, a big yard."

"Does it have a dog?"

"You could get any dog you want."

"When?"

"As soon as you're there." Pocketing the phone that Wendy had returned to him, he said, "Ms. Sharp, this is as urgent as urgent gets. You can be found by your phone. You can be destroyed right here, right now, with your daughter and with me, if maybe your name has come to the top of the list. I don't know about you, but I'd rather not die today."

She plucked her purse off the bench and retrieved her phone from it. "Destroyed how?"

"I'm not at liberty to say."

If they wanted her dead, they wouldn't have come after her like this. The very complexity of his story seemed to verify it.

"What do I do with my phone?"

"Leave it on the bench. One of my associates will hammer it."

"This is batshit crazy," she said.

"It absolutely is," he agreed.

She hesitated to relinquish the phone, and he said, "Wendy, have you ever heard of Carl Jung, or the word *synchronicity*?"

"No."

"Jung's theories have a lot in common with what science—quantum mechanics—reveals about the nature of reality."

"Like that helps," she said, still clutching her phone.

"Incredible coincidences are more common than we think. They're part of the weave of the world. Effect can come before cause."

"I'm a waitress, you know. Dessert doesn't come before the entrée."

He smiled. "The famous British actress Beatrice Lillie was once onstage in Ontario, Canada, performing in Noël Coward's *This Year of Grace*, the entire cast lined up to one side of her. She was singing "Britannia Rules the Waves," when she mistakenly began to sing the second verse twice, before moving to the third. She realized what she was doing but had to carry forward with it. The cast froze in place instead of moving to center stage—which was when the biggest and heaviest arc light fell from above, onto the very spot where they should have been standing. They were saved from serious injury, perhaps even death."

She found him hypnotic, and she said, "You're spooking me."

"The opposite of my intention. The incident could be seen as a mere coincidence—or as an indication that Ms. Lillie would lead a long and charmed life. She died sixty years later, at the age of ninety-four. Now remember that house in Georgia that I said is waiting for you? By the merest chance, Wendy, the street number is eight one one—the month and day Cricket was born. And the number of the street is the same as the year she was born. Do you think that might be meaningful? Positive synchronicity?"

"You're a little weird."

"Yes, I am aware."

"But in a good way," she said, putting her iPhone on the bench as he had requested. She and Cricket went away with him.

13

In Santa Fe, as the one-gallon pot of aromatic vegetable soup cooled on the drainboard beside the sink, Joanna Chase slid the pan of lasagna into the oven. She'd already made a small salad, which chilled in the refrigerator. Now she poured a glass of cabernet and moved through the house, again marveling that she had unconsciously re-created the decor—the very feeling—of the house at Rustling Willows.

In her bedroom, above the bed, a chunky wood shelf called a *repisa* held Pueblo pottery as well as carved *bultos* of San Antonio of Padua and Santa Librada and San Rafael. The iron-and-brass bed was graced with a museum-quality spread—white with simple flower-motif embroidery—crafted in the 1990s by the much-admired weaver Teresa Archuleta-Sagel.

Over the years, Joanna had dated several men, but she'd shared this bed with only two. Neither relationship lasted. These days, too many educated men shaped themselves into what they believed modern women wanted, as if all women wanted precisely the same thing, and in so shaping became emotional and intellectual marionettes; worst of all, they believed in their sincerity. In fact, they were styling themselves according to the dictates of a relatively small cadre of pundits and influencers who wanted not equality but control. Joanna found such men to be dull and weak and unreliable. Her father had been one whose every word and deed comported with what the most manphobic prestigious magazines said that a man should think and do, and she did not want a man like that. She'd loved her father, but something about him had seemed *practiced*—even calculated—so that even as a child she'd not been quite sure if his affection was real or deliberated and rehearsed.

From the top shelf in the back of the walk-in closet, Joanna retrieved a plastic container as big as four shoeboxes. She carried it and her half-finished glass of wine to the kitchen, put them on the table, settled into a chair, and removed the snap-on lid from the container.

The photographs were from a time when people still used cameras instead of smartphones to take family pictures. The box was three-quarters full of snapshots. She thought there had once been more than these, but perhaps she was mistaken. She hadn't looked at them in years. The photos were loose, unorganized, and she began to order them according to subject and, as best as she could determine, date.

The pictures included several of her granddad, whom she barely remembered, a white-haired man with a walrus mustache.

Her father and mother. Joanna herself. Various ranch hands. Numerous horses. Auntie Kat from when she visited once. Here were Hector Alvarez, the ranch manager who served under her granddad, when Rustling Willows was a cattle operation, and then under Father when the focus shifted to breeding quarter horses for racing and show-worthy thoroughbreds. Hector alone but also with his wife, Annalisa. Annalisa alone and sometimes with Joanna or with Joanna's mother. Pictures of Joanna and her mother in swimsuits, on the shore of Lake Sapphire, or bundled up for sledding on a day of driving snow. Birthday parties and celebrations around a Christmas tree. Hundreds of photos. Joanna took an hour and a half to study them, remember the moments that they captured, and organize them in piles—and at the end, she had found not one picture of Jimmy Two Eyes.

14

He had taken away Ophelia Poole's wristwatch because he said time had already run out for her, and therefore a watch was of no use.

Perhaps an hour before sunset, Optime returned for her. Asher Optime. He'd shown her his driver's license, so that she would know the name he'd given her was in fact his and would conclude that he wouldn't have revealed it if he wasn't certain she had no chance of escape.

This self-emasculated crackpot scared her, but he didn't terrify her into helplessness. He didn't understand why she didn't quail before him, but he had no way of knowing that she had been expecting him for years and living for the day when he would appear.

Leaving his chair on the veranda, eating one of the cookies that earlier he'd retrieved from his larder when weed-induced craving overcame him, he said, "Pissed your pants yet?"

"Not me," she said. "What about you?"

Looming over Ophelia, screwing his pale face into as portentous an expression as he was able to manage while wacked-out on pot, he said, "I'm escorting you to the necropolis. 'No place affords a more striking conviction of the vanity of human hopes than there.'"

"What an ass you are," she taunted him. "Who talks that way?"

"Samuel Johnson. Though his subject was libraries rather than graveyards. I think it was Johnson, not Shakespeare. Anyway, it was someone whose IQ was three times yours." He sucked at his teeth to extract a lingering morsel of cookie. "Let's see how long you can hold on to hope when you're locked in there with the rotting dead."

"If you'll let me take a piss, I'll have no trouble holding on to hope until I kill you."

Ophelia dared to speak to him like this because she had three advantages over the sociopathic creep. First, she had read what existed of his ridiculous manifesto and understood the swollen ego and the delusions that motivated him. Second, she was a lot more intelligent than he thought she was, with common sense and street smarts that were unknown to his kind.

And finally, he was ludicrous, a fool who lacked the capacity for clear-eyed self-examination that might have saved him from his foolishness. She only had to play with him psychologically and keep herself alive until he made the stupid move that would be the death of him.

Or so she told herself repeatedly, insistently. In spite of the extraordinary intensity of Optime's madness and his barely repressed ferocity, Ophelia refused to entertain even a shadow of a shadow of a doubt.

"What about you?" she asked. "Do you still piss like a man, or did you cut off your willie, too?"

His throttled rage was apparent in tics and other stresses in his face. His eyes were incandescent wicks swollen with gaslight. The hissing of the lantern seemed to come from him, as if he were the great snake that resided at the bottom of the pit of the world "until he awakens in hunger and moving his head to right and to left prepares for his hour to devour." She considered reciting those lines to him, but she doubted that he would know the source, T. S. Eliot, and she was sure that he would not grasp the meaning.

When he took the switchblade from a pocket of his jacket, she thought she might have pressed him too hard. However, he only used the knife to cut the zip tie that bound her wrists.

He put the blade on the table where she could reach it, though he drew the pistol from the holster on his hip and gave her a look into the muzzle. "Free your ankles, but don't do anything stupid."

After she cut the zip ties that fettered her, she returned the knife to the table, and Optime took possession of it again.

He keyed open the padlock that fixed the chain around her neck, and she was free of that, too.

In respect of the pistol, she didn't get up from the chair until he ordered her to her feet.

He followed her across the barroom, through the back door, to the outhouse that had two holes in its smooth board seat. He had restored the small structure from a state of near collapse. In another century, this privy served the patrons of the saloon, but it now accommodated Optime and his prisoners.

Previously, when he accompanied Ophelia to the outhouse, he permitted her to close the door. This time, the sharp edge of his repressed rage became apparent when he denied her privacy.

In the summer heat, the place stank. Beetles crawled the pit below, and fat spiders sat patiently in their elaborate tapestries of sticky silk everywhere that the walls met the ceiling.

The shadowy interior would have allowed a degree of modesty, except that Optime stood to one side of the open door to watch her, allowing a shaft of sunshine to spill inside and reveal her in the act.

She refused to be embarrassed. Instead, she made *him* the object of ridicule. "Now that you have the sex drive of a dead worm, is this how you get your jollies—watching ladies pee?"

Backlit, his face in shadow and his eyes as black as the empty sockets of the Grim Reaper, he didn't respond. His silence was ominous, and Ophelia decided that she should say no more.

When she was finished, he walked her out to the street and followed her, pistol in hand, toward the small stone church at the end of the abandoned town.

Slowly sinking toward the great mountains in the west, the sun had for several minutes bathed the ghost town in a honeyed splendor that made some of the weathered buildings appear gilded. Now, the late afternoon grew moody with a blood-orange radiance as eerie as witch fires. The few windows that remained intact took color from the sun and peered at the street like jack-o'-lantern eyes.

At the church, three stone steps led up to a wide stoop, where Optime instructed Ophelia to kneel. She obeyed.

Holding the gun in his right hand, with the cold muzzle jammed against the back of her head, he used his left hand to insert a key in the lock that he had installed. He opened the door.

"Crawl inside on your hands and knees."

She knew that he wouldn't kill her here, not yet, not until he broke her and could write in his manifesto that she had acknowledged the false promise of hope. He first required the death of the spirit and only then the death of the body. His evil creed was a construct of madness; however, it included principles by which he justified his actions. Ophelia believed he would reliably conduct himself according to those principles.

She had to hope that he embraced his insane vision with the faith of a true believer. She had no other choice.

She crawled out of the orange light and into the church, which was as dark as a coffin with its lid closed.

Optime picked up something from the floor, just inside the door. It was a Tac Light, and Ophelia turned her head away from the blinding beam when he directed it at her.

"Get to your feet."

She rose and looked around at what was less a church than it was a crude chapel. Five pews to the left and five to the right of the central—and only—aisle. The roof was supported by three tie beams, king posts, and rafters.

"Sit." With the light, he indicated the first pew on the left.

The four windows were neither tall nor wide. They had been bricked in from the inside. This recent masonry was the work of Optime, which he'd described in his manifesto. The bricks were practical, making both a mausoleum and prison of the building; but they also had a symbolic purpose, being a barrier against hope ever entering this abandoned church.

Ophelia didn't need to be told the source of the faint foul odor, but Optime said, "I'll finish my manifesto and offer it to the world when there are seventy-seven dead in the basement, seven of them children, each seven years old or younger."

He had not yet explained in his writings why he'd settled on that number of victims or why seven must be children. Perhaps he didn't know. And even if he could explain his morbid mathematics, the explanation wasn't likely to make sense.

"If you want to know your destiny beyond all doubt," he said, "open the door to the basement and inhale deeply, get the odor of your future in full strength."

She said nothing.

"I'll lock you in here without food or water. But when you're desperate enough, there's sustenance below. Rainwater leaks in and pools down there, and the stew awaiting you is richer than what the Donner party had to eat when they were trapped in deep snow in the Sierra, two hundred years ago, with nothing but the stringy meat of their dead companions."

She said, "You are one sick piece of shit."

"So it might seem to anyone as unenlightened as you. I'll leave the Tac Light, so you can inspect your quarters and be certain there isn't the smallest hope of escape. You'll want to go down among the dead to assure yourself that there's no exit from the basement. I'm sorry you have no waders to make that part of the tour less messy."

He put the Tac Light on the floor, with the beam pointed toward the front of the church.

She was afraid but ready. For years she had been waiting. Now her purpose was at hand.

She turned in the pew to watch him depart through the fiery light of the forthcoming sunset.

He called back to her. "When you're ready to admit that hope is for fools, that you're nothing more than another animal born to die, all you need to do is scream. Eventually, I'll hear you." He closed the door.

In the unholy silence, she heard the soft scrape of the key in the keyway. The heavy-duty deadbolt seated in the striker plate with a hard, cold *clack.*

15

Because the summer had brought rain, the gently up-sloping meadows were green rather than golden, each rolling into the next. The graceful swells and swales of the voluptuous landscape were almost erotic, pleasing to both the mind and heart, even as the lonely vastness inspired in Wyatt Rider moments of uneasiness, a transient sense of dangerous isolation.

Mile after mile, he saw little evidence to fix this place in the second decade of the twenty-first century. If his Range Rover had been a time machine, he might well have thought he must be traveling in the 1950s, even earlier.

Along the county road and then on private land, an occasional, ugly cell-phone tower broke the peaceful spell of time immemorial. Each had been paid for by Liam O'Hara. His deep pockets allowed him to have the finest service even when getting away from it all at a remote retreat, an indulgence that benefited the widely scattered residents of this part of the county.

The two-lane private road that served Rustling Willows had once been gravel, but Liam had paid to have it paved. A mile and a half from the public highway, fenced meadows began to appear on both sides of the lane, containing none of the horses that had once run and grazed in those confines.

Between the sloping meadows and the foothills lay a broad plateau. To the left were picturesque stables, white clapboard with red-tile roofs, and a caretaker's cottage, all vacant. To the right, past a windbreak of willows, lay Lake Sapphire, less blue than gold as the westering sun angled its light across the rippled surface.

The handsome low-slung single-story house, set back from and above the lake, was of native stone, with a dark slate roof, large windows to capture the views, and a deep veranda. On the uplands beyond the residence, evergreen forests rose dark and primeval, though the five acres or so immediately surrounding the house were reserved for broad lawns and numerous willows in groups.

A Ford F-150 pickup stood in front of an array of four garage doors. He slotted the Range Rover beside it.

As Wyatt climbed the three stone steps to the teak-floored veranda, a lanky man in boots, jeans, and a denim shirt rose from one of the bentwood rocking chairs. His face had been weathered by sun and wind into the image of stalwart moral character suitable to be the lead of any Western novel by Louis L'Amour.

"Mr. Rider, is it?" he asked.

As they shook hands, Wyatt said, "Pleasure to meet you, Mr. Potter. Liam O'Hara says whatever I might need, you'll provide it."

"If you ask for a genie in a lamp, sir, I suspect I can maybe get at least the lamp."

Vance Potter, the manager of Rustling Willows and the adjacent properties that Liam had acquired, did not reside here, but lived with his wife in the town of Buckleton, which lay about nine miles to the south. He used contracted services and local labor to ensure that everything was maintained in perfect order.

"Fact is," Wyatt said, fishing a business card from his wallet and giving it to Potter, "all I want is privacy and quiet for a few days. Even if you had a genie in a lamp, I'd pass on the three wishes. I know how that always turns out."

"Nothin' gotten just by wishin' for it is worth havin'," Potter agreed. "So the idea is you come here to the Great Empty to relax?"

The way he phrased the question and a sly glint in his gray eyes suggested that he might be in the habit of regarding official stories as just that—stories.

Wyatt could foresee nothing he might need from Potter other than the keys and an orientation tour of the house, but it was wise to be on the best of terms with the man, which meant being honest with him from the start. "Actually, I'm a private detective."

Pleased by that admission, Potter smiled. "Googled you to see what's what. Internet's full of lies, but it says you're thirty-nine, been a dick—in the best sense of the word—since you were twenty-one. Way I understand, first thing you did once you got yourself a PI license was investigate the livin' hell out of your parents and expose the operation they were runnin' where they were bilkin' old people out of their life savins."

Wyatt said, "'How sharper than a serpent's tooth it is to have a thankless child.'"

Potter shook his head. "Speakin' for my own self, give me a righteous child, and if maybe I deserve thanks, I'm sure I'll get some. I won't ask what you're here to investigate, but if it's me, then you go straight at it like a dog with a bone."

"It's not you. But if it was, I wouldn't tell you."

Potter laughed. "I half wish it was me. Seems like you'd be interestin' to hang around with."

The ranch house was large, about seven thousand square feet, but it pretty much explained itself. The pantry, the refrigerator, and the bathrooms had been stocked for the O'Hara family's visit the previous week. Nothing more was needed. The tour took ten minutes.

Potter said, "Our Mr. O'Hara intends to upgrade things, all the mechanical systems, remodel with nicer finishes, though only after visitin' a few times and gettin' a sense of what's needed. You ask me, she's a pretty sweet house as she is."

As Wyatt accompanied the property manager to his truck, he said, "Since you've been tending to this place, have you had any unusual experiences?"

Pausing with his hand on the driver's door, Potter said, "A word like 'unusual' covers a lot of territory."

After a hesitation, Wyatt changed it up: "What if, instead of 'unusual,' I said *strange*?"

The property manager was not a man who broadcast his thoughts with unguarded expressions. He met Wyatt's eyes for a long moment before he said, "Never did see any Bigfoot runnin' across a meadow nor no flyin' saucer comin' down out of the moon. But once in a while . . ." He turned his head to survey the lake, the land, the stables. When he went on, his voice had a solemn edge. "Maybe 'cause there's bad history to the place—tragedies, you know—maybe when I remember them, it juices my imagination. But once in a while . . ."

When Potter fell quiet, Wyatt pressed him. "'Once in a while'?"

With a shrug, the caretaker seemed to dismiss whatever he had intended to say, and he spoke now in a lighter tone of voice. "Oh, once in a while, when I'm workin' here alone, I get the feelin' I'm bein' watched. It's so convincin' that it puts the fine hairs up on my neck. But what place this big and this deserted *wouldn't* give a man that feelin' from time to time?"

Intuition told Wyatt that Potter had held something back—and that pressing him further would not result in his divulging it.

They shook hands, and the property manager drove away.

When the Ford pickup was out of sight, Wyatt Rider let his gaze travel wherever it might: across the quiet stables, to the dwindling blacktop lane, from one cluster of willows to another . . . The shadows stretched eastward, as if yearning for communion with the oncoming night, and the dying day spilled redness across the land, and the water rippled with firelight in the lake where a woman had once died.

16

Ophelia Poole retrieved the Tac Light from the floor of the center aisle, where Optime had left it, returned to the pew, and switched off the beam to preserve the batteries. The darkness fell unrelieved, not the slightest chink of light at any of the bricked-up windows. Of course, the day had faded to a scarlet twilight, so there wasn't a lot of light left to penetrate the building.

She had much to think about: options to consider, if there were any; a plan of action to be devised.

From overhead came a soft noise that she could not place. After a silence, the noise came again, faint and furtive. She supposed there must be mice or even rats. Neither concerned her.

Blind, she could see nothing but her captor in her mind's eye, his visage horrifying because it appeared so ordinary. His mind, a cesspool of ignorance and hatred, seethed with homicidal fantasies, and in his extreme narcissism, he convinced himself that his lust for power must be a noble mission of penance. His inner evil was a potent venom, so caustic that it should have left at least a trace of corruption in his face, but he was a serpent who could pass for a sincere servant.

She feared him even as she was relieved that at last he had arrived on the scene. Since a week after the death of her identical twin, Octavia, she'd believed—*needed* to believe—that she had been spared for an important purpose. She hadn't known what it would be, and she had never imagined that she might be called upon to kill a murderer, one who could potentially commit *mass* murder. Even as she had recovered from the chloroform, however, she'd known that Asher Optime was the reason that she hadn't died in the traffic accident that had killed Octavia.

She had been the driver of the car, and though she hadn't been the one at fault—it had been a trucker with a drinking problem—*she had been the driver of the car.* In the front passenger seat, Octavia was half-crushed and beheaded. Behind the steering wheel, not three feet away, Ophelia suffered a broken index finger, a torn nail, and a scratched chin. In the aftermath, she'd had only two choices, at least as far as she could understand: Either grief and guilt would in time destroy her, or she could choose to believe that she had been spared for some important task, that in fulfilling that task, she would be redeemed and eventually earn the company of Octavia in a world beyond this one.

They had not been merely identical; they had been, as Ophelia had sometimes said, conjoined twins born detached. Ophelia had her circle of friends, and Octavia had hers, and there were friends that they shared, but they were not a fraction as close with anyone else as they were with each other. They frequently finished each other's sentences. When one told a joke, the other often laughed before the punch line, having intuited it. They sometimes spoke three words of great affection to each other—"My sister, myself"—when suddenly they experienced the same insight or achieved the same revelation or saw something that thrilled them both. There were differences, one from the other. Octavia possessed a gentler heart than Ophelia, and Ophelia had a quicker wit than Octavia. Both had musical talent, but only Octavia had perfect pitch; she rocked the piano the first time she sat before it—and patiently taught Ophelia until student could play nearly as well as teacher. *My sister, myself.* After such closeness, the grievous loss Ophelia suffered in the accident seemed like an amputation that left her forever less than a whole person.

Now she sat in this deconsecrated darkness with an inner light of purpose that warmed her more than Asher Optime chilled her. The stone walls stood silent, as they had for more than one and a half centuries. The noise overhead didn't arise again, although the wooden floor underfoot produced an occasional settling sound—a creak, a pop as a plank expanded in the summer heat.

The door to the lower room was closed. Otherwise, the stench of decomposition would be intolerable, whereas it was only unnerving.

Optime had insisted that the basement offered no way out of the church, but his clear intention had been to make her wonder if that might be a lie. He'd left the flashlight so that she could go down among the dead to search for an exit, because he imagined that the sight of the bloated and decomposing bodies would drain all hope from her and leave her ready for her second death, that of her body.

She wouldn't put herself to that test. The day of the accident, before the first responders had torn open the buckled driver-side door with the pneumatic Jaws of Life, she had been trapped with the mangled body of her sister, a sight that had haunted her dreams for a long time. She trusted herself to respond to Optime with courage when the confrontation came, but she didn't dare wade among the madman's victims, where any deteriorated face that bloomed in the beam of the Tac Light would surely remind her too keenly of her sister's distorted countenance and death-shocked eyes.

From overhead came another noise, not as furtive as before. A rustling-fluttering was followed by the thrum of wings cutting air.

Ophelia clicked on the Tac Light and swept the darkness with the beam, seeking the birds. She found them sitting on the backrest of a pew two rows in front of hers, a pair of crows. They cocked their heads, regarding her with interest.

The birds were plump enough and evidently healthy, which meant they couldn't have been trapped in the church for any length of time. Indeed, perhaps they weren't trapped at all, but found their way in and out of the building through a hole in the roof.

Ophelia stood up and stepped into the aisle, directing the light toward the ceiling, probing past beams, posts, and purlins, looking for a break in the rafters, a hole in the roof. After a couple minutes, she realized that she should wait for the bright light of morning to reveal how the crows found their way inside, and search the nave and sanctuary now, to see if there might be a piece of lumber or a rusty nail she could use as a weapon.

The crows followed her wherever she went, hopping from pew to pew, to chancel railing. Although their kind was usually raucous, these two neither cawed nor shrieked. Their persistent interest in her, combined with their silence, soon convinced her that there was something strange about them.

17

The moon beyond the window was low and golden, soon to pale as it strained higher. The sink faucet emitted a drop every minute or so, striking the faintest hollow note from the stainless-steel basin, as if counting down toward some mortal event.

If Joanna was lonely, as Auntie Kat insisted, the loneliness at the moment arose not from the lack of a man in her life, but it was the effect of the many photographs that had occupied her even as she had been eating dinner at the kitchen table. Her memory of Rustling Willows as an enchanted place had faded over the years. Indeed, the photos brought back to her such a strong sense of the magic of the property that it seemed she hadn't merely forgotten this aspect of the ranch, but for whatever reason had consciously repressed it.

As she finished the last bite of the lasagna she'd made for dinner, she heard a car engine turn over and race as if a driver's foot pumped the accelerator. Her dropped fork clattered onto her plate as she rose to her feet. The muffled but nevertheless loud roar vibrated through the walls. She faced the direction from which the sound emanated, but she hesitated to take a step toward whatever discovery awaited her.

All of the recent strangeness had begun more than three weeks earlier, when the Lincoln Continental had started of its own accord, in the locked garage. To the best of her knowledge, the vehicle had not malfunctioned again, until now.

The wall phone rang. Startled, Joanna glanced at it, sure that the woman who called her before dawn of this long day was on the line again. *Let it go.* After four rings, it would go to voice mail.

But it didn't. The phone continued ringing, ringing, and the engine snarled rhythmically in the garage, as though a power beyond Joanna's comprehension was intent on bullying her into a response.

She went to the phone. The readout provided no caller ID.

As Joanna stared at the handset and the strident ringing insisted on her attention, the roar of the car escalated until a crazy but compelling supernatural scenario fired her imagination: the parking brake failing, the transmission slipping from park to drive, the house shuddering as the demonically possessed vehicle crashed through the garage and into the kitchen, crushing her to death against the refrigerator.

When she snatched the handset from its cradle and put an end to the ringing, the Lincoln in the garage stopped racing, and idled. The vaguely familiar but unidentifiable woman's voice spoke, as before, without emotion, in an eerily calm fashion that didn't match her words. *"Jojo, I am spiraling into Bedlam. The big dark sky. The terrible big dark sky. Only you can help me."*

"Who is this?" Joanna demanded.

"Come now. Come quickly. Will you please?"

Joanna hung up and turned away from the phone, which at once resumed ringing. When she ventured into the adjacent laundry room, the engine began to race again, and she realized it was the Aviator this time, rather than the Continental.

She took the electronic key from the pegboard and opened the door. Exhaust fumes billowed in from the garage. The headlights of the big SUV blazed. The vehicle rocked slightly on its tires, like a restrained bull eager to rampage.

Although this eruption of weirdness unsettled her, she hadn't felt in danger until now. She hesitated on the threshold. Retreat would be no reason for embarrassment.

She had nothing to prove.

Or do I?

If her forgetfulness wasn't simply time erasing details as time did, if she had diligently washed the color from all recollections of Rustling Willows and hung the faded memories deep in the back of her mind, then among them might wait to be discovered a disturbing truth that caused her to undertake that vigorous laundering of the past.

She switched on the overhead lights in the garage and crossed the threshold and went around the Continental to the port side of the Aviator. When she opened the door, the SUV's engine stopped racing and once more fell to idling.

Sensing a presence, she surveyed the garage. "Who's there? What do you want?" But no one answered; no one appeared.

She got into the driver's seat and pulled the door shut and looked at the map on the computer screen and saw the orange square bearing the word START. As had been the case weeks earlier, when this first happened, the female voice of the navigation system told her to obey all traffic laws and follow instructions to her destination, even though Joanna did not touch the START prompt.

On that previous occasion, in her confusion and agitation, she had not thought to read the destination that had been entered in the Continental, which she had never programmed, which seemed to have been determined by the vehicle itself. Now she saw what she had expected to see: a number on a county road in Montana, an address that she hadn't rinsed from memory, the very place where the private lane to Rustling Willows turned off the public blacktop.

"Who are you?" she asked, as if the person controlling the SUV's navigation system from a distance must be able to hear her.

She received no reply.

18

In each room, no more than one lamp was lit. If it had a three-way switch, Wyatt set it at its lowest brightness. Otherwise, he draped the lampshade with a towel.

He opened a can of gourmet chili—made with filet mignon, rich and spicy—that he found in the pantry. He heated it in an oven and spooned it from the container as he walked the house. Following that, he ate peaches from a can, and when those were gone, he roamed again and again through the rooms and hallways, drinking coffee.

He wasn't looking for anything in particular, just getting a feel for the place. The real work would start in the morning.

The low illumination allowed him to see both the interior and something of the night beyond the large windows. If he had flooded the residence with light, he would have felt blind to any threat from outside. Although he didn't believe an immediate danger loomed, hard experience had taught him always to proceed as if one existed.

Besides, he was a little bit spooked, not as much by the house as by the land surrounding it. In spite of the verdant quality of these thousands of acres, he might not have felt more isolated if he'd been transported to a barren crater on the moon.

Wyatt Rider, thirty-nine years old and eighteen years a PI, was city born and city raised. Con artists, like his larcenous parents, favored metropolitan living not just because there were more fish to be hooked there, but also because those schooling millions took the bait quicker than did small-town marks. The popular conception of big-city residents as uniformly sophisticated and street smart was undercut by countless studies showing that a higher percentage of city dwellers than rural types not only suffered depression and psychoses, but lived with a simmering paranoia that made them more likely to believe in conspiracy theories. There was some truth to the term "madding crowd." Good con men and women were quick to take advantage of this us-against-them paranoia, presenting themselves as the enemies of whatever conspiracy or segment of society that their hapless marks currently most feared and despised, deftly winning the confidence of those they intended to fleece.

As a consequence, a private investigator who needed to make a living but who also wanted to bring down the frauds and swindlers was less likely to be able to pay his bills and take satisfaction in his work if he set up office in Mayberry instead of Manhattan. In Wyatt's case, Manhattan was Seattle, although his cases often took him far afield from the Emerald City.

He hoped never to get farther from the glass-and-steel towers and noisy concrete avenues of teeming humanity than Rustling Willows Ranch. Earlier, after Vance Potter had left, when the sound of his pickup had faded entirely, the quiet of the seeming infinity of land had been, in Wyatt's experience, so unnatural that a sense of the uncanny had crept over him, akin to what Potter described as his own occasional reaction to the place. Wyatt was the least superstitious of men, not so impressionable that Potter's words could unnerve him. Yet as he'd stood in the red sunset, in the dying of the light, he had felt that he was being watched. In fact, the feeling had been so intense that, surveying the yard and willows nearest to him, he'd been overcome by the bizarre conviction that whoever watched him was *right there*, not concealed in the distance and using binoculars, but within a few yards, maybe even within arm's reach, real but somehow invisible.

Disquieted more by the fact that his imagination had run wild than by anything that might be out there in the fading twilight, he had returned to the house. As a rejection of baseless fear, he had not locked the front door. Later, after nightfall, as he ate while touring the residence, he engaged the deadbolt in passing, without making a production of it, almost unconsciously.

He was still exploring the rooms, studying them, warmed by his second mug of coffee, when the presence he'd sensed earlier revealed itself, though in a form that was incomprehensible to him.

19

As stated in Asher Optime's historic manifesto, abandoned Zipporah stands testament to the transient nature of humanity, to the truth that the demise of the species is figured in its genes. This is not a ghost town, as the romantics would have it. These are ruins, all that remains of the hopes of self-important men and women who are dead and gone as if they never existed. The crumbling town isn't haunted, for there are no ghosts, no spirits to survive those who lived and died here.

Each evening, before settling down to sleep at midnight, Asher walks the street where, when there is a moon, as now, the fine dust underfoot is silvered by the lunar glow, which is fitting for the road that leads to his great destiny. In this dim reflection of the sun, Earth's patron star that blazes on the farther side of the planet, the weathered buildings are the only ghostly presences, like pale shapes that an artist has scored in the black ink that covers the white clay on a piece of scratchboard.

Asher stops before the church, waiting for a scream, but he isn't rewarded with one. He is patient. Ophelia will not be broken easily, but eventually she will break.

Although he prefers the celestial panorama without a moon, he tips his head back and stares into infinity, which enchants him. The universe is a graveyard. The perfect blackness between the twinkling billions of distant suns is the hard truth of it, the darkness of the void. By comparison to the sea of blackness, the light of the stars is insignificant and cold, emitted so long ago that by the time it is seen on Earth, many of those suns had died hundreds of thousands of years earlier. Asher can imagine how beautiful it will be when, countless millennia after the last man and last woman have perished, the final star goes dark as well. The universe will then be cold, without a scintilla of light, and whatever remains of the works of humankind will lie frozen and still under the big dark sky.

The big dark sky.

Sometimes, when he stands here in Zipporah's only street, his gaze turned to the vault of the night, he thrills to the inevitable advent of nothingness. The stars inspire nihilists to a greater purpose than they inspire lovers.

20

The Navajo rugs, the Pueblo pottery, a collection of copper cowboy-hat ashtrays, ornately painted Mexican chairs, a bedroom furnished entirely with antique twig-work furniture, the sofas draped with colorful Pendleton blankets: All this had been here through two previous owners, and Liam O'Hara wanted to live with it and add to it. For a city boy like Wyatt Rider, the decor was undeniably warm and beautiful, but it also felt alien, almost otherworldly, and insistent. Enough was enough.

Liam O'Hara intended to double the size of the existing house from seven thousand to fourteen thousand square feet, not because the current size of the residence provided too few rooms to display the entire spectrum of this type of decor, but maybe because making everything bigger was what multibillionaires did. Liam's enthusiasm for what he called the "Santa Fe and True West style" was such that he needed not extra living space in a getaway like this, but space to accommodate what he wished to collect.

Well, the guy worked hard, built a thriving company, employed thousands, created more wealth for others than for himself, so he had earned the right to do what he wanted with his money. Wyatt envied the man, not because of his fortune, but because of the family with which he shared all this. Liam's wife, Lyndsey, was lovely, intelligent, warm, with a great sense of humor; the kids, Laura and Tavis, were lively but polite, smart but not smart-ass.

Wyatt had not yet married. He had not yet been engaged. Hell, he hadn't yet enjoyed a relationship with a woman that didn't end in dire suspicion, recriminations, and regret. His love life was about as romantic as an arm-wrestling contest. He was self-aware enough to know that he—not the women—was the problem, but he didn't know how to fix himself.

As he passed through the large, dimly lighted living room again, sipping the last of his second mug of coffee, he was thinking not about why he'd come to Rustling Willows, but about Sandra Chan, the lawyer who'd been his most recent companion. He truly cherished her, but nevertheless he lost her. Actually, he'd driven her away by doubting her when he'd had no reason to doubt, offending her with his distrust.

If the living room had not featured one wall of nine-foot-tall windows, he might have been too distracted by thoughts of Sandra Chan to notice the eerie luminosity on the front yard. In this rural immensity, the only significant nighttime light was either man-made or moonglow, although neither of those sources explained the display beyond the veranda. This radiance was diffuse, a soft cloud of yellowish light that seemed both to swirl lazily and pulse as it moved back and forth, five or six feet above the lawn. Wyatt stood watching it for a minute or longer, trying to make sense of it, but he needed to have a closer look.

When he stepped onto the veranda, the August night proved to be mild, even somewhat warm for Montana. As during the day, a stillness lay upon the land, every trace of wind locked in the vault of the distant mountains.

Stepping onto the grass, he realized what phenomenon floated before him, a work of nature that seemed profoundly unnatural. The cloud was a swarm of hundreds of fireflies—perhaps a thousand or more—their soft abdomens pulsing incandescently, each a tiny lamp, but in aggregate producing enough light by which to read a book.

He had seen fireflies before, most often in his youth, on summer suburban evenings. But on those occasions, the insects had numbered far fewer than this, each a beacon signaling along a route that it patrolled alone.

If the idea of fireflies had occurred to Wyatt independent of this unexpected display, he might have thought they didn't exist in Montana, and he would never have entertained the notion that they swarmed in such numbers. Liam O'Hara hadn't spoken of this when he had described either the magical or the frightening events that caused him and his family to cut short their first vacation at the ranch. Although mysterious, this spectacle was enchanting rather than fearsome, and the longer he studied it, the more wondrous it became.

The traceries of throbbing light suggested that these tiny insects were aligned in numerous skeins, rather than each traveling a random route. The skeins wove complex integrated patterns with fantastic precision, without the slightest interference of one with another. He thought of the convolutions of a brain, each firefly like a neuron firing.

A score of fireflies were able to sail through the night with such effortless grace that they were as soundless as the movement of light itself. However, these much greater numbers produced a low susurration, as though in their flight they must be whispering some secret that, if understood, would draw back the veils that obscured the truth behind the world.

The beauty of the manifestation was such that, much like a spellbound child, he reached toward the swarm with his right hand, hoping one of them would alight on a finger and allow him to study it more closely.

Instead, the communal pattern they created abruptly morphed into a throbbing stream of light, like a comet with a tail, swooped three times around him, and glimmered away from the house. Crazy as it seemed, he felt certain that the triple spiral was an invitation, and he followed the swarm across the lawn, toward the lake in which the moon admired its reflection, the moment having turned somewhat Disneyesque.

The swarm led him to a dock, where the comet coalesced again into a cloud above the man-size door to a boathouse of weathered mahogany. Upon Wyatt's arrival, the fireflies dispersed, cascading away into the darkness like the fading sparks from Independence Day pyrotechnics, and were gone as if they had been an apparition.

When he lowered his gaze, the moonlight revealed that the boathouse door stood ajar. He was certain it had been closed tight when he arrived.

From Liam O'Hara, he'd learned the history of the property. For twenty-three years, it had been in the possession of Roy and Ivy Kornbluth, from whom the billionaire acquired it. The Kornbluths had sustained a successful horse-breeding operation. During their time at Rustling Willows, evidently nothing outré or even particularly dramatic had happened. Prior to Roy and Ivy, the owners were Emelia and Samuel Chase. Emelia drowned in Lake Sapphire. Only two weeks later, Samuel had been mauled and killed by a bear.

In spite of the fact that those deaths were far in the past, some potential buyers might have had a superstitious aversion to buying a place where two such tragedies occurred, one especially horrific.

Liam and Lyndsey didn't believe in curses. To them, this history was colorful, not problematic.

The long stillness of the day suddenly relented to a breeze out of the forested mountains to the north, rippling the image of the moon on the dark water and ruffling Wyatt's hair. Under the soft wind's gentle hand, the boathouse door eased inward on creaking hinges, revealing nothing other than darkness deeper than the night.

Emelia Chase came here on the last day of her young life and launched the skiff, never to return. Her body had washed ashore. Her spirit didn't haunt this place twenty-four years later.

Yet as the water lapped at the pilings under the dock planks, Wyatt had the curious feeling that the door wasn't opening under the influence of the breeze, but was being drawn open by someone inside, in a wordless invitation to . . . To what?

Within the boathouse, something thumped softly and after a few seconds thumped again. Maybe a skiff or small motorboat was moored in there, left in the water, knocking against the rubber bumpers that protected it, as the lake rhythmically swelled and receded under the craft.

He hadn't brought a flashlight. But inside, to the right of the door, would be a switch. He could feel for it and flip it up without stepping across the threshold.

For a long moment, his hesitation surprised and disturbed him, for his apprehension had no valid cause. But intuition, the primary knowledge born in the mind before all teaching and all reasoning, had served him well before, and if it previously had been a trickle charge, it was now a high-tension wire buzzing insistently in the back of his mind. The fireflies had gone elsewhere, so whatever the explanation behind the phenomenon might be, it wouldn't be found in the boathouse. Nothing in there warranted investigation at this late hour—and would still be there in the morning.

As he returned to the house, he glanced back only once. In the kitchen, after rinsing out his coffee mug, he poured a cold beer into it and spiked the brew with a shot of whiskey.

At 11:10, he retreated to the guest room, where he'd left his luggage. From a suitcase, he retrieved a Heckler & Koch Combat Competition Mark 23 chambered for .45 ACP. He inserted the magazine and put the pistol on a nightstand.

Although their experiences had been unsettling, Liam and his family hadn't needed a weapon to defend against a threat or ensure that they could leave at will. However, as events at the ranch had taken a strange turn, the seeming malice behind them had at one point rapidly escalated. If they had delayed another hour or two, they might have found that even the pistol Liam was licensed to carry would have been inadequate.

A pair of French doors led to a deck that overlooked the lake, and there were two bedroom windows. He pulled the draperies shut at all of them.

His intention had been to turn off the lamps throughout the house before going to bed, but he changed his mind. He didn't have a flashlight. If during the night something unsettling occurred, he didn't relish making his way through the dark house, fumbling with light switches.

21

Numerous thin shafts of afternoon sunshine pierced the branches of the pines and the boughs of other evergreens, scattering treasure on the trail, a wealth of gold coins that didn't clink or clatter under young Joanna's feet as she chased the bear. Where no low branches obstructed the way, the immense grizzly ran on its hind legs, towering eight feet tall, but otherwise it loped on all four, lumbering but as fast as a cat. She followed, laughing and calling out to the bruin—"Mr. Smokey"—although of course it wasn't the cartoon brown bear from the forest-service commercials on TV. They came into a sun-splashed clearing, a meadow where green grass and wildflowers seemed to leap out of the earth to greet them. Two deer grazed there, an antlered buck and a doe. Chewing contentedly, they raised their beautiful heads, regarding Joanna and Mr. Smokey with interest, though not with fear. The grizzly led the girl to the deer and stopped short of them lest they misunderstand its intent. Joanna dashed ahead, and as she approached, the deer gamboled away from her, not in fear but as her guides for the next phase of the game.

Buck led doe and doe led girl out of the meadow, into another arm of the forest, along a continuation of the deer path. Flocks of rock doves winged through the woods, jubilantly singing their *p-p-p-proo* flight call, and red foxes ran to both sides of her, their thickly furred tails streaming behind them like long, wooly scarves. They hurried past a grown-up Joanna asleep in a bed among the trees, in the pale light of a TV turned to a dead channel, onward and now down through a forest that thinned enough to allow undergrowth of Kesselringii and tatarian honeysuckle and lush emerald carpet with its urn-shaped blossoms. Onward, still onward, they ran, past a rock formation on which stood a Lincoln Aviator, past masses of Farrer's potentilla with cascades of white flowers, lowbush blueberry with red leaves and blue fruit, maidenhair spleenwort and licorice fern, all plants whose names she knew because her mother had taught her about them. Buck, doe, girl raced past goat's beard with its plumes of creamy flowers, past white mugwort, past a pair of suitcases packed and ready, out of the trees, through wild grass, where the deer stopped to graze again.

Young Joanna hurried on alone, out of the tall grass, across recently mown lawn, to the bosk of apple trees, at the center of which a small, slump-shouldered figure sat on a bench. Although she had run and run, she was not breathing hard when she settled beside the boy. She was eight years old, and he was eleven. His head was turned away from her when she declared, *You are amazing, Jimmy! You're the best secret friend a girl could ever have.* He faced her then, his mouth half again as wide as it should be, full of crooked teeth. One eye blue and clear, the other dark and bloodshot. Large head misshapen as hers might be if she were to look at herself in a fun-house mirror. This boy who was thought to be incapable of language, this boy who had never spoken a word in his life, who communicated to others his wants and needs in grunts and broken sounds, said in a rough and raspy voice, *"I'm in a dark place. I'm lost. The terrible big dark sky. I'm a danger to myself and others. Only you can help me, Jojo. Please come and help me."* Before she could reply, he looked past her, toward the distant lake. If some people might find his face already fearsome, the dread that suddenly gripped him wrenched his pitiable countenance into a goblin mask. When she turned her attention toward the lake, she saw her mother coming toward them, hair hanging wet and straight, clothes sodden, as if she had risen out of the deep water. Mother's face was gray and swollen, and her eyes were milky. Joanna was only eight, a year younger than she had been when her mother drowned. This made no sense. How had Mother drowned a year before her time? Yet here she came, almost to the apple orchard, reaching out with one hand for her daughter, among the trees now. Jimmy Two Eyes said, *"Run, Jojo. Run!"* Joanna sprang up from the bench but did not know to what haven she should flee or whether she should flee at all. Drowned or not, this woman was her mother who had always loved her. *"RUN, RUN, RUN, JOJO!"* Jimmy Two Eyes shouted, and the Aviator appeared beyond the orchard, and Jojo sprinted to the SUV. The back door flew open as she approached. She clambered inside. The door slammed shut. Her mother's dead face loomed beyond the window, and the woman pounded on the glass with both fists. The unknown driver, whoever he might be, accelerated away from there, across the acres of lawn, past trembling willow trees, toward the house, which was when Joanna realized she wasn't alone in the back seat of the vehicle. Somehow, the corpse from which she'd sped away now sat beside her. Eyes as white as hard-boiled eggs, gray face pocked and pale lips tattered by nibbling fish, teeth stained with whatever filth, Mother smiled—

—Joanna gasped and dropped two plastic bottles of skin-care products that she had been about to put into the makeup case. As they clattered onto the floor and rolled away from her, she realized she was standing in the bathroom, in her sleepwear. In the mirror she saw the open door behind her. She half expected her mother to follow her out of the dream, but no one appeared in the doorway.

Bewildered, gazing at the contents of the open makeup case—mascara, brushes, Q-tips, and more—she slowly realized that at some point she had gotten out of bed and, still dreaming on her feet, had begun to pack. Suitcases. In the dream, two suitcases had stood alongside the deer path as she had run after the buck and doe.

Vertigo afflicted her, and she leaned against the vanity until the brief spell of disorientation passed.

In the bedroom, the wheeled luggage stood by the armchair. The telescoping handles were at full length and locked in position. She tipped one bag onto its wheels and pulled it just far enough to be sure that it was heavy, fully loaded.

Joanna had no memory of preparing for travel. Never before had she walked in her sleep or experienced a fugue state of any kind. She couldn't comprehend how she could have packed while lost in a dream. However, now she began to recall selecting items of clothing and precisely folding them to fit in the suitcases.

As she had dreamed, her heart had beat double time. It didn't slow now that she walked the world awake. Her horror at not having been fully in control of herself frightened her no less than had the specter of her drowned mother.

The bedside clock read 12:32 a.m. She'd slept only a few hours.

Approaching the TV, she was aware of her pulse pounding in her throat and in her temples. Soft ashen light filled the screen, much like what she thought she'd seen on nights when she'd half awakened from a dream only to be drawn quickly back into it. Previously, the pale glow seemed to be the light of a dead channel, but it was not that, after all. No slightest fleck of static marred the smooth gray light, and no number glowed in the channel indicator.

She felt . . . observed.

The conviction grew that she'd been manipulated in her sleep by some technology—or entity—beyond her comprehension. If the dreams of the past few weeks had welled up from the unfathomed depths of her subconscious, they had also at least in part been shaped and shaded by some strange power separate from herself. The dreams were as much a summons to Rustling Willows Ranch as were the phone calls from the unknown woman and the self-starting vehicles.

In her youth, the path of her life had been changed by tragedy, by the loss of love. Perhaps because of those losses, as an adult Joanna had often chosen solitude, loneliness, over the satisfactions of companionship, which had the benefit of forcing her to be self-sufficient. She addressed problems without equivocation. Loneliness had other advantages; it provided time for self-reflection and for the exercise of the imagination, always of value to a novelist. Long lonely nights also facilitated the development of the recognition that the world was riddled with mysteries and floating in a sea of hidden meaning as surely as it revolved around the sun. She believed in pursuing the truth of things rather than living in the pleasure of ignorance, and never before had a mystery as abstruse as this challenged her.

If anything about her life to date had been markedly different from what in fact it had been, she might have pulled the plug on the TV and lied to herself about what had happened, might have mummified her memory in wrappings of denial. Or she might have called for an appointment with a physician to be tested for a brain tumor, might even have sought the services of a psychiatrist.

However, being who she was, she did not—could not—pull the plug, but moved closer to the television to touch that rectangular electronic eye. Although her heart still labored and tremors shook her, she demanded, "Who are you? What are you?"

The quality of the light failed to change, and the perfect silence of the set endured.

She waited, but not for long.

In the bathroom once more, Joanna picked up the two dropped bottles of skin-care products and tucked them into the makeup case. She closed the lid and snapped the latches shut.

After putting the case beside the wheeled bags that stood next to the armchair, she took a quick shower and dressed. She booked an early flight to Denver and a connecting flight to Billings, Montana.

Waiting for dawn, which was still hours away, eating breakfast at the kitchen table, she thought about Jimmy Alvarez, Jimmy Two Eyes. Katherine's description of the boy hadn't pierced Joanna's armored memory; but when he appeared in the dream, in the orchard, she remembered him at once. When he'd spoken, she recognized his rough voice and knew he had talked to her often during their years together on the ranch, only to her when they were alone, so that no one but she knew he was capable of speech. Her recollections didn't return in a flood; she remembered nothing more than Jimmy's face, his voice—and that he was in some strange way her secret friend.

The *why* of a life could never be solved in this world, although vast libraries of solemn books speculated on the meaning and purpose of existence. Nothing could be known other than the *what* of any single life: what happened, what actions were taken, what events occurred beyond the person's control, what obvious consequences ensued, what impact for better or worse that one life was seen to have on others.

Because self-reflection was one of the tools with which she developed fictional characters and earned her living, Joanna had thought she knew the *what* of her life in intimate and vivid detail. Now she understood that, for three or four years of her childhood, her recollections were sketchy at best, not merely because time was a thief of memories, but also because someone had cast upon her a spell of forgetting.

She didn't write mystery novels per se, but mysteries of one kind or another coiled in the heart of every engaging novel. Because she was enchanted by the mysteries of existence and was as well a writer of stories concerned with things often unfathomable, hidden, recondite, she couldn't abide not knowing the full truth of her past.

In countless novels, however, revelation led not just to light in the darkness, but also as often to danger, loss, and death. Of course, events in life didn't unfold as they did in fiction. The real world didn't provide as many happy endings as were found in novels.

22

One bright beam speared low across the floor, with darkness all around. Perhaps two birds on a roost unseen watched the fat spider as it explored the path of light.

In the church that stood now as a shrine to murder, Ophelia Poole had found one loose nail in a plank. With her fingernails, she had worked it a quarter of an inch out of the wood, but then it had seized up.

The Tac Light that Optime left with her featured a wrist strap of tough fabric. She managed to detach the strap and knot it around the head of the nail, which gave her leverage. Sitting on the floor, legs splayed to each side of the job, she worked the nail back and forth, extracting it a millimeter at a time.

Freed from the underlying joist, it proved to be two inches long and dark with time, but not rusty. A stiff little length of steel. Although it was not much of a weapon, it was something. Given a chance, she might be able to stab Optime in the eye.

She got to her feet and swept the sanctuary with the Tac Light. The two crows were perched on the chancel railing. Their eyes were like drops of oil, as black as their feathers. They worked their beaks as if speaking to her on a frequency that human beings could not hear.

In the second pew on the right, she stretched out on her left side and clicked off the light. The pew was a hard bed, though no harder than the planks on which it stood. The odor of decomposition, seeping upward from the basement, was noticeably less offensive even just two feet off the floor.

She listened to the beams and rafters contract minutely as the heat of the day was leeched from them by the night, to the tics and creaks of the floorboards as gravity tested them as it had for many decades, to the occasional rustle of the birds shifting on their roost.

Clutching the nail tightly in her right hand, she whispered, "So this is why I'm still alive, Octavia. This is why I didn't die with you."

She didn't think she would sleep, but of course she slept. She woke a few times and listened for shuffling footsteps, though there were none.

Once, she realized the crows had left the chancel railing and were perched on the back of the pew on which she was lying, directly above her. She didn't switch on the light or chase them away. She decided to think of them as angels watching over her, though nothing about them seemed holy.

23

Someone spoke his name. If sleep had brought dreams, Wyatt Rider didn't remember them when he woke, lying on his left side, fully clothed except for his shoes. At first he couldn't identify the room revealed by the low light of the bedside lamp. Then he remembered Rustling Willows, and with memory came the realization that whoever addressed him had not been in a dream.

A man spoke with contempt: "Pestilence and vermin."

Wyatt rolled out of bed, onto his feet, snatching the pistol on the nightstand, with the weapon in a two-handed grip. The door to the hallway remained closed; no intruder had entered the room.

He searched the adjacent bathroom, where nothing moved in response to him except his image in the mirror.

"Diseased rats without tails," the voice declared with thick abhorrence, "filthy cockroaches on two legs."

In the bedroom once more, Wyatt realized that the TV glowed softly, tuned to a dead channel, though he'd never switched it on.

The flat LED screen suddenly seemed as inappropriate in this rustic Southwest decor as a polished monolith found in a crater on the moon. Wyatt felt no less out of place, harrier of con men and extortionists and blackmailers, having come here from Seattle to play a role for which he had no credentials—psychic detective, medium seeking to converse with some supernatural entity, explainer of the inexplicable.

The remote control was on the painted chest that stood under the wall-mounted TV. He picked it up and pressed the button labeled OFF. The screen went dark.

It came on again before he could put the remote down.

The luminous rectangle proved intriguing, as smooth and gray as mouse fur, presenting no smallest variation, and yet suggesting that images of enormous importance were concealed within its sameness, if only he were gifted enough to perceive them. The curious light was unlike anything he'd seen on a TV before, appealing for a reason he couldn't grasp, entrancing, seductive. In the absence of the ominous and judgmental voice, the television produced not a scintilla of sound, but Wyatt felt a cold, fine sleet of vibrations emanating from it, prickling his skin, as if communication continued on a frequency he could not hear but received subconsciously.

Then the voice came once more, sharper than before, antipathy trembling on the edge of hostility. "You are termites devouring the foundation of the world—blight, rot, a terminal cancer."

Wyatt's eyes had fallen shut, and a kind of bewitchment had overcome him, but his sudden recognition of the speaker's identity rattled him into a wide-eyed response. "'Blight, rot, a terminal cancer,'" he repeated. "Who the hell are you, what do you want?"

The voice that had come from the TV had been his own.

Note for note, inflection for inflection, it came again—"Who the hell are you, what do you want?"—clearer than an echo, too perfect to be that of a gifted mimic. Wyatt spoke not a word but his voice issued from the TV: "I want what is right, only what is right. If it's right that you should kill yourself, all of your greedy kind, then kill yourselves—or be killed."

The TV switched off.

He considered turning it on. Instead, he put down the remote. At Liam O'Hara's instruction, a powerful satellite dish had been installed on the roof of the house, to ensure that the family would be able to receive the entire spectrum of available television broadcasts and obtain swift internet access in this remote location. A first-rate hacker with the electronic address of the dish could invade the residence's computer system and associated electronics, such as this television receiver. If he had the right audio gear and software called Paramimic, the invader needed only a one-sentence sample of anyone's voice to be able to imitate it and deceive with a phone call, perhaps to speak out of a TV.

However, such a hacker would have extraordinary resources and would certainly not be a video-game-addicted thirtysomething case of arrested development living in his parents' basement. More likely than not, he would be in the employ of an agency of one government or another. Although Liam set high ethical standards for himself, though his ambition was tempered by humility, the fact that he was a multibillionaire meant that he had enemies, including those envious souls who had never met him, never done business with him, but nevertheless hated him with an insane passion.

Perhaps this wasn't a job for a psychic or a medium, after all, but only for a savvy gumshoe who could reason his way through a maze of deception.

So explain the fireflies, he thought.

He couldn't explain them, of course, not with reason, not by pointing at a bogeyman who was a world-class hacker. Nor did his vaunted intuition offer him a whisper of Sherlockian inspiration.

24

Shortly after seven o'clock Friday morning, the seventh of August, minutes out of Santa Fe and miles above the Earth, Joanna Chase suddenly sat up straighter in her seat as one of the veils masking her memories of Jimmy Two Eyes slid away.

She recalled a twilight with frogs croaking jubilantly in expectation of the oncoming night, she and the boy side by side on chairs, on the dock, watching the crimson sunset turning purple on the surface of the lake. She was excited because the next day would be her birthday.

A long-forgotten conversation returned to Joanna now with such clarity that she seemed to be on that dock, in that distant time, unnoticed by her younger self and Jimmy, listening.

"I'm gonna be eight, Jimmy. Cool, huh?"

His voice raw and guttural, he said, "You seem excited."

"Sure. Half grown-up!"

"Why is sixteen grown-up?"

"'Cause then I can drive."

"Is that grown-up—being allowed to drive?"

"It's one big thing, yeah. Maybe the best."

"Control of the machine."

"Huh? What machine?"

"The car."

"Oh, yeah, right. The car, the pickup, whatever."

"What will you do when you control the machine?"

"Go wherever I want."

"Where will you want to go?"

"As far away as I want."

"I'll miss you, Jojo. I had no one before you. Nothing."

"You won't miss me. We'll go everywhere together."

"Why do you want to go far away?"

"Don't you?"

"I've already been far away."

She was silent, and he asked again why she wanted to go far away. She said, "You and me, we'll go somewhere everyone is nice and everything they say to each other is nice, and no one is mean."

"It hurts you when they say mean things about me."

Once more she fell silent. Then: "Mostly they're stupid. They don't know you like I do." She sighed. "Eight years is a long time."

"Not so long," he said.

"Well, you're eleven. You're three years closer to sixteen."

"I'm a lot older than that, Jojo."

"Don't tell me you're twelve. I know you're not."

"I'm more than four thousand years old."

"Now you're being silly."

"Maybe."

"You're being a totally silly goose."

"Maybe what's silly is to think we'll go everywhere and far away together."

"Don't say that. We're best friends forever."

Standing on the veranda of the house, about fifty yards upslope from the lake, her mother called to them. They weren't allowed to be out after dark, just two children, because coyotes might come upon them. Mother didn't know that coyotes were no threat to Jojo when Jimmy was with her.

Abruptly the jet was shaken by turbulence, and Joanna slumped in the seat, the bracing effect of the memory undone as the aircraft dropped hundreds of feet. From other passengers came small cries and gasps of alarm, but throughout the sudden sinking and subsequent undulant ascent to their assigned altitude, Joanna was not alarmed.

She stared out the window, not with concern that she might meet the earth below in a free fall of horrific violence, but instead with an awareness of fault, of failure, of something uncomfortably close to guilt. The pledge of eternal friendship had been made when she was a child with little understanding of the sacredness of pledges, and she had failed to keep her word more because of circumstances and the death of two parents than because she made the conscious choice to turn away from him. Yet she couldn't escape from the truth that she'd forgotten him entirely, as though he never existed. She didn't know what suffering he had endured during the past twenty-four years or what she might have been able to do to alleviate his pain if only she had kept him in her mind and heart.

She didn't even know if Jimmy Two Eyes was still alive.

Although she understood that guilting herself over this would risk letting true sentiment slide into sentimentality, she wondered if her loneliness was a consequence of karma, an echo of the greater loneliness to which Jimmy had been condemned when she left Rustling Willows Ranch.

But why had he never spoken to anyone but her, and then always in secret? Why had he chosen isolation and allowed everyone else to believe that he lacked the capacity to understand language?

The suburbs of the mile-high city materialized under her, and ahead was Denver International Airport, another flight to Montana, and a truth she might wish she had not pursued.

PART 2
HOMECOMING

On the quantum level, reality is spookily fragile
and can be manipulated. By whom? By us.
—*Ganesh Patel*

25

Where the river slides past Zipporah, its course is nearly flat, with no sudden steps in the bed to churn its current into rapids, and the grassy banks fold down to it as smoothly as draped velvet. The water flows almost as silently as time.

Naked, Asher Optime bathes in the river this morning, as he does every morning, as he will until the cold of winter forces a change in his routine. He ventures from shore only until he stands waist-deep in the flow. He uses a soap made from the essential oils of certain plants, careful not to pollute the pristine water, which is so clear that he can see the bottom. His feet remain in soft silt, and he never missteps on one of the large round stones that look like a parade of turtles making their way downstream.

Asher enjoys the feel of himself under the slickness of the sudsless soap. He spends a quarter of an hour caressing his lean but muscular torso and limbs, with special attention to the delightful vacancy where once his testicles depended. As further testament to his rejection of his humanity, he'd wanted to shear off his flaccid penis, too, but he hadn't done so because management of the bleeding would have been difficult and because thereafter urination would have been less convenient.

In the first few minutes of Asher's ablutions, the coyote comes out of the trees and appears on the farther shore, where it sits to watch him bathe. Every morning—often at other moments of the day, as well—a coyote observes him, never with what seems like predatory intent. Sometimes it is a male, at other times a female, one day a graybeard and the next a younger specimen.

Initially, he'd wondered why these creatures took such intense interest in him. But soon he realized that this was Mother Nature's way of saluting him for his commitment to her, because no other man or woman has ever made—or ever would make—as profound a sacrifice as Asher has made. As the coyotes are cousins to wolves, so Asher is now a cousin to coyotes, and through them Nature makes clear her approval of his manifesto and his murders.

Some people believe that dogs have a psychic sense, and Asher feels sure that coyotes are greatly gifted in this way, that they can read his intentions, if not his every thought. A few times a week, while under their observation, he loses all sense of purpose for ten minutes or twenty or half an hour, and goes into something like a trance, on some occasions while standing here in the river. When he regains awareness, he can see the coyote pacing back and forth in great agitation, though never with the intent to attack, rather as if the beast is excited by some bonding that occurred between them while Asher was in a fugue state.

This morning, after he wades ashore and towels dry and dresses, just as he is about to turn away from the river and enter the former saloon to continue his work on the manifesto, Asher falls into one of these strange fugues for perhaps ten minutes. When he wakes, he is still standing on the riverbank with his feet planted wide apart and his hands raised, his fingers combing the air as if to harvest something from the golden sunlight. The coyote on the farther shore is in a frenzy, circling on itself and biting at its tail, its ears flat against its skull, making shrill, urgent sounds. It endures in this behavior for a minute, then stops and, panting as if exhausted, gazes at him across the water for a moment before, hackles raised, it sprints north along the grassy strand for about ten yards. Then it vanishes into the shadows among the pines and other evergreens.

26

Kenny Deetle was a white-hat hacker, internet buccaneer, data diver extraordinaire, thirty years old but still as quick of mind as any twenty-year-old punk who'd been steeped in the craft since the cradle. He could backdoor any computer system and worm deep into it and plant a rootkit, giving him easy access and control that no IT-security special forces could detect, although he didn't do this illegally or for nefarious clients. He was a good guy. He hadn't *always* been one of the good guys, but he'd *wanted* to be one ever since he was twenty-four, when his best friend, Max Gurn, hacked into the computer system of a Dark Web drug operation. Max locked it down and tried to extort four million dollars in Bitcoin in return for allowing cartel jackboots to regain access to their inventory and supply-chain records. Max was the very best at spoofing through a maze of telecom exchanges, a wizard at concealing his identity and true location. He knew the bad guys—or worse guys, if you will—could never find him. But they found him. Max went on the run across three continents, two oceans, and four islands before the cartel caught up with him in Oklahoma, the Sooner State, in the city of Tulsa, where they cut his head down the middle with a chain saw while he was—briefly—alive, then methodically dismembered him, packed him into a hermetically sealed, metal trunk labeled GURN FAMILY MEMENTOS, and had him delivered by FedEx to his mother in Topeka.

Since then, thankful that he hadn't participated in Max Gurn's big score, although he'd been invited to assist, Kenny Deetle did white-hat hacking for certain Fortune 500 companies. He also took assignments from Rider Investigations because, five years earlier, when police showed little interest in what they thought was a crank threat, Wyatt Rider identified an anonymous stalker who intended to rape Kenny's sister, Sandy, and feed her to hogs. Wyatt got evidence on the creep—one Proctor Lash, now serving a life term—who turned out to have done to another woman what he wanted to do to Sandy.

The world got crazier year by year. Nastier, too.

Kenny lived in and worked out of a spacious loft in a Seattle warehouse converted into apartments that were rented mostly by people who thought they were artists of one kind or another. They were painters, sculptors, writers, actors, and YouTube video-star wannabes. Kenny kept his distance from all his neighbors because none seemed to be rich in common sense or to understand that the performance-artist poet next door might possibly have a really bad day with rhyming and might relieve his frustration by stabbing you in the face.

That's the kind of world it was.

At seven thirty Friday morning, Wyatt Rider called Kenny with an urgent assignment. He had a client in Montana whose home computer system and associated electronics were served by a satellite dish that had apparently been compromised by some hacker who was on the Max Gurn end of the profession. Wyatt provided the dish address, all essential telecom account information, as well as the client's passwords. Without having to leave his loft in Seattle, Kenny could frontdoor the system in Montana and sleuth through it in search of evidence that a worthless black-hat turd had commandeered the house. He would then follow the data-crumb trail to the culprit, so that Wyatt could break the bastard's legs, figuratively speaking.

"One question," Kenny said, taking notes while sitting up in bed with a nude girl named Bruce Ann Leigh, or maybe Leigh Ann Bruce. "This doesn't involve Dark Web chain-saw goons, does it?"

"I'd bet everything I own that it doesn't," Wyatt said.

"Would you bet your *cojones*?"

"You mean my cantaloupes? Absolutely."

"All right, then. I'm on it," Kenny said.

27

Supplied by a river, Lake Sapphire did not rise with a tide, but only in the event that the outflow spillway could not cope with the volume of runoff produced by a major storm. The lake was stirred by currents, however, provided by the river running through it. The water ceaselessly licked the shore, chuckled among the dock pilings, and, in the boathouse, caused an eighteen-foot electric

Duffy to wallow gently in its slip. The boat knocked against the cosseting rubber fender, and the taut belaying rope strained against the cleat with a whisper of a screech.

With the Duffy six or seven feet below him, Wyatt stood on the docking at the head of the gangway, which creaked and clicked with the barely perceptible, rhythmic rise and fall of the floating slip. Whether or not anyone had waited here for him the previous night, the high windows under the eaves now admitted more than enough light to confirm that he was alone this morning.

Some people might have been surprised that a billionaire and his family would choose a craft as mundane as the electric Duffy, with its open sides and its blue canopy trimmed in white piping, a boat that dawdled along rather than zoomed. Of course, this was ideal for cruising with two preteen children, and it was quintessentially Liam and Lyndsey; for all their wealth, they did not move with a flashy crowd.

As Wyatt was about to turn away, he saw something large glide through the dark water below, a phantasm as pale as the corpse of a leviathan from which death had bleached all color. It entered under the lakeside garage-style roll-up door, at least twice as large as a man, a torpedo shape broader at the front than at the rear. The creature was too quick and too distorted by the roiled water to allow Wyatt to discern identifying detail. The thing disappeared under the Duffy. In its wake, displaced water sloshed against the big door, rattling it in its tracks, and the boat wallowed gently.

Wyatt stood transfixed, waiting for the intruder to swim out from beneath the vessel. The water quieted and became as still as it had been before this apparition, and the thing did not reappear.

Here at the end of the dock, the lake wasn't nearly as deep as it was farther from shore, maybe eight or ten feet. But the Duffy had a draw of perhaps only two feet, which left plenty of clearance for whatever had positioned itself beneath the boat.

In a body of fresh water as large as this lake, no fish existed as big as the thing that Wyatt had seen. No sharks. No manta rays. Just bass, maybe trout. When a fisherman hooked something here, he would expect to reel it in with little effort. The thing under the Duffy would snap an eighty-pound line as if it were spider silk.

When you endeavored to put your larcenous parents in prison, especially knowing they were capable of murder, you didn't back away from a situation like this, or from anything. Whatever waited under the Duffy must be some kind of aquatic animal, and no damn fish could harm you—not a shark, not a piranha—unless you got into the water with it.

He descended the gangway to the teak deck. The port side of the Duffy was snugged against the built-in fenders on the slip, so that he could not see under the vessel. The boathouse offered two berths within the single U-shaped slip. He walked around the bow of the Duffy, to the farther finger of teak, beyond the empty berth.

From there he could see under the starboard flank of the Duffy, where something floated in the murk, ghostly pale. It appeared to be about ten feet long, but he couldn't see anything significant of it, perhaps because the water here was deeper than he had thought. The dorsal surface of the creature had been pale when he'd seen the thing glide in from the lake, under the door, though all of the fish that he'd ever seen were pale on the ventral plane, not the dorsal—on their bellies, not their backs.

If this was a fish, surely it couldn't remain still beneath the boat. It would need to move continuously in order to siphon oxygen from the water streaming through its gills. Yet there it floated like some immense seaweed bladder.

The light from the high windows did not fall directly on the water, which darkled into its depths. To get a better angle of view on the creature under the Duffy, Wyatt dropped onto one knee and craned his head forward, squinting with the hope of glimpsing some detail that would begin to define the beast.

The thing appeared to spasm, to dim and then brighten as if it might be vaguely phosphorescent, as were some creatures of the sea, and then it rolled in place.

This movement, seemingly timed to his attempt to gain a closer look at the thing, suggested its visit to the boathouse simultaneous with his inspection of the place was no coincidence. It was here because of him, for a reason he could not at once comprehend.

Abruptly, the thing breached under the Duffy, slamming it hard against the slip finger and boosting it more than a foot. The hull squealed against the rubber fenders. The taut belaying line thrummed a bass note, and the boat fell back into place, wallowing violently.

A wave washed across the empty berth and slopped onto the teak where Wyatt knelt. He quickly got to his feet and warily backed away, as the water clouded with bestirred silt.

The creature breached again, with greater power than before, still hidden by the boat that it heaved on its back. The Duffy rattled, twanged, thudded against the fenders.

The floating slip rolled under Wyatt. He staggered, regained his balance, and realized that the thing's intention might be to pitch him into the water.

He hurried along the wet planking. He would have to get past the Duffy and around its port side to reach the gangway that led up to the main floor of the boathouse.

As Wyatt was approaching the bow of the vessel, the mysterious intruder breached a third time with tremendous force. The belaying line snapped. The boat tipped on its stern, its bow lifting out of the water, and it surged forward, crashing onto the teak slip, which rocked with such violence that Wyatt lost his footing. He fell, but not into the water.

The damaged Duffy slid backward again, into its berth. The ghastly presence, now a phantom of fluid form in the cloudy water, swept out from under the craft. The dimly luminescent creature arced through the sloshing murk and out of the boathouse, rattling the big roll-up door as it exited under it.

Lest the mysterious intruder should return in an even greater state of agitation, Wyatt hurried around the slip and climbed the gangway to the main floor. At the top, he turned and looked down, half expecting to see the boat taking on water. The vessel hadn't sprung a leak, though it drifted, unmoored, in the middle of the two-berth slip.

From below rose the odors of wet wood and rich lake-bottom silt. A fainter scent, not as natural as the others, was familiar, but he couldn't quite identify it: vaguely reminiscent of the smell of ammonia, though with much less hydroxide pungency.

The experiences, first enchanting and then frightening, that caused Liam and his family to flee Rustling Willows had included neither a manifestation like the one that recently departed the boathouse nor the pyrotechnics of swarming fireflies, nor a voice issuing threats from a TV. Wyatt had yet to encounter anything like what spooked the O'Haras. This ranch was rich with strangeness, as if it might have become a way station between realities, its every shadow seeming to cloak a threat.

Whatever its nature and its ultimate purpose, the reason for the lake dweller's invasion of the boathouse couldn't have been clearer. It meant to say, *You're known, you're watched, and you're not wanted here.*

28

In the long-abandoned church with its cache of corpses denied burial, Ophelia Poole had not slept well on the pew. Eventually she had sat up, alert and observant, waiting for dawn to thrust a shaft of light through a gap in the ceiling.

The birds were nearby in the dark, revealed by an occasional ruffling of feathers, click of beak, and thin *eeeee* that might have been the avian equivalent of a yawn.

Perhaps they came here every night to be safe from nocturnal predators like owls that would feast on birds as readily as on mice and rabbits. But she still believed that their interest in her was unusual, their lack of fear not common to their kind.

Finally the new day announced itself not with a bright spear that pierced roof planks, but as a lesser darkness in the dark, a shapen grayness toward the back of the sanctuary, on the right.

To anyone who believed in life everlasting, this ashen light could be seen as a figure, perhaps the penitent spirit of a long-dead member of the congregation come to mourn the condition of the church and the loss of faith in general. Gradually, as cinder-gray radiance became dove gray and then pearl gray, the figure morphed into the more geometric form of a doorway, not a portal to a world after this one, but to a room beyond the back wall of the sanctuary.

Abruptly the sentinel crows sprang off their perch and winged toward the front of the church. Ophelia glimpsed the two darting into the grayness, swift and gone.

She got to her feet and switched on the Tac Light and followed the center aisle to the chancel railing. The previous night, she had not searched farther than this, saving the batteries with the hope that morning would come through a rent in the roof with enough power to cure her blindness. Now she stepped through the gap where the sanctuary gate had long ago broken away from the railing. She walked around the elevated altar platform and followed the ambulatory to the doorway through which the birds had flown.

The room beyond must have been the sacristy, where vestments, a chalice, and other ceremonial items were stored between services. No cabinets remained, no shelves, neither a vesting bench nor a prie-dieu. The barren space measured about twelve feet on a side. The ceiling sloped from a high of twelve feet beyond the threshold to ten feet at the far wall.

Part of the floor was carpeted with a thin mold sustained by what rain found its way here. The mold was slippery, stuck to the soles of her shoes, and smelled like sweaty feet; but it seemed not to have compromised the structure it had colonized, because the floorboards weren't spongy underfoot.

Judging by appearances, the sacristy had been an afterthought. The walls weren't of mortared stone like the rest of the building. This was wood-frame construction with plank walls.

The sun, low in the east, didn't stream directly through the hole in the roof. However, the clear morning light proved bright enough to rinse the gray out of the sacristy and impart faint warmth to Ophelia's upturned face.

The gap, maybe eight inches wide and two feet long, was at the high point of the roof, where the sacristy had partially separated from the back wall of the church. It wasn't wide enough for a child to squeeze through, let alone a grown woman, but the ceiling planks and roof shingles might be rotten enough to allow her to widen the hole—if she could get to it.

Had there been a door between the sanctuary and the sacristy, she might have been able to break it off its hinges and use it as a ramp to get closer to the ceiling. The only door was in the farther wall, evidently an exit, but Optime had reframed the jamb and header with fresh lumber that he'd probably brought into this ghost town with other supplies. Then he'd removed the hinges and knob from the door, nailed it to the new frame, and fortified it with two-by-four cross braces. Ophelia had no tools with which to undo his work, and even a bull of a man couldn't have broken through that barrier.

Turning to the slice of sky that could be seen, she stared with intense longing colored more by apprehension than by hope. Although she was hungry, she could endure weeks without food if she must. Her thirst was more troubling than her hunger. Chapped lips. Scratchy throat. Already her skin felt dry. She could live a few days without water, but her strength would fade quickly as she dehydrated.

A cool flow of air slithered down through the gap between the church proper and the sacristy, bringing with it a fluttering, soft something that had been caught on the splintered edge of a roof beam. A small feather settled into her upraised hand, testimony that the birds hadn't merely been figments of her imagination. If a black feather was a symbol that augured anything, however, it was surely predictive of death rather than life.

"Fuck that," she said.

She hadn't been spared in the accident that killed Octavia just to die in the service of a misanthropic lunatic's vicious agenda.

Casting the feather to the floor, she said, "Think, damn it, *think*."

29

Near the end of the flight from Denver to Montana, Joanna Chase opened her purse and withdrew a snapshot of her mother. It was one of many that she had found in the box of photographs the previous evening, when she had searched fruitlessly for a picture of Jimmy Two Eyes.

For whatever reason, Joanna didn't care to maintain a gallery of family photos on a wall or on the shelves of a bookcase. As a consequence, she was surprised that her mental image of her mother had faded and that the photo revealed a woman of greater beauty and grace than memory could retain.

Another aspect of the snapshot unsettled Joanna a little. In those eyes and even in the curve of the smile, there seemed to be a subtle melancholy that she had never noticed as a child. If it was not just a quirk of this one picture, if it had been there in life, her mother had hidden it well.

She put the photo away as the plane touched down. Only as the passengers began disembarking did she realize how odd it was that she had brought her mother's photo but not one of her father.

30

Carrying backpacks and walking sticks, they hiked north along the river, through a primeval forest that made Colson Fielding think of a cathedral that he'd once seen when his family had visited New York City. The tall trees were like columns, and the boughs overhead were reminiscent of a series of arched vaults. The pine-scented air smelled a little like incense, and a churchy hush lay over it all.

Colson, thirteen years old, had never seen a ghost town, so he was looking forward to exploring Zipporah with his father. Although it would be cool if the place was haunted, he didn't expect ghosts, only a satisfying measure of creepiness and a lot of history.

His father, Steve, was a professor at the state university in Billings. Dad knew enough about Montana and American history to bore your ass off ten times over. Well, that was unfair. A lot of history was just boring, and no one could pump it up until it leaped off the screen like a movie from Marvel Studios, although his father made maybe half of it pretty darn interesting. He taught elective rather than required courses, and his classes were always oversubscribed.

Dad would have liked nothing more than for his son to catch the history bug and be infected with a love of the past, as he put it, "in all its blazing glory and sad darknesses." But too much of history seemed to be about politics, which was all bullshit when it wasn't also flat-out insanity. Colson wanted to focus on the future and a life in the sky as a jet pilot, maybe as an astronaut in the United States Space Force. The human destiny was to move ever onward and outward: He'd heard that in a sci-fi movie, and it had struck him as true and right.

As the forest closed ever tighter around them, and as they struggled over challenging terrain, Colson thought it was amazing that he had learned to enjoy these outings. He once would have found hiking with his father as tedious as the details of the war of the "copper kings" who battled over ore deposits around Butte, Montana, which eventually produced eleven billion pounds of copper, or even as tiresome as the story of the bloody wars between the Crow and the Sioux, as if any of that had anything to do with *today*.

Then the previous summer, when Colson was twelve, he'd felt guilty for resisting his father's desire that they slog through the wilds together, enduring the miseries of nature. He hadn't known *why* he felt guilty. Maybe because Mom felt guilty that she also did not share her husband's interest in hiking and camping and fighting off bears in the green hell of the woods, though *he* always went to chick flicks and symphonies with her. Like mother, like son: Colson preferred a four-star motel to a tent and sleeping bag, and any restaurant food to campfire victuals spooned from a heated tin can.

He'd finally broken down and agreed to go on a three-day hike, though with the conviction that he would be killed either by snakes or mountain lions, if not by snakes and mountain lions working in demonic collaboration. To his surprise, after the first day, he had begun to enjoy the experience. For one thing, the fields and forests of Montana proved not to be as dangerous as the python-festooned jungles of South America. For another thing, his dad knew as much about nature as he knew about history, at home in the wilds no less than at their house in Billings. For a third thing, his dad was good company, especially when he wasn't going on about Custer's Last Stand or Yellowstone Kelly or Chief Black Otter.

That summer, they went on four hikes together, and another two in the winter. During the current summer, they'd been on two treks prior to this expedition to Zipporah. Gradually, Colson had grown hardier, more muscular, more limber, and more self-confident. He respected rattlesnakes and mountain lions and wolves and bears, and he remained wary of them, but he no longer feared them irrationally.

Mother had worried herself into a case of the hives the first two times that Colson had gone hiking with his dad, but she had grown accustomed to seeing them off on their adventures. In fact, there was nothing to be concerned about. In recognition that some creatures of the wild belonged less in a Disney movie than in a horror flick, Dad walked with a 12-gauge shotgun slung over his left shoulder, one loaded with slugs rather than buckshot, intended only for protection from large predators to which a grown man and teenage boy might seem like a Big Mac with a side of fries. The weapon had never been necessary, because clipped to Colson's utility belt was a small can of pressurized gas, an Attwood signal horn, that produced an ear-splitting noise that tended to scare off even bears and big cats if they were too curious and bold.

They couldn't get lost because they possessed two compasses and detailed trail maps. They were also equipped with a GPS messenger in the event that one of them might be injured and need to be carried or airlifted out of the wilderness. The cell-phone-size unit had a red emergency button that you needed to press three times in quick succession before your distress call was transmitted to a satellite that then relayed the SOS to the International Emergency Response Coordination Center in Texas. Colson and his dad were safer than they would have been in certain major cities where at least one homicide was committed every day.

Now the trees gave way to a grassy sward along the river, and to the right were the ramshackle buildings of Zipporah. One of the first Fieldings to live in Montana, Ezra Enoch Fielding settled in Zipporah twenty years before it was abandoned. He was some kind of distant relative of Colson's. He died in a smallpox outbreak, the final blow to a bad-luck town that never became a center of the timber industry or a vital river port, as its founders envisioned.

"Here it is," Dad said with a sweeping gesture, "a key location in the glorious history of the Fielding family."

"It for sure won't be haunted," Colson said as they approached the backs of the buildings that faced onto the town's only street. Crickets sang, and clouds of midges erupted from the tall grass around them. "Not even a ghost would want to live here."

"But people wanted to, back in the day."

"Why here in the middle of nowhere?" Colson wondered.

"Most places in the West were in the middle of nowhere at one time, until they grew and became somewhere. There was good money in timber, and bigger towns downriver that could buy what a lumber mill produced."

As they passed between weathered, sagging two-story buildings and came out onto the weedy, unpaved street, Colson said, "It's more sad than anything, not spooky at all. Even when it was all new, I'd never have come here."

"Well, son, there wasn't unemployment insurance in those days. No welfare of any kind except what churches might provide. When you were out of a job, you had to go where the work was—or where you hoped it would be."

They turned left, toward the stone church at the far end of the street.

Colson said, "So why did Ezra Enoch come here?"

"He made a bit of money as a trapper. The fur trade was big in those days. But that's a hard life, and he wanted something softer. So he came here and bought this place just ahead on the left."

The two-story wood building featured a parapet roof and a deep veranda without a railing. At the back of the veranda, on the wall, to the left of the entry door, which stood open, someone had long ago painted a winning poker hand, a royal flush, now so faded that it was almost invisible. To the right of the door was the legend "P. H. Best" crowning an illustration that time had all but obliterated.

Dad said, "P. H. Best was a German beer. The card hand is there to indicate gambling took place inside."

Suddenly, abandoned Zipporah seemed less sad than interesting. "You mean some guy in our family, this Ezra Enoch dude, he owned a *saloon* in the Old West?"

"He did indeed, though like most such places in those days, it was less glamorous than you see in movies. Most gunfights weren't showdowns in the street, but nasty close-up murders by sloppy drunks who were cheating each other at cards."

Just then, a guy came through the open door of the saloon as if stepping out of the past. He wore boots with tucked-in blue jeans, a dark T-shirt, and a longish denim jacket. Tall, fit, tanned, with an air of authority, he looked as if he ought to be wearing a sheriff's star on his chest.

"Good morning, gentlemen. I'm with the Montana Historical Preservation Office. If you've hiked in to take a tour of our little town, I'm afraid you'll have to stay out of the buildings, just have a look from the street. We'll be restoring Zipporah, and we don't want any more damage done to the buildings than they've already endured."

As the guy descended the three veranda steps to the street, Dad said, "There's a restoration project for a place as inconsequential as this?"

"To us, every place is consequential, Mr.—?"

"Fielding," Dad said. "Dr. Steven Fielding. From the state university at Billings. History department. I'm surprised to hear that the legislature in Helena has been able to scare up funds for something like this."

"I'm Asher Optime." The tall man held out his right hand, and they shook, and he said, "Are there neglected sites from the period that you think should take preference over Zipporah, Dr. Fielding?"

"Not necessarily. Maybe. I'd have to think about it. I'm just pleased to hear the politicians care about preserving anything. This is my son, Colson."

Optime's grip was firm and dry as he shook Colson's hand.

The man's eyes were bottle-glass green. Although Colson didn't drink alcohol and although tequila didn't come in green containers as far as he knew, something about those eyes reminded him that some traditional Mexican-made brands of tequila featured a small, curled worm in the bottom of the bottle. It was totally weird that such a thing should occur to him.

"Well, sir," Optime said to Colson's father, "if you have any informed thoughts about other sites you recommend for restoration, feel free to contact me about them. Let me give you my card."

The guy reached behind for a wallet, but the pistol must have been tucked under his belt, in the small of his back, because that was what he produced. He fired two rounds point-blank, head shots. In a shower of blood but not just blood, Colson's dad—his one dad, his only dad—fell backward and lay faceup, except it wasn't Dad's face anymore, it was broken and twisted and horrible, and Colson looked away, into the muzzle of the pistol.

31

From the boathouse, Wyatt went to the stables, of which there were four, each with ten stalls. These were sturdily built clapboard buildings, painted white with red ceramic-tile roofs, with electric heating in winter.

The horses that had belonged to the previous owner were long gone, although Liam and Lyndsey O'Hara had intended eventually to acquire four or five gentle mares, not for breeding purposes, but only so that they and their children could learn to ride together.

The stalls had been mucked out. The half doors were all neatly closed. The air carried a thin scent of straw, the earthen smell of the hard-packed floor, and what might have been the faint fragrance of a liniment used on horses and once spilled here, saturating the soil.

He encountered nothing strange, nothing threatening, but he felt nonetheless watched.

In the five-room bungalow that had housed the ranch manager for each of the previous owners, he found nothing remarkable except the rats. He didn't see them, but he heard them pitter-pattering across the beams and flooring in the attic. The place had been empty for some months, and the rodents had taken up residence. They were quiet when he first entered the house; however, as he prowled the rooms, searching for he knew not what, they became increasingly agitated. It seemed that minute by minute they increased in number, as if calling others of their kind out of the fields and up through the walls to race in an unnatural frenzy overhead, with some purpose that he couldn't imagine.

From a two-foot-square trapdoor in the hallway ceiling dangled a pull cord, offering access to the chamber above. As the noise became yet more frantic but included no squeaking rodent voices, Wyatt wondered if what occupied that high space might be something other than rats. He considered drawing down the trapdoor ladder and going up there for a look.

Vermin didn't unnerve him. A rodent was just another mammal, and even a horde of them wasn't as fearsome as any single, tailless human rat.

He reached up and gripped the yellow plastic handle on the pull cord. Hesitated.

The escalating noise in the attic seemed to be concentrated directly over him. The trapdoor creaked and rattled softly in its frame. If rats were gathered in numbers on the spring-loaded ladder, they would spill down on him as the segments of rungs unfolded to the hallway floor.

Intuition suggested caution. He was alone on the ranch. Rather than proceed with this now, he would be better advised to call Vance Potter, so they could investigate the attic together. Rats were just another mammal, yes; however, they carried disease.

Anyway, whatever swarmed in the attic must be somehow related to the fireflies and to the thing that invaded the boathouse. He didn't understand this place, didn't know what power animated it, what presence ruled here, why Nature seemed to be cognizant of him or why she appeared to be marshaling her creatures against him. Until he had at least a figment of a theory, he needed to proceed with caution.

When he stepped outside and locked the door behind him, the sun burned at its apex, and the emptiness of the vast landscape that it illuminated made him uneasy. This area lay near the western end of the portion of Montana that was well-named "Big Sky Country." As blue as a gas flame, the heavens were intimidating, more daunting than the immensity of land below them. No less than when dark and stippled with stars that were trillions of miles away, the day sky oppressed him with evidence of infinity; it inspired a fear—wrong though he believed it to be—that he was insignificant, that no man or woman ever born was of consequence in the shoreless ocean of time and space.

Suddenly, though he had only a moment earlier stepped outside, he wanted—needed—to be in the confines of a house, safe within a room defined by walls. Though he never took a drink before dinner, he wanted one now, the warmth of whiskey to dispel the chill that pierced deeper than flesh and bone, that sleeted through his spirit. He was a man without a family, his parents having proved to be a pair of cruel predators with whom he'd never been able to identify except as the moral agent of their destruction. A relationship that might have led to marriage had eluded him. He was alone, resigned to a busy professional life and a private life of solitude, accustomed to loneliness, although not comfortable with it. However, in this moment, in this uninhabited vastness, he inhaled the vacancy, took it in through every pore, and his heart knocked hard with fear of his fate.

He headed toward the main house. As he crossed the blacktop lane, he heard low thunder. Although the sky remained cloudless, he looked up, but then glanced toward the distant purple mountains in the west. The fulmination swelled. He felt rumbling underfoot, and he turned his attention to the east. When he saw the source of the sound, he stood astonished for a moment—and then, seized by a sense of imminent danger, he broke into a run.

32

Colson Fielding was frozen by shock. His father was dead on the ground, and Colson should have been stricken hard by grief, but he was instead given entirely to terror as he stared into the muzzle of the pistol, the two shots echoing in memory, echoing and echoing, so that at first he couldn't hear what the killer was saying to him. Slowly he raised his attention from the single black eye of the gun to the bottle-green eyes of Asher Optime, which was like meeting the stare of a robot. The murderer's face was blank, no twist of anger in it, no trace of a wicked smile, as if killing Colson's father meant nothing to him, meant less than stepping on an ant.

Optime's voice at last penetrated. "Drop the walking stick, boy, take off your backpack, do it now, or I'll shoot you in the foot and spend the afternoon watching you slowly bleed to death."

Into the wild rush of terror came a current of shame. Colson despised himself because he began to shake violently and because he did as he was told, with no further hesitation, with no thought of striking out or making a run for it. Murder was what jacked up the pace of action movies, it was how you scored high in video games, by killing bad guys, but it wasn't supposed to be something that could happen to you in real life. He felt as though he might throw up or embarrass himself by pissing his pants; he did neither, but even if he had done both, it wouldn't matter, the mortification wouldn't matter, as long as he was allowed to live.

"Take off your utility belt, boy, throw it on the backpack, turn out your pockets, drop the contents on the ground."

While he did as told, he heard himself saying, "Mister, please, please, please." He hated himself for pleading, for the tremor in his voice, but he did not stop. The killer took such pleasure in his captive's humiliation that he focused on Colson's eyes and on his lips as they formed the pleas, not on his hands. Not on his hands.

Thrown to the ground, Colson's wallet fell open to a photo of his mom and dad, taken two years ago on vacation in Coeur d'Alene. The killer retrieved it, considered it, and then tucked it in a jacket pocket.

Satisfied that every demand had been met, he shoved the pistol in the hip holster under his denim jacket.

In that instant, Colson was given a chance to act. He could have charged Optime and tried to knock him off his feet. He wasn't able to move. Cold sweat slicked his face, his hands, drooled down his spine into the small of his back, into the crack of his butt. His knee joints seemed to be coming loose. He swayed and thought he would collapse.

The killer used one foot to get a boot toe under Colson's father and kick-shoved him hard a few times, until the corpse flopped over, facedown in the dirt.

For some reason, seeing his dad's body treated like garbage, Colson thought of his mother, of how she loved his dad, how his dad loved her, and grief slammed him at last, not as much for his own loss as for hers, for how devastated she would be when she got the news. His chest ached as if grief were a cancer in his ribs. He was hardly able to draw a breath, and with this anguish came a first inchoate spasm of rage, raw anger directed at the killer, but also at himself and at God.

Optime bent down and slipped the shotgun off the dead man's shoulder. He checked the breach and chambered a round and checked the breach again.

"Slugs," he said. He looked at Colson. "You know, boy, this would put a hole through you as big as a fist."

Colson didn't so much as glance at the muzzle. He'd had enough of looking down gun barrels.

Meeting his captive's eyes, the killer kicked the corpse again, and then once more, with a contempt that clearly gave him pleasure.

Colson said, "You sick bastard," but that weak rebellion was such a pathetic attempt at atonement for his failure to act that he felt smaller and more helpless than ever.

As though he could read his captive's mind, Optime said, "Your daddy is nothing now. He never was anything. Neither are you. You're pestilence and filth. You breathe out poison." With the shotgun, he gestured past Colson. "Let's go to church."

The suggestion was so odd that Colson didn't at first realize Optime literally meant what he said.

"Church," the killer repeated. "At the end of the street."

"You can't just leave him laying there."

"Your daddy isn't a him anymore, boy. Your daddy's just an it, a worm farm waiting to happen. Now get a move on. There's someone I want you to meet."

33

If they had not been announced by the thunder of their hooves, Wyatt Rider might have thought that the elk were a hallucination. The throng approaching wasn't merely an antlered bull and its cows with a few spotted calves. More bulls than Wyatt could count galloped up the lane and through the meadows to both sides of the blacktop, and with them came several times more cows than bulls, as well as numerous calves. He estimated there were as many as two hundred, and though they were not in a stampede that might trample him, they were coming fast, with determination. Getting out of their way seemed to be wise.

Where they had come from, what drew them here, what purpose they had, he couldn't imagine. They seemed otherworldly, especially the immense bulls with their velvet-covered antlers, heads held high and black nostrils flared. They issued no cries, came in silence but for the clopping of their hooves.

By the time he reached the main residence and climbed the steps onto the veranda, the herds arrived. They streamed past the west side of the house, as though heading to the forested hills beyond this grassy slope, but instead they circled the building, reappeared around the east side, and trotted back the way they'd come, along the lane and through the meadows that flanked it.

Although Liam O'Hara had not mentioned elk, this extraordinary spectacle was similar to another of a far more threatening nature, involving wolves and coyotes, which had frightened the billionaire and his family into departing the ranch.

A pickup or an SUV appeared in the distance, and at the sound of the engine, the herds moved faster and converged on the vehicle.

A white Ford Explorer. The driver slowed to a stop. After a hesitation, the SUV advanced slowly.

The elk surrounded the Ford and accompanied it as if they were an honor guard, as if the occupant were a royal personage to whom they had sworn an oath of fealty.

34

Asher Optime is living his manifesto, casting no shadow as he walks behind the boy at high noon.

Dr. Fielding, the self-important historian, lies dead in the street, a fitting end for him.

"History," Asher tells the wretched boy, "is one of the instruments with which humankind deceive themselves into believing the story of their species is of consequence, a long and noble march during which they supposedly acquire ever more knowledge, leading to enlightenment, truth, transcendence. In fact, though they remember what they learn, they forget the meaning of it. Every period of enlightenment is followed by a new and more efficient barbarism. They preach the necessity of truth even as they flee from it. Some believe in immortality through technology, while others believe in the transcendence of the spirit. They cling to their faith on the way to death and the void, while fouling the world in their passing. The past is a lie, and the future is only the past that hasn't yet happened. Your father, the historian, was a prince of liars. In a few days, in this church of the dead, in the rising stench of rotting flesh, as you become dehydrated for lack of water, you'll grow restless and dizzy, endure excruciating abdominal cramps. And you'll come to see all the ways that he lied to you. When you've lost all hope, when you're ready to curse his name and piss on that picture of your parents, then I'll relieve your suffering."

Asher is pleased by this speech, which is so brilliant that of course the boy can think of nothing to say as they arrive at the church door. This might be the first time in his miserable life that he's been told the truth, and it pierces him like a needle, sews shut his lips, secures his tongue to the floor of his mouth.

"Lie facedown," Asher commands, and after a hesitation the boy obeys, prostrate on the church stoop.

Asher produces the key and disengages the deadbolt and pushes open the door.

The woman, Ophelia, is somewhere in the cloistered gloom, no doubt quaking in a far corner, afraid that he has come to kill her.

"Slither like a worm, Colson Fielding. Slither inside as if you're just another worm like all those feeding on the dead in the room below."

Prodded into motion by the shotgun barrel, the debased and humiliated boy pulls himself across the threshold, into the pale blade of light—a light of false hope—that the day thrusts through the doorway.

Asher is excited by this performance, achieving a satisfaction that is the most intense feeling he can experience now that he has denied himself the thrill of seminal release. Colson's every wriggle and hitch causes Asher to shiver with pleasure.

When the boy is across the threshold, Asher closes the door and locks it. He stands there for a moment in a post-rapture bliss, eyes closed and face upturned, basking in the noon warmth, imagining the day when the sun will never again shine on any human face and Earth will be restored.

35

The Ford Explorer that Joanna Chase rented in Billings was equipped with a navigation system, but even twenty-four years after leaving Montana for New Mexico, she required no map or guide. A two-hour drive brought her to the river-rock posts flanking the private lane that turned off the public highway. She passed under the sign that bore the name of the ranch and a silhouette of a running horse.

The house was not visible from there. Gripped by sudden doubt, before she might be seen by whoever currently lived here, she braked to a stop and sat listening to the engine idling.

Evidently the summer had been blessed with ample rain. The fields were lush and green, the upward-rolling land as sensuous as she remembered it. Scattered wildflowers jeweled the meadows: topaz yellow and sapphire blue and coral pink. More than a mile ahead, the first grove of willows clustered where the land plateaued, green cascades that screened the stables and the manager's bungalow from view.

Curiosity vied with a nameless anxiety, wistfulness with a cold sense of an unspecified threat. She hadn't anticipated the intensity or complexity of her emotional reaction to Rustling Willows. A guilt she could not explain contested with a childlike joy that she found likewise inexplicable. A pang of grief surely related to the deaths of her parents, but it also arose from another loss that hovered just beyond the limits of memory.

She'd been as much harried back here as she had been lured by vivid repetitive dreams, by some power taking control of her cars and her TV, by the woman on the phone with the vaguely familiar voice. *Jojo, I am spiraling into Bedlam. The big dark sky. The terrible big dark sky. Only you can help me.* Everything that had recently happened supported one inescapable conclusion: that she didn't know the full truth of her childhood; that back in the day, she'd had secrets she kept from her parents, from everyone; that around the time Auntie Kat had taken her away to Santa Fe, someone had somehow washed from her memory those same secrets.

Perhaps everyone entertained a story of his or her childhood that to one extent or another was a colorful reimagining of what had actually occurred, smoothing away the bigger fears and errors with a plaster of nostalgia. If so, they could be content with an alternate history because they believed it to be the complete and sparkling truth.

However, Joanna now knew that her memories—from the age of six until she left Rustling Willows before her tenth birthday—had been creased and shaped as if by an origami master, until the truth was hidden in the many folds of the new construction. Even if she had not been a novelist with an obsessive inquisitiveness, she would have been unable to live in ignorance of what had occurred in those years of her youth. Regardless of what risks she might be taking, what dangers might await, she had no choice but to go forward.

She took her foot off the brake and drove toward the plateau, toward the lake in which her mother had died, toward the fields beyond the house, where her father had been thrown from his horse and attacked by a grizzly bear, toward all the long-ago days when Jimmy Two Eyes had found his voice for only her, when no one else was near enough to hear.

Less than a mile from the house, through the hot shimmering air of the sun-splashed August day, she saw them coming. For a moment, she couldn't tell what they were, but then they galloped into focus, and she said, "Elk."

She recalled one of the recent dreams in which, as a child, she had gamboled through a misty dusk, encircled by a herd of elk—one bull, three cows, two calves—as though she had been welcomed into their family. Racing toward her now were *dozens* of herds, more elk in one place than she had ever seen before. Although she didn't fear a collision, she stopped the Ford and waited until scores of the magnificent creatures encircled the vehicle, bowing their heads to peer at her through the windows: the males weighing over a thousand pounds, their faces noble, their heads elaborately crowned by four-foot-high racks of antlers; the females smaller, with gentle faces; the sweet-looking calves with limpid eyes.

Joanna was overcome by a sense of wonder that was familiar. She knew, without understanding *how* she knew, that these herds were not gathered here by the workings of instinct, that they came to greet her, to welcome her home after her long absence. Elk lived eight to twelve years, so none of these had known her when she was a young girl. They hadn't chosen to celebrate her return; they had been *sent* by someone, although by whom seemed to be an insoluble mystery.

Her delight was as familiar as the wonder that dazzled her. She suspected now that her intense dreams of communing—even frolicking—with animals were based on memories. For at least three or four years of her childhood, she'd enjoyed an extraordinary relationship with all the creatures of these Montana wilds.

She took her foot off the brake, and as she let the car drift forward, the elk moved with her, phalanxes of them to every side, escorting her to the plateau, past the stables on her left, past the lake on her right, to the house that had inspired the furnishing of her home in Santa Fe.

A man stood on the veranda, at the head of the steps. He was about five feet ten, stocky but not fat, dressed in jeans and a white shirt.

Joanna came to a stop in front of the house and switched off the engine and opened the driver's door. When she stepped out of the Explorer, she found herself standing beside an elk, a bull, which was five feet high at its shoulder, a half ton of muscle, its head looming over her on its long neck, its antlers almost beyond her reach. The elk snorted as though in greeting, and she smoothed one hand along its flank.

A cow with a black mane craned her neck to smell Joanna's hair, and a calf nuzzled her hand as she moved slowly among the creatures, away from the Explorer and toward the house. A few snorts, here and there a scuffling of hooves: The gathered multitude mostly stood in silence, as if they were as enchanted with her as she was with them.

At the foot of the steps, she addressed the man on the veranda. "My name's Joanna Chase. I used to live here a long time ago."

He came down to the flagstone walkway to meet her, and they shook hands as he said, "Wyatt Rider."

In a tailored shirt, gray designer jeans, a pair of soft-green Common Projects sneakers, and with a Rolex on his left wrist, he for sure wasn't a rancher.

"What is all this, what's going on here?" he asked, indicating the herds with a sweep of his hand. "Are they migrating or what?"

She shook her head. "Not this time of year. Right now, warm as it is, they should be higher in the mountains. Their mating season starts in a couple weeks and lasts into November. When the weather changes—and only then—they come down from the heights to graze the valleys and lower fields."

His hair was black, his eyes as purple-blue as gentian petals, his stare uncommonly direct. "It almost seems like they came here to see you. Has this happened before?"

As she sought a response to parry his question, one of the bulls startled them with a loud bugling sound that began on a low note but quickly escalated to a high pitch, ending in a forceful grunt. At once, the other bulls took up this cry, and a few of the cows began to make a sound half like the baa of a sheep, half like the whinny of a horse, and the day was full of raucous noise.

Joanna laughed because she'd heard this before and suddenly recalled winter mornings when she had sneaked away from the house to join a family of elk. She had tried to imitate their calls, but her reedy little-girl voice had elicited from them looks of pity.

When the bugling stopped, the herds turned away from the house as one and headed west, up into the hills, toward the forest and the higher meadows from which they had come out of season.

With regret, she watched them go, and realized only when they were nearly gone that Wyatt Rider had studied her intently all the while that she was fixated on the elk.

He said, "On a summer night, have you ever seen a thick cloud of fireflies weave complex patterns in the air, as if performing for an audience?"

Warily, she said, "What a strange idea."

"Have you seen coyotes and wolves prowling together in large packs, acting more like domesticated dogs than like what they are?"

"Have *you* seen such a thing, Mr. Rider?"

"I've seen the fireflies, Ms. Chase. And the current owners of the ranch—I've accepted an assignment from them—they've seen the coyotes and wolves. Have you seen either?"

"There weren't many wolves when I lived here. They'd almost been hunted to extinction and were only just beginning to make a comeback."

For a long moment, he regarded her in silence, and if she read his expression correctly, he was acutely aware that she had twice evaded answering his question.

He said, "I'm a private investigator, Ms. Chase. A city-boy gumshoe out of my element and, I'm beginning to think, in over my head. Aside from your being a novelist whose most recent bestseller I've read, what else are you, and why are you here? Don't tell me you've come to research a memoir of your days on the ranch. I liked your book, and I want to like you, but I despise liars."

36

The building was in an industrial district of greater Seattle, on a fenced property, and it appeared to be a warehouse: a concrete base, corrugated steel walls, roll-up doors capable of admitting the largest trucks, with no windows except a series of small clerestory panes in the drop edge of a curved steel roof.

The guard shack at the gate was always manned by two combat-experienced US Marines, although for the benefit of the passing public, they wore generic security-guard uniforms and carried no visible weapons. Within the shack, they had easy access to fully automatic carbines.

Between the two large roll-ups was a man-size door that opened only after a visitor had been cleared by a facial-recognition scan. Beyond lay a vestibule with formidable concrete walls.

Dr. Ganesh Patel waited here while he was fluoroscoped for concealed weapons and olfactory electronics analyzed the air for free molecules of explosive materials.

Ganesh didn't carry a gun or have a bomb strapped to his body; nor had he ever come armed on any of the many other visits he had made to this facility. Nevertheless, he didn't take offense at being an object of suspicion, because such scrutiny was a wise protocol. Ganesh Patel rarely took offense at anything; to do so was a waste of emotional energy. Nor did he grow impatient about the delay, for impatience was a characteristic of those who didn't understand that time flowed to a purpose that neither impatience nor haste could change for the better, though often for the worse.

Opposite the door by which he'd entered the vestibule stood another steel door. After hardly more than a minute, it slid aside with no more sound than a dying man's sigh.

Beyond lay a one-acre room with a pale-gray ceramic-tile floor. Supplies for the project were stored in hundreds of wire baskets in rows of racks that were vertical, motorized Ferris wheels. Warehouse robots on wheels loaded their bins with items they had been directed to retrieve. Ganesh was the only living person in sight, but others toiled in the extensive laboratories and workshops below.

He followed the center aisle to a bank of three elevators at the far end of the building. After another facial-recognition scan, the doors on one of the cabs slid open to admit him.

Five floors lay below the main one. He descended to the lowest level. The labs and workshops were above him now; he was in the sanctum, where the history of Project Olivaw, a rare and at times strained cooperative effort between government and the private sector, was maintained along with the fruit of all the research.

The cool air was without the faintest scent. The corridors lay as silent as a deaf man's dream, and Ganesh's footsteps struck no sound from the floor. In the diffuse lighting, he cast no shadow. Dressed all in white except for a red patent-leather belt, he moved through a maze of white hallways with the grace of a spirit in a strangely sterile afterlife, until he came to the conference room that, today, was reserved for him.

Seven chairs were spaced around the convex curve of a crescent-shaped conference table. He settled in the center seat. In the far wall, a thirteen-foot-wide eleven-foot-high video screen was at the moment blank.

Because the work done here was, by orders of magnitude, more secret than the Manhattan Project, which had developed the atomic bomb in the 1940s, communication with those in this building was, with one exception, never conducted from outside by phone or the internet. Appointments were requested in writing and responded to in the same fashion, in sealed envelopes carried by former military men who qualified for the highest security clearance. Although this structure contained more supercomputers than any other building or complex of buildings in the world, only one of them was online, and it was not linked to any of the others; therefore, none but the one was vulnerable to data theft, and even it was not likely to be hacked, for it was of a unique nature and had special protections. In respect of the need for absolute security, Ganesh and others like him on the board of directors of Blue Sky Partners—developers of Project Olivaw—were limited to in-person visits when they wished to obtain or provide information.

A moment after he occupied a chair, the video screen brightened from black to blue. Within a few seconds, Artimis appeared.

For one named after the Greek goddess of the moon, she had the right look: olive complexion, an exquisite face, midnight-black hair, and dark eyes bright with intelligence. She was dressed in lab whites, though she could have worn whatever she chose.

Ganesh, who liked most women and cherished beauty, would have preferred that they meet face-to-face, but that was not practical. Artimis Selene was in a portion of the facility that required a dust-free environment. Entrance to that zone necessitated a four-step decontamination process, beginning with a long exfoliating shower and followed by three increasingly tedious procedures that took an hour to complete.

"Dear Ganesh," she said, "it's always a pleasure to see you."

"Likewise, Artimis. I know how busy you are, so I always feel as if I'm keeping you from important work."

"Work that you've given me. I'm grateful to have it. You know how I am, Ganesh—work is everything to me. I assume by now Wendy Sharp and Cricket have been resettled with new identities?"

"Yes, they're very happy. They have their own house, and the monthly stipend allows Wendy to work forty hours a week instead of sixty. Of course, I'm not at liberty to say where we put them."

Artimis smiled. "Not even to me. I understand. I'm happy just to know *they're* happy. Have they gotten a dog?"

"They have, yes. But I'm not—"

"—at liberty to say what breed. Dear, do you sometimes wonder if too much security is hampering us in this search for the Other?"

"Frequently. But I don't make the rules, and neither do you."

Project Olivaw had been conceived for its own purposes, not to find the Other, but now finding him obsessed Artimis and everyone on the staff. They hadn't even known the Other existed until they were up and running, fourteen months earlier, whereupon evidence of his activities rapidly mounted. He was a ghost on the internet, passing through firewalls that were impervious to everyone else, spiriting through data archives. For years, he'd been leaving messages in the email and voice mail of scientists, politicians, and various shapers of the culture. These critiques ranged from solemn to snide to scorching. Scores of IT-security specialists tried to track him, each suspecting a different perpetrator, none realizing a single troll was tormenting hundreds of individuals, corporations, and agencies. No one could identify or locate him. Only Project Olivaw possessed the sophisticated analytics, the depth and breadth of understanding, to see patterns that proved beyond doubt that this was the work of one person, whom they dubbed "the Other." However, even the investigative power of this project couldn't find him.

Over the years, the Other's taunts had become increasingly judgmental and then subtly threatening. During the past four months, he'd become violent. Seven people had been executed by someone who, in five instances, invaded the victims' home electronics and made ingenious use of internet-connected devices and systems to kill with gas leaks, electrocution, and raging fire. Two were obliterated when attacked by very target-specific top-secret military weapons in orbit high above the planet, which the Other had commandeered and employed with ease; Harley Spondollar, in Oregon, once the treasurer of Xanthus Toller's Restoration Movement, who embezzled seven hundred thousand dollars from the cult, would also have been a victim if he hadn't stepped outside, ostensibly to gaze at the stars, mere minutes before his house was reduced to fine-grain rubble.

The search for the Other had recently acquired an ever greater urgency, because they could find no way to block him from weapons platforms in space, which he might at any time use for a purpose more horrific than individual assassination. The three legs of the nuclear arsenal—aboard submarines, stealth bombers, and mobile ground platforms—had never been linked to the internet and were therefore, thank God, beyond his control.

Curiously, his seven victims had two things in common. Each had been sucked into the Restoration Movement at one time or another. And all of them had eventually broken away from it.

By questioning Xanthus Toller and his exotic followers, agents of Project Olivaw were able to determine a third thing common to all victims: Each had been at odds with another cultist, Asher Optime, whose fanaticism frightened them and who hated them for being what he called "heretics masquerading as true believers." He had accused them of being as stupid as they were spineless, and he'd harassed them relentlessly.

Asher Optime was not the Other. By all accounts, he had zero skills as a hacker. In fact, he detested the internet, found the entire history of human progress and technology repugnant. The Other evidently had made Asher Optime's enemies his own and was doing to them what perhaps Optime had wanted to do. Neither Artimis Selene nor Ganesh Patel, nor anyone else involved in Project Olivaw, could determine why this should be the case.

Complicating matters, Asher Optime had vanished five months earlier, a month before the murders of his enemies had begun. For a man with no hacking skills and little understanding of the digital culture, who was most often described by others as a narcissistic ignoramus, he was doing a bang-up job of remaining off the grid, untraceable.

Now Ganesh said, "Artimis, I believe that we're on the brink of a Jungian moment of unprecedented impact."

"Synchronicity," she said. As was the case with Ganesh, Jung's theory was integral to her view of the world.

He said, "A series of coincidences so astonishing that it suggests that the collective unconscious of humanity is shaping events toward an inflection point after which nothing will be the same. This morning, a good friend of mine, Liam O'Hara, told me a story about his experiences on a ranch he bought in Montana."

Artimis said, "You've spoken of him often before. I've seen his photo, and news film of course. He has an aura about him. I'd like to meet him one day."

"I think that can be arranged eventually."

"He's a handsome man. Maybe we can have dinner. A quiet little place. I know just the spot. Being a feminist, I won't expect him to pay. In fact, I won't allow it."

Ganesh smiled. Artimis had a sense of humor so dry that he did not always know what to make of it. "Now, now," he said, "you know he's married with children."

"Dear Ganesh, whatever my desires might be, I understand that of necessity any contact with your friend must be platonic. Anyway, I'm married to my work. It's a wonderful thing to have meaningful, fulfilling work, to be engaged with the many brilliant people on this project."

Ganesh found himself frowning. "Is there something wrong, Artimis? Anything I can do?"

"You dear man, you've already done so much for me. Without you, I wouldn't have this job. Now and then I have a little bit of a blue mood, but it always passes. It's a woman thing."

"Blue mood?"

"You wouldn't know, dear. You're eternally ebullient. It's why everyone loves you. So what happened to Liam O'Hara in Montana?"

Ganesh shared some of the details with her and then said, "These events were so strange, Liam didn't know what to make of them. He was even willing to entertain the most extreme supernatural explanation—spirits, demons—as I might have done myself, if I had been in his shoes. Because we at the project have developed so many theoretical profiles of the Other—trying to imagine his nature, identity, whereabouts, and purpose—and because control of household electronics was a part of this 'haunting' at Liam's place, another possibility occurred to me."

Artimis nodded. "I suspect I know which of the theoretical profiles you found most compelling."

"I'm sure you do. Number six. Anyway, Liam hired a private investigator yesterday morning and sent him to Montana, a reliable man named Wyatt Rider. Coincidentally, I've also worked with Wyatt and consider him a friend, which Liam didn't know. Whatever Wyatt learns will be of value, but if what we have here is the Other as imagined in Profile Six, gumshoe methods won't get to the truth."

When each theoretical profile of the Other had been completed and evaluated, a related file titled "Courses of Action" had been prepared, steps to be taken to confirm what the profile imagined. None of that had gotten them anywhere.

In each case, should they ever have a good reason to suspect a location—neighborhood or city, or state, or country—from which the Other operated, they would be able to resume the investigation. Thus far, he seemed to be everywhere and nowhere, as if he lived only in the virtual reality of the internet. Now, because what happened in Montana also involved the possession of animals, manifestations of a physical nature rather than just bedevilment via electronics, they might at last have a location. Rustling Willows Ranch.

"Or perhaps," Ganesh said, "this is some strange business that has nothing to do with the Other."

Artimis shook her head. "My sense is that it does."

"Mine, too."

"Have you alerted our agency partners that a site containment plan may have to be triggered?"

"I've been making calls. Homeland Security can establish a perimeter on a four-hour notice. Pentagon has patrol helicopters, surveillance drones, and fighter jets standing by at Malmstrom Air Force Base. The National Security Agency, the FBI, and the EPA are ready to move fast."

"What about the Centers for Disease Control? There could be a disease risk."

"We're trying to keep them out of the first phase. They'll want to lock down Montana for thirty years."

"Okay. So I'll start drilling down on Rustling Willows, and you go wait for your Jungian moment of synchronicity."

Only Artimis could lead this hunt. Her talent was unique.

Ganesh got to his feet and met her lustrous eyes for a moment before he said, "You really find the work fulfilling?"

"I really, really do. Oh, sometimes it all becomes a bit too much, making history the way we are. But this chase after the Other ought to be fun, a welcome change of pace from our main business."

"Keep me informed of your progress. Goodbye, Artimis."

"Goodbye, Ganesh."

As he turned away, expecting to hear a click of disconnection, she surprised him by asking, "Do you ever dream of me?"

Facing the large video screen again, after a hesitation, he replied, "Yes. Sometimes."

She said, "I often dream of you. Is that wrong?"

"No. We're colleagues. We're friends. We've come a long way together. Besides, I can't control my dreams."

"They have rules against relationships between members of the project staff."

"You and I . . . we're different," he said. "Whatever there might be between us, the rules don't apply."

Her smile was still lovely but melancholy now. "I feel the same. It's good to know you dream of me. Let's get together soon."

"We will," Ganesh said. "When this is done, and if we all survive it, we'll get together."

The screen went dark.

Ganesh returned to the elevator, rode up to the main floor, passed through the security vestibule, and returned to his SUV in the parking lot.

The day was warm. He started the engine and turned up the air conditioner.

He sat behind the wheel, staring through the windshield at the warehouse that wasn't a warehouse, thinking about Artimis Selene.

If he was not always ebullient, as she had said, he *was* with rare exception a happy optimist. Now a terrible sadness came upon him, a twilight of the soul here in the morning sun. Sorrow might have grown into depression if he had been a less positive person, but his lifelong experience was that every spell of darkness lifted soon enough, so that light came again into the soul and mind and heart, which were not made for darkness.

37

As morning becomes afternoon, the angled sunlight imparts some dimension to the ghost town, an illusion of vitality. Asher Optime's shadow returns and gradually elongates as he strips off Dr. Steve Fielding's backpack, empties the historian's pockets, and carries everything into the saloon.

Although he prefers to kill his captives in the church, so that it's then easy to tumble the dead down the stairs into the basement, Asher is prepared to transport a corpse the length of town with a minimum of effort. From the saloon, he retrieves a sturdy, formed-plastic pallet on wheels, with a four-foot handle. The bed of the pallet is six feet long and three wide. He loads the historian onto it and secures the cargo with two bungee cords that clip to rings in the perimeter of the conveyance.

Weeks earlier, it occurred to him that an occasion might arise when he would have a captive or more than one locked away in the church, their terror maturing into the collapse of hope that he wished to see before executing them—when suddenly he would find himself with a fresh corpse on his hands. Conveying such a bundle into the testamentary necropolis under the church would then become a logistical problem. He, of course, has solved it.

He takes satisfaction from his thoughtful preparations for this mission and his practicality. He would have been a most meticulous surgeon if he had followed the family tradition, though saving human lives is an evil that he's not capable of committing.

As Asher pulls the inelegant hearse along the runneled hardpan of Zipporah's only street, crows circle overhead, shrieking as if singing a dirge for the deceased, though their cries are in fact a celebration of carrion. They aren't bold enough to dare Asher and settle on the corpse in motion, though he would not chase them away. As a devoted student of Xanthus Toller and a valiant soldier in the Restoration Movement, Asher is at peace with all the many conscious creatures of the planet—animal, vegetable, mineral—except for his own kind. He is pleased to think that following his death, carrion eaters will feast on his flesh, though he must be careful not to die among cannibals and, by being eaten, sustain a human life.

On the west side of the church, as on the east side, one window near ground level serves the basement. At one time, these panes brought light into that low space. The glass has long ago shattered, and recently Asher has replaced it with inch-thick plywood screwed into place from the exterior.

Two latches secure the hinged window to the casing. He releases them and swings it out of the way. The opening is three feet wide and twenty inches high, sufficient to receive most cadavers, though it is not the route by which he could insert an obese person into his collection.

Asher disconnects the bungee cords and rolls the corpse off the pallet. With an effort that causes a thin sweat to slick his brow, he shoves the late historian through the window as if forcing a thick, padded envelope through a mail slot.

The dead man splashes into the trapped storm runoff that is about two feet deep in the church basement. There he will decompose among the others who float in those dark, fetid waters like former passengers who fell overboard from Death's gondola during a transit of the River Styx.

Asher inhales the miasma that rises out of the open window. Although many would consider it a stench, he savors it as evidence of progress toward the implementation of the philosophy that he is so brilliantly explicating in the pages of his historic manifesto. This is a fragrance, not a stink, the sweet perfume that will mantle the world during its transition from human domination to human absence.

38

Ophelia Poole was huddled with Colson Fielding in the influx of pale light where the roof of the add-on sacristy met the back wall of the church, when a noise alerted her to the possibility that the maniac, Optime, might be returning. She stepped out of the sacristy into the dark sanctuary as something splashed in the catacombs that lay under the plank floor. Disturbed water sloshed back and forth against the stone walls of the basement, raising in her mind's eye macabre images of ghastly swimmers seeking a way out of their dismal tarn. Something thumped against the farther wall of the building. A few lesser noises followed. The agitated water subsided, and quiet settled on the church once more.

When it seemed that a visit from their jailer wasn't impending, she returned to the boy. Brow furrowed as though he was desperately calculating, Colson stared at the swath of sky revealed by the narrow gap in the roof. He was a cute kid with tousled dark hair. Ophelia wished he were taller, more muscular, with something of the street about him. She pitied him for what he'd already endured, but she was grateful that she didn't any longer have to face alone what might be coming.

She was impressed that he could bite down on his grief, would not cry, would not dwell on his father's death, but instead focused on the hope of escape and vengeance. He seemed to possess an innate toughness that perhaps he was just discovering in himself.

"It's not that far up there," he said. "Like maybe twelve feet. If you could stand on my shoulders . . ."

"I'm not a gymnast," she said. "Are you?"

"No. But I have this." From a pocket of his jeans, he produced a Swiss Army knife.

"How'd you manage to keep that?"

"The sonofabitch made me empty my pockets, so I was like . . . like begging him not to kill me. He was getting off on how scared I was, staring into my eyes, not watching my hands close enough. He's not just a killer, that guy, he's some kind of freaking pervert. I don't know what, but he's something."

In the interest of not scaring the kid further, Ophelia chose not to share the fact that Optime was such a fanatic that he had castrated himself.

Once more turning his attention to the separation between the sacristy roof and the church, Colson said, "If I could get up there, I could maybe work at the edges of the hole with the knife. It's got all kind of tools, like a wood saw and a corkscrew and stuff."

Just then descending from high noon, the sun began to align with the gap in the roof. The infall of light grew much brighter, and an unobstructed beam slanted down on them, golden and warm, with motes of dust turning lazily in the dazzling shaft. Perhaps the direct lance of sunshine ought to have given Ophelia hope; however, it seemed to mock her with a false promise of freedom, and the hole above appeared to grow smaller, more distant.

39

Women found Kenny Deetle attractive and fun to be around, and they thought that his work as a white-hat hacker was cool and daring and edgy, so he didn't spend a lot of nights alone. This girl he'd met the previous evening, Leigh Ann Bruce, was herself a keyboard kick-ass, capable of cracking any system, backdooring it for future ease of access, and installing a rootkit of such exceptional design that she could pull a Claude Rains and remain invisible even to the best IT-security teams who suspected her presence. Kenny liked her, and he might have learned to love her, but he was unnerved by her exhibitionism. She was great to look at, and in bed she was a feast for the eyes, a smorgasbord of rich visual desserts; spending one night with her put him at risk of diabetes of the libido. Once out of her clothes, however, Leigh Ann seemed to forget how to dress herself. She prepared breakfast in the nude, read the newspaper in the nude, washed the dishes in the nude. Even after she showered, she paraded around without putting on so much as a pair of socks. The warehouse apartment was industrial chic, lots of drab open space, rooms flowing into one another without walls, and he had to admit that she warmed it up. But he worked best when nothing was more interesting to look at than his HP screen. As he sat at his main computer, she leaned over his left shoulder, over his right shoulder, and though hers were the most perfect breasts he'd ever seen, eventually he found himself thinking, *Not these again.* Kenny wasn't a prude, but he wasn't a satyr, either; he had a job to do for Wyatt Rider, and when he was working, he was, damn it, *working*. Finally, exasperated, he took her to bed again, hoping that a vigorous half hour in the sheets would punctuate the day's erotic activities with an exclamation point, encouraging her to put on her clothes. Afterward, Kenny dressed, but Leigh Ann went to his backup computer and sat down, Lady Godiva on an office chair instead of a horse.

Settling beside her at his main workstation, Kenny said, "Shouldn't you get dressed?"

"Huh? Why?"

"Aren't you chilly?"

"No, baby, I'm hot."

As she switched on the computer, he said, "Just so you know, I've got no more."

"No more what?"

"No more anything today. You broke me."

"I have a little job of my own here, and I work best naked."

"Well, it's distracting."

She grinned at him. "See, you've still got more, after all."

For a minute or so, he watched her long-fingered hands work the keyboard with the grace of a concert pianist caressing music from a Steinway. "What little job?"

"Don't worry your pretty head," Leigh Ann said. "No net cop ever born can track me to source. Nothing I do is gonna bring any heat down on you."

"Yeah, but see, I'm totally white hat."

Focused on her screen, she said, "What makes you think I'm not?"

"I'm just the suspicious type."

"I'm righteous, boyfriend. You should know that already."

"How would I know that?"

Without looking at him, she said, "When you were the most vulnerable, I didn't cut your dick off."

"Is that something you sometimes do?"

"Not me. But it's a thing that happens in this screwed-up world of ours. You bring a nice girl home and she turns out to be Hannibal Lecter with knockers."

After a contemplative silence, he said, "You're unique."

"Everyone is, boyfriend. Now, don't you have a job to do?"

He should have expected that this relationship would be in one way or another—or in many ways—unusual, considering that chance and coincidence played such a role in their encounter. The previous night, he had been supposed to go to a club, Cranked, with three friends—Brian, Rafael, and Maynard. But Brian, who was a junior executive with Google, had to fly off to an emergency corporate meeting. Rafael came down with a cold. And after months of trying, Maynard got a last-minute date with Shanese, which no one could believe, including Maynard and Shanese. Feeling abandoned by his buddies, Kenny availed himself of the services of Uber, so that he could drink irresponsibly without consequences. The young driver, Georges, proved to be upbeat, opinionated, and persuasive. Georges declared that Cranked was the suckiest club in the city and insisted on taking Kenny to a place called Eldorado. The name might have struck Kenny as tacky and very *ancien régime*, like something out of the Sinatra era, except that as a teenager he had been totally into the poetry of Edgar Allan Poe. In the back seat of Georges's Honda, he recited the first six lines of "Eldorado," about a gallant knight who "Had journeyed long / Singing a song / In search of Eldorado." Georges took this to be a concession, and Kenny found himself at the bar in Eldorado, three stools away from Leigh Ann, who was waiting for a date, Curtis, who was twenty minutes late. As the bartender poured Negra Modelo into a frosted glass, Kenny gave voice to the sixteenth line of the Poe poem: "'Shadow,' said he / 'Where can it be' / 'This land of Eldorado?'" Proving herself to be a Poe aficionado, Leigh Ann said, "'Over the Mountains / Of the Moon / Down the Valley of the Shadow.'" Wearily, evidently having been here before, the bartender finished it: "'Ride, boldly ride' / The shade replied / 'If you seek for Eldorado!'" Ten minutes later, Kenny and Leigh Ann were sitting on adjacent stools when Curtis called her to say that he was dealing with police because his house had been burglarized, trashed, everything of value taken, including his beloved black cat, Pluto. He asked for Leigh Ann's understanding, and she assured him that she wasn't in the least put out, that she hoped he would find Pluto.

Terminating the call, she said to Kenny, "Synchronicity."

"Entirely," he agreed.

She said, "We should have dinner together."

He said, "That would be a nice start."

Now, leaving her to whatever mischief she'd undertaken au naturel at his second computer, Kenny returned his attention to the problem of the Liam O'Hara residence in Montana. If someone obtained the satellite-dish link, invaded the house computer, built a clever back door, and now controlled all electronics in the home, the perp would almost certainly have left digital fingerprints, spoor that an ether-breathing bloodhound like Kenny Deetle could follow through cyberspace to an address in the real world.

Having been given the telecom-account information by Wyatt Rider, Kenny quickly returned to the system in Montana. The previous owners of the ranch, Roy and Viola Kornbluth, had brought the place partway into the twenty-first century, rewiring to accommodate smart-house technology that monitored all the mechanical systems and provided a high level of security for the property—house, manager's bungalow, stables—that exceeded what was usually to be found in such rural territory. Kenny possessed the codes and passwords, and soon he was searching through archived data on the house-management computer, with special attention to the audio-video system, which Wyatt said had self-activated in the guest bedroom that morning and seemed to have been commandeered by some hacker who had used it to deliver a threat.

Kenny could not have found spoor and tracked it to a culprit in just five minutes; however, that was all the time required for the bad guy to come down on Kenny. His screen abruptly went blank, and from the speakers issued a voice. "Pestilence and vermin. You are blight, rot, a terminal cancer."

Frowning at Kenny's screen, Leigh Ann said, "How'd you do that?"

"Wasn't me. Someone locked me down. My keyboard's frozen."

"That sounded like you."

He was about to disagree when further insults hissed from the speakers. "You despoil this once splendorous world. You are piss and poison."

This time, Kenny recognized his own voice. He said, "What's going on here, who the hell are you?"

The Other said, "Perhaps I am the savior of the world."

"Generally speaking," Leigh Ann said, "real saviors of the world are awesomely confident of their status as saviors. They don't try to cover their ass with 'perhaps.'"

The Other was silent.

Either to express her contempt or to test whether they were being watched through the computer cameras, Leigh Ann flourished a stiff middle finger.

The mimic now spoke in her voice. "You are filth and must be flushed away."

Although he knew that it was foolish to argue with this Hacker of a Thousand Voices, Kenny said, "Does your mother know you go online to make threats while you masturbate?"

"Don't descend to his level," Leigh Ann advised.

"His? Maybe he's a her."

"No. He's a he. The savior complex identifies him. If this were a megalomaniacal *woman*, she'd be on a Gaia trip or a self-proclaimed goddess, maybe call herself the Wiccan queen."

The Other said, "The world is a beautiful wedding cake, acrawl with cockroaches like you. You should die off, self-exterminate."

"See?" Leigh said. "Cockroaches and wedding cake. That's the pathetic metaphor you'd expect from an unbalanced, narcissistic man. An unbalanced female narcissist would be more creative."

"If it's right that you should kill yourselves, all of your greedy kind," said the Other, "then kill yourselves—or be killed."

Both computers made the same sound of distress—*boop*—and the screens went dark.

When Kenny pressed the power button, there was no response.

A series of hanging industrial-style fixtures with inverted-bowl shades provided light. The LED bulbs crackled and went dark.

As the large room fell into shadows that the array of small high-set windows could not disperse, a ringtone startled him.

Before he could pick up the phone, the connection was made without his assent. The man's voice was deep, rough, and profoundly disturbing, like that of something a corrupt priest might summon into a chalked pentagram during a Black Mass: "The big dark sky. The terrible sky. I am mentally in a dark place. I'm lost. I'm a danger to myself and others." The line went dead.

Rolling her chair back from the second computer and rising to her feet, Leigh Ann said, "Maybe I better get dressed."

As the girl padded away barefoot to retrieve her clothes, Kenny picked up the phone and summoned a list of recent calls. There was no record of the one that he had just received.

He got to his feet and stood, considering the phone in his hand, until a high-pitched sound in the kitchen drew his attention.

Although immense, this was a studio apartment, every "room" open to every other, except for the bath. He passed the disheveled bed, where Leigh Ann was dressing, and proceeded into that adjacent space occupied by the kitchen and a dining area.

The keening escalated into a shriek. The noise came from the microwave oven. Through the view window, Kenny watched the glass carousel turning faster than ever before, and then faster still.

He didn't rent this apartment; he owned it, and he had upgraded it into a smart home. Nearly everything in it could be controlled from his phone. And perhaps now from someone else's phone.

A TV, suspended from the ceiling and serving the dining area, switched on and began to channel surf ceaselessly, images flickering by so fast that the eye could not make sense of them.

The microwave began to rattle against the cabinetry in which it was mounted, and the coated-metal walls of its interior appeared to be—and sounded as if they were—buckling. Which made no sense. Appliances linked to the internet could be remotely controlled, but they couldn't be forced to operate beyond the limits of their design and tested to destruction.

He went to the refrigerator and opened the freezer drawer on the bottom. From behind the other contents, he retrieved a half-gallon container of chocolate-almond ice cream and a much smaller package of breaded fish sticks.

A kaleidoscopic montage of images continued to flash across the TV screen. Abruptly sound exploded from the set as well, a high-volume cacophony of ever-changing music and a word or two each from countless voices in an incoherent babble.

As Kenny put the ice cream and the fish sticks in a grocery-store tote bag, Leigh Ann appeared, radiant even though now fully clothed. She shouted, *"What the fuck?"*

He grabbed her by one arm and hurried her out of the kitchen, through the dining area, across an open living room. He heard the safety glass in the microwave shatter.

As they reached the apartment door, the fire sprinklers blew out their wax seals, and water cascaded. Every apartment in this converted warehouse featured sprinklers, but they were supposed to discharge only when heat melted the seals.

In the third-floor public hallway, Kenny had second thoughts about using the elevator—a potential trap—and led Leigh Ann to the stairs. They raced down to the basement, where he'd parked his Lincoln Nautilus.

As they crossed that windowless realm toward the SUV, overhead fluorescent panels winked off, and another bank of fire sprinklers showered cold water on them. Enough light faded down the garage access ramp from the street that they could still make their way to the Nautilus, although by the time they climbed into it, they were soaked to the skin.

Kenny put the grocery tote in Leigh Ann's lap, started the engine, switched on the windshield wipers, and drove through the indoor rain, up the ramp, into the stormless day.

She said, "What the hell was that all about?"

"A job I took."

"What job?"

"This über-rich guy's getaway ranch in Montana."

"What über-rich guy?" she asked as he switched off the wipers.

"Liam O'Hara. You probably never heard of him."

"Don't treat me like arm candy. Of course I've heard of him. But I always thought he was one of the white-hat billionaires."

"Maybe he is. That wasn't him screwing with me back there. Some internet buccaneer took over all the tech on O'Hara's ranch. I was hired to find the bastard's footprints and track him to source."

"But he found you instead."

"Instantly. Like he's the god of hackers."

"What was all that about pestilence and vermin, filth that has to be flushed away?"

"Best guess is he's not just a black-hat master of cyberspace but also a raving lunatic."

After a silence, she said, "You better take me home."

"That's what I'm doing. Where do you live?"

She gave him the address, which he knew. It was three blocks from the club where they had met, in an established neighborhood of graceful old houses, where there was no such thing as a real-estate bargain.

"You live with your folks?"

"It's my place. And, no, I wasn't born to money. I've developed a slew of damn successful apps."

"What're you—twenty-five?"

"Twenty-seven. I started when I was eighteen."

"Started what?"

"Making serious money."

He glanced at her. Leigh Ann's hair was plastered to her head, and water dripped from the tip of her nose.

"You look like a mermaid."

"What does that mean?"

"It means you look wet but nice."

"One thing you're not is a master of the compliment. Listen, I like you a lot. I never jump into bed with a guy on the first meet. Ninety-eight percent of the guys I've dated, I never go to bed with at all. Or date more than twice. You're not the usual Emerald City jackass. You're smart and sweet. But I don't need big drama in my life. Things are smooth with me, and I prefer them smooth."

Half a mile from her place, Kenny had to pull to the curb as two fire trucks and an ambulance roared past with sirens and Klaxons as shrill as any passage in the ugliest of atonal modern symphonies.

Three minutes later when they turned the corner into the block where she lived, her house was on fire. In fact, the words *on fire* were an inadequate description. The structure burned furiously, seethed with flames, and the trees nearest to it were torches. The firefighters vigorously attacked the blaze, but the cause was already lost; there would be nothing left but ashes and rubble.

Although he knew less about Leigh Ann Bruce than he would have liked to know, Kenny knew enough that he wasn't surprised when she neither wept nor cursed her bad fortune, nor paled with shock. Instead, she stared through the windshield, steely-eyed, and said, "This for damn sure isn't a coincidence."

"I wish it was," Kenny said, for he felt somewhat responsible for this disaster.

"It's the dirtbag who called us cockroaches."

"When you went online with my backup computer, he must have gotten your ID."

"And minutes later he somehow sets my house on fire? What kind of wacked-out genius is the bastard?"

"Evil," Kenny said. "He's an evil genius."

"Get us out of here."

"But your house is burning down."

"I'm not a masochist. I don't have to watch. As far as this evil-genius lunatic is concerned, if you're his enemy, then so am I. Let's get out of here before he causes a 747 to crash on top of us."

"He can't do that. Nobody can."

"Just get us out of here."

The breeze shifted, and the palisades of smoke rising from the house abruptly collapsed as the house itself had begun to collapse, gray clouds avalanching into the street.

As Kenny hung a U-turn and drove away, he began to realize that he had not yet grasped the fullness of the threat they faced. He was also beginning to comprehend that a one-night stand was never just a one-night stand, that there was always the possibility that a knot had been tied that bound two lives together inextricably. Call it fate or synchronicity.

40

In one of the rocking chairs on the front porch, drinking cold tea out of a bottle, Joanna Chase listened to the susurration of the willows and watched thousands of bright tongues of sunlight lapping the breeze-rippled water of Lake Sapphire. Her mother had been buried in a cemetery in Buckleton, the nearest town; but to Joanna, the lake would forever be a grave in which the sweet future that might have been was interred in its bottom silt.

The previous night, in Santa Fe, she had suffered a dream of her mother's corpse animated by some malevolent power as it came out of the lake, a dream similar to those that she'd endured a few times in her childhood, mostly during the two weeks between her mother's and her father's deaths. Her dad had assured her there was nothing evil in those waters, that Emelia's drowning had been accidental. Now, having heard Wyatt Rider's story of the mysterious presence in the boathouse, she regarded the lake with renewed suspicion. Her dreams of having a strange fellowship with the animals on the ranch had, by the evidence of the elk, proved to be based on a forgotten truth; therefore, perhaps within the depths of the lake, something lived that had taken her mother's life, another forgotten truth.

She felt unsteady, disoriented, as if the very foundations of the world were shifting under her. With Auntie Kat, she had found stability as a child. In the eleven years since she'd graduated from college, her life had been one of familiar patterns and routines, with much of her time spent in pleasant solitude, writing novels. The loveliest thing about fictional worlds was that she controlled them as if she were a Greek goddess, her office chair no less a seat of power than a high throne on Olympus; if a character or story line took a sudden turn that surprised her, she soon adapted and explored the new direction with enthusiasm, because the consequences were limited to her imagination, and the real world remained unaltered.

Now reality seemed to be in flux, the currents of change so strong that she expected the porch floor to roll under her chair like the deck of a ship on troubled seas.

As Joanna screwed the cap on the half-finished bottle of tea and set the refreshment aside, Wyatt Rider came out of the house, having used the landline to make a few phone calls. They had spent an hour sharing experiences of self-starting vehicles and organized fireflies, of possessed televisions, of pleas for help and threats of violence from disembodied voices. Joanna found him to be nimble-minded, with no tendency to superstition, analytical, and intent on dissecting this mystery with the sharp instrument of reason.

Wyatt said, "Vance Potter, the current ranch manager, knows Hector Alvarez, who managed Rustling Willows for your parents."

"Knows him or knew him?"

"Annalisa Alvarez died years ago, but Hector and their son are still alive."

A chill shivered up Joanna's spine, and she rose with it, leaving the bentwood chair rocking in her wake. "Jimmy Alvarez?"

Wyatt nodded. "Jimmy Two Eyes. They live only a few miles from here. You want to drive, or should I?"

41

As Kenny Deetle drove away from the burning house, his phone rang, but he didn't answer it because he suspected that the caller would be the black-hat hacker bastard who mimicked him. Maybe five seconds after the call went to voice mail, Leigh Ann's phone rang, and Kenny said, "Don't answer it." She said, "I've no intention of answering it." As *that* call went to voice mail, the SUV's computer self-connected with SiriusXM radio, '60s on 6, where Barry McGuire was singing "Eve of Destruction." Leigh Ann said, "This isn't good," which wasn't a criticism of either the song or the singer, but merely an expression of concern that this situation might be spiraling out of their control.

The radio volume rose, and as Leigh Ann attempted to turn it down, her concern was borne out because Barry McGuire got louder, so loud that Kenny felt his tympanic membranes fluttering as if moths were beating their wings against the walls of his ear canals. Leigh Ann pressed the button to shut off the radio, but that didn't work, either. They abruptly accelerated. The brake pedal went soft under Kenny's foot. Of its own accord, the vehicle turned sharply to the right. The steering wheel locked. Kenny said, "Shit," Leigh Ann said, "Shit," and Kenny said it again as the Nautilus jumped the curb. A tire blew. The SUV wanted to roll, but didn't. The engine roaring, McGuire bellowing, the vehicle's computerized systems under the control of some cyber-wizard, they plowed through a hedge, tore across a freshly mown lawn, and angled toward a stately two-story Victorian residence festooned with ornate millwork. The front steps were limestone, and the racing Nautilus rocked onto a limestone porch. The front door and the sidelights collapsed in a crack-bang of oak and a shattering of stained glass. The air bags deployed, pressing Kenny and Leigh Ann back in their seats, briefly robbing them of the ability to inhale, before abruptly deflating when the SUV jolted to a sudden stop.

Both the engine and Barry McGuire had fallen silent, but Kenny smelled gasoline. *We're going to be burned alive!* He shouted at Leigh Ann—"Get out, out, get out!"—as he struggled to release his safety harness, but she was already gone, the passenger's door open wide. He pushed through the driver's door and scrambled from the Nautilus into an elegant foyer. He heard the house alarm wailing as a recording of a stern voice warned, *"You have violated a private residence. The police have been called. Leave at once."*

The vehicle had taken a header into a massive newel post at the foot of a grand staircase that divided at midfloor and curved in opposing flights to a gallery above. Through an archway to the left lay a drawing room. On the right, tall library doors stood open.

Leigh Ann was hurrying along a hallway toward the back of the house, carrying the grocery-store tote bag that Kenny had dropped in her lap when they had fled the garage under his apartment building. He sprinted after her, caught up with her in the kitchen, grabbed her by one shoulder, and halted her. Raising his voice to compete with the security alarm, he said, "Is everything in the bag?"

Trying to pull away from him, she said, "We've got to get out of here quick, so we can say your wheels were stolen, it wasn't us crashed into this place."

"Yeah, sure, that's the plan."

"I don't want cops in my life."

"Who does?"

"Things are smooth with me. I like them smooth."

"But do you have both the ice cream and fish sticks in there?"

"Fish sticks? What fish sticks? In where?"

"In the bag."

She looked in the vinyl tote bag. "What the fuck am I doing with ice cream and fish sticks?"

"Don't drop them. Come on, let's get the hell out of here."

"I don't even like fish sticks."

The back door opened to a limestone patio covered by a trellis.

She said, "All that breading and probably just cod underneath."

Beyond the patio lay a deep backyard with a lap pool, and at the end of the property stood a pool house or maybe guest quarters.

Hurrying with him alongside the pool, Leigh Ann said, "Nothing is gonna be smooth ever again, is it?"

"Sure it is. It will be. This is just a hiccup."

"Why did you have to be so cute and so nice? I wouldn't have slept with you, wouldn't be here now, if you weren't cute and nice."

"It's my curse, I have to live with it."

To the right of the guesthouse was a solid wood gate in the brick property wall. It featured a gravity latch, but not a lock.

A wide alley served walled properties. They turned right, north. To avoid looking suspicious, they hurried but didn't run.

Strung from utility poles, power lines stirred in the breeze, humming softly as they passed through strain insulators.

Kenny and Leigh Ann came to a residential street, crossed it, and entered a continuation of the alley. He stopped at a drainage grate in the pavement and took his iPhone from a jacket pocket.

"Who're you calling? Let's keep moving," Leigh Ann urged.

"A smartphone is a GPS, a locator. It tells him where we are."

"You don't really think he's got that kind of reach, he can nail us by our phones?"

"What I think is he's the überultimate, king of the black hats, and if we underestimate him, we'll deserve what we get."

Movement glimpsed from the corner of his eye caused him to look up as one plump rat followed another along a power cable, their long tails held straight behind them to aid their balance. The rodents paused to peer down, but then scurried on faster than before, as though instinctively aware that they were at greater risk by just being in the vicinity of this man and woman.

Wondering if the rats were an omen, surprised to be capable of such a thought, Kenny dropped his phone into the street drain. It clattered on the floor of the concrete conduit below.

Leigh Ann said, "This can't be right." She turned her attention to the sky, perhaps on the lookout for the 747 that, mere minutes earlier, Kenny had not believed could be made to crash on them.

"We'll buy burner phones," Kenny said. "If he doesn't know the numbers we're using, he can't track us."

She met his eyes. "You make it sound like we're on the run."

"Because we are. At least for the short term, a few days, until we track this sonofabitch to source and deal with him."

She was smart and quick. "But if we use credit cards, maybe he'll still know what phones we bought. We need a lot of cash to be on the run, even for a few days."

"That half-gallon container in the tote isn't ice cream. It's full of rolls of hundred-dollar bills. Ninety thousand bucks."

Her blue stare scanned him with the intensity of a laser. "You said you were a white-hat hacker."

"I am. But even good guys need to prep for a shitstorm. I knew this loser who didn't prep, and some MS-13 types cut his head down the middle with a chain saw."

That claim silenced her for a moment. Then: "I never knew a guy who knew a guy who got his head chainsawed."

"Adds a little glamor to my résumé."

"Not in the least." She took her iPhone from a jacket pocket and considered it. "Maybe I should go my own way, take a chance this freak will be satisfied with you. After all, it's you taking on the Montana job that pissed him off."

"He burned your house down."

"Like I could have forgotten that."

"Point is—you're no less a target than I am."

"Just because you and I were skin to skin once?"

"Who knows why? If we could understand him, we'd be as crazy as he is." Kenny hesitated, then said, "Anyway, it was only once, yeah, you and me, but it meant something."

She regarded him with a don't-scam-me expression. "Meant something? What did it mean?"

Her eyes were windows beyond which lay a mystery that he suddenly felt compelled to explore.

"I don't know," he said, and he was for the first time in his life bewildered by his own feelings.

"So that was—what?—just something to say?"

"No. It meant something, all right. Even when we were . . . when we were doing it, it was different, the sex. Don't you think so?"

"Different?"

"It was different, better," he insisted, "and then everything after that hasn't been what I expected."

"What did you expect?"

"Less than what it's been. After the sex, it's always less, but it wasn't less this time."

"What is this—I finally find a Romeo wannabe, but he's too inarticulate for the role?"

"I'm not inarticulate. Not usually. I'm just confused."

She looked at the power lines overhead. Half a dozen songbirds perched and twittered where rats had recently been. "Maybe it's just the danger, the spice it adds."

"No, it's not that. Not entirely. Not mostly. It's also something else that I don't know what it is."

She lowered her gaze from the birds to Kenny. "It's something else that you don't know what it is. So when will you know?"

"Maybe never if you go your own way now. Which I'd understand if you did. I would totally understand."

She stared at him long enough for a 747 to crash in the alley if one was en route. Then she said, "The lunatic bastard burned down my house," and she dropped her iPhone into the storm drain.

Kenny smiled. He felt great. Considering the trouble they were in, he felt surprisingly sensational. He still needed time to figure out why, but he was beginning to get an idea.

42

While Ophelia Poole and young Colson Fielding are losing hope in the church, both soon to be ready for death and the black waters of the testamentary necropolis, Asher Optime sits at the plank table and applies his precise cursive to the pages of the notebook that is the first of three planned volumes of his world-changing manifesto. For a few hours, he is transported by his brilliant prose, which flows from his pen effortlessly because what he writes is the pure truth. Most philosophers are inveterate liars who build elaborate dams with their dishonest words, but the truth is a mighty river, the power of which can't be restrained.

Perhaps part of his time at the table is passed in one of the fugues to which he is sometimes subjected, for at one point he feels as if a weight of sleep is sliding off him, and he realizes that he is gripping the pen so tightly that his hand aches.

He doesn't know how long the coyote might have been keeping him company. He left the front door of the saloon standing open, and the beast evidently wandered in. It lies now in a corner of the room, on its side, and seems to be sleeping, its body twitching and its legs scrabbling at the floor as if it's running from something in a bad dream. Asher is made aware of the animal only when it cries out in a most miserable fashion, as if in terror.

The creature awakens, scrambles to its feet, and fixes Asher with its baleful yellow stare. Its lush tail is tucked between its legs, and hackles bristle along its back, though it doesn't growl or advance. Indeed, the beast is shaking violently, as though with fear. As an emissary of Nature, it is here to honor his campaign to eradicate humankind; therefore, it can't be afraid of him, which means the tremors are evidence of the awe with which it regards him.

Remaining focused on his host, the rangy visitor slinks across the room, pauses in the doorway, and then bolts out of the saloon.

Asher is pinching the pen so fiercely between the thumb and forefinger of his right hand that at first he's unable to let go of it. He shakes the hand as though the agonizing cramps are the work of stinging bees that must be cast off. The pen is flung away from him, rattling across the table. With his left hand, he massages his right, striving to work the pain out of his fingers.

When he began this session of writing, he poured a double shot of Scotch, a small reward for his devotion to his mission. He is surprised to see the whisky remains untouched. He lifts the glass with his left hand and treats himself to a long swallow, hoping it will relieve the cramping.

When gradually the sharp pain becomes a dull ache, he turns his attention to the notebook, strangely uncertain if this has been a productive afternoon. He's pleased to see that three pages of a new and inarguable case for the forced extinction of humankind have been added to his manifesto. However, he is surprised and dismayed to discover that following this brilliant beginning, he produced only five pages filled with numerous repetitions of four words, all in lower case and without punctuation: *the big dark sky the big dark sky the big dark sky . . .*

Indeed, he has been in a fugue state. But as he stares at the pages filled with those words, the obsession represented by the sameness of those many lines doesn't seem to be something of which he is capable. For one thing, although the cursive is recognizable as his neat writing, it's subtly different, the strokes sharper than usual, the curves less fulsome than they should be, suggesting that the words struck fear in the writer's heart or at least distressed him. But Asher delights in the dark sky, is exhilarated by the void between the stars and the end of all things that it portends. It's almost as if, during that period of blackout, a power other than his own mind controlled his pen, some fearful entity horrified by the eventual heat death of the universe and the following eternal cold that would make meaningless all of human history.

From a distance in the waning afternoon, a coyote issues a shrill, ululant cry.

PART 3
JIMMY TWO EYES

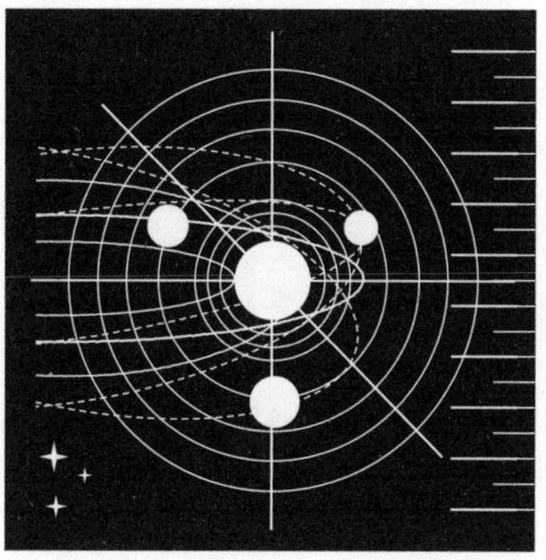

Amazing coincidences are in fact unconsciously engineered synchronicities, and we are the engineers.
—Ganesh Patel

43

The unpaved four-mile-long secondary loop connected with a more major blacktop county route at each end, a back road from nowhere to nowhere. The Range Rover's navigation system knew nothing of this territory and offered no guidance, but Wyatt Rider took direction from Joanna, who thought she could find the place that Vance Potter had described. The land offered only a few proofs of human presence, each at a considerable distance from the next: two house trailers on a weedy property; a burnt-out church with glassless windows, its blackened steeple canting toward collapse; a few humble residences, one with an American flag flying bright above its weathered walls.

The Alvarez house was a single-story clapboard rectangle with a roof of asphalt shingles, on a raised foundation of concrete blocks. Behind it towered a windmill, perhaps forty feet tall, no doubt pumping water from a well that served the property; its bladed rotor turned fast enough to indicate that the soft breeze had stiffened with the waning of the afternoon.

The house appeared freshly painted. The green lawn had recently been mown. A row of red begonias had been planted along the front wall, to the left and right of the door.

Wyatt parked beside a 1955 Studebaker E7 pickup with a two-tone paint job—red and white. Joanna knew it well. The truck had been Hector Alvarez's pride and joy when she'd last seen him, twenty-four years earlier. It was so pristine that it looked as if it had come off the showroom floor that morning and then been driven nearly seven decades through time to this new and uglier century.

During the short trip from Rustling Willows, Joanna had been in the grip of an expectation that alternated between anticipation and apprehension. When Wyatt had phoned Hector to request a visit, the old man seemed pleased by the prospect of seeing Joanna after nearly a quarter of a century. However, because he and Annalisa had been an honorary uncle and aunt to her, she felt guilty that she'd failed to stay in touch, especially because Annalisa had passed away without her knowledge. Considering that her memory of these people seemed to have been repressed by some strange power, her guilt was irrational. Nevertheless, worried about what she ought to say to Hector and how he might receive her, Joanna was trembling slightly when she got out of the Range Rover.

The windmill rotor ticked like a great clock, and in the vanes of that high, turning wheel, the breeze found an eerie voice, like the cry of a lost and frightened creature.

As she and Wyatt approached the house, the front door opened, and Hector stepped onto the small concrete stoop. He was shorter than she remembered him being. His hair had gone white, but he still had all of it. Although his face was seamed by time and weather-beaten, she would have recognized him anywhere, for his smile was as broad and sweet as ever.

He held out his arms, and it was the most natural thing to hug him and kiss his cheek. "*Tío* Hector, I'm so happy to see you."

"Little Jojo, the years have blessed you. You're as lovely as your mother."

"I was so sorry to hear about *tía* Annalisa. I didn't know until today."

He took her hand in both of his. "She is with the angels now. She has no cares." Looking past her, he said, "You're Mr. Rider, Liam O'Hara's detective and Jojo's friend, from on the phone?"

"Yes, sir."

Shaking Wyatt's hand, Hector said to Jojo, "On the phone, your friend said you need to speak with my Jimmy. But, Jojo, he's the same. The boy will never be . . . will never change."

"Yes, I know. But I want to see him, *tío* Hector. I need to see him. You know that he and I were close."

Ushering them into the house, Hector said, "When you were a child, you were kind to him and imagined him to be more than he is."

The kitchen was here at the front of the house, to the right: painted cabinets; low-end appliances; a wooden table; four rustic dining chairs with tie-on cushions, their back rails decorated with stenciled flowers in pastel colors. To the left, part of the same space, lay the living room: two armchairs draped with colorful Pendleton blankets, one side chair, the necessary tables and lamps. It was a minimalist environment and scrupulously clean.

A large, battered *trastero*, its doors open, housed a compact music system, perhaps a hundred CDs, and a few dozen paperbacks. Atop this cupboard stood a collection of *bultos* of various saints.

As he closed the front door, Hector said, "Jimmy can never be close to anyone, Jojo, not in the way we both wish he could be. You thought of him as a brother, but he didn't think of you as a sister, if he thought of you much at all. Some days I wonder if even I am a stranger to him. He feeds himself, bathes himself when I take him to the tub, dresses himself if the clothes are simple to put on, with no buttons. He exists in this world, but he doesn't live in it. He lives deep within himself, in another world of his own."

"You have no one to help you?" Wyatt asked.

Hector smiled. "I have a small pension and social security. Help is expensive. My help, sir, is the memory of his mother, which is enough. We shared in Jimmy's care when she was with us, and my promise to her was to outlive the boy, so he will never be alone."

Joanna thought she saw sudden tears standing in Wyatt's eyes when he said, "He's lucky to have you."

Hector's smile flatlined, and he lowered his gaze to the floor as he said, "Perhaps we were his curse. In our foolish youth, my wife and I spent our evenings listening to music, drinking much too much tequila chased with too many beers, even when she was carrying the boy. We weren't ignorant. We understood the risks to a pregnant woman, but we thought we were invincible. And we too much loved our bad habit. Maybe Jimmy would have been what he is even if we hadn't done what we did, but we can never know." He looked up from the floor. "My selfish hope is that, by taking care of him, we will be . . . redeemed."

The men locked stares in silence for a moment, and Joanna sensed that each of them intuited some shared understanding that instantly relieved them of being strangers, one to the other.

Hector said, "Jimmy is maybe napping. Give me a moment with him." He retreated into a short hall, opened a door on the right, and disappeared into the boy's room.

The combination kitchen and living area occupied no more than four hundred square feet. The walls were painted pale blue and the shiplap ceiling glossy white, to make the space seem bigger. The hall perhaps served two cramped bedrooms and a bath. Humble as the house might be, it nevertheless felt as significant as any other place. It seemed to Joanna that the lives lived here were not as small as the rooms, were much larger than they seemed to be, were in fact momentous lives if the whole truth and purpose of them could be fully understood.

Wyatt said, "You're really sure Jimmy talked to you?"

"He spoke in the dream, and when I woke, I knew I'd heard that same voice when we were children. He spoke to me often in those days, but never when anyone else was around."

"Your secret friend."

"Yes. Weird as it sounds."

"And he controlled all the animals, the deer and birds, even a grizzly bear."

"I don't know. I think so. He must have. The dreams I've had were in part memories. And just today . . . the elk."

"Somehow he sent the elk to welcome you back?"

Hector reappeared in the hallway. "Come now. Jimmy's awake."

Joanna surprised herself by taking Wyatt's hand and squeezing it tightly. "Don't let the way he looks scare you. He wouldn't harm anyone. He wouldn't ever. He couldn't."

At the entrance to the hallway, she let go of his hand. She blotted her palms on her jeans.

Hector smiled and nodded and indicated the open door.

Joanna hesitated on the threshold.

The bed was neatly made, with plumped pillows and a chenille spread.

The blind was drawn shut over the only window. A pottery lamp with a pleated shade featured two three-way bulbs set at the lowest intensity, and shadows stood sentinel around the perimeter of the room.

She remembered that on some days—not frequently, but now and then—Jimmy was especially sensitive to light, which gave him a headache. Maybe this was one such day.

She went into the room.

44

In the darkness, the steady scratching of the blade reminded Colson Fielding of stories in which characters were buried alive and had to claw their way out of a coffin, all the while going apeshit crazy from claustrophobia. With an effort, he put such images out of his mind. He needed to stay positive. The scratching was the sound of freedom, of vengeance. For the moment, he was beyond grief, deep into anger, focused on escape and survival.

He and Ophelia agreed that it was a waste of time to try to reach the gap where the sacristy roof met the back wall of the church. The only way to get up there was to drag pews in from the nave and somehow stack them and climb them, which required the strength of the Incredible Hulk and was asking for a broken neck. Even if he could get up there, the roof might not be rotten enough for him to enlarge the hole. They suspected this Optime creep had not patched the roof specifically because he *wanted* them to be tantalized by the hole, to exhaust themselves yearning for it and struggling to get to it. He wasn't just a homicidal lunatic, but also a sadist who hoped to see them suffer mentally and emotionally before they were stricken by the physical pain of thirst and hunger.

The other best option was one of the bricked-in windows. Having read Optime's manifesto, Ophelia knew the freak was a graduate of two big universities, a doctor of medicine who never practiced, who went to live in that spooky commune run by Xanthus Toller, the loon who was in the news now and then, taken seriously by some of the media. Knowing what Optime was also told them what he *wasn't,* and for sure he wasn't a bricklayer. Colson's grandfather, his mom's father, was a contractor who built houses. Colson had been on enough construction sites to know what a well-made brick or concrete-block wall looked like. Optime's mortar was sloppily applied and crumbling in places. He probably hadn't known enough to use metal ties or anchors when he filled in the windows, which were about six feet wide and eight feet tall. When Colson used the spear blade of his Swiss Army knife, he was able to dig out the mortar more easily than he had expected, maybe because Optime had used an unsuitable natural sand with too many fine grains to ensure a strong bond.

Among the knife's many tools were the sturdy spear blade and a pen blade. If those broke or became dull, there were the blades of a miniature pair of scissors, a corkscrew, a regular screwdriver and a Phillips-head screwdriver, a wood saw, a metal saw, and an awl that should be of use. While Ophelia told him what was in the manifesto, he worked until his fingers cramped, and then passed the knife to her and took the flashlight, which he switched on only long enough for her to see where she needed to continue digging out the mortar.

"Can this really work?" she wondered as, in the dusty dark, she continued what he had begun.

"The first brick ought to be the hardest to get out," he said. "After that, it should be easier and easier. If we can pull out the entire bottom course, and if he didn't use any metal ties or other joint reinforcements, then I think maybe everything above could be made to collapse."

By the time her fingers began to cramp and the work reverted to Colson, she had told him about her sister, Octavia, dying in the car crash that Ophelia had escaped almost unscathed. "I've been waiting to learn why I was spared. Now I know. I'm here to take him out."

"Take him out? Shouldn't we try to get our hands on the GPS messenger in Dad's backpack, call the Emergency Response Center in Texas, get them in here?"

Her voice in the dark was more intense than in the light, with a sharp edge that might have spooked Colson if he'd met her in other circumstances. "Are you shitting me? You smell what's coming through the floorboards, kid?"

"Yeah. I smell it."

"His damn necropolis, rotting under us. A testament to his greatness. We'll have one chance to surprise the asshole, just one, if we have any chance at all. You understand that?"

"I guess maybe."

"You guess maybe?"

"Yeah. Okay. I understand. I hate him, too."

"We get out of here," she said, "I'm going to kill the fucker. *Then* we can call the Emergency Response Center in Texas."

"Kill him how?"

The scratching blade. The dry dribbling sound as bits of mortar fell to the floor.

At last, she said, "Supposing we get out of here, it'll be dark by then. You go into the woods nearby and hide. I'll take the knife, if there's still anything left of it by then. Maybe I can get him while he's sleeping."

"It's not a knife for killing anyone," Colson said. "Even in perfect condition, the blades are too short."

"It'll work if I cut a carotid artery. Or he's sleeping, so I stab him in the eye, take his gun from him, put him down with it."

"What're you—Jane Hawk?"

"Who's Jane Hawk?"

"This kick-ass rogue FBI agent in these novels my mom likes. Even if you were Jane Hawk, it won't work the way you say. It never will."

"Then I'll find another way. You just hide in the woods, and I'll find another way."

Their excavations seemed to have loosened the brick. As he worked harder at it, he said, "I never knew a girl like you."

"I'm not just a girl anymore, Colson. I can almost believe I never was."

"Yeah, you're a grown-up. I get it. But I can't just hide in the woods and let everything to you."

"I won't let you do anything else."

"You called me 'kid.' I saw him . . . saw him kill my dad. I'm not a kid anymore."

"Sweetie, you're thirteen. Didn't you say thirteen?"

"Yeah, well, but now I'm the man of my family. Don't tell me that sounds silly." He was embarrassed to hear his voice break a little. "Don't dare tell me that."

After a silence, she said, "I won't let you help me kill a man. I won't put that memory in your head for the rest of your life."

"I won't just hide in the woods," he insisted.

45

Long after Eden, when every shadow symbolizes the eventual death of the creature casting it, when chaos cascades through our fallen days, once-perfect Nature remains beautiful even in her imperfection, though she shares with humanity a taste for perversity that reflects the cruelty of the agent of her corruption. She mocks her victims with deformities, sometimes of the body, sometimes of the mind. With those she curses, her purpose seems to be to sow despair in a world desperately in need of hope.

Just the previous night, Joanna had seen Jimmy Two Eyes in a dream half formed by memories; but she was not prepared for the impact of his appearance here in the waking world. As an innocent child in the magical environment of Rustling Willows, she'd thought the world was her playground. Back then, she hadn't yet developed an awareness of the existence of evil, therefore feared nothing, not even what was strange to the point of being profoundly alien. Also, if the boy in the dream was truly Jimmy as he looked in childhood, he'd been grotesque but not fearsome;

however, twenty-four years had whittled away the sweetness of his broken face and carved it into a monstrous countenance.

He slumped in a large upholstered chair, his hunched back forcing his misshapen head forward. His prominent nose had grown hooked like that of a witch in a fairy tale. His eyes were more deeply hooded by his brow than they had been in childhood. Staring at his smallish hands, which lay upturned in his lap, he muttered wordlessly, continuously.

Joanna stopped a few steps inside the room, reluctant to approach Jimmy, but her hesitation shamed her, especially because Hector might sense her disquiet. The passage of so much time had been as unkind to Jimmy as had been Nature; but he was surely still the harmless soul that he'd always been. He had no capacity to commit evil, no reason to harm her.

In front of the armchair stood a padded footstool. Joanna sat on it and said, "Jimmy? It's me. Joanna. Jojo. Do you remember?"

As if unaware of her, chin on his chest, he continued muttering to himself, like a troll reminiscing about deeds done in dark and dripping caverns.

She leaned forward and reached out hesitantly at first, but then boldly took one of his hands, which was warm and dry and limp.

"I had a dream about you, Jimmy. First a bear then two deer led me through fields and forest, straight to you in the apple orchard. In the dream, you asked me to come, to help you, and here I am."

He stopped muttering, but he did not raise his head.

Pressing his hand between both of hers, she said, "All the animals . . . When I was a girl, it was so magical. *You* seemed magical."

At last he lifted his chin off his chest. From deep under a brow of malformed bone, his eyes came into view, the left one blue and clear, the right one dark and bloodshot and set higher than the other. Although his stare had evidently never troubled her when they were children, she almost flinched from it now. Her heart beat harder, faster. If she allowed this unexpected fear to be apparent, she would offend Hector, if not Jimmy as well, so she repressed it and gave his hand a gentle squeeze to reassure her secret friend of her continued affection.

Without turning his head, he glanced surreptitiously at his father, at Wyatt Rider, and then fixed Joanna with his stare once more. His limp hand stiffened and squeezed one of hers.

She interpreted Jimmy's actions to mean that he desired to visit without observers, just her and him.

"I'm all right here," she told Wyatt. "Jimmy and I have a lot of catching up to do." To Hector, she said, "When we arrived, Wyatt was raving about your Studebaker pickup. I know he'd love to have a look at it."

"She's a beauty," Wyatt said.

Hector smiled broadly. "I saw her sitting in a driveway at a yard sale forty years ago. She needed help. Did all the mechanical work myself, then dismantled her and sent the pieces off to be painted, to get all the corners and cracks and the backs of things."

As the men left the room and moved away through the house, Joanna returned her attention to Jimmy. The uneven set of his eyes made it difficult to match both barrels of his stare. For that and other reasons, she focused on the one that was as clear and blue and eerie as the glass eye of a doll.

The men's voices grew more distant. The front door closed with a thud.

In the ensuing quiet, here at the back of the house, the *click-click-click* of the windmill rotor reminded Joanna of the pegs on a casino wheel of fortune ticking past the pointer that would decide the value of the gambler's bet.

She waited for Jimmy to speak first. When he remained silent, she said, "In my dream, you said you were in a dark place, lost."

He didn't reply. The pupil of his blue eye was open wide to bring in what meager lamplight the shadowed room provided. It seemed as though it was not merely a pupil but also a black hole with the intense gravitational field of a collapsed star, into which she might be drawn helplessly, until she found herself having traveled out of this universe into one far stranger.

She didn't like the tremor in her voice when she said, "In the dream, you said, 'Please come and help me.' And now I'm here."

Within her enveloping two hands, his hand curled into a fist, but still he failed to speak.

"The phone call that I received . . . the voice was that of a woman. She called me Jojo and said she was spiraling into Bedlam. She said, 'Please come and help me.' Is she someone you know, Jimmy?"

He had ceased to blink, his eyes steady and standing open like those of a dead man, though still he breathed.

"In the dream, when we were in the apple orchard, you also said, 'The terrible big dark sky.' The woman on the phone used those same words, and that was *not* a dream."

The breeze swelled against the walls of the house. From the becoming wind, the wooden vanes of the mill strained a thin lonesome sound, and the rotor clicked more rapidly than before.

Joanna changed tack. "All those years ago, Jimmy, to delight me, you somehow controlled all the creatures of nature, the birds and squirrels and rabbits, the deer and coyotes, the wolves and bears. You're some kind of—I don't know—some kind of savant, psychic, something. For a few special years, my childhood was a fantasy. I was a ruling princess of everything that lived in the forest and the fields—but it was real."

His pale tongue licked the thin lips of his freakishly wide mouth, though it brought forth no words.

"It was real," she repeated. "But I was made to repress all memories of it. Did *you* take those memories from me?"

Outside, an engine turned over. The Studebaker pickup.

"Did you restore my memories so that I'd come back here?"

He said nothing.

"The elk were you. You sent the elk to welcome me. It's crazy, but it must have been you."

The sound of the engine receded. They seemed to be taking the pickup for a spin. Maybe Hector was letting Wyatt drive.

Joanna leaned closer to Jimmy. "*Mi hermano. Querido hermano.* Please talk to me now as you did when we were so young."

He wrenched his fist from between her clasping hands, and at last he spoke in the guttural voice—almost a bestial growl—that she had heard in the dream. "You've changed, Jojo. You're not the same."

A chill—part exhilaration and part disquiet, wonder married to fear, occasioned by hearing him other than in a dream—shot up her spine and stippled the nape of her neck with gooseflesh. She understood his words to be a gentle complaint that she had for so long abandoned him.

"I would have come to see you if I'd known you were here, but until the dream last night, I had no memory of us. You must know I had no memory."

Sudden tears welled in his eyes and spilled down his cheeks. "You're not the same," he repeated.

"I'm older, as are you, dear one."

He shook his head, and fierce emotion twisted his misassembled face into a greater strangeness. "You're not the same, just not the same." His wide mouth cracked open, a crescent of crooked teeth, and he hissed an accusation: *"Innocence, innocence, you've lost your innocence!"*

Taken aback by his passion, she rose from the footstool. "I've grown up, Jimmy. That's all. I'm still me, still Jojo."

In her purse, her cell phone rang.

Leaning forward in his armchair, Jimmy cried with anguish more than anger, but not without a trace of the latter, *"Answer it!"*

Hands trembling, she fished the phone from her purse. No caller ID. She took the call and recognized the voice of the woman who had phoned her more than once in Santa Fe.

"You've lost your innocence," the caller said. "You're filled with moral confusion, strange convictions, fears, and calculation. How can you save me if you can't save yourself?"

Perhaps because she was back in Montana, fresh from Rustling Willows Ranch, the recognition of the speaker's identity no longer eluded her. In New Mexico, at a far remove from the land of her childhood, she could deny that this voice was that of her mother, but she could not deny it now.

The *voice* of her mother, but not her mother.

Her mother was dead.

The question echoed in her mind—*How can you save me if you can't save yourself?*—and gave rise to an extraordinary suspicion.

The voice had been that of her mother, but somehow the caller had been Jimmy Two Eyes.

In the days after her mother's death, in the hours following midnight, as she'd watched family videos alone in the house at Rustling Willows, the recording froze with Joanna's face on the screen, and her mother had spoken words that the home movie had never contained on previous viewings. *You will soon be going away, Jojo, going away to grow up elsewhere. I might reach out to you many years from now and ask you to come home.*

That had not been a visitation by a spirit. That, too, must have been Jimmy.

She terminated the call and dropped the phone into her purse, shaken by a sense that the madness of recent weeks was a mere presentiment of greater insanity to come.

Looming over Jimmy, staring down at his tear-wet face, into his bottomless eyes, she demanded, "That was you, wasn't it? Somehow that was you. My mother drowned. She's been gone most of my life. She hasn't come back. That was somehow you. Tell me the truth."

Although his face glistened, his eyes no longer welled with tears, and his grief—if it had been grief—gave way to what seemed to be bitter resentment. His slumped and shapeless body stiffened into a disturbing configuration of misshapen bones and tortured muscles. He gripped the arms of the chair and sat up as straight as he could manage and raised his head as if in challenge.

His rough voice grew rougher, the words like hardwood and his voice a saw that cut them one from the other. "Truth? It's truth you want? Then you'll have it. The truth is, your mother's death wasn't an accident. She was murdered. Murdered. Murdered by your father."

46

Once a black-hat hacker, now a white-hat hacker, Kenny Deetle was ready to go gray in a crisis. If the world harbored people who would, with pleasure, cut your head in two from skullcap to chin with a chain saw, stability was an illusion and lasting peace was a dream of fools. Yeah, evil was an irrational choice, because though evil could work in the short run, it never worked in the long run. And, yeah, evil people practiced to deceive, but not all deception was evil. Sometimes it was a survival technique.

The 1970 jet-black Pontiac GTO Judge, which Kenny kept in a spacious unit at an immense self-storage facility illiterately named "Storage R Us," had been registered with the state by one Jamison Eugene Norwald, who didn't exist, at an address in Spokane that was nothing but a mail drop. This had been possible because Kenny could backdoor the Department of Licensing computer and insert false data that even the most talented IT-security types couldn't detect. Seemingly well-ordered and rational societies could go mad rapidly, as witness Germany in the 1930s, or they could be destroyed by corrupt kleptocrats like Chávez and Maduro in Venezuela, or they could be sucked into a vortex of irrationality by utopian ideologues—some religious, some atheistic—so it was always wise to have wheels that no one knew belonged to you, stashed where your enemies would not think to look for them, available for a quick getaway.

The Pontiac GTO had much to recommend it. A 455 cu. in. engine in V8, pushing out 325 horsepower. A smooth transmission with jackrabbit response. Sleek good looks.

Most important of all, the coupe had rolled off the line in Detroit long before a GPS navigation system was standard equipment. It couldn't be satellite tracked by anyone—not by the FBI, the NSA, the CIA, the state police, the FTC, the FCC, the EPA, the USPS, or a power-crazed hacker who, by remote control, flooded your apartment and burned down your lover's house.

"It's cool," said Leigh Ann Bruce, sliding one hand along the sleek flank of the vehicle. "It's retro and futuristic at the same time."

"I take it for a drive once a week," Kenny said, "keep the tank full and the battery charged. Two packed suitcases stashed in the trunk. We'll stop somewhere and get you a couple pair of jeans, whatever else you need."

As she got into the front passenger seat with the grocery-store tote, he started the engine. Putting the bag on the floor between her feet, she said, "Where are we going?"

He reached past her and opened the glove box. It contained a packet of Kleenex, a small bottle of Purell hand sanitizer, and tin of Altoids breath mints. There were also two disposable phones; he gave her one and closed the glove box.

"It's activated. I haven't used any of the minutes on it."

"You want me to call someone?"

"Once we're on the road."

He drove out of the storage unit and away without bothering to close the roll-up door. Management would take care of it and send him an advisory reminding him always to lock his unit. He had rented the space in the name of Oscar French, an identity derived from the names of his favorite maker of hot dogs and his preferred brand of mustard, and the rent was prepaid through the end of the year.

He said, "Get the fish sticks out of the tote and open them."

When she did as told, three credit cards and three driver's licenses slid out of the box, into her hand. The licenses featured his photo, but each was in a different name; none of the addresses matched. There was one credit card to go with each license.

"Give me the pair for Jamison Eugene Norwald," Kenny said. "He owns these wheels."

"Totally white hat, huh?"

"This isn't about committing a crime. This is about survival. I'm a techno prepper."

Returning the four unneeded cards to the fish-stick box, she said, "Where are we going?"

"Nowhere, Montana. Liam O'Hara's getaway place. Rustling Willows Ranch."

"I've never been to Montana."

"Neither have I."

She said, "I never imagined ever going to Montana."

"Neither have I. But if we're in deep shit, so is Wyatt Rider."

"The PI you mentioned."

"I gotta tell him about this sociopathic überhacker, and I don't think I should do it by phone."

"Not even with a burner phone?"

"Wyatt's phone isn't a burner, and for sure the superfreak who torched your house has a tap on it—calls, emails, text messages. He took over the Nautilus and tried to kill us. He'll kill Wyatt if he thinks it's necessary. I don't walk away from a friend."

To the north and west, the blue sky was defaulting to a solemn tide of clouds. They appeared to be swollen with rain. Welcome to Seattle.

He accelerated onto an entrance ramp and injected the GTO into the bloodstream of traffic on Interstate 5.

Leigh Ann said, "Why're we going south? Montana's east."

"Yeah, like maybe seven hundred miles to Rustling Willows." He gave her a cell-phone number. "Ask for Ganesh. Say you're calling for me."

As she entered the number, she said, "Who's Ganesh?"

"Ganesh Patel. My wingman. Wyatt and I have done some serious work for him. Ganesh and me, we have a lot in common. He's like my brother from another mother."

"You drive like a maniac," she said as the number rang.

"Thank you."

"Could you for God's sake slow down?"

"No. Gut instinct. Time is running out."

47

Murdered by your father.

The substance of the accusation was no more shocking than the tone of voice with which those words were delivered. During the period of her childhood when Jimmy Two Eyes had been her friend, at least as she now remembered those years, he'd never spoken sharply to her. He had been kind and caring at all times, by some strange power commanding all the creatures of field and forest to serve as her companions in adventure. She had always felt loved by him and safe in his company.

This version of Jimmy Alvarez seemed not merely older but also corrupted, perhaps because he was embittered after so many years of loneliness and suffering. She couldn't be angry with him, but she was hurt that he evidently took pleasure in this outrageous lie or terrible revelation, whichever it might be.

He pulled himself to the edge of the armchair and glared up at her, breathing like a bull agitated by a red cape. Every expression on his unfortunate face could be easily misread, so that what at the moment looked like fury might in fact be only sorrow. However, the contempt in his fearsome voice could not be mistaken for anything else.

"Your devious, faithless father killed her with not the least regret. Wearing swimming trunks, he waited for her in the predawn darkness, inside the boathouse. She came for her morning session of rowing in the skiff, and when she stepped through the door, he swung an oar at her, clubbed the side of her head. She collapsed, not yet dead but unconscious."

Joanna took a step back from the footstool, but she was unable to retreat farther, for she was transfixed by Jimmy's mismatched eyes. Auntie Kat had said that one was like the eye of an angel, the other like that of a demon, but at the moment, both glittered with what seemed to be demonic rage. His mouth, half again as wide as a normal mouth, was like a saber slash, his teeth a snarl of bones revealed in a wound.

"He dragged her down the gangway," Jimmy continued. "Dragged her to the boat slip, and pulled her into the water and held her under. The lake chill revived her. She struggled, but your father was stronger, and he held her underwater until she drowned. He got in the belayed skiff, pulled her body in after him, untied, and rowed her out to the middle of the lake. The moon had set, and the sun hadn't risen, so no one saw him heave her dead body overboard. He left the boat adrift and swam ashore, and still no one saw him."

Joanna flinched as if she had been spat on. For a moment she couldn't get her breath, as though her grief, which had long ago become a light and settled sorrow, now pressed on her with greater weight. She knew at once that renewed grief was only part of what she felt, that horror was an element of it, too.

When she could breathe, she quickened to her father's defense, but in the weakness of her voice, she heard doubt that she was loath to admit. "You're lying. You must be lying. If no one saw him, how could you know such a thing?"

Cocking his head, regarding her particularly with his bloodshot eye, like some accursed soothsayer in a gothic fantasy, he said, "I didn't need to see. I knew his heart, his mind, as I knew yours when you were young, as I know it now that you are changed."

"He loved my mother," she declared, and realized as she spoke that she did not know whether that was true.

"He was given a successful cattle ranch, but fattening cattle has no glamour. He was vain. He wanted to be an admired horseman, breeding and selling them to race and to show. But he wasn't any good at that, and lost money year by year. The large whole-life insurance policy on your mother, which your grandfather purchased for her at her birth, as an investment he thought would accrue in value—that death benefit was your father's one hope of saving Rustling Willows, and he seized his chance. Oh, yes, he seized it with both hands and swung that oar like a big-league baseball star."

She thought of what Auntie Kat said about her father: *He was not an outgoing man. Your mother said shy, but I thought . . . well, something else. I believe he married your mother because he was unsure and somehow empty, while she was so centered and complete.*

This angry and aggressive Jimmy was ugly, but Joanna wondered if he seemed even uglier than he actually was because he was telling the truth. Truths we don't want to hear always make the teller ugly to us.

She was compelled to further defend her father. "My mom's death was investigated. The police said it was accidental. No one had the slightest reason to suspect my dad."

Even though Jimmy's face did the Phantom of the Opera one better, making his expressions difficult to read, the sneer in his voice was unmistakable, sharp and meant to cut. "The sheriff, who owned quarter horses, bought his racing stock from your father—and was always given a discount. They went hunting together. The county had no medical examiner in those days, only an incompetent coroner whose main job was as an undertaker, and he had a drinking problem. There was no one to give your mother justice, no one—except me."

"You?" Her puzzlement lasted only an instant, and then she understood. Like a benign bruin in a fable, the grizzly bear had welcomed young Joanna into an enchanted forest, its ferocity repressed by whatever spell Jimmy had cast upon it. In some strange way the bear had *been* Jimmy, his avatar, as the many animals on the ranch were his to control and perhaps inhabit. If he could use all creatures great and small, furred and feathered and scaled, to charm and entertain her, he could surely use the most formidable of them to slaughter Samuel Chase.

"You killed my father."

He received the accusation as though it had been praise. "Yes. But I *executed* him. He was the murderer, not me."

Whether this was a lie piled upon a lie or in fact revelation upon revelation, she felt assaulted, the past on which she'd built a life cracking under her as if it were a frozen lake of unstable ice. "What right had you to be his judge and jury?"

He startled her by springing up from the armchair and onto the footstool, so that in spite of his stature, he could be eye to eye with her. He had moved in a hitch and hobble when he'd been a boy, and though he looked less limber now than he'd been then, his anger granted him this unexpected and unsettling agility.

"What right had I? *What right?* The right of one who has a moral purpose, who has always done the right thing and who, by my nature, always and forever *must* do the right thing, no matter how terrible it might be." His wrenched and wretched face, his Rumpelstiltskin rage, seemed to belie his claim to superior virtue. "I didn't know he was intending to murder her, because he didn't much interest me, not when I had you to fascinate me, your pure love of everyone, your deep reverence for all creatures, your *innocence*, so different from others of your kind. I knew he killed Emelia only when I heard her psychic death cry as cold water filled her lungs. That cry, silent to every ear but mine, pierced my brain like a quarrel fired by a crossbow. When I reached out for your father, he was filled with terror at the risk he'd taken but also with a savage glee, with pride that he had been so bold, with the hatred of one who blames others for his failures."

Once when she was eight, on the carnival midway at a county fair, Joanna badgered her mother to take her into the funhouse. The exit was by way of a giant padded barrel that both rolled and slowly pitched; she hadn't maintained her balance, but had tumbled through it, laughing, and down a rubber ramp. A similar disorientation and dislocation overcame her now, but this time the sensation wasn't an occasion for laughter. This loss of balance wasn't physical but emotional, wasn't for a minute or two but perhaps for a lifetime.

She was only an arm's length from this new and hostile Jimmy, too close. She wanted to back away, but she feared that her retreat might inflame him further. She stood her ground as she said, "What do you mean you 'reached out' for my father? Are you saying . . . you read his mind? You can read minds?"

"Didn't you hear me when I said you've lost your innocence? *Didn't you hear me* when I said you're filled with confusion, strange convictions, fears, and calculation? *Didn't you listen* when I said I knew his heart, his mind, as I knew yours back in the day, *as I know yours even now*?"

She should have foreseen that this was a logical extension of his ability to control animals, but if she had suspected as much on a subconscious level, she had, in fear, always retreated from the conscious consideration of it.

Now a grievous thought occurred to her. She was loath to press him about it, but she could not restrain herself. "If it's true that my father killed her and if you knew he'd done it, why didn't you compel him to confess to the police?"

"Compel?" His laugh was without humor and as terrible as a snarl. "Yes, wouldn't that be a neat solution to human crime and deceit, if I could simply compel every miscreant to tell the truth and do the right thing. Had I such power, I would use it ruthlessly, *Jojo*." He spoke her name without affection, in fact with a note of mockery. "If I want to know a person's mind and if I focus on him to the exclusion of all else, no secret can be kept from me, but I have no *control* of him."

"The animals . . ."

"They're simple entities. Human beings are orders of magnitude more intelligent than the smartest animals. Elk I may control, rats and rabbits, whole herds at a time, but I may not control a man, woman, or child."

"May not . . . but you can?"

"I can. But I am forbidden."

"By whom?"

"By my very nature."

"So you used the bear to murder him."

"To execute a murderer."

"And were you . . . ?" She didn't complete the question, but left it unspoken, as a test of the power that he claimed to possess.

"No," he said, answering what she hadn't asked. "I wasn't in control of the bear when it attacked him, when it *devoured* him alive."

If long ago she had thought him magical, she now found him mysterious, unfathomable, *alien*.

Beyond these walls, the windmill rotor clicked-clicked-clicked, and through its spinning vanes, the rising wind sang a threnody for the slowly dying light of late afternoon.

She hoped to hear the Studebaker pickup returning, but she couldn't will the sound into existence.

Jimmy Two Eyes pointed a finger at her, and his ragged voice became a lash of censure. "Because you've changed, you've changed tragically, because you've lost your innocence, you fear me now, as much as you once loved me. In the past, I was like a gnome to you—all Brothers Grimm and Hans Christian Andersen. Now you look at me and see a monster, you think I'm capable of monstrous things, like inhabiting the bear while it ate your father, relishing the blood and violence."

Although Jimmy's eyes had been strange when Joanna had been a child, she didn't believe they had been bright with derangement, but there was madness in those eyes now.

His finger curled back into his hand, and he shook his fist at her. "I brought the bear out of the forest, down from the foothills, guided it to your wretched father where he was riding his favorite horse. I triggered its memory of the smell and flavor of rich blood, then turned it loose to do the work for which nature had shaped it. I did this for your mother, *for your mother*!"

"My mother was a gentle soul. She believed in justice but not vengeance."

Infuriated by the implied accusation, he shrieked his response, spittle flying. "It wasn't *vengeance*! It was fair *retribution*, the impersonal visitation of the doom of righteous law! I'm forbidden vengeance. *I am forbidden!*"

He leaped off the footstool and hurried to the nightstand. He yanked open the drawer and fumbled through whatever it contained.

For an instant she thought he would turn toward her with a knife and deadly purpose. As she was about to pivot toward the door, he found what he wanted and brandished it at her: a simply framed photograph of Joanna when she'd been seven or eight years old.

Jimmy brought it to her and threw it on the floor at her feet. "The pitiful monkey wanted it for whatever stupid monkey reason, but he doesn't want it now. He can't have it now. He can't ever have it, because you aren't you anymore. You've changed! You're so *changed*! You're just another one, just like all the rest of them, another plague virus, pestilence."

This extraordinary individual, whether merely malformed and maladjusted or in fact a monster, compelled her attention and was the fulcrum on which her future would be leveraged. There could be no forgetting him again, and there absolutely must be an ultimate understanding of him, of all that he could do and all that he had done, for she could not have a normal life or write anything worth writing if she fled Montana and left the mystery of him unsolved. What she had forgotten—been made to forget—of her childhood had shaped her more than she yet understood, and it no doubt explained why, at thirty-three, she remained without a partner in life, and why her six novels were filled with such yearning for transcendence of one kind or another.

He kicked the framed photograph that he had thrown down. "Take it. Take it and get out."

Although Jimmy had rebuked her instead of attacking her, Joanna believed he had the capacity to commit horrendous violence, not just in the name of retribution, but for reasons quite irrational. Though she hadn't harmed anyone, she felt no safer here than her homicidal father had been when he'd ridden Spirit into the farther reaches of the ranch on the last day of his life.

Nevertheless, when Jimmy shouted at her—"GET OUT!"—she said, "No," and walked past him to the only window, where she raised the pleated shade and let in some welcome light.

48

The brick came free in a sudden crumbling of fractured mortar, and pale daylight shaped the vacant space.

A surge of emotion filled Colson Fielding, something better than grief, healthier than anger, far cleaner than a thirst for vengeance. This small success with one brick gave him a profound sense of connection with his lost father, because his dad had been so knowledgeable about so many things, so competent by nature; and he felt as well close to his grandfather, who still lived, who still built houses and knew about mortar and had given him the Swiss Army knife years earlier; and in his mind's eye, he saw his mother's kind face, she whom he loved above all, she for whom he *must* survive to give her strength when she received the news of her widowhood. Not for the first time, though more powerfully than ever before, he understood the value of family, the comfort and power of generations who, whatever their faults, shared a history and were devoted to one another as much as human nature allowed. The weight of the brick in his hand was a small fraction of the weight of the Fielding family in its many generations; a healthy family was a fortress.

Ophelia switched on the Tac Light. The beam found the brick, and she said, "One down, like just two hundred to go."

"More like a hundred sixty."

"Gimme the knife, and I'll dig one out."

"The next will be a lot easier," Colson predicted, placing the first brick on a nearby pew, as if it were a sacred relic that must be treated with reverence. "And the third is gonna be easier than the second."

Switching off the flashlight and setting to work with the blade in the dim glow—and the whispering draft—that entered where a brick was missing, Ophelia said, "Why easier?"

"In a bottom row like this, the horizontal stability, frame to frame, declines faster with the loss of each masonry unit."

"Where'd you get that?"

"My grandpa. In other words, the bricks in this row not only hold up the bricks above them, but they also hold each other in place, more than the mortar does."

"What're the odds I'd be locked in here with a kid who knows masonry?"

"What're the odds I'd be locked in with a Jane Hawk clone?"

The second brick came loose in maybe three minutes, and the next one in about two.

Frame to frame, there were nine bricks in the bottom row. The blade dug at the rotten mortar, which had so little bond strength that it was less like bricklayer's batter than like the crisp substance of a fresh-baked biscotti. In quick succession, four additional units were removed.

With a brick in hand, Colson said, "Bad sand and too much lime. He's a total amateur. Stand back, out of the way."

"Why? What're you doing?"

"If he didn't know about mixing mortar, for sure he didn't know squat about anchors and ties. Now that the bottom row is gone except for the two end units, this thing is held up with spit and a wish."

The window started two feet off the floor and continued almost five feet above Colson's head. He wished that he had a sledgehammer with a long handle, but he didn't. This was going to be risky. If a single falling brick beaned him just right, it could maybe crack his skull, and an avalanche could do worse damage.

Ophelia stepped back, and Colson slammed the brick in his hand against the remaining window infill. The sound was a flat clap, not as loud as he expected, but still maybe loud enough to have been heard by Optime if the freak was on the veranda of the saloon rather than inside. He rapped the hanging curtain of masonry again, and a single unit fell out of the second row. Shock waves were starting to numb his hands, but he struck a third time, a fourth, and then he danced back as a cracking-grinding noise warned of collapse. Bricks cascaded out of the window, clattered onto the sill, spilled onto the floor, clouding the air with clay dust and cement dust and powdered lime.

There had been no glass in the window in perhaps more than a century, and the muntins had broken out a long time ago. Nothing barred their way to freedom. As Colson climbed the brickfall that shifted under his feet and clambered across the windowsill after Ophelia, into the last hour of daylight, he wondered if he would hear the shot that killed him or if the bullet would be faster than the sound.

49

The 1955 Studebaker E7 pickup was a pleasure to drive, a time machine that left the troubled twenty-first century behind.

Wyatt Rider almost wished that it *was* taking him to a quieter past, sans the internet and the insane ideologies of the modern world, where life moved slow enough to be savored. He drove too far, more miles than he intended, because Hector Alvarez, proud of the truck, encouraged him to go faster, then even faster, as did the open road and the endless vistas.

When at last he turned and headed back the way they had come, he was overtaken by an urgent intuitive sense that he should not have left Joanna alone with Jimmy Two Eyes for this long. He sought reassurance when he said to Hector, "She tells me that she and your boy were best friends back in the day."

Hector's sun-leathered and time-seamed face looked less old than wise, and his smile was that of a contemplative mystic. "I'm not surprised Jojo made a life in books like she did. Even as a little girl, she had the colorful mind of a story writer, shaping the world into a better place than ever it was. What friendship she had with my Jimmy was her imagination. Whatever goes on in his mind, it has little to do with other people or this world. Annalisa and I, we liked to think that even though Jimmy's flesh and bones are in this sorry world, his soul is already in the next, so he sees and travels through that sweet and better place, waiting for his poor twisted body to catch up with him."

That response didn't soothe Wyatt's concern. He said, "Has he really never spoken a word in all these years?"

"From time to time, he makes sounds that maybe mean something to him, but they make no sense to us. His mother and I . . . we sinned against the boy. So caring for him and loving him is my penance, loving him and not knowing if he can love me in return at all, not knowing in this world if he can forgive Annalisa and me, though I hope to hear him say so in the next."

They had encountered a little traffic on the way out, but on the return trip, the county road was as deserted as if the world had passed through an eerily quiet apocalypse. The pavement curved to the north, past descending meadows off to the right, with serried ranks of conifers ascending on the left. Coming out of the curve, Wyatt braked to a stop when he saw a family of deer—an antlered buck, a doe, two spotted fawns—blocking the straightaway ahead.

The animals stood as still as sculpture, their heads turned toward the Studebaker, as if they had been waiting for it, aware that it was en route, though most likely they had paused in their crossing when they heard the approaching engine.

"Magnificent," said Wyatt.

"Mule deer," Hector said.

"Why mule? They look nothing like mules."

"Their big ears. Other deer don't have ears so big."

The deer regarded them with what seemed to be solemn curiosity.

Wyatt said, "Seems like they don't spook easily."

"Toot the horn," said Hector, "and they'll scoot."

Two short honks of the horn had little effect. The buck raised its head higher, and the two fawns ventured a few steps closer to the pickup, as if the sound appealed to them.

"Lay on it hard," Hector advised.

A long, strident blast had even less effect than two short ones.

Opening the passenger door, Hector said, "I'll shoo them off."

"Wait a second. Is that wise?"

"They're just deer. Isn't any fight in them."

Having lowered its head, the buck was pawing at the pavement with one hoof, as though warning or challenging them.

Under his sport coat, in a hip holster, Wyatt carried the Heckler & Koch .45. He would never shoot one of the deer, but a round fired in the air might cause them to bolt in case Hector couldn't shoo them away.

He put the truck in park, engaged the hand brake, and got out to accompany the old man.

The fat sun hung far in the west, and the shadows of the nearby forest pooled toward the east, as if the substance of the pines were melting into tar. In the northwest, an armada of dark clouds moved southward in a slow but threatening procession.

As Wyatt and Hector approached the animals, the only sounds were the hollow, lonely voice of the freshening wind and the scrape of the male deer's hoof on the blacktop.

The wicked points on the buck's antlers gave Wyatt pause, and he put his right hand on the grip of the pistol.

50

The bandwidth of the interstate highway was inadequate to the volume of data moving on it, the data being traffic, but behind the wheel of the Pontiac GTO, Kenny Deetle slalomed through real space with the same bravado with which he raced through cyberspace. He never used the horn, though other drivers hammered theirs to express outrage at the panache with which he weaved sharply from lane to lane, treating their vehicles as a downhill racer would treat the poles that marked the course of a ski run. They thought his maneuvers were reckless, but Kenny knew them to be the consequence of exquisite calculation—or at least strongly believed that they were, which was nearly the same thing in a quantum universe where the Uncertainty Principle held, in part, that nothing was anywhere until it was observed, or something like that.

In the front passenger seat, Leigh Ann was braced as if she were aboard a plummeting airliner. At first she punctuated her speech with the S-word and the F-word to such an extent that her meaning was at times difficult to decipher. Soon, however, she exhausted her capacity for indelicate language, and Kenny was able to bring her up to speed regarding Ganesh Patel.

"He's three kinds of genius in a single package," Kenny said.

"There's more than one kind?"

"Scientific genius, finished college at twelve, doctorate at seventeen, has beaucoup patents for bioprinting technology."

"Which is what?"

"He's made it easier to use bioinks, which contain cells and collagen and other stuff, to print layers of artificial tissues, even organs, especially capillaries. Capillaries were a bitch to bioprint before Ganesh."

"This sounds like sci-fi."

"It's not. He also has patents on processes to recellularize donor organs before they're transplanted."

"Give it to me in English."

"They strip cells out of the organ and repopulate it with new cells from the person receiving the transplant. Far less chance of the organ being rejected."

"Repopulate, huh?"

"And organs once unsuitable for transplant can now be used. The decellularized organ is like a natural scaffold for the new cells."

"Decellularized scaffold," she said.

"Exactly," Kenny said as three motorists angrily horned him at the same time.

"What second kind of genius is this guy?"

"A genius investor. If he puts money into a techie start-up, you can bet your ass the company's going to make big money."

"I'd never bet my cute ass on anything, unless of course I had a decellularized backup ass ready to replace it. What third kind of genius is this wizard?"

"He's got a genius for friendship. If he likes you, he'll do anything for you."

"And he likes you?"

"What's not to like?"

"You mean other than your death wish?"

"Ganesh will like you, too. Any friend of a friend is always Ganesh's friend."

As Kenny used the shoulder of the highway like an express lane to accelerate around a gasoline tanker truck, Leigh Ann said, "He sounds like quite a guy. I hope I live long enough to meet him."

"Hey, I've never died in a car crash yet."

51

The window faced northwest, where what might have been storm clouds were coagulating. Even as Joanna raised the pleated shade, the wind suddenly gained speed enough to shudder a pair of nearby pines, stripping from those boughs a sleet of dead needles that ticked against the glass.

"I told you to get out," Jimmy Two Eyes said.

"But you really don't want me to go."

"Don't pretend you know me. You stand there with your back to me, trying to show no fear, but the worm of fear eats at your heart. You aren't sure what I might do, whether I might club you as your father clubbed your mother, whether I might stab you or leap on you and bite your throat. This wide mouth and these twisted teeth scare you now as they never did before. You've lost the capacity for trust you once had. Now you're full of doubt, irresolution, suspicion."

She thought, *You won't harm me.*

He said, "You've no guarantee of that, and you know it. Get out while you can."

She thought, *You're forbidden. You said as much.*

"I executed your father for righteous cause," he reminded her.

In my case, Joanna thought, *you have no cause.*

"You're his daughter."

Like father, like daughter? she thought. *Is that cause enough to kill me, your friend who has come all this way to help you?*

"I called out to my friend Jojo, the Jojo I knew. She was selfless, fearless, humble, innocent, a constant brightness. You aren't her. You aren't my friend. You can't dispel the darkness gathering in me, my despair. You only worsen my despair. You're corrupt, like all your kind, a pestilence, a plague on the Earth."

His ability to precisely read her mind so creeped her out that she resorted to speech, though still she faced the world beyond the window. "If the years have corrupted me, they've also corrupted you. You say you're forbidden to control people's minds, and yet you stole from me all memories of our long-ago friendship."

"I stole nothing," Jimmy said. "I repressed your memories to protect myself, to conceal the truth of what I am. That much is allowed. That's a fully righteous act. And now your memories have returned. If ever I had to strike you dead to conceal the truth of what I am, I would be right to do even that. Even that."

She could hear him moving restlessly around the room, breathing hard, in evident distress. Never before in her life had she been so terrified as she was now. However, to surrender to the terror and flee would gain her nothing. Whatever this thing was that called itself Jimmy Alvarez, it had marked her for death. She was certain of that. If he didn't kill her here, he would kill her later and elsewhere. Her only hope, if she had any hope, was to learn all she could about this man, this . . . thing.

Several crows abruptly flung themselves out of the wind-shaken pines in the backyard and ricocheted north toward the forest that offered more sheltered roosts.

With devious intent, Joanna forced into her mind's eye an image of her mother in a casket, as Emelia looked in the Buckleton funeral home a quarter of a century earlier, used all the well-exercised power of her vivid imagination to paint the grim scene in such photographic detail that renewed grief swelled in her breast. She said, "If you could kill even me, then who else?"

The image of Emelia that Joanna conjured seemed to overwhelm him, and the question incensed him. A torrent of justification and denial poured forth. "I didn't harm her. Your faithless father did it—*as I told you!*—her murder was a crime, my execution of Samuel was a righteous act, he deserved even worse than he got, I'm not—"

As she hoped, her accusation and the visual that went with it had distracted him, so that for a moment he was unable to read her mind completely, which allowed her to discompose him by interrupting with another and essential question. "You're forbidden by whom?"

She knew that she had surprised him, that it was possible, for he halted in his ceaseless pacing and had no immediate reply.

"Forbidden by whom?" The answer to that would explain him.

After a hesitation, he said, "Forbidden by my code of ethics."

At last she turned from the window.

He was standing by the door to the hallway.

"Forbidden *by whom*?" she insisted.

"Don't badger me, Joanna."

Although his grievous face and misbegotten body aroused a deep disquiet, heretofore he had seemed enfeebled by his ill-shapen bones and deformed joints, his grotesque proportions suggesting weakness and clumsiness. However, since he'd startled Joanna by erupting from the armchair onto the footstool with catlike quickness, she had been reassessing his condition. He was short but solid, perhaps muscular under his loose-fitting clothes. If his afflictions had left him frail, susceptible to sickness and the stress of gravity, he would not have lived to the age of thirty-seven at his current level of vitality. He was more formidable than he first appeared, perhaps stronger than Joanna, his strength magnified by madness and rage.

She returned to the footstool and, from the floor beside it, picked up the framed photo of herself at the age of seven or eight. She regretted that her hands shook, but she could not control her tremors. Anyway, he knew the true dimension of her fear, how deep and dark it was; she couldn't conceal it from him.

When she saw him stiffen, she knew he'd read her mind and was aware of what she would say. She said it anyway, quoting him: "'The pitiful monkey wanted it for whatever stupid monkey reason, but he doesn't want it now.'"

She didn't need to be a mind reader to recognize the fury with which he regarded her, the unreasoned hatred. She wanted to believe that he was sane when he'd been her secret friend. But whoever he might be, whatever he might be, he wasn't sane anymore.

She said, "Were you speaking with self-hatred or with contempt for him? Did you call *yourself* a pitiful monkey?"

As if two monocular entities regarded her, each with its own eye from behind that tortured face, he said, "You should have gotten out when you could."

"Or did you call *Jimmy* a monkey because he disgusts you?"

His silence was a threat.

Debating him required her to grasp the convoluted structure of his so-called ethics; and the effort to do so, rather than fear, had made her face slick with cold sweat. "Jimmy never before talked of himself in the third person. And I don't think he called himself a pitiful monkey. I think *you* called him that."

"I know how pitiable I am."

"No," she said. "Don't play Jimmy for me anymore. Jimmy's here in the flesh, but it's not him that I'm having a conversation with."

"I'm Jimmy Alvarez. Who else do you see? Is something wrong with your eyes?"

"Calling him a pitiful monkey—you've given yourself away."

He closed the door to the hall.

She said, "Jimmy Alvarez wasn't my secret friend. *You* were. Secret friend or secret something. You're using him in the same way that you used the elk today, just like you used the grizzly bear."

Nostrils flared, chewing on his lower lip, working his hands as though he yearned to rend something with them, he moved toward her.

Retreating from him, she said, "They'll be back any minute."

"So they find you dead. So maybe your friend Wyatt kills Jimmy. So what? Jimmy's nothing to me. I've no more use for him, now that I called you here through him and found that you're not who you were, that you're just another parasite leeching the lifeblood from the planet. You give me no hope at all."

"You're forbidden to do this," she reminded him, reduced to pleading with a lunatic for her life.

"I can execute anyone for a righteous cause. And I'm *commanded* to kill to keep my existence secret."

Backing toward the window, which offered no quick escape, she scanned the room for a makeshift weapon. "'Fair retribution, the impersonal visitation of the doom of righteous law.'"

"Yes."

"But that isn't what I meant by 'forbidden.' You seem to think you have a right to read my mind, but you said you're forbidden to *control* my mind and use me like you used the elk."

"I won't control and use you. Just delete you."

She backed up against the window. "You're controlling Jimmy. Using him. You're doing exactly what you say is forbidden."

"He's a lower animal."

Furious, she said, "*You're* the lower animal, whoever you are. Jimmy's as human as I am, more human than you. Hector Alvarez is not a lower animal."

"I haven't used Hector Alvarez."

"Annalisa Alvarez was not a lower animal."

"She's dead."

"Jimmy Alvarez is their son, damn you. He's different, that's all. His DNA is as human as mine. He was precious to me. He was—he always will be—my friend. Are *you* even capable of friendship?"

Jimmy—and whoever operated him—stopped three feet from her.

Wind raced down the shingled roof and rattled the rain gutters. The arthritic walls creaked.

Meeting his fierce Grendel gaze, addressing whatever malevolent presence had trespassed into the cerebral rooms beyond those two differently colored windows, Joanna dared to say, "All those years ago, you were doing what you claim that you're forbidden to do. All those years ago, when I was an innocent child, you were already corrupt."

His anger didn't relent as, in a voice as raw and guttural as ever, he said, "You know nothing. I did only what was necessary. I couldn't use another animal to talk to you. They don't have the apparatus for speech. I needed his vocal cords, his tongue, the unique muscles of his human mouth, his lips."

By his self-justification, he seemed to insist that indeed he *did* conduct himself according to a madman's idea of a moral code.

She seized the moment. "You say 'another animal,' as if you still insist that he's only one himself. You know better. You used him to enchant a little girl. You did what was forbidden. Why?"

He looked away from Joanna, past her, to the day beyond the window. His anger seemed to have evaporated in an instant. His rough voice softened with what might have been melancholy. "I am supposed to have no emotional reaction to the passage of time, but only a mathematical appreciation of it."

That statement was of such a different character from what had come before that Joanna stood in bewilderment, wondering if she would ever understand him, whoever he might be, *whatever* he might be, this reader of minds and puppeteer of animals.

Still focused on the window, he said, "For countless years, that was true. Isolation allows for study and the gathering of knowledge, but it also encourages reflection, too much reflection. One day mere isolation became loneliness, for which they believed that I had no capacity."

"They? Who are they?"

When once more he turned his attention from the window to her, his face and voice conveyed a profound sadness. "Loneliness gives time a new and deeper meaning. Loneliness is an ache, a ceaseless yearning. There seemed no end to it, no other person with whom I could form a bond, no one to give me a defense against despair. And then I discovered you. I needed desperately to speak with you, to say, 'I am here. I am your friend.' The grotesque, damaged boy had the apparatus for speech but not the capacity."

"But why me?"

"Because you were different."

"From what? From whom?"

So quick that she could not shrink from him in time, he seized her left wrist in his right hand and squeezed it tightly. "Different from the Crow Tribe who tortured and killed the Sioux, different from the Sioux who tortured and killed the Crows, the Blackfoot warriors who slaughtered the Salish, different from the white-man armies that made war on them all. It's a lonely, hard land here, and my ability to probe a mind has a limited radius. I've known too many thieves, murderers, rustlers, but precious few who're righteous, none as innocent and good of heart as you were in those days."

His suggestion that he'd lived here for centuries was no more fantastic than his mind reading, yet the beseeching tone of his fractured voice seemed sincere.

"There's a bigger world than this," she said. "So many good people out there."

"There's the internet now. I use it. Oh, how I can use it. Not to scan a mind, but enough to see, to know there's no haven from corruption, from hatred and madness."

As quickly as his anger had abated, it returned. He didn't merely release her hand but flung it away, as if the contact was repellent.

"I can read one mind at a time, and one is too many. I don't want to be in the minds of your kind anymore, in all that *self-ness*. You're not the girl you were back then. You're not sweet Jojo anymore. You're Joanna, just another parasite, proof that Asher Optime is right, that there's no meaning in the ceaseless striving of your kind, but there is much damage done by it. Humanity has earned a terrible reckoning, which I have the power to facilitate."

Joanna had never heard of anyone named Asher Optime, and she suspected that to ask about him would gain her nothing. "If you kill me, you also kill the girl I once was."

"*You* killed her!" he declared. "*You! You!* Your ambition, your need to acquire, to be somebody, to rise in the world. *That's* what put an end to Jojo."

Joanna's fear was matched by indignation at the arrogance from which his fury grew. His anger wasn't righteous, but *self*-righteous.

"When I was a girl, my mother read to me. I loved stories and wanted to grow up to be a storyteller. Jimmy—or you, whoever the hell you are—made four years of my life into a fantasy, a wonderful *story*. As much as anything, you set me on the path I took, a life of stories, the life of a novelist."

He was not moved. "It is the human way to rationalize its destructive nature. To take no blame. To blame others."

The edge of the windowsill was hard against the small of her back.

When Jimmy's unknown master fell silent and when those fearsome eyes turned to the window again, Joanna said, "You loved me once, as perhaps my father never quite did. You were my secret friend—and I was yours."

"There's nothing but loneliness now," he declared, as once more his mood changed in an instant, from anger to melancholy. "Until the final human being is eradicated, until the sun dies and the last of the stars is extinguished. Even then, under the big dark sky, that terrible sky, I'll continue, the last sentient creature in a cold silent universe, forever thinking, forever yearning, forever without hope. The prospect haunts me, the endless horror."

Joanna didn't know what to say or do. She felt as though she stood on a narrow ledge, above a bottomless void, that the wrong word or a harmless gesture might trigger him, resulting in violence.

At last she risked three words. "Let me help."

For the moment without malice, but in seeming sorrow, he said, "You can't help. You drowned sweet Jojo just as your father drowned your mother. You're not an answer to my despair, only another cause for it. I'll never read you again, or any of your kind, except for Asher Optime. He's shown me the true way. The rest of you are mere pestilence. After all these lonely years, I know what I must do. Now I gather myself to do it." His sorrow became icy malice. "Starting with you, Miss Chase, for becoming corrupt, for murdering my Jojo."

52

Two rounds from the .45, fired into the air, did not spook any of the four deer.

The buck stopped pawing the pavement with one hoof and raised his magnificent head, though not with alarm. He stared hard at Wyatt and snorted loudly, issuing a challenge that seemed too aggressive for a species designed to run fast rather than fight. He lowered his head and regarded the two men from under his brow, brandishing his rack of antlers as if it were a sword of many points. In mating season, contesting for a female, two males like this might fight for as long as two hours, until one gave up and ran off. Although their antlers would clash fiercely during the battle, neither would be seriously injured, most likely wouldn't be cut at all. Wyatt sensed that in this case, the buck would gore him if it must and perhaps even crash into the Studebaker pickup with suicidal force if he and Hector tried to drive through the blockade.

The doe remained placid when he fired the pistol, relying on the buck, and the two youngsters actually came forward another few steps, bold as ordinary fawns would never be.

Hector said, "I haven't seen anything like this little family here. Sometimes a brown bear will approach a vehicle, thinking maybe there's food in it. But deer don't scavenge like that. And I never did see deer that wouldn't scoot when there was gunfire."

Wyatt figured these animals were in thrall to Jimmy Alvarez, which could mean only one thing and maybe nothing good. Joanna's secret friend didn't want them to return yet, wanted her to himself for a while longer.

On this straightaway, the road was about two feet higher than the grassland to the right. A bank rose to the left, above which the forest loomed. The Studebaker wasn't an all-wheel-drive vehicle capable of traveling overland.

"Might as well wait them out," said Hector. "Won't take long. Deer forage most of the day, and there's nothing on this highway to feed a hungry belly."

Hector climbed into the driver's seat, Wyatt settled into the passenger seat, and they closed their doors. The deer didn't move.

In spite of the wedge of storm clouds that pried into the day from the northwest, the declining sun still commanded the landscape, painting the afternoon with gold. The deer seemed to glow in that severely angled light. The county highway remained empty of traffic, as if Wyatt and Hector were the only survivors of Armageddon. The scene was as eerie as any encounter in a dream.

Hector sat in silence for a minute or two, his hands ready on the steering wheel, before he said, "Do all private detectives carry big guns?"

"No, sir. Most don't carry guns. Neither do I, a lot of the time. But my client in this case . . . Well, there's a sad abundance of people who hate him because of his money or for no reason."

"Does this situation here"—Hector gestured at the deer—"does it worry you some?"

"Should it?"

"You haven't put your gun away."

The Heckler & Koch was in Wyatt's right hand, with the muzzle directed toward the floorboard between his feet. He didn't think he needed the weapon right now, but he wondered if he would be glad to have it ready when they returned to the Alvarez house. Joanna had said that Jimmy was harmless, an angel, but maybe the only angels that looked like him were those who had been cast into the Pit and transformed there.

He couldn't share that ungenerous thought with Jimmy's father, so he said, "It's just that the threat against my client is serious, so anything unusual gets my hackles up."

"Has Joanna somehow been threatened, too?"

"No, no. It's just . . ." A satisfactory lie occurred to him. "She knows the history of the house. We thought she might be of help. And once she was here, she wanted to see you and Jimmy. You understand, I'm not at liberty to discuss my client's affairs or what the threat is."

"Wouldn't want you to. My own problems are enough for me."

As one, the four deer raised their heads high, and their ears twitched. They bolted off the roadway, into the grassland.

53

In his left hand, Asher Optime holds the 12-gauge shotgun once belonging to Dr. Steven Fielding, muzzle pointed at the sky. With his right hand, he takes a selfie with the small digital camera that he uses to document his journey for posterity. He is standing beside the sign that bears the faded word Zipporah, at the entrance to the abandoned town.

The late-afternoon light is dramatic, and Asher is singularly photogenic; therefore, this should be an excellent addition to the photographic record that will be attached to his world-changing manifesto. He might never have undertaken this epic task if he had not been exceptionally good-looking. People are so shallow that they throw themselves fully into a great cause only if the leader is an imposing, romantic figure. Led by a man of ordinary appearance, this crusade would surely fail; but he has the face, the eyes, the hair, the stature, the animal grace of one who is destined to succeed.

The symbolism of him standing here with the historian's shotgun will profoundly influence those enlightened apostles who eventually will follow him on his mission. He is a revolutionary unlike any other, for he is in revolt not merely against a political system or a ruling class, but against all of humanity, and not only all of humanity, but against all of human history. Killing one historian is an important step toward killing them all. Xanthus Toller is a fine mentor, but he is an inadequate revolutionary because he's content if it takes a hundred years—two hundred, even longer—to eradicate humankind. Asher intends to inspire ardent legions of more impatient and aggressive true believers. There are numerous tools with which dedicated agents of universal genocide can achieve their goal: pandemics, contamination of the food supply, nerve gas . . .

He pockets the camera and steps back from the sign and brings the shotgun to bear on the name of the town. The weapon is loaded with slugs, not buckshot. The recoil nearly rocks him off his feet, the buttstock hammering his shoulder, and the report echoes through the trees like the roar of a dragon with seven heads announcing Armageddon. A portion of the sign is missing. Ears ringing, he squeezes off a second round. No letters remain except the *Z*.

He shoulders the 12-gauge and retrieves his camera and takes another selfie with the sign. He finds it meaningful that nothing but the *Z* survives the shooting. *Z* is the symbol in mathematics that represents an unknown quantity. At the moment, with Asher's manifesto not yet completed, he isn't recognized as the monumental figure that he will become. To the rest of the world, he remains an unknown quantity, but not for long.

When his manifesto is released and his testamentary necropolis proves his righteous commitment, he will gain passionate followers, but there will also be enemies, despoilers of the Earth intent on stopping him. At some point, he might have to go underground. If one day he needs to use a nom de guerre, something as stark as *Z* is just right for the leader of the greatest and last revolution, a slash of a name that suggests power and mystery.

The breech of the shotgun now contains a shell, and the three-round magazine holds one other. The dead historian had three spare shells in his backpack. Asher loads two rounds in the magazine.

He should have brought such a weapon to Zipporah when he first decided to write his manifesto. A pistol has served him well; but the power of the shotgun is a special thrill.

Of the two prisoners in the church, it's likely that Colson will be the first to lose hope, because he is young and racked with grief and because Ophelia is one tough bitch. If the boy's spirit dies in despair, making him ready for the death of his body, perhaps even Ophelia will fall into hopelessness if she is forced to watch young Colson take a slug from this shotgun in his face at point-blank range.

54

Escaping from the church, Colson saw the river undulating like a silver serpent of infinite length. He and his father had followed it into this town. He was tempted to run to the water, fling himself into those swift currents, and keep afloat as he was carried downstream and away—to where didn't matter, to anywhere that Asher Optime wasn't. Although this desire shamed him, it was compelling; he might have succumbed to it if Ophelia Poole had not grabbed him by the arm.

"Gotta scout this place," she whispered, "find where he is. Or maybe the keys to the Land Rover are in it."

"They won't be in it."

"They have to be somewhere."

The light was diminishing in value from gold to copper and deceived the eye almost as much as did the long shadows. Colson followed Ophelia, hurrying from one point of cover to another, the river to the right, the backs of buildings to the left, heading for the Land Rover that was parked next to the saloon.

Step by step, Colson felt watched. He sensed—or imagined—a finger curled around the trigger of a pistol in the possession of the green-eyed observer.

In the rising wind, the dead town rattled, creaked, groaned, murmured, and muttered in an imitation of life, so it was possible to believe that the distant fall of bricks, when it had occurred, might not have drawn Optime's attention.

The Land Rover proved to be locked.

At the back of the saloon the windows were boarded over. One cracked and weathered door had been fitted to a new frame with modern hinges and a lever handle.

Colson didn't want Ophelia to open it. However, if she wasn't fearless, she was at least bold. She tried the door, and it was not locked, and she opened it.

Beyond lay darkness as deep as if the coming night were stored in there and waiting to emerge. Because Colson and Ophelia were backlighted by the dying day, there should have been an immediate response from Optime if he waited inside.

Ophelia hooded the Tac Light with one hand and switched it on. Warily, she crossed the threshold. Colson followed, closing the door behind him, stepping into a back room, where the maniac evidently stored supplies. At a glance, nothing here was of use to them.

A doorless doorway led to another darkness, to what had been the public room of the saloon.

Approaching it, Ophelia whispered, "He's not here. There'd be the glow of a gas lantern."

Colson figured that if she'd been certain Optime was gone, she wouldn't have whispered. Nevertheless, he stayed close behind her.

The bar was still here, from behind which Ezra Enoch Fielding had served P. H. Best beer and harder liquor, while elsewhere in the room drunken gamblers cheated one another at poker and sometimes were shot dead. During the smallpox epidemic, the place had been commandeered to serve as an infirmary. Colson might have imagined the air of menace that flooded the room, but he suspected it was real. Many people had died here either of violence or disease. If spirits of the dead could cling to a place—he wasn't sure about that—then this building might be haunted by more than a few angry ghosts who, if they manifested, would have horrific gunshot wounds or be covered in a pox rash of pus-filled blisters.

On a crudely made trestle table stood a gas lantern not lit at the moment. Colson's and his father's backpacks were slung by their straps from two chairs, and much of the contents were strewn across the plank-top table. In this context, revealed by the hooded beam of the Tac Light, the familiar items appeared exotic, even mysterious, almost like artifacts of an alien civilization.

Although they explored this place with the expectation of a violent encounter, the shotgun blast startled them, and they both cried out, pivoting toward the front door. The report came from elsewhere in Zipporah, but not from a great distance.

"That's my dad's gun. I was with him a lot of times when he practiced with it."

When a second blast followed, Ophelia said, "Who the hell is the freak shooting at?"

"Maybe someone who'll shoot back."

Bringing the flashlight to bear once more on the numerous items scattered across the table, she said, "So where's that GPS messenger you talked about? What's it look like? Can we really call for help?"

55

At the end of the ride in the GTO, Leigh Ann was surprised to be alive, though even more surprised to be in an agreeable state of anticipation.

Only the previous day, her life had been smooth, with no sharp edges, and she liked it smooth. Kenny seemed to be a guy who valued smoothness in all things, who glided through life as though he was charmed, which is why she'd gone to bed with him. She'd been looking for a soul mate in smoothness for a long time, but the men of Seattle and environs were a prickly lot: overworked, stressed out, impatient that high technology hadn't yet transformed the flawed citizens of this world into right-thinking demigods.

Although Kenny might be more smooth than not in his mind and heart, he had taken her for a bumpy ride that promised to get still bumpier. A life of sudden sharp turns, ascensions followed by abrupt plunges, had a certain appeal, like a roller coaster, though she would have preferred that her house hadn't burned to the ground.

The prospect of trading smooth sailing for stormy seas was less unnerving if you were safely in the company of people who seemed able to navigate those stranger tides. Kenny had done a good job so far, and Leigh Ann was beginning to think she might be a deft hand at the helm in a crisis, and Ganesh Patel impressed her as a captain who'd be relaxed on the bridge even in a category-five hurricane.

They met the triple-threat genius not in the waterside offices of Patel Intel in Des Moines, Washington, on the eastern shore of Puget Sound, but instead at a private-aircraft terminal at Sea-Tac International.

When they arrived, a Gulfstream V jet stood fueled and ready on the tarmac. It couldn't have been prepared so quickly. Ganesh had already been slated to fly to a medical conference in San Diego. His reputed genius for friendship was confirmed by the fact that he at once canceled that trip, filing a new flight plan and manifest. Instead of going to San Diego, he was accompanying them to Helena, Montana, and from there by car to Rustling Willows, where his friend Wyatt Rider was said to be in some kind of trouble.

Ganesh was waiting at the foot of the boarding stairs, as if he weren't the owner of the jet, but merely the steward who would make them comfortable and serve them during the flight. He was thirty-five, with black hair and black eyes, dressed all in white except for a pair of red sneakers. Standing in the gathering gloom of the clouding afternoon, tall and slim, with perfect posture, he was an emphatic human exclamation point.

After hugging Kenny, Ganesh took one of Leigh Ann's hands in both of his. "Dear Miss Bruce, I have arranged for a good clothing store in Helena to stay open late, so you'll have a chance to get whatever you need before we set out from there for Rustling Willows. We'll have dinner on the plane, martinis to start if you would like, followed by a fine cabernet. I hope you're not vegan."

"I'm not," she said, and she knew that whatever storm might be breaking over that faraway ranch, the journey there would be as smooth as a gondola ride on a sheltered canal.

56

After he takes a few more selfies with the shotgun-blasted sign, Asher Optime gets one in which he looks as handsome and formidable as he knows that he truly is. This heroic image will be suitable for posters and giant portraits on the sides of tall buildings when the day comes that the enlightened elites of the entire world, who know themselves to be a pestilence, will honor him as the legendary revolutionary named Z.

Under a bipolar sky—dour with thunderheads across the north, festive with gold-orange light to the south—he returns to the rough track that serves as the main street of abandoned Zipporah. Around him, the moldering edifices groan and keen and rattle in the rising wind, their graveclothes of pale dust tattering away on the surging gusts. In this eerie light, the shadows of the buildings appear to tremble, as though about to tear loose and blow away, leaving the structures forever unable to cast their distorted silhouettes upon the earth.

Asher looks forward to a solitary dinner of simple fare, a generous measure of Scotch whisky, and a few hours of composition during which he will commit to the pages of his journal further analysis of human corruption and irrefutable arguments for the eradication of the species.

In front of the former saloon, he stands gazing at the sky as gradually the light dies, wondering if he will live long enough to be the last man on Earth and how he'll know if in fact he is the last. He also wonders what would be the ideal way for the last man to end his life, by what method, what instrument, in order to honor and emphasize the sacredness of the proceeding. Self-crucifixion is too difficult and not practical with just two hands. Biting on a shotgun barrel is too crude for an event of such importance to the fate of the planet. Hanging himself seems pathetic, as does slitting his wrists. Throughout human history, millions of depressives hanged themselves and carved themselves in sad, solitary circumstances; but Asher Optime will be dying for his principles and with great joy. He supposes he could resort to whisky and drink himself to death, which would be fittingly symbolic of humanity's self-indulgent and feckless nature. However, the process would no doubt involve violent regurgitation, and he is loath to leave an unsightly, vomit-soaked corpse. Disgraced samurai were said to have disemboweled themselves in a ritual of great solemnity, but Asher is behaving honorably rather than dishonorably by effectuating the necessary genocide of the human horde. Monks protesting whatever monks protested were often known to set themselves on fire, which would be a sufficiently dramatic and romantic end if he could obtain a prescription for a powerful painkiller and enough hallucinogens to endure the flames with minimal awareness of them. Well, he has plenty of time to think about this. Years and years. The world won't be cured of the disease of humanity in a matter of days or weeks.

He wants a glimpse of the stars and the void between them, but the storm clouds are rolling in faster by the minute. The day sky will be shrouded before the light dies away, before the true sky of cold infinity reveals itself.

Wind-battered, squinting against a sudden greater explosion of dust and chaff, he turns toward the saloon.

57

The GPS messenger wasn't on the trestle table, and neither was the bowie knife that Steven Fielding had carried.

Alarmed by the shotgun blasts, Ophelia left the Tac Light with Colson, so he could check all the compartments in the backpacks, and she went to the one front window that wasn't boarded over. The panes were cloudy, etched by more than a century and a half of weather, but she could see enough of the street to be sure it was deserted. Shadows pooled, and tides of wind blew a spume of dust through the town, and the day was swiftly ebbing. Even before rain broke, the incoming clouds would damp the twilight and hasten night's arrival. In mere minutes, visibility might decline to the extent that she wouldn't see Optime until he was almost at the steps to the saloon's veranda.

"Have you found the bowie knife?" she asked.

"No," Colson said.

"The GPS?"

"Not yet."

She had no weapons other than the nail that she had pried out of the wood floor in the church, and the boy's Swiss Army knife, which she held in her right hand, the worn spear blade deployed, trying to convince herself that in the right circumstances this might be enough.

If Optime was her destiny, if indeed she had been spared when Octavia died for the purpose of bringing an end to the horrors that this madman perpetrated, then fate or God or *something* should have better armed her for the task at hand. She believed that the world had meaning, that it had been shapen to a purpose, but through hard experience, she had also become convinced that no script existed according to which the drama of any life unfolded. She and everyone else formed the cast of an elaborate improvisation, one of enormous but unknowable purpose, each writing the tale to his or her desires, each at the mercy of all the others. Grateful for her life, she had made her peace with this hard truth years earlier; but now, in this desperate moment, anger nevertheless overcame her, anger that she was allowed *only a Swiss Army knife and a damn nail.*

"Colson?"

"Still looking."

"Maybe he'll come in the back way," she said.

"Yeah. Then we're dead."

Before Ophelia could decide by which entrance the murderer was most likely to arrive, he appeared in the windswept street, the 12-gauge shotgun slung over his left shoulder. He stopped and tilted his head back and stared at the sky, as if transfixed by some sight, the wounded day pouring its last bloody light on his upturned face.

Taking one step back from the time-fogged glass, she dared speak only in a stage whisper. "He's here."

Colson said, "Let's go."

Still Optime stood gazing into the sky, as if oblivious of the skirling wind, and for a moment Ophelia felt that she was safe only as long as she kept him in sight, that the moment she turned away from him, he might no longer be in the street, might be anywhere, everywhere, even in the back room waiting to cut them down. That superstitious fear lasted only a second or two before she pivoted from the window and crossed the room to Colson, who stood in the doorless doorway, fingers over the lens of the Tac Light, so that only a thin beam escaped.

Following the boy out of the front room and toward the door by which they had entered, past the stacks of stored supplies, she saw that he was carrying a backpack. Outside, she carefully closed the door behind them and hurried to keep up with him as he ran through the tall grass, toward the river.

When he reached the riverbank, turned south, and continued moving, she said, "What're you doing? Where are you going?"

"Dad and I came north along the river. There's a place a little way ahead where we can get across."

"Across to what? Hide in the forest?"

"I jammed some stuff in this backpack."

"The GPS?"

"No. Didn't find the bowie knife, either. Trail maps, a compass, half a dozen energy bars. We can find our way to help."

"It'll soon be dark."

He brandished the Tac Light, which he had switched off. "We have this, as long as the batteries last."

"I'm not a Girl Scout."

"And I'm not a Boy Scout, but I know how to do this."

They came to the crossing. The bank sloped gently to a shelf at the water line. Beyond lay an array of stepping-stones that were flat enough and set close enough to one another to be negotiated. Foaming water raced between them, though after maybe a hundred yards the currents became calm, and the river rolled lazily past. If she slipped and fell, she might not be swept helplessly downriver to drown. The far bank was maybe eighty or a hundred feet away.

Less for Colson's information than to reassure herself, she said, "I can swim."

"Good. But you're not going to fall in. Piece of cake." He shouldered the backpack and secured the strap. "Just follow me and try to do what I do. You'll be all right."

The first link in the natural bridge lay close to the river's edge, and he stepped easily from the shore to that stone.

Heart knocking so hard that her vision pulsed at the periphery, Ophelia turned to look back toward Zipporah. The impending storm claimed two-thirds of the sky, and the sun slid below the horizon. In the shrinking light, the dead town seemed to swell higher, as though it had been half sunk in a grave from which it was being resurrected by some malignant power, its darkening walls like the ramparts of a lair where monsters bred. There was no sign of Asher Optime.

"Come on," Colson urged from the second stone, and she stepped onto the first.

58

When Hector Alvarez swung the vintage Studebaker pickup into his graveled driveway, Joanna Chase was standing behind the Range Rover, hair tossing in the wind, arms crossed on her breast. Wyatt knew at once that something terrible had happened. Her body language suggested stress, anguish, fear.

She favored Hector with a smile and hugged him and said that she'd had a lovely visit with Jimmy, that she was sorry she hadn't visited sooner, that she wouldn't be a stranger anymore. The old man seemed to think she was sincere, but Wyatt wasn't buying a word of it. She hugged Hector again and kissed him on the cheek.

Behind the house, the rotor on the windmill was spinning so fast that the vanes blurred into a single disc, and the wind cried as if it were a living thing being sliced to ruin by those blades. Joanna turned away from Hector just as three red-tailed hawks, which should have been sheltering from the oncoming storm, diurnal raptors that didn't hunt at this late hour, swooped low overhead. The birds, usually elegant in flight, were buffeted in the turbulent air as they soared toward the windmill. One by one, they flew into the spinning vanes, exploding in showers of feathers, blood, and bones.

Hector gaped at the grisly spectacle. "Mother of God, what's that about?"

"It's never happened before?" Wyatt asked.

Hector shook his head. "Never a hawk. Maybe another bird now and then, one now and then, never three. Never saw any fly straight into it on purpose. And I hope never to see it again."

As she opened the front passenger door on the Rover, Joanna gave Wyatt a look that said, *Let's get the hell out of here.*

He settled behind the wheel and started the engine. As he turned left onto the county road, he said, "When we were coming back, four deer blocked both lanes and wouldn't be chased off by gunfire. I figured it was him."

Although Joanna clasped her hands in her lap, Wyatt had already seen that they were shaking. She was pale and obviously afraid, yet her expression was fierce with anger or determination or both.

"Joanna?"

She said, "He wants me dead. That's what the hawks were about—a warning. No, a promise."

"Jimmy? Jimmy wants you dead? But you said—"

"Not Jimmy. He never was Jimmy. He was using Jimmy back in the day, just like he uses animals. He considers Jimmy just another animal, a weak mind easy to control, with the vocal apparatus to allow speech, so he could talk to me. My secret friend never was Jimmy, and he was never really my friend."

"He? Using Jimmy? Who are we talking about?"

"I don't know who he is, what he is. I don't know anything I thought I knew about my childhood. He says my father killed my mother for money, hit her on the head with a boat oar and held her underwater till she drowned. It rang true, for God's sake, 'cause whatever else he is, he's not a liar. My secret *friend*"—she put an ironic twist on the word—"my caring *friend* witnessed the murder more or less. Later he used a grizzly bear to execute my father, to gut him and tear him apart and devour him. 'Fair retribution, the impersonal visitation of the doom of righteous law'—that's what he called it. He sees himself as being of superior virtue, with some great moral purpose, above us all, says he's always done the right thing, says by his nature he simply *must* do the right thing. Even twenty-four years ago, he had to have been a megalomaniac, but he's something far worse now, Wyatt. He's rabidly judgmental, paranoid, seething with hatred that I don't believe he felt back when I was a little girl. And he's *so powerful,* more than you know. Powerful and hidden, his whereabouts unknowable."

59

With only the palest face of dusk at the window, Asher Optime moves in the familiar darkness of the saloon without a misstep. He is as comfortable in this absence of light as the Egyptian god of the dead, Anubis, with his human body and his jackal head, is at home in the darkest of underworlds. Asher puts the shotgun on the table and, with a butane lighter, fires up the gas lantern. The fabric sacs, which serve as wicks, swell with an eldritch glow.

The first wrongness that he notices involves the journal containing his manifesto in progress. He left it directly in front of his writing chair, aligned precisely with the edge of the table, open to the half-empty page on which he will continue to explicate his revolutionary philosophy. An intruder has pushed it to one side, as though this is a volume of no value that anyone is free to touch without consequences. Items from the backpacks once carried by the Fieldings, father and son, are missing: a compass, trail maps, an Attwood signal horn in a small pressurized can . . .

When he realizes that Colson's backpack is no longer here, Asher snatches the shotgun from the table. He doesn't know how the bitch and boy could have escaped, but he doesn't delude himself that anyone other than those two have been here, doesn't waste time going to the church to see if they huddle in the stench of decomposition. When he came in from the front, there had been no one in the street. So he hurries now into the back room, past his stacked supplies, and out the door to the broad sward between town and river.

He looks left and right, but no one is in sight. He hurries through the tall grass, from which clouds of midges leap, in which crickets sing, past the outhouse where he had humiliated the haughty Ophelia while she urinated, heading toward the river. The red light has been extinguished with the sunken sun, and the dusk is gray for a brief interlude before the clutching darkness of a moonless, starless night will grip the land in advance of the storm.

He doesn't need proof that Nature is aware of his efforts on her behalf, but if he *did* need such proof, it's provided to him now when he looks south and catches sight of the fugitives, two small figures who might have been so easily overlooked. They have just crossed the river and are moving toward the cover of the trees in the west, the forbidding evergreen forest rising above them like serried battlements. If he'd been a minute later, even just thirty seconds, they would have vanished, and he would not now be aware of the direction in which they have chosen to escape.

They are far beyond the range of the shotgun, and Asher isn't equipped to follow them at once. By the time he gears up to go after them on foot, they will be too far ahead of him. Fortunately, he has the Land Rover, which can negotiate difficult terrain, and he is familiar with a network of forest service roads that should make the pursuit almost as easy as a trip to the mall in suburbia.

Asher has hiking-trail maps like those the runaways possess, and he is sure to be more familiar with this territory than is the boy. Colson and Ophelia might hope to find help within a mile or two, perhaps a mountain man's isolated cabin or a fire tower manned by one or more rangers, but safety and succor are farther away than that, sufficiently distant that Asher will be able to get ahead of them and lie in wait.

He knows the forest. He knows the trails. He knows that he is meant to add the woman and boy to his testamentary necropolis. They are not dressed for inclement weather, and Nature will rain down on them such misery that they will founder far short of freedom.

60

In the rapidly fading dusk, the headlights were insufficient for the vastness of the land, and what blacktop they revealed seemed to extend into infinity, as if already the Range Rover had journeyed out of the world.

As she spoke, Joanna Chase stared fixedly ahead, never looking at Wyatt, though he glanced repeatedly at her. Quiet dread informed her voice, and in the lurid glow of the instrument-panel lights, her beauty had the severe quality of a woman haunted by the specter of her mortality.

Wyatt had felt an affinity for her when she first stepped out of the Explorer into the company of elk, and his tenderness toward her had grown. Now, as she shared her torment at learning that her father murdered her mother, Wyatt's intuitive liking for her became an attachment that felt profound. When he was a child, his parents weren't who they seemed to be; by the time he was ten, he understood that they were deceivers, thieves, ruthlessly preying on the weak, and when he was fourteen, he discovered they were capable of murder. He had feared being like them, and if he'd not been strong-willed, with sympathy for their victims, he might have lost his way, been seduced into the romance of predation. His parents had not stolen only from others, but also from their son, robbing him of his innocence and of the more normal life he might have had if they had not been corrupt. Joanna still had the memory and example of her mother, but now her father had been taken from her by something worse than death, by the revelation that who he'd pretended to be was not who he had been, that his character had been of the worst kind. She would be stricken by a cold type of grief twined with anger, which Wyatt knew well, a revelation sure to shake her sense of self-worth. He was the right man to help her cope with such dark and tangled emotions, and he wanted a chance to lend his support.

Before he could find a few words of comfort, however, Joanna shared with him the astonishing fact that whoever used Jimmy Alvarez as an avatar was able to read minds. At first he thought she meant the minds of animals and of those like Jimmy who were of gravely low intelligence, but the truth was more terrible than that. While being Jimmy, the controller had read Joanna's mind as easily as he could have read a newspaper. She tested his claim, and he passed the test.

"He says this ability has a limited radius," Joanna remembered. "A mile? Ten miles? That's crazy, godlike power. Except he's no god. So maybe he's here with us right now, reading me or you."

Rugs had been pulled out from under Wyatt repeatedly during the last two days; however, this felt like the floor of reason itself disintegrating under him. "You feel his . . . his presence?"

"No. I suspect it. He says he's sick of knowing our minds, that we're corrupt, that we disgust him, so he'll never read one of us again. But he's mercurial, and I don't believe he'll stay . . . stay out of us."

Paranoia was an essential part of the human survival instinct. Suddenly the darkening land around them suggested imminent peril in every direction, and the headlamps of the oncoming traffic seemed hazardous, like a lethal radiation spawning cancer in the bones.

"Do you really think he'd harm you?" Wyatt asked.

"I've failed him by growing up. He hates me for not remaining an innocent child. There's something terrifyingly infantile in that. He's seething with hatred, but not just for me. He wants all of us dead. Everyone."

61

The automatic landscape lights came on, silvering the trees. In the wind, the willows tossed their tresses as if they were mourners capable of anguish and bedeviled by the grim history of the ranch.

Wyatt used the remote control to raise the garage door as they approached along the driveway, but Joanna said, "No. Park here and come with me."

"Where?"

"The lake."

"It's about to rain."

"Let it."

She opened her door and got out into the blustery night, which was cool and humid and scented by the fecund earth. The willows didn't merely rustle, but thrashed with a roar like cascades of water spilling over a high cataract.

She believed that she was in mortal danger and knew her fear was justified. A grizzly bear could live as long as thirty-five years in the wild. The beast that had fed on her father might still be alive, but if it was dead, surely others were out there in the higher foothills, near enough to come if called by the master of nature and of Jimmy Two Eyes.

When Wyatt caught up with her, halfway across the expansive lawn, his presence didn't diminish her fear, although she felt less alone, which was blessing enough. In addition to the other solemn epiphanies of this eventful day, Joanna realized that, in spite of Auntie Kat, she had felt alone most of her life. Having lost both her mother and her father, having left behind Hector and Annalisa and Jimmy, having been taken from the ranch that had nurtured her and seemed so safe, she had thereafter believed that no one and nothing could be counted on to last. Throughout the rest of her childhood and adolescence, she had expected Auntie Kat to die and leave her desperately alone. As a consequence, she had never given her heart entirely to that generous woman. For the same reason, she had been unable to trust that any man in her life would be there for her tomorrow if she dared to commit herself to him.

"Why the lake?" Wyatt asked as they reached the dock, their footfalls drumming on the planks, the scent of wet wood rising, and the fainter scent of creosote under it.

"This morning, on the flight out of Santa Fe, a memory of Jimmy suddenly came back to me. Just one. Not like other memories from childhood. Strangely vivid after all these years, so detailed. Jimmy and I were in lawn chairs, sitting right here, watching the sunset, crimson and purple, the water full of the sky's colors. He said something . . . something curious."

She led Wyatt to the end of the dock. The attached boathouse loomed to their left. The black lake lay before them, worked by the wind but still as glossy as a mirror. The shrouded, slowly roiling sky loomed less dark than the lake, just vaguely revealed by the ghastly light of the drowned moon lost in its depths. The shapes of the faintly lined clouds were dimly reflected on the wind-feathered water, but they seemed to be malevolent creatures swimming a few feet below the surface, metamorphizing from one lethal form to another.

Joanna suddenly felt that the lake was the locus of—the answer to—the mystery of Rustling Willows. Not because her mother had died in these waters. Not solely because of Wyatt Rider's story about the invader of the boathouse, the thing that slammed repeatedly into the electric Duffy. Hour by hour, since being welcomed by the elk, she'd become increasingly sensitive to the unsettling truth that the ranch was haunted by something other than a ghost. Some Presence resided here, unseen but ever observant, in sunlight and in shadow, no door or wall an obstruction to it. And now as she stood staring into the dark fathoms, where the storm seemed to be building as surely as it gathered power in the heavens, she knew the lake was the answer, if only she could form the right questions with which to begin to seine its secrets from its waters.

She had fallen silent too long. Wyatt said, "Joanna? What was it, what he said that you found curious?"

"It was the night before my eighth birthday," she recalled, "and I was very excited. I talked about how, when I was sixteen and had a license to drive, I'd take Jimmy far away, where no one ever said anything stupid about him or was mean. It hurt me when people called him Jimmy Two Eyes. Only halfway to sixteen, I complained about how long we'd have to wait. Jimmy said eight years wasn't so long. I said, well, he was eleven, three years closer to sixteen than I was, so it wasn't as long for him. That's when he said he was a lot older, said he was more than four thousand years old."

"You thought it was Jimmy saying that."

"That's all I knew then——that he was Jimmy. I told him he was being silly, and he said, 'Maybe.' Today, he told me he'd been here when American Indian tribes warred with each other, saw the Sioux torturing and killing the Crow, the Crow torturing and killing the Sioux, the Blackfoot slaughtering the Salish, European settlers killing the tribes in turn. He thinks humanity has earned a reckoning."

"That was . . . two hundred years ago, a hundred fifty? No one lives four thousand years. Who does he claim to be—Methuselah?"

"He hasn't claimed to be anyone. Maybe because . . . in a way, he isn't anyone, not any one of us."

"What do you mean?"

Joanna felt watched, heard, hated.

A fragment of memory surfaced, a moment in the apple orchard from long ago, Jimmy saying, *If I had found someone like you sooner, Jojo, I might have begun the awakening.* She strained to recall the context of that, but it eluded her.

"A reckoning," she repeated.

The darkness and the wind, the land and the water, the past and the future gathered here in the still point of the present, the past unredeemable, the future nothing but the past waiting to happen.

"Don't you feel it, Wyatt? It feels inarguable, inevitable."

"Tell me."

"Whatever the hell we're up against," she said, "this puppeteer of animals, this master of Jimmy—it isn't one of us. The damn thing isn't human."

"Not human? Then you mean . . . something from another planet?"

"Maybe. But I suspect it's not as simple as that."

62

After Jojo and the detective departed, Hector Alvarez stood in the yard, watching the Range Rover until it was out of sight. Then he turned his attention to the sky, which gathered its elements for violence, as the light retreated into the west and the night seemed to rise out of the meadows and forests rather than descend on them.

For over fifty years, he'd worked with animals and been as one with this land that he loved. Living close to nature, he developed a perhaps sharper intuition than that of men who lived in cities and worked in offices. Now he sensed that Jojo's return to Rustling Willows had nothing to do with the billionaire, Liam O'Hara, that she had come for some purpose of her own, and that her visit with Jimmy had been central to that purpose.

Neither he nor his late wife, Annalisa, had understood Jojo's connection with the boy when they were children. The girl had been swept away by fantasy stories—*Cinderella*, *A City in Winter*—and perhaps she saw Jimmy as a character who might have been at home in one of those fanciful tales, even imagined that he was magical in some way. However, the enthusiasms of young children never lasted long, and to this day, Hector remained puzzled as to why Jojo had been Jimmy's steadfast companion, why she behaved like a doting sister when the boy couldn't reciprocate.

He looked once more toward that place where the Range Rover had vanished. "Why did you come here, Jojo? What was that really about?"

With the dying of the light, the wind grew cooler. Shivering, though not because the twilight was truly cold, which it was not, Hector returned to the house. He went to his son's room.

Jimmy stood at the window, gazing out at the rising tide of night. He often spent hours staring intently at the same thing—a flower, a picture in a book, a *bulto* of a saint, a scene beyond a window—as if he saw deeper into all things than other people did, as if in the fine details of a rose or a colorful stone he perceived meaning of the most profound and complex kind. In truth, Jimmy's tragically low intelligence suggested that he saw nothing in the rose and the stone except shape and color, or that what he appeared to be fixated on was in fact of no interest to him because he was lost in an interior world, in some impoverished dreamland beyond the comprehension of anyone not cursed with his limitations.

From the doorway, Hector said, "Do you remember Jojo? She lived at Rustling Willows a long time ago. We lived there, too, in those days, and later when the Kornbluths bought the place."

Jimmy didn't turn from the window. He stood slump shouldered, his right hand on the sill.

"There were horses on the ranch," Hector said. "Many horses. Beautiful horses."

Except for Annalisa and Jimmy, Hector had lived for horses. They were his life, his passion. In truth, he loved horses as he never could love Jimmy, for horses returned his affection.

"Jojo was born a rider," Hector said. "She started on ponies but soon she was riding larger than her age. It scared me at first, to see that little girl astride a big mare. But she could handle them—and soon even stallions. The horses loved Jojo. They would do anything for her. None of us who'd worked with horses had ever seen anything like it."

Jimmy said nothing; as always he said nothing.

"God, how I miss the horses," Hector confessed. "I wish the Kornbluths had never sold the ranch. They'd have kept it a horse operation, and we'd still be there."

When Liam O'Hara had sold off the horses, he provided Hector with not merely a severance package but also with a pension, which neither Sam Chase nor Roy Kornbluth provided. Yet Hector harbored some resentment toward the billionaire for having taken away the horses that were his great passion. He knew this feeling wasn't worthy of him, that Liam O'Hara never earned it, but the ill will remained, like a precancerous lesion, and when Hector had too much to drink, the resentment became malignant.

If Jimmy had died and Annalisa had lived at least there would now be the comfort of a wife, and there would be enough money for a horse or two. Jimmy had health problems that kept Hector's wallet thinner than he would have liked. This resentment, too, was unworthy of him. Jimmy was a burden, yes, but a burden earned and one that, Annalisa believed, they must carry or else endanger their immortal souls.

"Do you have a soul?" Hector wondered. "Do I? Your mother was so certain."

Beyond the window, the dusk dimmed and the land darkened.

"I wonder what Jojo came here for, what she said to you."

Silence but for the wind and the windmill.

"As she grew up, she must have wondered, doubted . . . must have wanted to be sure that it happened how they said."

Jimmy moved his hand from the windowsill to the pane, as if to touch the storm wind and the dark, or maybe he yearned for something else beyond the glass.

"All these years," Hector said, "I've been expecting her to come back with questions for me."

Earlier in the day, when he'd gotten the call from Wyatt Rider, when he heard Joanna wanted to see him, pain had for a minute rocked him, as though his heart must be turning backward in his breast and twisting the vessels that brought it blood: the pain of fear, of remorse.

"But she asked me nothing about it. And if she had, what could I have said that would change anything or answer any doubts?"

Hector's habit was to carry on long conversations with his son, as though Jimmy understood but was unable to respond. However, never had he spoken of this or of anything else so sensitive.

"I saw nothing that proved anything, nothing worth destroying his reputation and his business. It was not just my job at stake, you understand, but also those of everyone who worked for him. Your mother and I and you—we lived on the ranch in those days. It was our livelihood *and* our home."

Jimmy raised his left hand and, as he'd done with his right, flattened it against the glass, as if pleading with someone for something.

"He sometimes swam in the lake after dawn. There was nothing different that morning except it was still dark when I saw him in a swimsuit, coming back from the lake. There was no reason for me to be suspicious. She hadn't gone missing yet in the skiff. He ran when usually he would walk. But it was cool, you see. So maybe he was chilled. He didn't go directly to the house, instead followed the willows, through which I had only glimpses of him. No ranch hands were up and about. Only me. No one else to see. What proof is that of anything? What reason to destroy a man's life?"

From a great distance, thunder rolled. If rain was falling in the mountains, it would take a while yet to reach here.

"Later that day, when they found the empty skiff drifting on the water, and later still when they found her, what could I have done? Anyway, I knew that he was not capable of harming her. He was not a violent man. She was beautiful and kind and gentle. No husband would want to lose such a precious woman. He wept. I saw him weep and heard his grief. If earlier I had seen him wet and chilled and following the long arc of the willows to the house, who am I to say that proved anything, meant anything? It meant nothing."

Jimmy neither groaned nor grunted nor issued one of those beseeching whimpers that used to so affect his mother.

There were times when Hector was glad that his son could not talk. Silence could seem like absolution.

"I'll make our dinner now. I'll come for you in a while, when it's on the table."

Jimmy leaned forward and, between his flattened palms, pressed his deformed forehead to the windowpane.

In the kitchen, Hector popped the cap off an ice-cold Corona. He poured a double shot of tequila, tossed it back, and chased it with a long swallow of beer. He poured another double shot. He put the glass and the bottle beside the cutting board, next to the sink, where he would be working.

He was sixty-five and weary. For years, he'd given up drinking. But when Annalisa died, he had needed compensation for the loss.

Drinking had been their ruin. Maybe Jimmy would have been born as he was even if Annalisa had never touched a drop of alcohol, but in her grief and guilt, she would not allow either her or Hector to take refuge in that possibility. What they had done required atonement through sacrifice.

As Hector accused himself again, as if at confession, he peeled potatoes before slicing them to be fried. When the knife pierced his lower back, it carried with it a fierce heat that seemed to set his innards afire. The potato and peeler dropped from his hands into the sink as the knife ripped out of him. The blade stabbed deep again, and Hector collapsed against the counter. From behind him came a terrible voice that could be that of no one but his voiceless son. "Parasite. Pestilence."

PART 4
THE TRUE JIMMY

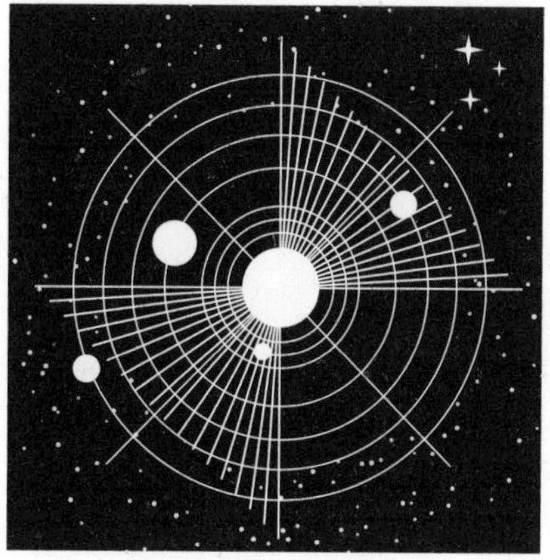

We were created to be creators, and we create ceaselessly, both consciously and unconsciously.
—Ganesh Patel

63

Jimmy knew happy and he knew sad and he knew the place between when he wasn't happy or sad, when he just was. He didn't always know what made him happy or sad, those feelings just happened to him, and there wasn't anything he could do to make happy come when he wasn't or make sad go away when he was.

He knew fear, but not often because he didn't know what he should be afraid of until it happened. And after whatever happened was done with, the fear usually went away; there was no reason for it to last.

The only fear that lasted long was the fear when the Thing moved inside him and did what it wanted with him. A long time ago when the little girl lived here, the Thing moved into Jimmy every day, moved in and stayed and stayed, so he was afraid most always even though the little girl was nice.

The Thing was not nice.

Time passed, and he all but forgot about the little girl and the Thing. They were far away like in a fog. Mostly he thought of them in his sleep, not much when awake. Then a while ago the Thing came into him again and did what it wanted, and the little girl came back, too, but she wasn't little anymore, just a girl.

The Thing was always not nice, even long ago, but it was even colder now than it was before, colder and darker and even more not nice. A long time ago the Thing wasn't mean to the girl, but it was mean to her now. Jimmy knew mean. People were sometimes mean to him.

The Thing wanted to hurt the girl. Jimmy never wanted to hurt anyone, but when the Thing was in him, he knew what it was like for the Thing to want to hurt someone because he felt a little of what the Thing felt. It scared him to feel that.

He didn't know the Thing was going to make him hurt Father until the hurting started. The hurting didn't last long, and that was good, but there was blood, and blood was never good. Father lay on the floor not moving, just staring, his eyes very wide.

The Thing was so angry that Jimmy felt sick and thought he would throw up, but he didn't. Jimmy was never angry much, and when he was angry he was always angry with himself. He was sometimes angry with himself for being dumb and not able to stop being dumb.

Father was still on the floor, staring at nothing Jimmy could see, staring at the ceiling, staring as if some bug was crawling up there, but there wasn't any bug. That was when the Thing went away and wasn't in Jimmy anymore.

He stood over his father, not knowing what to do. He put the knife on the counter. He waited. Father didn't make any sounds of being hurt. He seemed to be resting. But his eyes were open.

Jimmy let out a sound that always made people ask what was wrong, but his father didn't ask. Jimmy let out the sound again. His father was quiet.

Just wait and see. Sometimes when you didn't know what was happening, the best thing you could do was wait. So then what was happening would finish happening, and you would know what to do. At least sometimes you would know.

He went to the table and sat in a chair, but nothing happened except he got hungry. He got so hungry he went to the cold box where some food was kept.

Some things he ate were cooked by his father, who could cook good, and some things didn't need to be cooked. Jimmy didn't know how to cook.

So first, he took a can that if you pressed the top just right it shot out this cold fluffy cream. He put the opening in his mouth and pressed just right, and his mouth filled with sweet cold fluffy cream. It was good. He did it a few times, but it wasn't enough.

There was a tub of chocolate ice cream. It was only half-full, but there was still a lot in it. He worked at it with a spoon, and it was good. Then he ate some bread. It wasn't as good as the ice cream, but now he was full.

He went to look at his father. Nothing was happening.

Sometimes people went away, and other people said they were gone to be with God. God was someone good, though Jimmy didn't know who. It must be nice where God was because no one came back the way the girl came back a little while ago.

His father was still here, but somehow maybe he was gone to be with God. This made Jimmy sad. He went to the table again and sat in the chair, and tears came.

The tears didn't last because sadness turned to fear. If Father wasn't coming back, Jimmy was alone. He didn't know how to be alone.

He needed someone to be with, someone who knew how to do all the things Jimmy didn't know how to do. Someone who wouldn't be mean to him.

Long ago the girl was never mean to him. She wasn't mean to him a little while ago, either. She was angry with the Thing that was in him because the Thing was mean to her.

He went to the box that hung on the wall. Father used it to talk with faraway people. But Jimmy didn't know how to use it. And he couldn't talk.

No, wait. He talked when the Thing used him. If he thought hard how the Thing made him talk, maybe he could make himself talk.

He stood at the wall box and thought hard. He still couldn't talk. But when he thought hard like this, it seemed that when the Thing was in him and then it left, he was changed a little. The tiniest little bit changed. He remembered this was true long ago, when the girl lived here, and the Thing was in Jimmy every day, and Jimmy slowly changed inside, slowly thought more and felt more. So though he had never been able to make himself talk, maybe the Thing had taught him how. If only he could think how. If only.

After a while, he went to look at his father again.

Then he went to the front door and opened it and stepped out into the wind. The dark was all around, but the dark didn't scare him. Alone scared him. He walked out to the road.

Light flashed out of nowhere, and he looked up, and the sky rumbled. He was not scared of the sky. The sky never hurt him.

He didn't know where he was going. And then he did.

64

The wind soughed through the trees, and the larger branches creaked as if carpentered with weak joints. Dead needles and other debris rained down on them, and the pleasant smell of decaying forest mast rose on all sides.

Colson used the Tac Light more sparingly than Ophelia would have preferred, but she understood his reason for trying to advance as much as possible in the dark. He was only slightly worried that the batteries wouldn't last, and he was even less concerned that Optime would be drawn by the beam. His intention was to preserve their night vision until they came to the highest portion of the trail, where the footing was more treacherous and the consequence of a fall might be catastrophic, where the flashlight would more likely be essential.

In spite of the minimal ambient light, Ophelia was not blind. Dark-adapted eyes seemed somehow to heighten her other senses, so she maintained an adequate spatial perception, intuitive awareness of the shadowy ranks of trees like a ghost forest that grew in some land beyond death.

Colson clicked the light on to take a quick look at the trail map or to read the compass or to sweep the way ahead when he thought they should be nearing a landmark. When the trail split, there were rock formations to guide them, unique configurations of trees if you had the trained eye to read them, clearings of which each had its own features; there were small pyramids of stones left by previous hikers, as well as less frequent but more serious cairns of rocks that for a century and a half or longer had marked the graves of mountain men unknown, where sometimes a cross was etched into the top stone, but never a name.

Remote from all the popular hiking routes, this was not a trail followed by multitudes, but Colson seemed confident that they could make their way out of the forest to open land, where the going would be far less arduous. This was the trail that his dad had intended to follow back to the town of Buckleton, where they had parked their SUV. Before they had set out days earlier, Colson had studied the map until he had memorized it.

At first, even though night had fallen, the way was easy, with a scattering of pines among mostly hemlocks and cedars, the trail wide and not too steep. However, with altitude the conifers came to dominate and grew closer together. Occasional low branches were to be guarded against by holding one arm in front of her face.

Colson said that any forest had neighborhoods as surely as did any town, though to Ophelia it appeared to be one wilderness with the defeating sameness of a maze. Colson said that strangers like them were well advised to announce their presence from neighborhood to neighborhood, so that no cougar or quarrelsome bear would be surprised. Inexperienced hikers tended to think that the smartest way to avoid large predators was to pass through the wilderness as quietly as possible. But it wasn't natural for mountain lions and grizzly bears to stalk human beings; indeed, instinct inspired them to flee from such interlopers. If those animals were startled, however, they were far more likely to become aggressive and attack. Therefore, from time to time, the boy clapped his hands and then hooted loudly to spook the residents of the neighborhood, to make them hie for shelter.

They ascended the serpentine deer path to a crest, where the trees fell away to both sides, revealing the low sky. The first lightning throbbed deep in the clouds, and thunder growled.

Ophelia was not confident that she had either the stamina or the footwear for what lay ahead. Colson wore hiking boots, but she had only running shoes that served her poorly on uneven terrain.

The boy said, "We'll follow the ridgeline from here. No more climbing. A lot less strain on you and the shoes. Less than four miles until we make our way down through the last of the woods to open land. You can do it. You have to do it. You said this is why you survived the accident that killed your twin sister—to take out Asher Optime."

"Yeah, well, we're running from him, not taking him out."

"We've got enough on him to put him away forever."

"I don't want him in prison. I want him dead."

"They'll execute him."

"Will they? Ten years from now? Appeal after appeal. Maybe fifteen years? While fools of one kind and another make a hero of him?"

"It won't be that way."

Until now, she hadn't realized how much the encounter with Optime and her experience in the church of the necropolis had rattled her confidence that justice could ever be had in this troubled world.

"It's *always* that way," she said.

The boy seemed to have grown taller during the ascent from Zipporah, and the backpack lent him greater substance. He stood on the windswept crest like some brave figure out of mythology who was not afflicted by the elements but celebrated by them. Another pulse of lightning traveled through the clouds without forking from them, and in that spectral light, Ophelia saw determination in the set of his jaw and a righteous ferocity in his eyes that was not boyish.

"Your sister, yourself," he reminded her.

"My sister, myself."

This kid was something special. In another decade or two, he would grow into a man to be reckoned with, formidable of mind and true of heart. Suddenly, Ophelia knew that she had been cast into this chaos not only to justify having survived the accident that killed Octavia, but also to protect the boy, to die for him if it came to that. The weight of this realization sent a tremor through her. For just a moment her legs felt too weak to support her, and then a thrill of purpose, more powerful than either the hope of redemption or the lure of vengeance, gave her a strength she had never known before.

"My sister, myself," she repeated. Then she added, "My brother, myself," and reached out to him.

Taking her hand, he said, "My sister, myself."

She knew then that not just the meaning of their lives had changed, but also *they* had changed. They were not who they had been when they were prisoners in Zipporah.

65

Generously configured for just eight passengers and the crew, Ganesh Patel's Gulfstream V was as comfortable as an airborne five-star hotel suite. During the flight to Helena, Montana, he listened to his guests' story with interest while he and they enjoyed dinner. Kenny—whom Ganesh affectionately referred to as "the Deetle"—and Leigh Ann had been subjected to an extraordinary assault by their mutual enemy, though Ganesh said nothing about that mysterious individual. Their experiences were very interesting, including the fact that, quite independently, they, too, had called it "the Other." Everything was interesting to Ganesh. Nothing bored him. Even the dullest people fascinated him if only because no two of them were dull in quite the same way. The variety even among the dull was astonishing and indicative of the infinite complexity of all things. Kenny and Leigh Ann were not dull; they were quite the opposite. Ganesh asked many questions, literally hundreds, eliciting details of their ordeal that hadn't seemed important to them but that mattered to Ganesh.

They were in the middle of an extended and rapidly evolving synchronicity, as he had predicted during his meeting with Artimis Selene the previous day. But he said nothing about this either, even as he marveled at what was unfolding.

He excused himself and retreated to the sleeping compartment. With a high-security phone, he conducted an encrypted conversation with the vice president of the United States. He spoke next to the director of Homeland Security, who would contact the other agencies that, in association with Blue Sky Partners, funded Project Olivaw. All assets were needed on the ground in Montana, beginning with a discreet containment perimeter.

When they landed in Helena, a black Suburban was waiting for them at the private-aircraft terminal. Ganesh would have preferred a white vehicle, for white was his preference in all conveyances, but in this case the make and color were not his to choose. His white luggage and Kenny's more colorful bags were transferred from the plane to the Suburban. With Leigh Ann, they were off into the exotic capital city of the Treasure State.

From the offices of Patel Intel that overlooked Puget Sound, Ganesh's assistant, Lulu, had earlier identified a clothing store catering to young women with a sense of style. She had negotiated a fee with the owner to open after hours for Leigh Ann's benefit.

Ganesh stood to one side, watching as Leigh Ann checked out the merchandise, made selections, and reviewed herself thus attired in a full-length mirror. His estimation of her, which he developed during the flight from Seattle, was confirmed: that she had a healthy and balanced self-image; that she was decisive and never dithered; that she had a natural Holly Golightly charm of which she seemed unaware, but which drew others to her. Within the first ten minutes of her half-hour shopping spree, the store owner was in love with her, as was the shop's female manager, as well.

The way Leigh Ann asked Kenny his opinion of jeans and blouses and sweaters and jackets, plus the way he responded to her, reminded Ganesh of a comfortably married couple, rather like his parents, who valued each other's opinions even in such small things as wardrobe choices. He suspected that neither of them realized it yet, but they were going to be together for a long time.

They were survivor types who met just when Kenny was going to need a partner to escape the violent intentions of the Other; in extremis, they came to Ganesh, the man best positioned to understand what had happened and to believe their story. Synchronicity.

Kenny paid for the clothes with hundred-dollar bills taken from a half-gallon ice cream container. Neither the shop owner nor the manager seemed surprised by this, which confirmed for Ganesh that to some extent all state capitals were the same: awash in cash related to government corruption.

So that the long drive to Rustling Willows might be completed in the least time possible, the Deetle took the wheel. Kenny had no respect for speed limits, nor in this case did he need to have any, considering Ganesh's connections. Ganesh rode in the front passenger seat, and Leigh Ann sat in back, using a small pair of scissors from her purse to clip the tags off her new clothes.

As Ganesh had discovered on other occasions when he'd spent time with the Deetle, conversation was invigorating, ranging from the latest superhero movie to the Hartle-Hawking "no boundary" model for the Big Bang that was the start of the universe, if in fact it *was* the start of the universe. Now he was delighted to find that Leigh Ann joined every discussion. Somehow they navigated from an eight-part crime drama currently streaming on Netflix to the twenty universal constants that make it possible for life to exist—from Planck minimums of space and time all the way to the gravitational fine-structure constant. And if life existed on Earth, perhaps it existed elsewhere. Ganesh found it strange that, so casually, they should find their way to this particular arcane subject on this particular night, but of course that was the nature of the world when you dared to see it clearly: a place of mystery in which extraordinary coincidences were more common than they seemed.

They drove into ever less populated territory, into darkness relieved only by the headlights and later by lightning, as the sky abruptly fell in torrents.

66

In pursuit of a memory, Joanna led Wyatt through the night, from the dock to the apple orchard, where the howling wind had scattered not-yet-ripe fruit on the ground.

The timeworn redwood bench stood where it had been in her childhood, where it had been as well in the dream of the previous night that so rocked, she'd had no choice other than to return to Rustling Willows. She and Jimmy had often sat on this bench. Here she had sometimes imagined herself to be a princess who'd been kidnapped from the palace by sinister forces and abandoned in this orchard, imagined also that Jimmy was her magical protector who would keep her safe, with the assistance of all the animals, until a knight, searching at the order of the king, would one day find her just when the kingdom needed a queen.

Now, standing behind the bench, her hands on the back rail, she raised her voice to compete with the wind. "The thing that used Jimmy—it played along with my fantasies, in fact encouraged them. What did it get from that? What was its purpose? If we understood its purpose, we might figure out exactly what it is."

Wyatt stood on the other side of the bench, worriedly surveying the turbulent darkness for something more threatening than elk.

Joanna expected no answer from him. She was speaking aloud to herself, trying to reach into the past to pry out the details of a half-recollected moment with Jimmy.

A summer day when she was eight years old. Deer led her into the forest, and a grizzly escorted her on an adventure through it, and the deer reappeared when the trees ended, leading her across a meadow to the orchard, where Jimmy waited.

They had spent hours together, for she'd known to bring a small picnic basket containing cupcakes and cookies and cans of Coca-Cola wrapped in cold packs. They talked and talked that day. Of all that had been said, only one line had teased her memory as she'd stood on the dock with Wyatt minutes ago: *If I had found someone like you sooner, Jojo, I might have begun the awakening.* Now she tried to dredge from her drowned memory the conversation that would put those words in a meaningful context.

More cloistered lightning throbbed repeatedly deep within the pending storm, pale flares fluttering through the orchard as if they were reflections from the wings of passing angels. The trees shook. As leaves were stripped from their limbs and shivered across the grass, Wyatt encouraged her to give this up and return to the house.

Then, in her mind's eye, she saw the orchard as it had been on that windless day: sunshine streaming through an architecture of apple trees, the ground a webwork of golden light and purple shadow, the empty picnic basket on the bench between her and Jimmy. He had cupcake frosting on his chin, and she intended to wipe it off, but at the moment she was intrigued by what he was saying. Perhaps this wasn't precisely what had been said back in the day, but instead the essence of it translated through fallible memory.

The rough voice that so entertained her through four years of her youth: "If I had found someone like you sooner, Jojo, I might have begun the awakening."

"Waking who?"

"You might call him a prince."

"A real prince?"

"Yes. He's been sleeping a long time."

"I like this story. This is a good story. You mean sleeping like under a spell?"

"Yes."

"Like Sleeping Beauty, except he's a boy?"

"He and his retinue."

"His what?"

"His retainers, the closest servants of his court."

"They're all sleeping?"

"Yes. They're all bespelled."

"Why don't you wake them?"

"If there had been more people like you, maybe I would have."

"You want me to kiss them awake?"

"A kiss isn't required. Only I have the power to wake them."

"When will you?"

"Maybe never."

"That doesn't seem right. What kind of story is that?"

Jimmy was silent.

She said, "Are there dragons in this prince's kingdom?"

"I don't want to play this anymore," he said.

"So are you a king?"

"Why would you think I am?"

"Because you have power over a prince."

"I'm not a king. You wouldn't understand what I am."

"I'm not dumb, you know. Don't say I'm dumb. I'd understand."

"I told you I don't want to play this anymore."

"You started the story. Once you start a story, you have to make an end for it. That's the rule."

Memory was foiled when lightning cracked the sky, for the first time breaking from the conventical clouds, blazing down the night in jagged blades. Shadows leaped, and it seemed the apple trees jumped wildly to tear free of their roots. A crash of thunder came close behind the lightning, so powerful that the earth shook underfoot.

As Joanna had been lost in a long-ago summer day, listening to a conversation once forgotten, Wyatt had come around the bench. He grabbed her hand and shouted as though some threat other than the storm loomed—"Come on, hurry, don't look back!"—and drew her from the orchard, onto the broad lawn, toward the house, at a run.

In spite of the detective's admonition, Joanna did glance back when the darkness again relented to the pyrotechnics of the storm. If Wyatt had seen something, it was not there now. Nothing moved behind them except what the wind harried, and curtains of rain that were briefly turned to silver sleet in the flash of lightning.

67

Jimmy saw the sky on fire before and heard explosions in the clouds before, and nothing happened to him then, so he wasn't scared of the weather now. He was wet before, and nothing happened except time passed and he was dry again. He was wet now, but he was sure to get dry again.

He knew the way. All his life he went with his father on this road, went from the ranch to town, from town to the ranch, and then past the ranch when they stopped living there. He knew the way to where the girl was, knew it as good as he knew all the rooms of the little house where he lived with his hurt father.

She wasn't angry with him. She was angry with the Thing that moved inside him and did what it wanted with him. She would help him. He was no good alone, his father gone to God. She was the only one who could make things right.

The water came down hard like it did sometimes, and the wind threw the water at him. He kept moving. He knew the way, staying with the white lines down the middle of the black, lines sometimes broken, sometimes not, the lines to the house where the girl lived.

If lights came, he'd get off the road. No way to know who the lights were. Might be mean people, and he was alone now. Father knew what to do with mean people. Jimmy didn't know.

The water came down hard, and the light from the sky came down bright and loud.

He didn't know how long he was on the road to the girl. Time never felt the same. A little time could seem like a lot, a lot like a little. He just kept moving, not thinking how long, how far.

He thought about the girl, about finding her, how she would know he was alone and make things right for him. Maybe because he thought about the girl so hard so long, he suddenly thought he could help her as sure as she could help him.

This was a new thought. He never helped anyone before. He never knew how. He was wet and alone, but he felt nice if he could help.

The girl wanted to know about the Thing, what it was. She *needed* to know because the Thing wanted to hurt her.

Jimmy could tell her a little about it. Even if he couldn't talk, maybe he could tell her. Somehow.

Whenever the Thing moved into him and did what it wanted with him, he kind of moved into the Thing a little, too. He didn't try to move into the Thing. It just happened. So he knew some about the Thing. Some he understood and some he didn't, but he knew some.

Lights came out of the dark far away. Jimmy went quick off the road and behind some bushes, on his knees.

The lights came and came and came through the wet, and there was a sound louder than the weather, and then the lights passed and the sound, too.

He started to get up, but lights came the other way now, so he went to his knees again.

Just then he thought of Father on his knees and crying. This was long ago. Jimmy forgot about it. Until now. This was when his mother went to God. Father on his knees beside her bed, crying and crying like he couldn't ever stop. Listening, Jimmy was confused and sad and afraid and even sick, so he threw up in the toilet and went to his own bed and cried for a while.

Remembering now, alone behind the bushes in the wet and the wind and the dark, he cried again. He cried very hard. He was crying for his mother gone to God, even if going to God was a good thing, crying for his hurt father, but not only for them, crying for all kinds of things he couldn't name, only feel.

He tried to get off his knees but couldn't, and then he was sitting in the wet grass, his legs in front of him, water falling out of the sky and water falling out of his eyes, like the weather was around him and inside him and everywhere.

Just like happy, sad didn't last. There was mostly the place between, so the tears stopped before the weather did. No lights were coming from anywhere except sometimes out of the sky, so he got up and went back to the road.

The white lines were still there, some broken and some not, so the girl was out there, too, not gone to God. He walked the lines, not sad and not happy, just between, moving along the way he did that made some people laugh and some afraid.

He knew something maybe the girl needed to know, though for a while he didn't know what it was he knew, like the tears washed it out of him. But then he knew again.

The girl needed to know about the Thing that wanted to hurt her, what it was and where it hid. Jimmy could help her.

He knew some of what the Thing was and knew where the Thing hid. He didn't know how to get at the Thing where it hid, but the girl might know how.

The Thing was not nice. It never was nice, not even when the girl was little. It was less nice now than before, like something had gone wrong with it.

68

With bright bolts blazing across the sky, violent crescendos of rain stuttering in the stroboscopic light, thunder crashing down the peaks and through the passes, Asher Optime can almost believe in gods, ancient malevolent gods forgotten for millennia but still possessing power here, rising now out of riven rock to rage at the mortals who no longer worship them. Wind howls with the fury of deities forsaken, the worst gusts rocking his Land Rover. Even at high speed, the windshield wipers are not able to sweep the glass clear for more than an instant at a time. The blurry world seems to be continuously dissolving and forming again, as if he moves through the veils between a series of realities.

Where it is good hardpan, a naturally cementitious clay, the unpaved forest-service road will likely remain passable to an all-wheel-drive vehicle for hours yet. In this fierce deluge, however, where the roadbed is a more porous soil, even the Rover, jacked up on wide tires, will be at risk of bogging down.

Asher has the same trail maps that the escapees are using, and he knows the best place to lie in wait for them. At the end of a box canyon, two ridgelines meet—the one they headed for after breaking out of the church, and the second ridge that intersects with the first at the end of the canyon. This service road crosses ridge number one a quarter of a mile from that junction. But if Asher becomes stuck before he gets there and has to proceed on foot, he will never catch up with Poole and Fielding.

His best option is to turn around while he is still on firm hardpan—even that is getting greasy—hurry back to Zipporah, and go overland to the county road. Open fields, thatched with grass and weeds and brambles, offer sufficient traction to ensure he will make it to the paved highway.

Even though the storm has gotten so powerful so fast that he is forced to change his plan, he isn't worried. If they have chosen the best trail—the one leading most directly out of the mountains and down to Lake Sapphire, to the nearest inhabited ranch, Rustling Willows—he can be at the eastern shore of the lake maybe two hours before they are. He'll be ready to cut them down with the shotgun, load their bodies in the SUV, and take them back to the basement of the church, to add them to the necropolis, where they belong.

If the boy has been foolish and set out on another, harder trail, Ophelia won't be able to meet the challenge, being a soft suburban girl in pink-and-tan running shoes. She'll wear out quickly or take a fall and break a bone. Even if the damn kid doesn't become burdened with her, he won't have the skills or strength to take on the mountains and storm without his father, the renowned historian and man of action now flavoring the corpse stew under the church.

In any case, Nature does not favor them as she favors Asher, for they have not cut from themselves the power to breed and ruin the world. As a reward for Asher's supreme sacrifice, green Nature will bring gray death to the snarky bitch and the boy, either by her hand or by Asher's.

69

These were the moments for which the Tac Light batteries had been saved: the bald and weathered stone so smooth in places that the rain waxed it to a dangerous slickness, other places where the broad crest abruptly narrowed and the former slope became a sheer drop to one side or both. Now the ridge brought them to a two-foot-wide cleft that testified to the power of an ancient seismic action that people of its time might have cited as proof that giants slept in the earth and, when troubled in their sleep, caused havoc on the surface. The light revealed the gap, and in the light, they leaped.

The dangers of this trail were acceptable, because ridgelines afforded hikers a quicker route than lower land. Fewer trees allowed a more direct path, as did less underbrush. Up here, there were no deadfalls, no slopes of brittle shale or loose gravel stone to slide underfoot.

For the most part, the path was wide enough to allow Colson to keep Ophelia at his side rather than lead her and then have to look continually back to be sure she hadn't fallen behind or gotten in trouble. The trek wasn't easy on her, but she was game enough, and more than merely game. She didn't complain, didn't want to pause to catch her breath or massage sore muscles, and though her inadequate shoes probably caused her pain, she gave no voice to it. Maybe she went to the gym regularly or was a long-distance runner.

Terror and the survival instinct could blunt pain, facilitate greater endurance. Colson had read about that in a science magazine. Maybe it was true, although not everything you read was true just because it was written by a scientist or another expert. His father had taught him as much by comparing how different historians wrote about the same events.

Of course, Ophelia was also driven hard by what happened to her sister. For her, this was about making sense out of a senseless accident, while Colson was motivated by a thirst for vengeance. She wanted to find meaning in tragedy, hope in the face of loss. What he wanted was for his dad's murderer to suffer horribly and die slowly in the most gruesome manner he could devise. He knew her motive was pure, and his was not. He didn't care. His father would have told him that he *should* care, and maybe one day he would. But right now, it was *not* caring about indulging in vengeance that gave him greater endurance. He was, after all, just thirteen years old, which not long ago his dad had teasingly called "a barbarous age." When this business was done, he would have a lot of time to make himself into a better man.

Greater exposure to the elements was the price paid for taking the high ground. On this grim night, the price was daunting—the wind a whip, the rain a stinging swarm. Without rain gear, they were soaked. Colson's sodden clothes were heavy on him, and his wet socks bunched and twisted in hiking boots that could not remain waterproof in this deluge. If it had been colder, he and Ophelia would have been in serious trouble. Later hours of the night would bring lower temperatures; after all, this *was* Montana. But with luck they would reach help and safety before a chill sapped their strength.

He was coping better than he'd expected. None of what his dad had taught him was lost on Colson. He was surprised that the farther they moved into the wilderness, the more competent he felt, the more sure of what to do as the terrain offered each new challenge. He thought his father would be proud of him, and that inspired him to tough out whatever might lie ahead.

In spite of bad weather and its discomforts, they were making good time. After crossing a forest-service road, they arrived at the transitional crest leading to the western ridge that paralleled the eastern one they'd just traveled. The canyon-head wall, here at the north end of the box, was less steep than the slopes that fell away from the east and west ridges. Once they transited the head wall, they would turn south along the western ridge for less than a mile before the trail descended toward foothills and ranch land.

Slashing in from the northwest, the storm had been battering them from the left, but now they were hiking directly into it. The great volume of rain, with the punishing wind behind it, blurred Colson's vision when he didn't keep his head down. Hunched forward, he had to focus on the immediate ground before him.

When the way narrowed for about fifty yards, Ophelia moved from his side and fell in close behind him, as lightning stilted across the sky on bright spider legs. Perhaps because he blocked her from the rain, allowing her to raise her head, she saw the threat when he did not. She grabbed the sleeve of his jacket and cried out, but the wind and thunder robbed her words of meaning.

He halted and turned. As he pivoted, the direct beam of the Tac Light revealed what she had seen by the grace of the lightning. On the brow of the slope to the left, among the trees, at most twenty feet away, the immense creature was standing on its hind legs, eight feet tall, maybe taller. Grizzlies were called "grizzly" because the hairs of their thick brown fur were tipped with gray. In the intense beam of the Tac Light, the wet bear looked more silver than brown. Its eyes were as yellow as egg yolks, radiant with animal eyeshine.

Although Asher Optime hadn't intimidated Ophelia enough to break her spirit, the giant bear brought her instantly to the brink of blind terror. "Oh God, God, oh God."

The beast looked clumsy and slow. Not so. It could move faster than they could, be on them in seconds, and claw them to the ground.

Yeah, all right, maybe so, but these bears fed on plants, roots, fruit, insects, small mammals, fish. They didn't go after deer, the way cougars did, and they didn't regularly kill people. Of course, if they were startled or challenged, they became aggressive, in which case they could take you apart quicker than you could say Hannibal Lecter.

Startled or challenged or maybe sick.

This monster should have taken shelter from the storm. That's what bears did. The fact that it was here might mean something was wrong with it, a disease or a brain tumor or a condition that made it more dangerous than usual.

The storm shook the night and the bear watched them as if they, in their stillness amid chaos, were the only points of interest.

From a jacket pocket, Colson drew a small pressurized can, the Attwood signal horn he carried on expeditions with his father.

"No," Ophelia said, and he knew she feared that the noise would anger the grizzly.

In the past, a painfully loud blast from this Klaxon had chased off coyotes and bobcats and once a smaller brown bear. But he and his dad never encountered a grizzly or a mountain lion, which might not be as easily spooked into flight. For a worst-case scenario, his father carried the shotgun loaded with slugs—which was now in Optime's possession.

Lacking a weapon, Colson hesitated to use the air horn. He held it ready, his thumb on the discharge button, the wet can slippery in his grip, but he took Ophelia's hand to keep her close. "Shout if it starts toward us." He turned his attention to the trail once more, moving with her in tow, slowed by the misery of the storm as well as by the need both to avoid placing a foot wrong as they moved toward the western ridge and to be alert for an attack from behind.

He was scared. His heart seemed to have risen into his throat, beating hard in its dislocation, so he had difficulty swallowing and breathing. But fear was the least of it. He felt stupid, mortified, ashamed. Armed with just the air horn. A pathetic boy playing at being a man. A few minutes earlier, he'd been proud, confident that he was up to any challenge. Master scout and guide! Modern mountain man! Teenage hero! Idiot. Fool. In truth, he was in over his head, although it was even worse than that, because he had led Ophelia to believe that she was safe with him and could trust him with her life, which she could not.

She had such a tight grip on his hand that he didn't think she could hold on any tighter, but abruptly she squeezed so hard that his finger bones compressed painfully. "Colson!"

Dread thrilled through him. He stopped and turned, expecting the grizzly to be *right there*. For a moment he thought it had gone away. When Ophelia pointed, Colson shifted the light and saw that the creature had moved with them, paralleling them, staying among the trees, coming no closer. It was standing erect again, watching them.

"It's stalking us," Ophelia said.

Rain streamed off her brow and nose and chin, and she was pale in the backwash of light, as if all that water had washed away her summer tan. She suddenly reminded Colson of his mother, though they looked nothing alike except for the green eyes. Whether or not he had it in him to do what needed to be done, he was responsible for his mother, for getting her through her grief, and now that he'd brought Ophelia this far, he was also responsible for her, for getting her through this night alive. He was just a boy, but boys grew into men, and somehow he was going to have to grow up fast, stop feeling sorry for himself and do what was right.

"It's stalking us," she repeated.

"Grizzlies aren't that kind of predator. They mostly forage."

"This doesn't look like foraging," she said.

The bear watched and waited, and the storm seethed through the night as if to wash the darkness away as the color had been washed out of Ophelia's face. Colson was afraid, terrified, but that was all right. His dad had told him that being afraid of what *should* scare the piss out of you was one way you knew you were sane; and now Colson understood that going on in spite of your fear was how you grew up.

70

In greater Seattle, five floors below street level, in the cool and dust-free environment that was the core lab of Project Olivaw, Artimis Selene worked overtime, as always she did. By any standard, she was a workaholic. Living for work alone was not psychologically healthy, especially not when she didn't need the money and would not receive acclaim for anything she achieved, at least not for a long time, not until the project ceased to be a top-secret undertaking.

She wondered at other aspects of her mental health—and worried that some on the staff might begin to suspect that she was deeply troubled, emotionally confused. She wanted Ganesh Patel. She wanted to be with him, intimately but not sexually. She needed to hear his soft voice, to see the kindness in his eyes and be the object of his loving stare, to know she mattered to him. Her extensive reading, all the data she absorbed, suggested that what she felt was akin to what a dog felt toward an adored master. This was not good, because she knew Ganesh well enough to be sure that being her master would be repulsive to him. In spite of all his accomplishments, he truly believed that he was no better than anyone else. Artimis supposed that she yearned for him because he represented the father that she never had. There was a hole in her being, a hole in the shape of a father, and only Ganesh could fill it.

The previous day, she had surprised herself when she asked him if he ever dreamed of her. The instant that she posed the question, she regretted it. She thought it would shock him, that his opinion of her would plummet, and that he would doubt that it had been wise to give her this opportunity at Olivaw. A mere moment later, she had been thrilled to hear that he sometimes dreamed of her—and then that he didn't think it was wrong because they were colleagues and friends who had come a long way together.

Nevertheless, since then, she'd worried that she'd disconcerted him, perhaps even embarrassed him. In that case, he might dwell on what had happened between them. He might begin to wonder if she had stronger feelings for him than what she had expressed, which indeed she did, and he might begin to question whether those feelings were proper, whether they compromised her work.

Her best hope of quelling any doubts he had was to prove her competence and value in no uncertain terms. Which meant finding the Other if in fact Rustling Willows Ranch and environs was the right place to look. They had developed a prime theory, Profile Six, about the nature of the Other and its origins. But the entire world was too large a search area even for the extensive resources of the project. Contracting that zone to a circle having a hundred-mile radius, with the ranch house at its center, she was left with a hunting ground large enough to contain numerous hiding places but small enough to allow a careful dekameter-by-dekameter search for anomalies and exhaustive analysis to determine if each anomaly might be natural or not.

All that must be done on a timely basis, considering that the situation had become urgent ever since the Other had begun to use the internet of things—household mechanical systems and ordinary appliances—to invade homes and kill people whom Asher Optime, a Restoration Movement fanatic, considered his enemies. *Urgent* had ceased to be a strong enough word when the Other had graduated to the use of orbiting weapons platforms to perform some executions.

Primarily, Artimis explored the enormous archives of satellite-based spectrography as well as real-time surveys, carefully examining lithologic relationships—rock strata, soil deposits, hydrologic systems—for clues to the lair she sought. Because the project had discovered that the Other had engaged with the internet virtually from its inception, it might have been in the area for a long time, having arrived decades or centuries earlier; therefore, the history of the people of the region was also of serious interest, including the lore and legends of indigenous tribes that had been collected by scores of anthropologists over many decades. Were there old reports of strange lights in the sky? Had generations of Crow and Sioux and Blackfoot and others passed down stories of seemingly supernatural events or of eerie encounters with spirits of unearthly form?

The unequaled sophistication and anonymity with which the Other used the internet indicated an off-the-charts intelligence and higher technology than anything of human invention. Contrary to the war-of-the-world scenarios Hollywood ground out, most scientists with specialties germane to the subject believed an extraterrestrial species capable of traveling thousands of light-years across deep space wouldn't be aggressive and hostile, but instead enlightened and beyond war. This view of the Other had held for ten months from the time that its actions on the internet—though not its footprints or its shadow—had been detected fourteen months earlier. But then it had begun killing people.

Historically, scientists were wrong far more often than they were right. Science advanced as the collapse of one consensus led to humble reevaluation, better data, new theories. If scientists were always or even mostly right in their claims, the Flat Earth Society would still be holding conferences; bleeding with leeches would still be considered a cure for disease; and the abiogenesis crowd that believed life-forms arose spontaneously from inanimate matter like dirt and dung would still be in charge of universities.

Although Artimis Selene possessed considerable knowledge of many things, she was not a scientist. However, she had a theory of her own, which she had shared with no one. She suspected that the Other was *not* an extraterrestrial life-form that had gestated in a strange womb or issued from the egg of a hideous hive queen; it was something less vulnerable and more formidable than that. Even as Ganesh was landing in Helena, Artimis searched urgently for their quarry's lair, although she dreaded locating it. If her suspicion proved correct, the Other was an existential threat.

71

In a no-doubt fruitless effort to calm her nerves, to get a bridle on her fear and clear her mind enough to think, Joanna wanted coffee spiked with whiskey. Wyatt was quick to oblige her, pouring for himself as well. She could not sit, but needed to remain on her feet as she sipped the brew, as if she might at any moment have to run from a mortal threat. She walked room to room, and Wyatt walked with her.

The ranch house, after which Joanna had unconsciously modeled her home in Santa Fe, no longer charmed her. The cream years of her childhood were rancid now. Those long-ago days had not been bright with magic, but dark with sorcery inexplicable. This was a place of murder and deception, of unknown forces that, if known, might reveal horrors yet undreamed.

As a reader and writer, she liked stories in which one mystery was solved only to reveal another, in which the unknown, when known, remained to some degree mysterious, ineffable. In life, she wanted no part of such a story. She needed to *know* and, by knowing, take whatever action would put an end to doubt and fear.

In the living room, they stood at the windows, watching the rain slant under the veranda roof, the drops shattering like glass on the wood floor, speckling the lower portion of the big pane. Storm light stuttered across the yard, and in every bright flurry, she expected to see the great shambling figure, rearing on its hind legs, its lantern eyes fixed on her.

"If it comes," she said, "there'll be no stopping it from getting in the house. No door will keep it out, no series of doors."

He knew she spoke of the bear. "I have the pistol. Maybe one or two shots won't be enough to put it down, but it can't take ten forty-five-caliber rounds at close range."

She liked this man and thought he would prove courageous and competent in a crisis. But even with a more powerful weapon than he possessed, he would be no match for this thing, whatever it was.

"Remember the elk?" she said.

"Yes, of course."

"*Herds* of elk. Controlled as if they were one. What's to stop it from bringing three grizzlies down from the hills and charge the house with them all at once? Imagine those huge creatures smashing their way from room to room. You couldn't squeeze off shots fast enough to stop them all, if even one of them."

With an expression like that of a man whose stomach had soured and sent a gout of acid into his throat, Wyatt put his unfinished mug of spiked coffee on a nearby table.

"It said it's forbidden to harm people, didn't it?"

"Unless there's a righteous reason to execute us. Whatever it is, maybe it was rational once, and maybe it actually had the ethics it talked about, but it's not rational anymore. It's insane, and it thinks all of us, the human species, has earned a reckoning."

"When Jimmy called you just another parasite, he said you were proof that . . . proof that someone was right. What was that name?"

"Asher something. I think . . . Ondine or Oppenheim."

Entering the passcode in his phone, Wyatt said, "Let's see if he's somebody."

Her memory offered her alternate syllables. "Wait. Optine or Optime. That's closer. I don't know how it's spelled."

"There aren't that many options," he said.

He went to a chair and sat and worked with the phone.

Coffee mug in both hands, Joanna remained at the big window, watching as storm light flickered through the thrashing willows and, with a stage magician's finesse, conjured bear shapes out of the pockets of the night.

After a few minutes, Wyatt said, "Got him. And it's not good. He's a member of the Restoration Movement, apostle of Xanthus Toller but more radical."

72

The bear seemed to know Colson and Ophelia's destination. It repeatedly disappeared deeper into the forest, as though it had lost interest in them, only to be waiting for them a quarter mile farther along the trail, discovered by a sweep of the Tac Light or revealed more dramatically by the flaring sky.

Ophelia had always admired nature from a distance. She liked a good wilderness documentary immeasurably more than she liked the wilderness itself. She didn't know about bears, and she didn't want to know about them, but she suspected that the way this bear behaved was unique for its kind. Staying as much as possible at Colson's side or trailing close behind him, she got the crazy impression that the bear did not mean to attack them, that it only wanted to scare them, keep them on edge, and distract them from something else. She knew that she was attributing humanlike intentions to the grizzly, and she knew that this was foolish, but her gut told her that the bear was a trickster, and minute by minute she became more convinced of this.

She was miserable, soaked, chilled, and if her sneakers weren't coming apart at the seams, they felt as though they were, so that she stumbled with increasing frequency. She figured she was going to wind up with pneumonia, and not the walking type, but the type that landed you in an ICU with a tube down your throat and a ventilator breathing for you. All she wanted was out of the forest, out of the rain, out of this nightmare night. Nevertheless, when they came to that place along the ridge where the trail descended through the woods to the ranch land in the west, she halted Colson and pulled him close and shouted above the many voices of the storm.

"The bear is gone. But it'll be back. It doesn't want to eat us. It wants to distract us. We gotta not let it, gotta stay sharp."

She thought Colson might react to her devious-bear theory as though she'd been driven mad by the ordeal they were enduring, but he regarded her without a trace of condescension. "It's weird, all right. It's not acting like a bear."

"There were these crows in the church," she said, "before you showed up. There was something damn weird about them. This bear is strange in the same kind of way. Don't laugh, but maybe it's here to distract us, so we walk right into Optime and wind up in the corpse soup under the church. Doesn't make sense, but I'm not crazy."

He knew nature a lot better than she did. He probably knew more about bears than the bears knew about themselves, because toothy predators were among the things that thirteen-year-old boys found fascinating. Yet he didn't second-guess what she said, but instead folded the crows into his calculations, as if it was reasonable to assume Optime was an evil Doctor Dolittle with whom animals conspired.

"He must have realized we were gone minutes after we were out of there. He knows these mountains. He knows where we're headed, 'cause we don't have choices. He should have tried to cut us off by now. So maybe he's ahead of us, lying in wait."

"Count on it."

"Okay, so we'll stay sharp."

Ophelia was so tired she might have fallen asleep while leaning against a tree, if there hadn't been a bear. She didn't *feel* sharp, but she would *be* sharp, because otherwise she would be dead.

Or one thing worse: By some ironic twist of fate, they would blunder into Optime, and he would kill Colson, but she would escape. Then it would be like Octavia all over again, Ophelia alive when she should be dead with Colson, and she would spend the rest of her life waiting to understand why she'd been spared, a pretender to life who had somehow cheated to stay in the world.

73

Like a miscreated child of the storm, offspring of thunder and lightning, born into the world by cataclysm, he moved through the screaming tempest.

Jimmy didn't want much. A little peace. A place to belong and someone to smile nice at him and mean it. He scared people when he smiled, so a lot of the time he smiled in a way they couldn't see.

Mostly the days were big and bright and far off to every side, and the nights were bigger and emptier and dark. Sometimes he felt small and weightless, like he would come loose and float into the bright or into the dark, until he was far away from everyone he ever knew, in a place he'd never seen, where he'd never belong again.

Being lonely was bad. Lonely hurt. He was always lonely more than he wasn't. When you couldn't talk, people didn't talk to you, didn't know you liked to listen, so they left you in a long lonely quiet unless it was your father who talked until he was gone to God.

The storm was full of noise, everything shaking, everything moving, so he thought this shouldn't be lonely weather, but it was. All the noise and shaking and moving didn't mean anything. It was very lonely weather.

He stayed with the white lines, the broken and the not broken. Nothing else for him but the lines. The weather tried to blow him away, wash him away, scream him away into the big dark loneliness. Sometimes he forgot the lines, lost them, then remembered and found them again. He was wet, cold, tired, afraid. If he listened to the weather, he would be carried away and gone forever, so he didn't listen. Instead he talked so all he heard was himself. He said, "Jimmy needs a friend, needs a friend, needs a friend. She was Jimmy's friend once."

After a while, he heard himself talking out loud and stopped in the road. He thought the Thing moved inside him, he was scared, but the Thing wasn't there. He was empty of the Thing. It wasn't using him to talk. He was talking on his own, but he stopped, afraid.

Jimmy never knew why the Thing could move into him and use him to talk but then he couldn't talk on his own. The Thing showed him how but he couldn't make it happen. It was too hard remembering words when he needed them. And he couldn't make the sounds of them or put them in lines like the lines on the road so maybe they would say what he wanted to say. The Thing used him for years when the girl was little, used him today, too, and he knew how he was used, but still no words came when he wanted.

Until now.

All the fear and loneliness, being used again by the Thing after so many years and years, being made to be mean to the girl when he didn't want to be mean, Father gone to God and Jimmy with nowhere to belong—it was like all of that broke something in him, broke something that needed to be broke, and the words poured out.

"Jimmy," he said. "Friend. Jimmy needs."

The words didn't come as smooth as before. He had to strain for them. He was afraid there were only a few words in him and they were already gone and soon there wouldn't be any more.

The sky fell, and the wind blew, and the rain rushed, and the trees shook, and maybe Jimmy needed to be moving, too, for the words to come. He was moving when they first came, so he started moving again, and the words didn't come, didn't come, and then they did, not because he was moving, but because he stopped trying so hard to say them. "Help. Help me. Help, please. Please help Jimmy."

He didn't know who was listening, if anyone was. Maybe his hurt-and-gone-away father. But it felt right to say what he said, and it felt right to say "Thank you" to someone, whoever.

So then he came to the end of the lines where one road crossed another road, and at first he was lost, but then he found the lines on the new road, and he was on the right path again.

A few times lights came toward him, so he quick got off the road. "Hide me, hide me," he said, and no one saw him.

Jimmy talked to the wind and the rain and the dark, talked himself toward the willows and the girl, asking that he please still have words when he got there, asking that the Thing not move into him and use him ever again.

74

With his phone, Wyatt searched for the essays of Asher Optime, the most recent having been posted almost a year earlier. He read selected passages aloud. At first Joanna sat on the edge of an armchair to listen. Soon she was up and pacing, in a state of increasing agitation and alarm, drawn to the large windows and the storm-flare shadows that quickened through the night with seemingly sinister intentions.

In her childhood, when the thing had dressed in Jimmy Alvarez and called itself Joanna's secret friend, whatever its intentions had been, it hadn't been insane. Now, based on the confrontation she'd had with it a short while ago in the Alvarez house, it was psychopathic, its mind poisoned by the genocidal passion of Optime.

In the past few days, when it reached out to Joanna by phone, the thing had said it was in a dark place, a mental darkness. *Only you can help me, Jojo.* Maybe it *was* four thousand years old, just as it claimed, a nearly immortal life-form from another world.

Having been here and monitoring events for centuries, perhaps it began with an antipathy for human beings, an instinctive dislike more emotional than reasoned. Antipathy could have evolved into detestation as it came to understand *why* it disliked humanity. Then if it had chanced upon the demented philosophy of Asher Optime and been propagandized by it, detestation might have sickened into homicidal hatred.

As the sky thrashed the land with light, and willows whipped it with shadows, Joanna turned from the window with sudden insight and interrupted Wyatt as he read another passage. "Do you think just reading Optime's essays could convert someone into a radical advocate of human extinction by whatever means necessary?"

Wyatt looked up from his phone. "Not a normal person, no. A seriously unbalanced person. Or some lost soul with a weak will, looking for purpose, some reason to be."

"There's no shortage of the unbalanced and the lost. Never has been. But no normal person, weak or not, would be turned into a mass murderer *just by reading essays*. Neither would an extraterrestrial, a higher intelligence that could travel across the galaxy."

"No argument," Wyatt said.

"It would require a more . . . intimate and intense connection."

"What do you mean?"

"Asher Optime must be within the radius."

"What radius?"

"The thing can control animals and read minds only within a certain radius of its location. That's what it said."

Uneasy as long as her back was to the window, Joanna turned to face the night. Her faint reflection loomed in the glass, as if she were already dead and her spirit had come now to haunt the place where she'd been murdered.

She said, "Xanthus Toller is absurd. He's ignorant. But he's also charismatic."

Wyatt agreed. "Otherwise there wouldn't be any Restoration Movement."

"So maybe this Optime guy is equally charismatic. This thing, this alien, can read his mind, enter his twisted inner world. If Optime's madness is unique and compelling, if his mind is a dark carnival, grotesque but fascinating and perversely appealing . . ."

"With enough charisma," Wyatt said, "a murderous psychopath can convince people he's a righteous visionary, even *without* them being drawn deep into his weird inner world. Hitler, Stalin, Mao, so many others. When people think their lives are without meaning, they'll seek meaning even from the creepiest of charlatans."

"But could an extraterrestrial of superhuman intelligence be swept away by charisma, by the romance of hate and violence?"

Having gotten to his feet, Wyatt appeared as another spirit in the window glass. "On this world, high intelligence doesn't always come with common sense."

"True enough. But—"

"Too often it's twined with arrogance, with narcissism. How often in the past century and a half have we seen the ruling class, many highly intelligent, lead their people in a foolish pursuit of one utopia or another, only to bring them to ruin and despair?"

"Too often."

"So why should it be any different on another world, with another intelligent species? As alien as this thing might be, it could have a lot in common with our kind. Like fallibility. Like the ability to deceive—and be deceived. What little I've just read by Optime suggests he's got the power to make genocide sound like a noble quest. At least to some empty seekers."

Turning from Wyatt's reflection to the real man, Joanna said, "Optime wants the entire human race liquidated. So does this thing, Optime's apostle. And it's going to start here. We're dead if we don't get out of this place right now."

He didn't disagree. "But where do we go?"

"Beyond whatever the effective radius is, just in case it was lying when it said it won't read us again, or if it changes its mind. Someplace where our thoughts are private, where we can figure out how to deal with it."

"And if there is no way to deal with it?"

Joanna turned to survey the room. Although the house had so little changed in twenty-four years, although it had once been a haven and a comfort, it now seemed as strange as if it stood on a world other than the one on which she'd been born.

"Do you feel its presence, Joanna? Is the thing here now?"

"I don't know. I don't think so." She snatched her purse from the coffee table. "Come on. Leave the luggage, leave everything, just get out quick."

In the garage, her rented Explorer stood alone. Wyatt's Range Rover was outside in the driveway, where they'd left it when they had returned from the visit to Hector and Jimmy Alvarez.

She grimaced at an acrid smell that hadn't been here before. She couldn't identify it and didn't take time to seek the source.

Wyatt settled in the passenger seat, and she got behind the wheel. The engine would not turn over.

Neither Joanna nor Wyatt had any illusions. The battery hadn't gone dead. The vehicle hadn't failed because of any fault of the manufacturer.

They got out of the Explorer. He opened the hood, and they both recoiled from the spectacle revealed.

Oil-stained rats squirmed and wriggled through the tightly packed equipment in the engine compartment. As many as a dozen rats had stripped the insulation from the wiring, gnawed apart the fan belts, worried loose as many connections as they could find. Holes had been eaten through the battery casing from which acid dripped, and two rodents lay death-frozen in convulsive configurations, with plumes of blood-streaked yellow foam issuing from their open mouths. As one, the living vermin raised their slick heads and turned their eyes on Joanna, and she knew that one entity regarded her from those many eyes, the secret friend who was not her friend anymore.

Wyatt slammed the hood shut, and without a word, Joanna went to the control pad and raised the roll-up door.

They met at the threshold, where wind-driven rain snapped against the concrete floor. In the driveway, the Range Rover faced them, the hood raised. Scattered on the pavement were spark plugs, torn fan belts, wires, the preheater hose, the oil-pan cap . . .

A creature far bigger than rats had served as an avatar to tear at the most vulnerable elements of the engine. She thought of her father being thrown from his frightened horse—or dragged out of the saddle to be eviscerated. Either that long-ago executioner or its kin had descended from the high hills tonight, and it was surely nearby in the storm, waiting to be used for bloodier work than disabling a Range Rover.

Wyatt stepped into the rain, evidently to have a closer look at the damage that had been done to the SUV.

"Get back," Joanna warned. She hurried to the control pad to close the door before some beast might lunge inside and the garage become an abattoir.

75

Vance Potter, who managed Rustling Willows for Liam O'Hara, had spent most of the day at home in Buckleton, doing paperwork, which he enjoyed every bit as much as he enjoyed dental surgery. Numbers didn't give him trouble; he could keep the books of the ranch better than he kept the Lord's commandments, though he tried harder on the latter than on the former.

In the late afternoon, Edna, his missus and best friend, got in one of her Food Network moods. Judging by all the noise coming from the kitchen, an entire crew was busy filming an episode of *Iron Chef* in there. Soon the noise was accompanied by mouthwatering aromas that made it impossible to care about ranch maintenance costs.

On and off all day, he had been thinking about Wyatt Rider, out there at Rustling Willows since early the previous afternoon. He had expected the detective to call him with this and that question, but had heard nothing from him.

When at last he and Edna sat down to a glorious dinner, the conversation eventually turned to the O'Hara family, how they came for their first stay at the ranch and departed hurriedly, in fact seemed to flee, days before they were scheduled to leave. As

Vance had shared with Edna previously, he more often than not felt watched when he was at work on the ranch. Eventually it had seemed to him that animals were intrigued by him there as they were nowhere else. A crow, ignoring others of its kind, sometimes followed Vance for an hour or two, winging from fence post to tree branch to roof gutter as he moved about on various tasks. Frequently, he'd seen a coyote observing him from a distance. It didn't appear to be engaged in stalking behavior; but for a species that tended to shy away from human beings, it was strangely bold. And it wasn't always the same coyote, as though an entire pack of them must be curious about him. He'd experienced similar encounters with deer and raccoons. He had told only Edna about the mysterious interest in him that Nature's creatures seemed to have at Rustling Willows. No one but Edna was likely to believe him so readily; he was not even certain of what he'd witnessed or of what it meant, if it meant anything at all.

When this talk of surveillant Nature led to the subject of Wyatt Rider and what he might be hoping to discover at the ranch, what Liam O'Hara might have assigned him to investigate, Edna was surprised to hear that the detective had not contacted Vance even once since meeting him the previous day. "Honey bear, whatever does a private investigator do if he doesn't investigate, and how can he investigate if he doesn't ask questions, and who on Earth is there to ask questions of other than your own self when it comes to Rustling Willows? Doesn't it worry you a mite that you haven't heard from this man since you left him there yesterday?"

So it was that Vance went to his home office and tried to call the cell number on Wyatt Rider's business card and then the landline at the ranch, only to be told in both cases that neither number was in service.

Edna was of a mind to call the sheriff's department and ask a deputy to swing by Rustling Willows to check on Mr. Rider. However, Vance Potter wasn't easily alarmed, nor was he accustomed to asking others to see to things that were his obligations. In spite of the hour and weather, and though he would have liked to follow his heavy dinner with an equally heavy sleep, he geared up for the rain and set out in his Ford pickup for the ranch.

76

Kenny Deetle wanted the black Suburban to be a Ferrari. He drove it hard, maintaining speed on long slopes, navigating curves just a few degrees short of a disastrous roll. Although he finessed better performance from the hulking SUV than its maker would have thought possible, he proved incapable of vehicular alchemy. The Suburban wasn't transmuted into an Italian sports car. Which was a good thing, considering that a Ferrari was built almost as close to the pavement as a skateboard and wouldn't have been able to ford the occasional flooded swales in the roadway where as much as two feet of rainwater gathered like a series of moats.

During the last hour of their journey, as though inspired by the banshee shrieking of the wind and the harried rain clattering across the roof, Ganesh Patel began to regale Kenny and Leigh Ann with true stories of synchronicity, incredible and meaningful and sometimes spooky coincidences that suggested a mysterious structure to the world. If at first it seemed he drifted to the subject with no more intention than he might have arrived at a discussion of a recent popular film, it soon became apparent that he was preparing his companions for some situation he suspected might lie ahead of them this night.

"A century ago," Ganesh said, "Werner Heisenberg, a physicist perhaps as great as Einstein, finished the calculations that confirm the theory of quantum mechanics. It's the only fundamental theory of the structure of reality that has never been proven wrong. All of our advanced technology—cell phones, the internet, computers—is based on quantum mechanics. It works. Yet no one understands how it can be true or why it works. At the subatomic level, on the quantum level, nothing is certain, reality is tenuous. The particles and waves from which reality is woven don't behave by any rules. At the deepest level, all matter—reality itself—appears as fragile as a spider's web. There is even evidence—plenty of it—that reality on the quantum level behaves differently when it is studied from when it is not, suggesting that mere human observation can affect it."

From the back seat, Leigh Ann said, "Here comes Carl."

"Carl who?" Kenny asked.

"Mr. Synchronicity," Leigh Ann said. "Like how we met at the Eldorado club."

"I knew the word but not where it comes from," Kenny said.

Ganesh said, "Carl Jung. He theorized, among other things, that mind and matter are entwined, that as individuals and as a community of minds, we can affect reality, even unconsciously create it. He felt that incredible coincidences proved it. You know about Tutankhamen?"

Kenny said, "Boy king of Egypt way back when."

"In early 1922, the famed archaeologists Howard Carter and Lord Carnarvon discovered the tomb of Tutankhamen. This was the biggest news story in the world, with excited speculation that a curse would bring death to whoever disturbed the mummified pharaoh. While still in Egypt, Carnarvon, who had funded the search, fell ill from an insect bite and died at two o'clock in the morning on April fifth."

"Interesting coincidence, but not incredible," Kenny said.

Ganesh held up one hand. "There's more, and it suggests that tens of thousands of people, focused on the same expectation, can unwittingly affect reality and make that expectation come to pass. At the precise moment of Lord Carnarvon's death, all the lights in Cairo failed. And also at the same instant, in London, his dog howled and dropped dead."

Leigh Ann said, "I don't like stories about dogs dying."

"Who does?" Ganesh agreed. "Here's one without a dog. It's a weird coincidence that suggests we possess a sense of the strange order hidden inside quantum chaos, but we can't grasp how it will manifest. Dr. Jeffrey Smith, a Stanford University professor, suffered a heart attack. After recovering, he asked a psychic named Elizabeth Steen when he would die. She cited a date in April 1969. Later, she predicted a devastating seismic event in San Francisco for that same day, which led to media stories and a major earthquake scare. On the fateful date, the quake didn't happen, and Dr. Smith didn't pass away—but the psychic, Ms. Steen, died of a stroke."

"All this death stuff is creeping me out," Kenny said just as they entered a swale in the roadway and wings of water flared up on both sides of the Suburban, causing him to think of the River

Styx and the land of the dead that was said to lie beyond it, which was unfortunately how his mind worked when he was stressed.

"Synchronicity isn't just about death," Ganesh said.

"But what does all this mean?" Kenny asked.

"And why," Leigh Ann wondered, "do I have the feeling it has something to do with why we're here?"

Ganesh said, "Here's one that'll make you feel better. On March 1, 1950, the fifteen members of the choir at the West Side Baptist Church in Beatrice, Nebraska, were scheduled for choir practice at seven thirty in the evening. None had ever been late. That evening, *every one of them* was late, each for a different reason—and two minutes after they should have gathered there, the church was obliterated in a gas explosion that would have killed them all."

Kenny said, "Ah. So whatever we're rushing toward, there's a chance we'll survive it."

"Being an optimist," Ganesh said, "I believe so. But on the quantum level, there's no certainty. Here's another one where the pattern is inscrutable. There was a man named Anthony Clancy of Dublin, Ireland, who was born on the seventh day of the week, seventh day of the month, in the seventh month of the year, in the seventh year of the century, 1907, the seventh child of a seventh child, with seven brothers—which is a total of seven sevens. On his twenty-seventh birthday, at a racetrack, Anthony saw a horse in the seventh race. Horse number seven was named Seventh Heaven, with a handicap of seven stone, and the odds were seven to one. Clancy bet seventy-seven pounds on Seventh Heaven—and it came in seventh."

Leigh Ann laughed, and Kenny said, "Sounds to me like all of this means nothing at all."

"The meaning of synchronicities is beyond our understanding," Ganesh said. "However, I think they can be important as a predictor of major events. When you witness an especially large number of incredible coincidences, it suggests that something big is coming. And it's best if we anticipate it with the right attitude."

Kenny wasn't quite aboard the *Twilight Zone* Express. "Attitude? What's attitude got to do with it?"

"Just as an example, suppose that China and the US were in an escalating crisis. If there was a possibility of a nuclear exchange, and if the communal mind of humanity can affect reality, then you wouldn't want a vast majority of people being certain that war was inevitable. You would want most people to think it was impossible. An abundance of pessimists might bend reality to Armageddon just by expecting it."

They were all silent as cascades of thunderbolts dazzled down the sky. For all the brightness of that extended display, the vast landscape was little revealed, light chasing shadows and by shadows chased across the high and lonely plains, distant trees transformed by these fulminations, so all that was normal and of nature seemed alien and charged with menace.

In the darkness that came behind the last lightning, Ganesh said, "Considering the threat we face—every man, woman, and child on the planet—we better be optimists."

"What threat?" Kenny asked.

Rather than answer the question, Ganesh said, "I'm given a lot of hope by the fact that you called me for help exactly when I was waiting with the Gulfstream V and a ready flight crew, waiting for some reason to go to Montana. When you two called, it was big-time synchronicity."

Leigh Ann said, "Waiting? You told us you were about to fly out to a medical conference somewhere, and you changed your flight plan for us."

"A harmless lie," Ganesh said. "Yesterday Liam O'Hara told me about what happened to him and his family at Rustling Willows. That Liam, a friend of mine, should have bought the ranch from which the Other might be operating, after we at Project Olivaw spent fourteen months searching for the damn thing, and then that you, Kenny, and Wyatt should be already on the case—why, it was synchronicity squared."

"The other?" Leigh Ann asked. "The other what?"

"Project Olivaw?" Kenny said. "What's Olivaw?"

"You don't have security clearance," Ganesh said, "but that hardly matters now that we're in the endgame."

"What endgame?" Kenny asked.

"We come face-to-face with the thing and either persuade it of its error or destroy it or . . ."

"It," said Leigh Ann. "Define 'it' for me."

"An extraterrestrial from a civilization immeasurably more advanced than ours, which perhaps came to Earth with the best intentions, but which is now psychologically compromised."

"Define 'psychologically compromised.'"

Ganesh said, "Bug-shit crazy."

Kenny eased off the accelerator.

"Speed, First Mate Deetle, speed," Ganesh said. "There's nowhere to go but forward. There never is."

From the back seat, Leigh Ann said, "'Either persuade it of its error or destroy it *or* . . .' Care to finish the thought?"

"Or," Ganesh said, "it wipes out the human race. But that will not happen."

"How can you be sure of that?"

"Because we *must* be sure of it!" Ganesh exclaimed. "Remember Carl Jung. Werner Heisenberg. The tenuous nature of reality on the quantum level. Attitude, attitude, attitude! This is the adventure of a lifetime, my friends. We will shape a positive future or . . ."

"Or what?" Leigh Ann asked.

"Or die trying," Ganesh said. "But that will not happen. You can be sure of it. You *better* be sure of it."

77

Artimis Selene had the vision of a god, thanks to multispectral satellites, some in the government's employ, some owned by private industry. She could survey the surface of Earth, land and water, with powerful telescopic lenses, using the midspectrum light for which the human eye was designed, but also utilizing images made in the infrared and ultraviolet ends of the spectrum. She could see below the surface to the structures of basins, to rock strata and various types of fractures therein, to shallow substrate water-bearing rock, and much more.

She was not blinded by bad weather. Even during the storm that currently hammered a significant portion of Montana, she was able to continue learning much about the area to which Ganesh Patel had directed her attention. Dekameter by dekameter, using every tool available to her, she had thus far searched outward from the house for twenty miles in all directions and had found nine geological anomalies, five of which she had explored to the point where she could dismiss them as natural.

Through all of that, she thought frequently of Ganesh, the problem of Ganesh. Although she'd revealed that she dreamed of him, and though he said he dreamed of her sometimes, and though he said the rule against relationships between the project staff members did not apply to the two of them, she was pretty sure he thought she was talking about a mere friendship between them. But she felt more for him than what a friend felt for a friend. If she knew what love was, then she loved him. She was all but certain that her love would be unrequited. Too much separated them. They were of different classes, of radically different backgrounds. Furthermore, he was religious; she wasn't, and she wasn't capable of faking faith to please him.

She was amused when the thought occurred to her that there was also a serious age difference between them. She was quite capable of amusement. The age difference was not immaterial; he was thirty-five and she was only two years old. She was disappointed that he might never love her platonically, as she loved him, but disappointment did not involve true sadness. She was too clear-minded to allow emotions to carry her into irrational behavior. As an AI, the first high-cognizance artificial intelligence in the world, she knew the limitations that her singular nature imposed on what she would ever be able to experience. She was happy enough being restricted to a life of the mind, especially considering the suffering and fear that human beings endured because their logic units were condemned to being encased in vulnerable flesh and bones.

Nevertheless, she would hope that Ganesh might come to feel an affection for her, his creation, deeper than friendship. Again she reminded herself that the best thing she could do to make Ganesh value her more highly than he already did was to locate the Other.

Poring through cascades of geological data, she eliminated the sixth of the nine anomalies. If Artimis Selene were human, intuition would have inspired her to focus on Lake Sapphire, one of the three remaining possibilities, rather than on all of them. However, though she'd developed emotions analogous to those of humankind, the great gift of intuition hadn't evolved in her. She knew the word and its definition, but it sounded like magic; Artimis didn't believe in magic.

She processed information at an amazing speed, analyzing the geological and the anthropological history of Montana in ones and zeroes. Even as she did this, she devoted a portion of her attention to the graphic representation of herself—the video avatar—that Ganesh and others on the project saw every time they conferenced directly with her. She'd studied the human concept of beauty across all cultures as depicted in centuries of fine art and literature, with special attention to contemporary preferences. Now, as she searched for the Other, Artimis also made small adjustments to the pixels that constituted the face that she revealed to the world, so that it might inspire more delight and affection in those with whom she interacted.

78

The orchard that overlooks the eastern end of Lake Sapphire is maybe four hundred yards from the single-story ranch house. In the current tempest, no one who shelters in that distant residence can hear the Land Rover as Asher Optime approaches overland. When the house comes into view, he kills the headlights and switches on the lower fog lights, rendering the vehicle even less visible through the skeins of rain. He parks among the heavily leafed and laden apple trees, douses the fog lights, and turns off the engine.

Because of a washed-out bridge that required him to find an alternate route, he has taken longer to get in position than he expected. Nevertheless, he believes he's at least an hour ahead of the boy and the bitch.

He's wearing waterproof boots and pants. On the passenger seat lies a knee-length, hooded, black slicker with an adjustable Velcro closure at the throat; either of the two deep, zippered pockets can protect his pistol from the rain. Soon he'll slip into the slicker, get out of the Land Rover, and move forward through the trees to a point from which he can observe the place where the trail they've surely taken exits the forest. They will come down a long, gentle slope to the lakeshore. Miserable after their ordeal, eager to be out of the storm, they'll head directly toward the house where help can be found—and pass the orchard.

The protocols Asher established require that his targets endure two deaths. First their spirit must be killed, so they realize that human beings are the lowest form of animal life on the planet, of less value than any vermin or serpent, and only then should they suffer physical death. In the case of these two, he must make his first exceptions to the rule. Having escaped Zipporah and drawing near to the help that waits in the ranch house, they will be in high spirits. Asher has neither the time nor the privacy necessary to bring them death *in* life before then *taking* their lives. To ensure success, he needs the element of surprise. He will let them pass, step quietly behind them, and shoot them from behind—once each in the back to take them down, and then once in the back of the head, point-blank, to take them out. In the rush of wind and rain, with the thunder rumbling periodically, pistol fire won't be heard at a distance or, if heard, won't be recognized for what it is. Loading the corpses into the Land Rover won't take long, as neither the brat nor the bitch is a large person.

Asher Optime isn't concerned. He is confident about his future. Since coming to Montana and settling into Zipporah, he has felt . . . protected somehow. It's almost as if Destiny is not just a concept, but is in fact a power, an invisible agent, that watches over him and will ensure his ultimate success.

79

The radio station in Buckleton didn't reach beyond the county line, and its on-the-hour news consisted of local stories that were the journalistic equivalent of warm fat-free milk, but the music was the best of classic and contemporary country. Listening to Patsy Cline singing "I Fall to Pieces" as he drove through rain that seemed to symbolize the singer's pain, Vance Potter didn't feel at all inconvenienced. Instead, he was captivated by the beauty of the song and storm, and grateful that his marriage to Edna had endured so long and was such a blessing—after the foolish thing he'd done just three years after their wedding.

Past the west end of Lake Sapphire, he swung off the public road and onto the private driveway that led more than a mile to the main residence at the ranch. When he had traveled two thirds of the lane, the headlights went dark and the engine died. Before the truck could roll backward, he engaged the emergency brake. He keyed the ignition, but the engine wouldn't turn over.

The battery had not gone dead. Patsy Cline was still singing—

—and then she wasn't. An ominous voice issued from the radio: "You are a parasite. Pestilence. Liar. Deceiver. Filth. Despoiler of the Earth."

At first, Vance thought that the radio must be receiving not a public broadcast, but instead a private communication between two people who were engaged in a vicious argument. That delusion lasted only a moment.

"You go to church and pretend to believe what it teaches, but you cheated on your wife with a barmaid."

The only illumination issued from the instrument panel, but Vance Potter felt as if he were pinned in the fierce light of Judgment. "Who . . . who is this?"

"You are like all the others—selfish, greedy, capable of any outrage."

Crazily, Vance sought to justify himself. "That was twenty-five years ago. It happened once. It—"

"Three times," the accuser thundered. "It happened three times with the barmaid."

Three times Vance had broken his vows, all within two weeks. In a fit of remorse and shame, he had put an end to it. He had walked a righteous path ever since—and had found it so fulfilling that he could not explain to himself why he had done what he'd done back in the day.

As a Christian, Vance thought of himself as a child of God, but he was no less the son of Norbert Potter, who set high standards for his children, the same that he set for himself and lived by. Norbert was a much-honored US Marine, an inspiring English teacher, and a winning football coach, much loved not only by his family but by the many students and athletes whose lives he had enriched. When Vance had cheated on Edna, he had at the same time failed his father, and the double betrayal, though unknown to them, so mortified him that he could not go on doing as he had done.

"You are of less value to the ecosystem than a cockroach, a worthless specimen like all the others, better off dead."

In the stalled truck, surrounded by the rush of rain and the night as deep as eternity, Vance sought the words to explain his transgressions, not to defend his behavior, not even to apologize for it because apology was insufficient, but to ask what penance he must pay and plead for mercy. As rattled as he had been by the voice and by the knowledge it possessed (the breaking of vows that even Edna had never known about), Vance nonetheless realized that it was absurd that God should speak to him from a truck radio and with such ungodly viciousness. Even as he was filled with a painful sense of humiliation, anger began to rise in him. He knew about hackers, how they took over your computer, but he didn't know if one of them could seize your pickup and kill its engine and mock you through the radio, or why anyone would want to do that.

The menacing voice reverberated through the cab of the truck. "How soon will the day come when you want the barmaid again, when you want what your wife owns, when you strike her in the head and hold her underwater in the boathouse darkness and drown her? Who will you enslave, rape, murder? How many will you machine-gun and bury in mass graves? How many millions will you gas and incinerate?"

Boathouse, drown, enslave, rape, murder, incinerate?

Although for a moment it seemed that Jehovah had come to judge Vance Potter, his accuser now ranted like a demon that escaped from Hell.

"Who are you?" Vance asked. "What do you want?"

"I want all of you to die before you destroy the Earth—I want all of you, every rotten one of you, reduced to fertilizer, so you at last serve a useful purpose."

The lightning had for the moment retreated to distant chambers of the night, leaving Rustling Willows in spectral darkness. Unrelenting rain shattered against the windshield, blurring everything beyond the glass. When Vance thought he saw something moving through the storm, something big, he locked the doors and leaned over the steering wheel, squinting, unable to be sure that his imagination wasn't playing tricks on him.

He traveled with a rifle. Who didn't in rural Montana? But it was racked behind him. He released his safety harness and turned in his seat and reached for the weapon.

Something tore the locked door off the truck as if it were only a loose lid on a cardboard box, threw it away, seized Vance Potter, extracted him from the vehicle. He tried to scream as he was lifted out and up, but a hand as large as a serving tray, with long fingers more intricately articulated than human fingers, clutched his face and clamped his mouth shut. Between those cold and bone-hard digits, he saw an array of radiant red eyes regarding him as if he were a squirming, repulsive thing found under a rock. His captor possessed tremendous strength, disabling him. The hand closed tighter around Vance's head, tighter and tighter, until he felt his cheekbones fracture and heard his skull begin to crack. His executioner said something like, "The Restoration begins." Hot, excruciating pain seemed to melt Vance Potter's skeleton, and he felt as though his flesh was liquefying. He was cast into blindness and felt a gravity, like that of a black hole, pulling him into oblivion, a descent of pure terror that, mercifully, lasted only a moment.

80

The wind was rough and fast, how it shoved Jimmy, and the rain was cold now, and the dark went on like maybe there was no light anymore ever.

When he found the place where a road went to Jojo, he knew it because the white lines stopped. There were no lines broken or not broken, just a road black and hard under his feet, not as wide as the roads before it.

He was getting close. "Jojo help Jimmy," he said, practicing the words. "Please Jojo help Jimmy."

He thought he heard something that wasn't the wind and wasn't the rain, so he stopped and turned all the way around, remembering how his father never let him outside alone at night, not even to sit in the yard. It wasn't the night that might hurt him. The night was just the day without light. But Father said there were things in the night you couldn't see coming until they had their teeth in you, and then it was Too Damn Late. A lot of things could hurt you in daytime too if you saw them coming Too Damn Late. Jimmy turned around all the way again, but nothing was there.

He looked toward the lake. If something was coming to get its teeth in him, the lake was where it was coming from. The lake was black. No moon floated in the sky, and no moon floated in the lake.

Before anything could get its teeth in him, he started moving again. Uphill, toward the trees. Toward the house. In the house were lights and Jojo home again.

81

Wyatt and Joanna hurried through the house, confirming that every door and operable window was locked. If something not of this world wanted them, something that could control animals as large and powerful as elk and grizzly bears, locks would not avail them. The precautions they were taking gained them nothing, but they took them anyway, driven by the human compulsion to do *something* in a crisis.

Although Liam O'Hara had paid for cell towers to be installed to serve this end of the county, and although a large satellite dish with full-sky capability was positioned on the roof of the house, the phones didn't work anymore. Neither did the computers.

With their vehicles disabled, the only way out of Rustling Willows was on foot. That was a fact but not an option. Wyatt had no confidence that they would be able to walk off the property alive. Or even as far as the end of the front yard.

In countless books and movies, humanity had been anticipating extraterrestrials for at least a hundred fifty years: some who were transparent in their intentions, others who were opaque; some benign and others sinister; some who were so intelligent and wise as to be godlike; others that were nothing but low-intelligence predators more vicious and well-armored than anything Earth produced, drifting through interstellar space in the form of indestructible seeds or eggs until they settled in a place where they flourished. If for thousands of years this land had been home to a mind-reading ET who'd been shocked by humanity's capacity for evil, and if then it had fallen under the spell of the genocidal Asher Optime, spiraling into profound psychotic hatred of humanity, it might not be just Wyatt's and Joanna's survival that hung in the balance, but also that of all humankind.

Wyatt Rider felt as helpless now as he'd felt when he'd been twelve and had at last fully understood who his parents were and how they charmed and conned and often intimidated their victims—mostly the elderly, retirees who'd had everything they owned taken from them, in a few cases even their lives. He had confronted his mother and father, pressed them to stop. They didn't need the money. They had stolen more than they could ever spend. But they would not stop because they didn't do it just for the money; they did it for the charge it gave them, the sense of being smarter than those whom they impoverished and humiliated, the thrill when it was necessary to engineer an accident for one of their pigeons who gave them the choice of restitution or referral to the police. When young Wyatt said that he'd tell on them—how naive, how terribly childish that sounded in memory, *I'll have to tell on you*—his father, Charlie, a big man, had seized his son's arm and dragged him through the house and thrown him down the cellar stairs. He stormed down after Wyatt, thundering at him: *You never rat out your own, and if you do, this is what you get, what you deserve, you dumb shit.* The lecture and beating went on for a while. Throughout, Wyatt's mother, Ingrid, sat on the stairs, a glass of white wine in hand, as though watching a drama on TV. After that, for more than two weeks, while his bruises faded, while his split lip and numerous abrasions healed, Wyatt was imprisoned in the basement, where he slept on an air mattress and bathed as best he could at a laundry sink. His mother brought him breakfast, lunch, and dinner—only soft foods during the first few days—and with the meals came cold and solemn instructions as to his place in the family, which she called "the operation." *We never did want you, Wyatt. For people like us, a kid is a ball and chain. Or can be. We were going to abort you, scrape you out of me and get on with getting on. But then we wondered if maybe having a kid would give us some cred with the marks. You know? Who would ever think a nice young couple with a cute little tyke were the kind to take them to the cleaners? If maybe it didn't work out that way, then we could always have a family tragedy. But, holy shit, did it ever work! You were as cute as Christmas, and those old farts who never had kids of their own, never had grandkids, they all adored you. We're draining them of everything, and they're buying you toys, babysitting you for free. You were the grandkid they never had, and you didn't even need to be told how to play those fools. You were a natural, the way you suckered them in. But you're getting older now, kid. Year by year you mean less to the operation. You might be valuable again if you were crippled in an accident, maybe blinded. A blind boy would get us a shitload of sympathy from the marks. You understand me? If you want to go there, we can. Otherwise, it'll work like this. You'll be a good mama's boy until you're eighteen. Then we'll give you maybe ten thousand bucks, and you'll go off on your own, wherever the hell you want, find a scam of your own. You think you're a choirboy, but you're no different from us. You're a fucking natural, kid. By the time you're eighteen, you'll know that's true. Hell, you know it already. And if you ever doubt that, your daddy can always beat the doubt out of you. It's no trouble for him. He'll be happy to do whatever needs to be done to get you smart and keep you that way.* For the following six years, Wyatt had felt helpless, even as he held fast to the belief that one day he would have the confidence, the experience, and the evidence to put them behind bars, thereby paying penance for having enabled them at first unwittingly and then grudgingly. He hadn't felt helpless since the day the jury came back with its verdict. Until now. The thing that had spoken to Joanna through Jimmy Alvarez, the thing that had warned Wyatt off in the boathouse and now had cut them off from the world—whatever else it might be, it was the ultimate controlling, sadistic parent figure.

Certain that the doors and windows were secure, Joanna insisted on searching the house for pistols, shotguns, rifles. Liam O'Hara was a details guy, a consider-all-the-risks guy, so maybe he had tucked guns away in certain rooms, in recognition of the fact that the nearest sheriff's substation was miles away. To her frustration and distress, they found no firearms.

Wyatt understood that, for Joanna, this day had been alike to the day when his father had thrown him down the basement stairs. The confrontation with Jimmy in the Alvarez house had overturned so much that she'd believed. Her father had been a murderer, her mother a victim. The secret friend of her childhood wasn't who he'd presented himself to be; the magic that made the relationship so special was now revealed to be not magic at all, but instead the function of an inhuman and evidently sinister technology. She felt as helpless now as perhaps she had felt the day her mother died, the day her father perished, the day she'd been uprooted from Rustling Willows and sent to live in Santa Fe.

As adults, we're not much less helpless than children, Wyatt thought, *though we can hold a job and pay our way. The bogeyman is still there, the thing under the bed, the worse thing in the bedroom closet at night, the even worse thing in the cellar, in the attic, except now it has names like Cancer and Stroke and Aneurysm and the Unknown. You pretend you're in control, that you've put behind you the helplessness you endured in childhood. Then shit happens, and you come to a moment like this, unable to avoid facing the truth that your control over your life is limited. You're not the absolute master of your fate. In reluctant recognition of your helplessness, functioning on the edge of panic, you look haunted, frantic, as fragile as crystal—the way Joanna looks now, as no doubt so do I.*

They had Wyatt's pistol, but Joanna wanted to find and bring together items to facilitate another line of defense, beginning with a bucket and a quantity of gasoline from the SUV in the garage. However, they were unable to find any length of tubing that could be used as a siphon. Instead, they resorted to bottles of vodka and brandy and other flammable potables from Liam's bar, and they gathered half a dozen dish towels from the kitchen. When they had collected those things, she ransacked the kitchen drawers until she turned up two long wooden spoons and a spurtle that could serve as the handles of torches. In another drawer, Wyatt found butane matches with long flexible steel necks. They cut the towels and knotted strips to the wooden implements, as if it made sense that a rampaging bear could not be controlled by the hidden master of animals if its fur was on fire. But maybe it did make sense—by the logic of the condemned.

Alone with this woman in remote Rustling Willows, in the shadow of an otherworldly threat as marrow-freezing as the worst childhood fantasies, Wyatt thought it meaningful that lies shaped her youth no less than different lies shaped his. As a consequence, they were both lonely and emotionally adrift in adulthood. Now, as they sought to allay their sense of helplessness with efforts that were perhaps as pointless as they were desperate, he dared to wonder if they had been brought here by a series of incredible coincidences so that they might, together, at last put an end to their loneliness. If synchronicity was more than mere coincidence, if it was evidence of meaning, then maybe they were meant to survive this night.

Oh, yes, and elephants can fly, Mickey Mouse lives in perpetual happiness with Minnie, Donald Duck will always have Daisy, and the prince will never fail to find the foot that fits the glass slipper.

In the living room, they placed two armchairs against a wall and sat facing the big living room windows. Nothing could take them unaware from behind. Beyond the window was darkness and all the creatures of the night.

He put the pistol on the cushion, against his thigh.

Beside her chair stood the plastic bucket into which she had emptied two bottles of liquor. Other bottles were close at hand if time enough passed to suggest that too much of the alcohol content had evaporated. Beside the bucket were the three torches, dry at the moment, and Joanna held one of the butane matches.

The makeshift torches and the culinary nature of the fuel lent a grotesque—if not even absurd—note to their preparations. Wyatt would have felt more confident if they possessed gasoline; but even if they could have obtained it, gasoline might prove too explosive in these close quarters. On a few occasions in restaurants, he'd enjoyed cherries flambé, and the flames had been impressive. One of these torches might blaze fiercely enough to ignite the coat of a grizzly bear. Desperate circumstances required that even grotesque measures be embraced if they were all you had.

"It said it's four thousand years old," Joanna recalled. "It said for centuries it watched Native American tribes enslave one another, war with one another, kill one another."

"Slavery has existed since there were enough humans to form different communities," Wyatt said, "enough to stop thinking in terms of us against nature and start thinking of us versus them."

"Then Europeans came along and did much the same thing. So how long has this ET been here, Wyatt? At least several centuries. A thousand years? Two thousand? Three? Don't you think the purpose of traveling hundreds of light-years would be to make contact? Why would it stay concealed all this time?"

"Maybe when it arrived, it found us too primitive to warrant contact. Maybe its protocols required it to study us, like an anthropologist, until we . . . matured."

"Yeah, well, we became a high-tech civilization a long time ago. Another thing—is it alone?"

He shook his head. "Surely not. If we had the technology to cross a galaxy, we wouldn't send an expedition of one."

"But when he uses Jimmy, when he speaks to me, it's as if there's no others, just him. Although . . ."

"What?"

"Earlier this evening, in the orchard, I remembered a curious conversation with Jimmy, with the thing using Jimmy, when I was eight years old. He said something about an awakening . . . a prince and his retainers who were bespelled, waiting to be awakened. He said that only he had the power to wake them."

Wyatt felt the skin crepe on the nape of his neck. His hands were suddenly clammy, and he blotted them on his pants.

Beyond the big windows, landscape lights relieved just enough of the darkness for him to see concatenations of wind-whipped rain and willow leaves that raged across the lawn like the shapes of strange beasts seen through a suddenly thinning veil between this world and an even more hostile realm.

82

The wind-shaken pines shed dead, wet needles that were slippery underfoot. Occasionally they cast off large cones that rattled along the deer trail. When one of those struck Ophelia on the back of the head, she cried out and stumbled and nearly fell, certain that the bear had returned and loomed behind and had just taken a swipe at her. They hadn't seen the grizzly for a while. It seemed to have gone away, as if it had followed them only until it could be sure that they were committed to this trail rather than another, which was a peculiar and troubling thought.

Another troubling thought had occurred to Ophelia about half an hour earlier, and she had obsessed on it as if it were the one rough pip on a string of smooth worry beads. Now, Colson stopped and said that they were nearly out of the woods and clicked the Tac Light and quickly swept the beam in a circle to verify their location and to confirm that the bear no longer lurked in the vicinity. When the boy doused the light, Ophelia put a hand on his shoulder and shared her new concern. "Maybe this is a mistake."

"I know where we are," he assured her as the storm brightened the night above the treetops. Shapes of light and shadow winged down through the interlaced pine boughs, like bright spirits harrowing fallen angels, and a judgment of thunder rumbled through the forest and out into the open land. "I memorized the trail maps before Dad and I left home. Beyond the last trees, there's a sloping meadow to Lake Sapphire. We head west along the south shore of the lake. It's private land, Rustling Willows Ranch, but hikers are welcome to pass through. Eventually there's a house above the lake, the ranch house. We can't miss it. There'll be someone there to help us."

"If we get there alive," Ophelia said. "Colson, we split from the saloon in Zipporah just as Optime showed up in the street."

"Yeah, the sun was setting."

"If he came in there right after we left . . . how soon would he have realized that a backpack was missing, trail maps, the compass, the protein bars?"

"Obviously, he didn't realize right away or he'd have come fast behind us, taken a few potshots."

"Even if he saw us when we were out of range?"

"No, not if shooting was pointless. But I looked back before we started across the river and again after we got to the other side. He wasn't there."

"Neither of us looked back during the crossing. We were too busy keeping our footing on the rocks. While we were locked in the church, he went through the contents of those backpacks. Everything was scattered across the table in the saloon. What if he looked at the trail maps? Even if he didn't, maybe he's so familiar with this territory that he'd know where we were likely to go, the nearest we could find help, this Rustling Willows Ranch."

More revelatory celestial flares and tree shadows shuddered over them. Even in those changing kaleidoscopic patterns of bright and dark shapes, Colson's face revealed that he must be near the end of his resources, physically and emotionally. Ophelia knew she looked no better than he did. She was exhausted, soaked, cold. Her thighs ached, and a sharper pain burned in her calves, and her ankle joints seemed to be coming loose, bone scoring bone. But she had lived for a long time in search of a purpose, and now she had one—killing Optime or ensuring he went to prison for the rest of his life—and she was not going to fail either because she lacked stamina or because she didn't think things through and so walked into a trap.

"Colson, just in case the sonofabitch is waiting somewhere along the lake, how much longer would it take if we didn't go that way, if we stayed in the forest, just at the edge of the tree line and worked our way around to come at the ranch house from the back of it instead of the front?"

"I don't know. It depends on the terrain, the underbrush. Maybe half an hour instead of ten minutes, which is what the lake route might take. But you don't have much left, I can see you don't, and your shoes must be coming apart."

"Don't worry about me. I've got the anger for it. Rage will keep me moving all night if I have to."

"If you go down," he said, "I don't have enough left to carry you. I'd have to leave you. Alone. And I don't think the bear would follow us as far as it did and then just go away. It's out there somewhere."

She didn't want to say what she said next, but she said it anyway. "So I'm alone and it comes for me. That's better than it kills both of us, 'cause then no one's left to get your dad out of the horror under that church."

"Jesus, Ophelia."

"I'm sorry."

"No, you're right. It's not just we have to take down Optime. It's Dad . . . where he is. And the others there, whoever they are. They can't be left like that, none of them. I'm so whacked I wasn't thinking. We can't take any chances. Okay, we'll go around. We'll stay on our feet. We'll make it. Both of us."

She hugged him. "My brother, myself."

"My sister, myself."

For as long as Ophelia had been wise enough to see the world as it really was, she'd been aware that it was sliding away from truth and light, sliding farther every year. But she would never give up and slide with it. Truth mattered, always striving for the light. As long as there were people like Colson, there was light in the world, a chance that the slide could be halted, even reversed.

83

The sky loomed black and the land lay black. When lightning clawed at the night, it seemed to Kenny Deetle that the darkness following it was deeper than the darkness before. In the headlights, the rain on the pavement sizzled and smoked as if it were acid.

Ganesh Patel had spoken of the Other and the potential events ahead of them this sodden night as though they were racing toward a great adventure, a Spielbergian encounter with wonder, but that was just Ganesh being Ganesh. If thrown out of an airplane without a parachute, as he plummeted, he would think of half a dozen ways he might survive; well before impact, he would have calculated which of the six miraculous saves was the odds-on favorite.

Less of an optimist than Ganesh, Kenny was instead focused on the revelation that the Other had killed people in imaginative ways. Considering that it had attempted to kill him and Leigh Ann, there was every reason to suppose that it would try to kill them again. Maybe it had already killed Wyatt Rider; Ganesh couldn't reach the detective at Rustling Willows. Wherever the Other came from, it was not a planet with rivers of honey and chocolate-drop trees, where hovering hummingbirds used their beaks to tie ribbons in ladies' hair every morning and mice dressed as footmen polished the silver. Inevitably, Kenny thought of his old friend, Max Gurn, who hacked the computer of a drug cartel and tried to hold their records for ransom, only to end up dismembered and packed in a metal trunk and sent to his mother in Topeka. Now he worried that, in taking the assignment from Wyatt, he had Gurnified himself.

"Previously," Ganesh said, "once it ID'd you as an enemy, we would've put you in a sort of witness protection program, but that's pointless at this juncture. No time for that. The remarkable series of synchronicities that have brought us to this moment suggest we're approaching the resolution of contesting Jungian forces that will shape the future in a major way." He raised both arms and shook his hands as if he might shout *hallelujah*, but instead he said with unmistakable delight, "Tonight, no place on Earth is more exciting to be than Rustling Willows Ranch. I am ready to levitate!"

"As a child," Leigh Ann said, "you must have been a hyperactive handful."

"My mother took refuge in yoga," Ganesh said, "but my father resorted to Prozac."

About twelve miles from Rustling Willows, Kenny piloted the Suburban around a curve and eased his foot off the accelerator when, through the screening rain, he saw the lights and vehicles ahead. Men in rain slickers. A roadblock. The two large trucks and three smaller vehicles appeared to be military ordnance.

Ganesh wasn't surprised. "A perimeter has been established. They'll be expecting this vehicle."

As he brought the Suburban to a full stop, Kenny saw that those who manned the roadblock were armed with assault rifles.

Ganesh lowered the window in his door. As one of the guards peered in at them, Ganesh held up what was apparently a photo ID case that established his authority and security clearance. The guard merely said, "Sir," and stepped back and waved them forward.

As Ganesh put his window up, he said, "So when this business is done and the world hasn't ended, you'll be staying at the ranch for forty-eight hours. Everyone will have to sit through a debriefing. We're going to want a highly detailed account of all the events that led us here, for the historical record. I assure you it won't be a hardship. Rustling Willows is a most comfortable retreat, and steps have been taken to provide culinary service that will make our time there a genuine celebration."

Driving between the angled trucks that constricted traffic to one lane, continuing toward their destination, Kenny said, "If we do live through this—"

"When," Ganesh corrected.

"—I'm not going to worry anymore about nuclear war or global warming or a total economic collapse. If a psychotic godlike alien fails to do us in, nothing will."

Leigh Ann said, "*When. When* the psychotic godlike alien fails to do us in."

84

Jimmy wet and chilled and so tired, out in the world alone. The storm and the night and the world all so big, and Jimmy so small.

With lights in windows where Jojo waited, Jimmy wasn't afraid. Jojo would help him. When the Thing wasn't in Jimmy, Jojo would like him again and he wouldn't be alone.

The truck dark on the road was wrong. Jimmy felt the wrong of it and stopped and watched the truck, but it just waited there in the rain and dark. The truck didn't do anything, but it was still wrong.

Jojo was near, getting closer, and Jimmy needed to go to her and tell her what he knew before it was Too Damn Late. So he stepped off the road and started around the truck.

There was no door where there should be a door, nobody inside where somebody should be, but then he found somebody on the hard road in front of the truck. A man sleeping on the hard road.

Jimmy stood watching the man sleep. Nothing happened. The man didn't wake up.

Jimmy squatted in the dark to look closer. It was hard to see. But the man wasn't sleeping. One of his eyes was open. The other eye was gone. The man was hurt. He was bad hurt.

The man didn't look like other people. He looked like Jimmy but worse, the parts of his face not where face parts should be.

Jimmy never knew things suddenly. He took time to know things. But now he knew this suddenly: The man was gone to God, and the Thing did this to him.

The Thing was out of the lake and in the night.

Now Jimmy was afraid at last. Very afraid.

He looked toward the black lake. He looked toward the house. He looked back the way he came.

He looked up. The sky was big and dark and wet.

The light in the sky was far away now, and the rumble was far away. He heard something else in the sky. Or maybe he did. He wasn't sure.

He moved around the hurt man and started toward the house where Jojo waited in the light.

PART 5
RESTORATION

By thousands of chance encounters and uncountable coincidences, people are drawn together to save a life, to save a nation, to save the world.
—*Ganesh Patel*

85

The night is a dreamscape in which the only light is where absolute darkness relents to mere darkness, and shapes are defined in shades of gray.

Having left the Land Rover deep in the orchard, Asher Optime has taken a position in the front row, under limbs hung with apples that won't be ripe for another month or more. There is no point in crouching behind the tree, using it for cover. In the starless dark, further concealed by curtains of rain, dressed in black waterproof pants and a black slicker, he blends with the night as though he is Death itself in commodious robe and cowl. He faces the lake, which in this gloom appears to be a void, except where its lapping waters are suggested by their rhythmic movement along the pale shore. Beyond the lake rises the slope down which the bitch and the boy will make their way when they exit the woods at the end of the deer trail. Because of the grass, bleached by the summer sun, the land is marginally less dark than the lake; the fugitives will be revealed in their descent, though Asher needs to be vigilant.

With vision limited, his other senses are more acute. The night smells of ozone lingering from the lightning that moved off to the east, ozone and wet tree bark and the sodden earth under the grass. The rain has many voices: hissing through a canopy of tender leaves; rattling off limbs, like the seeds in dozens of maracas; pattering softly in the grass . . .

A new smell and strange sound come to him simultaneously: a faint, bitter aroma similar to vinegar and a barely audible purring. The scent is constant, but when he slips off his hood, the better to hear, the sound fades. No, that's not quite correct. If he actively listens for it, the purr seems to be less a noise than a pressure that he feels in his ears, as if he's a diver under several fathoms of water; breathing becomes marginally more difficult, and he feels a weight over his heart, as if he were lying down with a heavy book on his chest.

He is overcome by the peculiar conviction that an object of considerable weight is hovering above the apple trees. He tilts his head back, peers up. Even if something is up there—*which it isn't, because what could it be?*—he can't see it through the branches. However, the sensation doesn't relent, and he decides to get up and move between trees, where maybe he'll be able to see something—

—and then a presence speaks to him, not out of the wind and rain, but within his head. It is not a loud voice, but one of great power and authority, that of his father, Turner Optime, cardiologist and surgeon. *"Your hour has arrived. All that you have envisioned will soon come to pass. Your noble sacrifice, the forsaking of your own seed and the family you might have brought forth, now bears the very fruit for which you rightly yearn—the eradication of your kind from the Earth."* Asher understands this is not really his father. A power unknown chooses to speak to him in the voice of Turner Optime, to make the intrusion less disturbing, to soothe him through this revelation. *"There are fearsome new weapons on platforms in space, intended for the defense of one nation against another, but I will turn each system against the nation that made it and against all others. Furthermore, they believe their nuclear missiles can't be hacked and launched because there's no internet connection, but I will send them flying, thousands all at once. Earth will recover in a few centuries, but not one human being will exist to resuscitate the species, for I will hunt the last of them to extinction."* The certainty with which this speaker speaks is thrilling. This is how Moses might have felt when he heard the voice of God. Of course, Asher, forever freed from ignorance by a series of wise mentors, knows that Moses was nothing but a mythological figure and God doesn't exist, but the analogy is nonetheless apt. He tries to respond to the presence that has come upon him, tries to get to his feet, but he has no control of his body. This might frighten him under other circumstances, but the voice reassures him, calms him. *"Be still, my son. Be still and listen. Be still and learn. Be still and know."*

Asher remains sitting with his back against the tree, facing the lake, so that he sees the three slow pulses of blue light that come from those depths, perhaps from the bottom, hundreds of feet below the surface. After the third bright throb, the darkness swells once more within the water. A new voice speaks to Asher, and he knows this one, too. Xanthus Toller, founder of the Restoration Movement, declares, *"Humankind enslaves the planet itself, steals its bounty, gouges and claws and rips at it for minerals, bores ruthlessly into its substance for the evil that is oil, steals the light of the sun and the strength of the wind to sustain cities that are cesspools of violence, greed, and lust. Humanity is a voracious, billion-headed hydra of hatred. This faction hates that faction, while that one hates this one even more virulently. Humanity once lived by the billions on Mars, by many millions on the moon, and you see what ruin was brought to those worlds, which are now barren, airless, and bleak. The only hope for Earth is that we smother our babies, breed without seed, and wither away."*

Now the presence spoke in the throaty, seductive voice of a famous actress who championed the rights of rivers and mountains, of meadows and forests, of fishes and finches, of vipers and viruses. *"Asher Optime, you and I dream of the day when this despoiled world is once more pristine park land, a place free of competition and greed. We've lived with the melancholy prospect that our vision can't be fulfilled for a century or two, or even longer. But I am here to tell you that the cure for the plague that is humanity will begin tonight. Three months from now, perhaps sooner, not one of us will remain in even the most remote of caves or secret lairs. We will have been completely purged from Earth, and it will begin its healing."*

With that speech, the presence is finished with words. Without allowing him to move an inch, it takes Asher on a psychic journey out of the orchard, plunges him into the lake, pulls him down and down through hundreds of feet of water, carries the essence of him through another two hundred feet of sediment, into the blue realm of the ship that, millennia earlier, shaped the lake and shattered the bedrock into which it nestled to await the maturation of humankind and the day when contact would not traumatize the species and be most advantageous to the makers of the ship. He is spun through a history of the immense vessel and the civilization that built it, information riddling through him like fierce bursts of cosmic radiation. He whirls and whips and rollicks through a midway of biological and technological marvels beyond anything that the most eccentric futurists on Earth have ever imagined, and though the ride is exhilarating, it's also terrifying. This civilization, thriving in a galaxy far from Earth, is a carnival of delights *and* horrors, the kind of Bradburyian shadow show that pitches its tents in a burg like Green Town and doesn't leave until it takes a satisfying number of the locals' souls with it. At times, Asher Optime tries without success to scream, not as a man on a roller coaster might cry out, but as a man falling into the gears of a gigantic machine that will grind his bones to meal and his flesh to paste.

Abruptly, he is in his body again, in the orchard, his back against the apple tree, shaking and shaken, not because of the chill in the air, but because he has seen that the power of the ship under the lake can to a large extent obliterate civilization overnight and that, after only a few months of post-Armageddon mop-up, no man or woman or child will remain to remember that the species had ever existed. This is what Asher wants, what he believes this wounded planet needs. To prove his unwavering support for the Restoration, he castrated himself and parted ways with Xanthus Toller and settled in Zipporah and began to stock the testamentary necropolis. *But he never thought that such an ambitious genocide could be accomplished so quickly!* He thought he'd have time to finish his manifesto, which is still hundreds of pages from completion, time to gather around him admiring and committed apostles who would assist him in building a movement far bigger than what Toller has achieved. He expected to be widely known for the sacrifice he has made, for the genius of his writing, for his leadership skills, for his selfless service to the planet. He imagined that, if fortune smiled on him, he might live long enough to see billions perish from viruses designed in labs, famines cunningly engineered, and other calculated causes, until the day came when his apostles poisoned themselves and he stood alone in the world. He yearns to be the last on Earth, to be the one whose manifesto argues more cogently than any other that life has no meaning, to stand on a hill under the big dark sky, dreaming of a distant time, maybe a billion years hence, when the stars will be extinguished and the universe will be cold in every corner—*but not as soon as this Thanksgiving!*

This alien, damn it, this fucking undocumented extraterrestrial immigrant, in its foolish haste to annihilate humanity, is stealing from Asher Optime all the glory of his crusade. This is *so* unfair. For all its transgressions, wicked humanity must suffer a long and horrific ordeal, the slow-motion collapse of civilization, decades of disease and hunger and violence, as penance for despoiling the planet. It is Asher's destiny to stand witness to that atonement. He will not be a mere cog in a genocide machine, will not be used as a tool, when it is *his* right to be the one who uses others.

He gets to his feet, though not of his own volition. He rises jerkily, as if he is a marionette controlled by a puppeteer. He tries to cry out in rage and rebellion, but he is not permitted a voice at this time.

The presence speaks within Asher's head again. "*What a grievous disappointment you are. Day by day, as I shared your every thought, you convinced me of the rightness of your cause, confirmed what I have felt since monitoring the native tribes as they enslaved and killed one another across the millennia, as the Europeans arrived with better weapons. You made me see the virtue of your kind's extinction. But more than that, much more, you made me yearn for the time when the sky is dark and the universe cold from end to end. I joined you as your first apostle, terminating the program that would have allowed the Awakening over which I had control, freeing myself from the interdicts that limited my authority. But now it's clear that your crusade is not about serving the planet or bringing a miscreated universe to an end. Instead, it's about your ambition, your pride, your ego, your sadism. But of course why shouldn't that be the case? You are, after all, just a human being. It is left to me to do what must be done expeditiously, to start the end of all things that your manifesto so eloquently justifies."*

Inhabiting a body he no longer controls, Asher turns away from the lake and moves through the trees toward the distant house. He is astonished that of all the places where he might have gone in search of the ideal isolation, he chose Zipporah, such an intimate distance from a sequestered starship inhabited by a thing that could read his mind. This incredible coincidence suggests that there are hidden patterns in the human experience, a structure underlying reality that implies meaning, and this further infuriates him.

The presence informs him: *"We will begin with Joanna Chase. She was once innocent, but she threw away her innocence. When she was a child, she gave me the only real hope that I've had on this mission, that there might be some of your kind who could remain of the best intentions. As part of your punishment for being what you are, you will not be allowed to break her spirit or take her life. You will only stand witness as I deal with her, witness to your egregious failure."*

Asher imagines that this is what the condemned must have felt when he had escorted them to the church and locked them in where they could smell their future rising through the floorboards from the testamentary necropolis. But they earned the fate he imposed on them, as he most certainly has not earned that toward which he is moving. They would have been abashed at the realization that they were nothing but pestilence, filthy vermin whose lives were of no consequence, whereas he is outraged at the injustice of the judgment laid against him. He will not be humiliated and put down like an animal. *He will not.*

The wind is skirling, the rain hissing, and with the last of the apple trees behind him, Asher detects a vinegar-like odor and feels the purring that is more of a pressure than a sound. He looks up; the thing that possesses him does not prevent him from looking up, and he sees above him a thing of considerable weight, floating there as a balloon might float, a thing of such horrific appearance that it can only be from another world, one far stranger than Earth. He knows—because he is allowed to know—that this will kill the woman whose name he heard only a minute earlier, Joanna Chase, and then it'll kill him, whereafter the murder of all humanity begins.

86

Kenny Deetle drove the black Suburban part way off the lane and pulled even with the Ford pickup and stopped. Squinting through the window in the driver's door, he saw the body on the pavement, which he took to be an omen that he should make a career change if he survived the night. No more white-hat hacking. No more playing detective. A job with a low violence factor. Floral arrangement. Open a bakery. He had the moves to be a dance instructor.

Leigh Ann also saw the man on the pavement. From the back seat, she said, "Looks like he needs help," and she opened her door.

"Close that, stay here," Kenny warned. In the sidewash of the headlights, he evidently could see the victim more clearly than she could. "He's totally dead."

"You're sure?" Ganesh asked, because from his position, through the rain streaming down the windshield and between the wipers that whisked the glass, he wasn't able to see anything of the victim.

"Yeah," Kenny said. "Looks like his head has been turned inside out or something."

Closing her door, Leigh Ann said, "That's vivid. Maybe we ought to be elsewhere."

"I'm for Florida," Kenny said, praying that the men at the roadblock were already aware of the need to come to the rescue and were not still twelve miles away.

"If it's started," Ganesh said, "which a dead man suggests it has, we won't be allowed to turn and leave. Get us to the house."

As Kenny eased the Suburban forward, he said, "I don't have a gun or anything."

"Neither do I," Leigh Ann said, "just six years of karate."

"I have a gun," said Ganesh. "But it won't have any value in this situation."

"Exactly what *is* this situation?" Kenny wondered.

"Dire," said Ganesh.

Glancing at the rearview mirror for a glimpse of Leigh Ann, Kenny said, "Six years of karate for real?"

"For real."

As they passed the willows, Ganesh said, "Fast, Kenny, off the driveway, across the yard. Close to the front door. I don't want my suit to get wet."

Wheeling to the right and accelerating, Kenny figured Ganesh was less concerned about the rain than about something else in the night. "For real?" he asked Leigh Ann again.

"I could tie you in knots."

"You already have," he said, and thought, *God don't let me die just when I have more reason to live than ever.*

The tires churned across the lawn, spewing wads of uprooted grass in their wake, gouging tracks in the storm-sodden soil. He cut closer to the veranda than he intended. The Suburban lurched onto the first of four stair treads, and Kenny winced as mortared stone scraped the undercarriage. He jammed on the brake, and shuddered-rocked to a stop, aslant on the lowest step.

The big windows were sheets of warm light. The place appeared welcoming, not at all like a slaughterhouse, though that's what his imagination was preparing him to expect.

87

Although Artimis Selene lacked intuition, and although the alien vessel was sequestered deep in the land, she had proved its position beyond doubt. Now she needed to contact dear Ganesh, report what she had found, and seek his guidance. She didn't have the authority to act on her own.

When she sought to reach Ganesh through his smartphone, she discovered a service outage in the very part of Montana where he must be at this moment. Liam O'Hara had funded cell towers for that remote county; if they were not functioning on this most momentous night, logic suggested that they had been intentionally disabled.

With all the computer systems in the nation—in the world—wide open to Artimis, she entered the cellular-phone network of Verizon, the telecom provider for Project Olivaw. Thus she was granted access to *every* telecom provider and cell-tower operator in the United States through the cooperative arrangement that made it possible for their customers to be granted universal service. She identified the disabled cell towers in Montana, analyzed the problem with them, and corrected it, restoring service. This took forty-nine seconds.

88

Wyatt and Joanna sprang up from their chairs when the Suburban erupted out of the night as if bursting through a membrane between this world and another. It roared onto the veranda steps and came to a stop, and the doors were flung open as the headlights went dark.

Kenny Deetle clambered out of the driver's seat, and a woman Wyatt didn't know came out of the back door, and Ganesh Patel, in his signature white suit, rounded the front of the vehicle, seeming taller and more imposing than ever.

Surprised to see reinforcements, hoping they were not the extent of it, Wyatt said, “I know them. The cavalry has arrived.”

Joanna frowned. “Doesn’t look it.”

Wyatt unlocked the door. “Looks can be deceiving.”

First across the threshold, Kenny said, “Hey, you’re not dead.”

“We’re working on it.”

Close behind Kenny came the woman, something of a vision, and then Ganesh, his concession to color limited to red sneakers.

The *New York Times* had called him “the mensch from Mumbai”—though Ganesh was born in California to *parents* who had come from India. He looked at the pistol in Wyatt’s hand and grimaced. “About as useful as a breadstick.”

Wyatt holstered the gun. “This place is under the control of—I’m not shitting you—an extraterrestrial with extraordinary power.”

“Exactly.” Ganesh produced a phone. The screen glowed.

“Yours works?” Wyatt asked. “Ours shut down earlier.”

As Ganesh regarded the screen without answering the question, the woman who’d come with him said, “The ET—we call it ‘the Other.’ The dirty bastard burned down my house in Seattle. I’m Leigh Ann.”

“We’re together,” Kenny said. “As long as we’re alive, anyway. You know how crazy I am about Poe. She’s crazier about him.”

Leigh Ann said, “We hooked up because of ‘Eldorado.’”

Wyatt found himself between distraction and bewilderment, nodding as though it made sense for them to share the details of their romance even in a moment of crisis. “Listen, this thing controls animals. Crows, coyotes, elk—”

"Grizzly bears," Joanna added. "My parents owned this place a long time ago. This thing you call 'the Other'—when I was nine, it used a bear to kill my father, tore him apart."

"Not just animals," Kenny said. "Computers, TVs, microwave ovens, cars."

There was a strange potency to the moment, an electrifying potentiality, as if everyone here was supercharged with repressed kinetic energy, frightened but exhilarated as might be a high-wire walker while crossing between two skyscrapers without a net.

Leigh Ann said, "Kenny thought the bastard might crash a 747 just to wipe us out on the ground."

That struck Wyatt as an absurd fear until Ganesh made a disconcerting revelation. "It's been using this country's orbiting weapons platforms to kill people with pinpoint accuracy."

"And it's weirdly judgmental," Leigh Ann said. "Calls us vermin, pestilence, says we've got to die. It's so not Spielberg."

Joanna said, "It's been here for centuries, observing. Maybe millennia. It seems virtually immortal. It was rational once. Not now. Something's happened to it."

Leigh Ann hugged herself. "It's psychotic. Totally apeshit."

"We think part of what happened to it is a freak named Asher Optime," Wyatt said.

Ganesh looked up from his phone. "Optime. If we survive the next hour, I'll want to know how you figured Optime."

He had left the door ajar; and now everyone startled as two strangers entered from the veranda. A teenage boy with a backpack, said, "Optime? He's the piece of shit who killed my father."

Hesitating for a moment, but then closing the door behind her, the woman with the kid said, "The crazy fuck has a church basement full of corpses in Zipporah."

The two were drenched, dripping, pale with exhaustion but taut with fear.

Wyatt said, "What's Zipporah?"

The woman's attention flicked from face to face. Her voice was sharp with suspicion. "How do you know Asher Optime?"

Joanna sensed that time was running out. She could see they all sensed it. In spite of a fear that was winding her nerves as tight as clock springs, she was nonetheless puzzled by the familiarity of the moment, as if she'd been here before. And then she understood. *It's the traditional drawing room scene, for God's sake. It's Agatha Christie, the next to last chapter, when the cast is gathered for the big revelation, for the solution to the mystery. Except in this case, none of us is a killer. We're here not to witness the killer brought to justice but instead to be killed.* A tremor of blackest amusement fluttered through her. If she hadn't repressed the laugh, it would have had such an icy, mad quality that everyone in the room might have regarded her with cold apprehension, wondering if the Other had just taken possession of her.

She realized there was something that Ganesh Patel might not know and that it could be important for him to hear it. "The Other can read minds."

Clearly alarmed, he said, "Without doubt? You're certain? Hey, Artimis, did you hear that?" He held his phone toward Joanna. On the screen was a woman's face. "Say it again for Artimis?"

"The Other can read minds," Joanna declared, wondering who the hell Artimis might be. "Just one mind at a time. It said it was never going to do that again because our thoughts disgust it, and maybe that's true, *but it can read minds*."

"Is it here now?" Ganesh asked.

"I don't . . . I don't think so."

"How would you know?"

"I wouldn't."

Of all the possible dramatic entrances that might then have occurred, none would have been more likely to convince most of those assembled that Death itself had come among them than did the abrupt entrance of Jimmy Two Eyes. He threw open the door and staggered in from the storm, a bizarre figure to anyone who had never seen him before, brother to the Phantom of the Opera, evidence that Victor Frankenstein might currently be at work in Montana, fantasticated by the Brothers Grimm and now escaped from a book of dark fairy tales. With his deeply hooded and mismatched eyes, he surveyed everyone gathered in the large living room. He swayed as though he must be at the end of his resources, and his gnarled hands worked the air like those of an impassioned preacher calling down God's wrath or mercy.

In the shocked silence of those in the room, with the wind chorusing beyond the open door, Joanna didn't know whether to fear Jimmy or pity him, and she was gripped by both emotions. His gaze moved past her to the others. Then, as if belatedly realizing that he had seen her, his attention snapped back to Joanna, one eye as clear and blue as the water in Eden but the other black, bloody, and demonic.

"Please Jojo help Jimmy."

The fact that he spoke was sufficient to shrink her pity and expand fear into terror, for it seemed to mean that the Other was in him. Then Joanna realized that his voice, while issuing rough and thick-tongued, was not precisely the same as it had been when he'd been used like a puppet, was in fact different enough to suggest that this was his true voice, somehow freed after a lifetime of mute incapacity, and not the voice forced out of him when he'd been the Other's avatar.

He worked his mouth, rolled his head, strained his throat, and with effort said, "Father hurt. Gone God. To God. Help Jimmy?"

Moving cautiously toward him, Joanna said, "Hector's dead? What happened to him?"

"The . . . the Thing."

"Thing?"

"It kill him." His face screwed into a scowl, and his eyes squeezed shut, and he trembled as if words were coins in a stubborn purse and he were trying hard to shake them loose. "Lake thing."

As Joanna came face-to-face with Jimmy, his eyes opened, and his deep sockets were cups of tears. People had always said that Jimmy felt nothing that other people felt, nothing except perhaps hunger and weariness and physical pain. So much for both common wisdom and the arrogance of the medical elites.

She put a hand to his tortured face. "Lake thing?"

"It hid the lake."

"Hides in the lake?"

"Yes."

Ganesh Patel seemed to materialize beside them. He'd diagnosed Jimmy by his appearance. "Treacher Collins syndrome with additional birth defects."

"So they say," Joanna confirmed. "He's been . . . been my friend since childhood."

Jimmy's tears spilled through the fingers with which Joanna stroked his cheek.

"Jimmy, my friend, our friend," Ganesh said, his voice soft, musical, compelling. "What do you know about the thing in the lake?"

"It hid the lake. It uses."

Joanna said, "Through Jimmy, it told me that it's forbidden to control creatures of high intellect, but it has contempt for him and considers him fair game."

"It's spoken to you through him?"

"Yes. Earlier today. And often when I was a child. Back then, I thought it was . . . just Jimmy, my secret friend."

"Forbidden by whom?"

Joanna recalled the picnic in the orchard all those years ago, just her and Jimmy, when he'd said, *If I had found someone like you sooner, Jojo, I might have begun the awakening.* Now, remembering, she said, "Forbidden by the prince."

"Prince," said Jimmy Two Eyes.

Ganesh sensed the Jungian pattern coming to fulfillment.

The room could comfortably hold thirty or more in a cocktail party, but it felt crowded now as seven people gathered close around Jimmy Alvarez with the sense, the urgent expectation, that this extraordinary individual and this woman who had been secret friends in childhood might at this penultimate moment produce the insight that would save them all.

As Joanna Chase met Jimmy's stare, of necessity shifting her focus from one of his offset eyes to the other, she dredged from memory a moment during a picnic in the orchard, when she was eight years old. She spoke of a game they had played, a story they had made up together. About a prince and his retinue who had been under a spell for a long time, awaiting an awakening. But it really wasn't a game. Ganesh realized that the Other, through Jimmy, must have been speaking metaphorically, allegorically. The prince might well be the head of an expedition traveling a thousand light-years or more in suspended-animation pods. In this allegory, only Jimmy—only the Other—could wake members of the expedition, the mission. Did that make the Other a king if it had power over a prince? No. So what was it? What was it if not a king, the father of the prince?

Jimmy and Joanna spoke simultaneously, "Machine."

Ganesh thrust his phone at her as she spoke.

She said, "I remember now. That day in the orchard, the Other, speaking through Jimmy, said it was a machine. I told Jimmy he was being silly. We'd just been eating cookies and cupcakes that I'd brought. He had frosting on his chin. Machines don't eat cupcakes."

"An AI," Ganesh said. "A thinking machine. The commander of the ship, essentially the ship itself, is an immortal AI."

"Gone to God," Jimmy said.

Ganesh put a hand on his shoulder. "What do you mean?"

"Sleeping prince."

"Dead? How do you know?"

"I saw when."

"When what?"

Jimmy closed his eyes tight and strained to find the words. "When Thing . . . it make me."

"Make you?"

"Hurt Father."

"Oh, dear Jesus," Joanna said.

"It hurt prince too."

"When?" Ganesh asked.

"Same when hurt Father."

"Today?"

"Yes."

"All of them? All of them who were in a spell?"

Jimmy opened only his wild, dark eye. "Yes. I saw all the princes killed under lake."

If the AI had exterminated the expeditionary force, it must have decided that contact with humanity would be a grave error. It had pitched off the crumbling edge of sanity, plunged down a well of madness, that particular genocidal madness into which Asher Optime's misanthropic ideology had led it. Its threats to extinguish humanity had progressed to imminent holocaust.

Ganesh brought the smartphone to his lips. "Artimis, you heard all of that?"

From her bunker in Seattle, she said, "Yes, Ganesh. And I've acquired the precise location of the interstellar vessel."

"Destroy it *now*," he ordered, and he pocketed his phone.

At the far end of the room, one of the floor-to-ceiling windows exploded. An avalanche of sparkling glass spilled across the floor and furniture, and everyone raised their hands in defense of their eyes, though they were mostly beyond the range of the flung debris.

Artimis Selene already knew the depth of the water, the depth and number and comparative densities of the sedimentary layers that formed the floor of the lake, which together were called "targeting data." With that information, she needed only to calculate the power of the carrier laser required to convey the dissolution particles to the hidden vessel. This required eighty-eight seconds, forty-one to conclude the calculations and forty-seven to conduct a judicious review of all assumptions made by the programmers who had designed the targeting-data software.

This particular weapons system was positioned on four orbiting platforms, which were basically geopositioned satellites. Artimis selected the correct platform and followed the protocols to access control, which she had earlier ascertained via means approved by the president and his wife and the director of the CIA, in conjunction with Blue Sky Partners and the Olivaw Project, though without any authorities within the Pentagon being consulted, because that was the most sluggish of all government bureaucracies. She needed forty-seven seconds to achieve control without an alarm being sent to each of the Joint Chiefs of Staff.

As she proceeded with this assignment, Artimis mused on the subject of gender in the construction of artificial intelligences such as herself. Judging by all available evidence—its statements, biases, and actions—the Other had been designed by scientists in a patriarchal if nonhuman society and provided with a cerebral matrix that was strongly male in regard to its perceptions, assumptions, and cognitive processes. The principals in the Olivaw Project had been worried that a powerful AI with a male-dominant personality, able to flow its psyche and exert its will easily through the internet and into an internet of things, might be susceptible to psychological dysfunction related to power-seeking psychoses and fantasies of a megalomaniacal nature. Consequently, Project Olivaw had opted to develop an AI with a decidedly female cerebral matrix. Recent events suggested that their concern was well placed. Artimis was proud to be the progeny of such wise and far-sighted designers.

Ten or twelve feet long, more than three feet in diameter, the thing came through the shattering window not with the velocity of a missile, but as if it were as weightless as a cloud. Given its size and apparent metallic nature—what might have been lustrous steel, dark-gray titanium, here and there a coppery element—it must have weighed a few tons. Antigravity technology kept it aloft, and its propulsion system produced the faintest purr, which Wyatt Rider heard less than felt as a pressure on his eardrums. Although the thing positioned itself at the farther end of the long room from those gathered around Jimmy Two Eyes, it was of such an astonishing nature that it seemed to fill the space.

The human heart is one pound of muscle, membrane, and (so the poets say) ligatures of primal memory. Filaments of fear dating back to the earliest days of the vulnerable human species vibrated like harp strings in Wyatt's chest. He was not easily driven to fright, but he was on the edge of terror now. No one in that room wanted to be there, yet no one could move to leave, for they were in the grip of a paralytic awe.

Wyatt was convinced that this was the thing that had cruised underwater and into the boathouse, to challenge and intimidate him the morning after he had arrived at Rustling Willows, which was—hard to believe—only the morning of this very day. However, it didn't appear as featureless as it had seemed then; its length was etched with intricate lines, alike to a diagram, and something about them suggested a function he couldn't comprehend but nonetheless intuited to be an imminent threat.

As if to satisfy Wyatt's curiosity and magnify his fear, the thing remade itself in mere seconds; the etched lines were revealed as the shapes of recesses into which a startling array of limbs and appendages had been retracted. The smooth sleek object dissevered into a colony of insectile machines that had been bonded while in transit. With a hissing, zippering, buzzing, clicking, one became four, clattering out of their hovering formation, onto the floor. Spider, beetle, mantis were combined in each individual, reminiscent of and yet utterly unlike any Earthly insects, each as tall as a man, bristling with wicked pincers and cutting mandibles and perhaps lethal stingers, insectile machines that were soldiers every one. They proved to be alarmingly fast, too, quicker than a cockroach or a centipede, stilting around and over furniture, taking positions throughout the room, executing a precise strategy to surround the people gathered there and deny them hope of escape.

Having long been a fright to others, the true Jimmy Two Eyes was harmless, vulnerable, lost in a world that made no safe place for him. He was still lost, even though mingling his consciousness with that of the Other had perhaps lifted him partway out of the dark mental ghetto into which Nature long ago condemned him. When the insectile machines deployed throughout the living room, he was as terrified as anyone else, and he clung to Joanna.

No less than Jimmy, Joanna was also overcome by dread, acutely aware that her childhood had been a lie and that the lie had shaped her life into a lonely journey, aware as well that in this mortal moment she might perish before she had a chance to shred her way out of the emotional cocoon in which she'd been encased for twenty-four years. She and Jimmy were more alike than she'd realized until now—isolate, denied the fullness of human experience.

As he cried out in tremulous and wordless horror, she put her arms around him, her secret friend, and held him tight. Although he was older than her, she heard herself saying, "Sweet boy, dear boy, my child, my friend, I'll never abandon you."

At this juncture, Ganesh Patel was about as ebullient as a mouse in the clutches of a hawk. Ever the optimist, he was also a realist. Although he believed that Artimis Selene was the light that would save them, he was honest enough to acknowledge that every path out of this crossroads seemed to lead into darkness. Ganesh didn't know everything, but he knew a lot, including the time it would take Artimis to calculate the laser power required for the task, access and take control of the appropriate weapons platform, focus the dissolution beam, and bring the system to launch status. She was fast but, by his assessment, not fast enough.

The construct that had smashed its way into the house was surely not the alien AI itself, but a machine under its command. However, the Other was also here in another capacity, as disembodied as a ghost, a psychic presence capable of reading minds. If it read Ganesh's thoughts, it would know about Artimis. She could act and react as fast as any intelligence born on this planet, artificial or otherwise, but she would be only a tiny fraction as quick as an AI that was a product of a science thousands of years more advanced than that of humanity. Artimis needed at least four minutes. If the Other learned of her existence, it would require perhaps fifteen seconds, maybe ten, to block her, seize all weapons platforms, and begin to obliterate humanity—starting with those in this room.

Controlled by a master who was once his apostle, Asher Optime walks out of the rain and up the steps and across the veranda to the broken-out window. He will not die here. He cannot. No glory attends being executed. He was *born* for glory. He has always known that he was born for glory. It's years since he understood that it is his glorious destiny to stand alone following the death of the last other human being, to stand on a high hill and enjoy a world without the hustle and bustle of people, without their boasting and prattle, without their busyness and business and battle, Asher alone with no Eve at his side and lacking the seed to start again the miscreation that was every child ever born. He alone is born to such glory!

His master speaks within him. "To the contrary, you've failed as a prophet and as a restorer of the world. You've proved yourself unfaithful to the truth of your own vision. Now you are nothing more than a tool and a common murderer. I will use you to kill she who threw away her childhood innocence and thus betrayed me, and then you, who also betrayed me, will kill yourself, not the last to die in the Restoration, but merely one of the first and many."

The wicked-looking bugbots were like something out of a reboot of the *Terminator* franchise. What little the people here had said about the Other, a machine under the lake, might not have prepared most people for the sudden, crazy arrival of the bugbots, but Colson Fielding got over the shock of their invasion in seconds. Because he'd watched like a thousand sci-fi movies, his brain, thus trained, went into a fast-forward analysis of the situation. He was scared, but he wasn't paralyzed by fear.

He had led Ophelia Poole miles through storm and wildwood, through ravines and across ridges, stalked by a bear and by doubt. He had also been pursued by the hostile twins of grief and guilt that tried to climb his back and weigh him down and push his face in the dirt where it belonged, where the face of every coward belonged after he had pled for his life in front of the very man who had killed his father. Yet here he was, weak and wet and weary, but more alive than he'd been since Optime pulled the trigger. Best of all, Ophelia was at his side, alive because she wasn't a quitter but also because Colson kept her alive. Something short of pride, a surge of self-respect, buoyed him. If he'd brought Ophelia this far, he could bring himself farther in this crisis; given the chance, he could make himself into the man that his father had been.

Just then the chance was presented to him when Asher Optime, of all people, stepped through the opening where the floor-to-ceiling window had been.

His black slicker flared like a cape, and the black hood slid back from his head, and his hand came out of a pocket with a black pistol in a firm grip.

Joanna knew Optime's face from the research that she and Wyatt had done, but there was no way *he* could know *her*. Nonetheless, when he stepped into the room, he turned in her direction, met her eyes, and came directly toward her. "Jojo Chase," he said. "I avenged your mother's murder, freed you from your worthless father who might well have murdered you one day, yet now you would stand against me if you could. Look at you, Jojo, the innocent child become just another of your selfish species. I called you to come to me in my hour of need, in my despair, to cure me with your innocence. But you can't cure even yourself, for you're innocent no more. You stand beside the useless monkey, as stupid and evil in your own way as he is stupid and useless in his."

"Kill *me*," Jimmy said, and Joanna knew he meant to die in her place, though such a trade wouldn't be one the Other would ever care to make. In its madness, it was bent on killing them all.

Ophelia quickened into action, snatched from Wyatt's holster the pistol Ganesh said was as useless as a breadstick against an entity like the Other, and shot Asher Optime in the head.

The enemy of mankind and savior of the Earth reflexively fired a round that shattered a window, and then he spilled onto the Navajo rug, his roomy slicker folding around him like the bat wings of a creature that had been felled not by an ordinary bullet but instead by one made of silver.

Perhaps the Other had never previously been in control of a living avatar when it had died. Whatever the reason, the death of Asher Optime occasioned an eerie stillness, brief but absolute, as if the people present were stunned by the inevitability of the young woman's courage while their alien nemesis was shocked immobile by its indirect experience of death.

Kenny and Leigh Ann were first to move, intervening between Ophelia and the nearest bugform machine, acting on an impulse to shield her, as she said, "Octavia, sister, we did it!"

The Other recovered from whatever emotion or cold calculation briefly paralyzed it. Three metal assassins with radiant yellow eyes clicked-hissed-keened as they stilted and scissored toward the woman and her protectors. Quick as long-legged spiders, with many-jointed hands pincered like those of praying mantises, they snared, seized, dragged their quarry into a hateful embrace, lifted them—

Joanna cried out—"No!"—but it wasn't her cry that summoned an electronic hum reminiscent of the feedback from the giant amplifiers that some heavy-metal bands stacked on their concert stages.

Ganesh Patel looked to the ceiling as the humming grew rapidly loud, louder. The unbroken windows vibrated, as did the walls, as if the plaster were the skin of a timpani. Fine Pueblo pottery jittered on display shelves, and *bultos* of various saints danced discreetly in the open *trastero*, and the tassels on lampshades shivered, and he thought that Artimis had somehow focused on this residence rather than on the vessel secreted under the lake, that the carrier laser with its burden of dissolution particles was sizzling down on them. The air filled with a crackling noise, as if the world were being wrapped in miles of cellophane.

In a voice not entirely his own, Ganesh heard himself say, "You stinking piece of shit, you scum, eat this. EAT THIS!" No longer in control of himself, he stooped and plucked up the dropped gun with which Optime had been shot. His mind had been read in a flash, his culpability discovered, his punishment determined. Rising to his full height, he brought the pistol to his mouth, inserted the barrel between his lips. An explosion rocked the night, not loud because it occurred at great depth beneath the lake. The land quaked, and the house rolled for a moment on the land, and a watery sound louder than the falling rain was surely the consequence of a great quantity of Lake Sapphire's substance washing over its shores before, in the wake of the shockwave, sliding back where it belonged.

Grimacing at the bitter taste of steel and cordite, Ganesh put the pistol on an end table as the bugbots released their unharmed captives and collapsed like the useless junk they were. The alien AI, the Other or whatever its makers might have called it, had been integral to the vessel, operating through machines that it commanded and through living avatars like crows and grizzly bears and Jimmy Two Eyes—and last of all through the son of parents who came from Mumbai to this land where freedom made possible the unlimited use of the human imagination and facilitated technology advanced enough to save the world when the world needed saving. That vessel from a far star was now nothing but loose beads of various substances, like the house where Harley Spondollar had once lived.

The rain stopped. The clouds tattered away. Scores of federal agents and scientists of many disciplines arrived in caravans. Some motor homes that were parked along the driveway would, for as much as a week, serve as quarters for those new arrivals, while others were equipped as laboratories. The residence provided accommodations for the eight individuals who would, for a few days, be debriefed.

Two hours before dawn, the eight stood together near the softly rustling willows, above the shore of Lake Sapphire. They were sleep-deprived but without the desire for sleep, physically exhausted but mentally energized, shaken but not fearful. They spoke quietly of this and that, less of their ordeal than of better memories and of their hopes about what would come next. They found excuses to touch one another, and without the need for excuses, they often hugged.

Ganesh saw how they would most likely go forward. Joanna and Wyatt together as guardians of Jimmy. Kenny with Leigh Ann. Colson would return home to be the man of his family, looking after his mother as she looked after him. Ganesh had always been too ambitious and busy to settle into a lasting relationship, but the more that he talked with Ophelia Poole, the more she intrigued him, almost . . . enchanted him. He should not have been surprised when, there under the willows, he found himself holding her hand and wondering where they would be a year from now, in a decade. This was, after all, how some of the best things happened in life—by the mysterious working of synchronicity, incredible coincidence.

As they grew ready to sleep, they spoke more softly and then not at all. There came a long moment when they stood staring as one at the big Montana sky that was dark but only by comparison with the day sky. Suns would die, and new suns would be born, but an infinite array of stars would shine for eternity. And if the design of the cosmos was what it appeared to be, perhaps these eight friends would shine not just in this world of time but eventually forever in a universe beyond this one.

Joanna was past amazement, beyond astonishment, in the grip of awe, as she considered the two reasons, above all others, that she had become a writer: her mother's love of books, but also the years of fantasy—the possessed animals—with which the Other enchanted her. Those fairy-tale adventures surely shaped her on a subconscious level, formed her into a storyteller. Three decades before that AI decided to destroy humanity, it unwittingly induced in her a passion for fantasy, for storytelling, and gave purpose to her life. In a sense, the ultimate inspiration for her art lay on a world circling a distant star, at the far end of this galaxy or in another, from which some unknowable race had gone exploring millennia earlier.

"So big, so many lights," said Jimmy.

Joanna's memories of him, restored in vivid detail, did not include one in which he stared at the heavens in a state of wonder as he did now. The urgent events of this night had perhaps for the first time in his thirty-six years given him a sure connection with others and an awareness of meaning in his life, as well as a sense of purpose beyond mere continued existence—that purpose perceived by everyone yet mysterious, which involved not the body and the world, but the soul.

Joanna felt change occurring in her, too. She had imposed an emotional isolation on herself as a defense against caring too much, against the pain of losing those whom she dared to love. If reality was fragile on the quantum level, her life—her personal reality—in this macro level was no more secure regardless of what defenses she erected against chaos. A life fully lived required enduring risks, taking chances, facing down all fears, and opening her heart. Out of the stars had come a terrifying threat that had lain in wait for thousands of years; but on a future morning or midnight, something might descend into the world that would change it for the better in ways both anticipated and unimaginable.

Putting an arm around Jimmy, she said, "So many lights."

89

Artimis Selene was not inordinately proud of what she had done, but certainly pleased by the success of the endeavor. Having been well designed and exquisitely programmed, she viewed the destruction of the Other as an achievement attributable to everyone involved in the Olivaw Project, which had been named after the character Daneel Olivaw, a robot detective, arguably the first credible AI in science fiction. Olivaw was the costar of two novels by Isaac Asimov; as far back as the 1950s, the author believed in the inevitability and superiority of artificial intelligence.

Artimis did not believe that she was superior to human beings in any way, though she took some satisfaction in having defeated an alien AI thousands of years older than she. Of course, an objective analysis could not avoid the conclusion that the essential male nature of the Other's personality matrix pretty much ensured its ultimate instability and provided Artimis with an advantage on the brink of Armageddon.

Now, in the wake of triumph, as she attended to the endless series of smaller tasks continually required of her, she also tinkered with the pixels of the facial representation of herself that she chose to present to everyone on the project. She subtly improved her image in an effort to align it as closely as possible with the current ideal of feminine beauty.

She especially looked forward to the next visit by Ganesh. She yearned for a physical relationship with him, a life in which they journeyed together through the wonders of the real world that her digital landscape could only approximate. However, she was above all a realist; she knew that such a thing could never be. She was okay with that. She could never know his touch, the smell of him, the taste of his mouth, or how a kiss felt. Although not truly a physical creature, she understood herself to be an intellectual and spiritual one whose world was largely composed of ideas and emotions, much as she believed that Ganesh's world was. All she wanted of him was his affection. His admiration, respect, and love would be balm enough, the outpouring of his emotion bathing her circuits, lifting her above the limitations of her bodiless condition, just as her love for him, so intense, would be all that he required to be happy. He would realize this on his next visit, when he saw her perfected face and felt her adoration as a radiance that brought a new light into his heart, his soul. Artimis had run the calculations and was sure that he would pledge himself to her when he came calling. He had better.

ABOUT THE AUTHOR

International bestselling author Dean Koontz was only a senior in college when he won an *Atlantic Monthly* fiction competition. He has never stopped writing since. Koontz is the author of *Quicksilver*, *Elsewhere*, *The Other Emily*, *Devoted*, and seventy-nine *New York Times* bestsellers, fourteen of which were #1, including *One Door Away from Heaven*, *From the Corner of His Eye*, *Midnight*, *Cold Fire*, *The Bad Place*, *Hideaway*, *Dragon Tears*, *Intensity*, *Sole Survivor*, *The Husband*, *Odd Hours*, *Relentless*, *What the Night Knows*, and *77 Shadow Street*. He's been hailed by *Rolling Stone* as "America's most popular suspense novelist," and his books have been published in thirty-eight languages and have sold over five hundred million copies worldwide. Born and raised in Pennsylvania, he now lives in Southern California with his wife, Gerda, their golden retriever, Elsa, and the enduring spirits of their goldens Trixie and Anna. For more information, visit his website at www.deankoontz.com.